CONTENTS

LEGENDS of WAR

SPARROW WARS IN THE GARDEN OF BLISS

BOOK 2

C. A. PORTNELLUS

SCRIPTOR HOUSE
THE EPITOME OF GREATNESS

Scriptor House LLC

2810 N Church St Wilmington, Delaware, 19802

www.scriptorhouse.com

Phone: +1302-205-2043

Published by Scriptor House LLC

Paperback ISBN: 979-8-88692-287-5

eBook ISBN: 979-8-88692-288-2

Legends of War: Book 2 of Sparrow Wars in the Garden of Bliss

Published by iUniverse-Copyright 2014

ISBN: 978-1-4917-4892-3 (sc)

ISBN:978-1-4917-4893-0 (hc)

ISBN: 978-1-1917-4894-7 (eb)

Library of Congress Control No:2014917545

DEDICATION

Pour ma Belle-Mère Lily, qui as un Coeur de Lionne et une humeur belliqueuse.

To all those who bravely fought and in memory of those who died

for a cause greater than their own both in foreign lands and at home.

You are the true legends of war; may you never be forgotten.

PROLOGUE

Shall we learn from war, no matter how devastating or comic it seems to the gods? Perhaps we are perceived much like the warring sparrows, insignificant creatures as we struggle and strive for supremacy in our lives. We engage in petty arguments or jealously fight for love and relationships. We attempt to conquer our world to mold it to our image and ideals.

Are we but puppets dancing to fate's hand? Is there such a thing as luck or fortune if we find it a rarity in our lives? We must only watch zealously as others excel, rising to celestial heroic fame or callously playing Russian roulette with fate.

Some believe that man is but a pawn in fate's chess game. Yet he struggles to prove himself more.

If a heroic man were to live forever like a god, he would still be but a dust mote in the heavenly creator's eye. His name and daring feats or victories are fleeting and perhaps recalled as legends by his peers. With all legends and heroes, their endeavors and souls must someday fade and be washed away clean like sand on a beach.

CHAPTER 1

Les Cauchemars

Beaumont, Texas
Sunday, May 23, 1943

Laughter echoed off the nearby crypts as beams of flashlights garishly bounced off the headstones. They ran, tripping on planters, leaping over stone markers and grave hillocks, and dodging through hedges and trees as they trampled fresh graves and flowers.

"Hey! Whose idea was this?—'Let's get drunk in Magnolia; nobody will kick us out!' Well, this stinks!" Barton bellowed after he fell down on a gravel-lined grave.

"Oh shut up, you big chicken-shit! You scared of little ole ghosts, Barre?" Louis cackled, his voice strident in the darkness up ahead.

"We're not kids anymore! This is stupid!" Barton yelled back.

"What a killjoy!" Garrett's mocking tone echoed among the crypts.

"I hate this place!" Barton grumbled. He got up, dusting off his knees, and blew on his skinned palms. Barton leaned for a moment against a headstone to catch his breath. E. Lucas probably didn't mind him resting here; he had been dead since 1898. Still, Barton felt a chilly, ghostly breeze rise from the misty ground and sinuously wind about his neck. He put back the stone angel that had fallen off when he crashed into the headstone and sauntered away, rubbing a sore elbow.

"Come on, guys," he moaned. "Let's go somewhere else. I gotta go to the bathroom."

Far-off noises and laughing helped to direct him closer to his friends. He certainly didn't enjoy wandering through this place alone. He staggered along, hiccupping and taking a few sips of the harsh whiskey, wishing they had more money for better booze. He was disappointed that they had been ejected from the Rusty Spur Cantina. At least it had been warm, and the place had peanuts and pretty girls.

"I thought this was gonna be a party!" Barton complained, hollering into the darkness. "Yeah, Louis says, 'We gotta cheer you up, little buddy.'... Shit!" He paused to belch. "I ain't feelin' cheery yet!"

"Look who we found! Bart! C'mere!" Louis yelled.

Barton trotted on a new trajectory through the cemetery toward his friends. "Who is it?" he called into the murky darkness.

"Old Pew-Bert Hubert. Remember him?" Louis giggled drunkenly.

"Hey! Let's piss on him!" Garrett suggested with a wicked laugh.

Barton met up with his taller, older friends to see brothers Garrett and Louis undoing their pants.

"Don't do that!" Bart grumbled. "That's sickening."

"Why? He was a sick, old creep! He gave me an F on my term paper. Well, here's your F, you old geezer!" Louis snarled and farted and then began pissing on the flower planter decorating the grave.

Snickering, Garrett joined in. "Yeah, I hated the old crumbum too. He sent me to the principal's office once cuz I was lookin' at Shirlee's paper."

Louis retorted with a loud laugh. "It wasn't just Shirlee's test you was lookin' at but down her blouse!"

Barton veered away as the brothers crudely reminisced about their old high school teacher, sending him rude drunken toasts.

"Up yer tail w' a rusty nail, ya old bastard!" The brothers shouted as they shared their whiskey.

Bart had never minded old Mr. Hubert—the man had given him an A.

He tripped along, feeling muzzy-headed. His stomach roiled from supper's greasy chili con carne and probably too much beer and whiskey. He padded along to a stone bench to sit and then stared out at the dark and dismal cemetery.

He hated the dead and anything to do with them. While he enjoyed scary movies, he preferred monsters because they weren't real, rather than things about the dead, like Dracula or the Mummy; even Frankenstein was too creepy. The hideous movie creature Nosferatu once gave him *cauchemars* for a week!

Bart slurped the rest of the whiskey and reluctantly wished there was more. He stood up and threw the pint bottle across the way as far as he could but didn't hear it break. Bart peered into the darkness, wondering why, sure that there would have been a loud noise. Disappointed, he then looked around, feeling very alone. He no longer heard his friends or any live sounds other than the rush of the night wind through the trees, a pair of bleeping frogs, and the drip of dew off the nearby stele. He looked about, wondering how to get out of this place. Where did they leave Louis's car?

All of a sudden, the fog seemed higher, and the place was dark and eerily lit by the swirling vapor and low moon. It felt like a movie scene from *The Wolfman*, lost out on the foggy moors. He moved on through the darkness with a sense of urgency, wondering if his friends were pulling a prank. Maybe they had left him behind here!

Barton tripped and fell again; this time, he quickly popped up only to stumble on a low-set marker some feet away. He ran between the headstones, feeling panic gripping him. "Oh God, don't leave me!" he mumbled as he drunkenly navigated through the mist. His breaths were coming in sharp gasps, tinged with worry and fatigue.

"Where are you guys?" he hollered, now feeling paranoid by the surrounding tall monuments and the sinister mist.

"Hey, Bart! Over here! Come see …"

He turned to the echoed call and picked up speed again, this time hopeful he would meet up with his friends. His foot hit something, and it ricocheted; there was the tinkling sound of glass. He looked about, thinking the area looked familiar. There was a narrow sign pointing to the cemetery lane, and he sighed with relief. However, he crept along, feeling his way through the low-lying shrubs and tombstones, and found the bottle he'd thrown.

"Oh, that's weird; it's not busted." He picked it up and sipped at it to catch just a drop. Smacking his lips, Bart put the bottle in his jacket, thinking he shouldn't leave it behind. As he sat down to rest on a stone crypt, he noticed the pale pink granite headstone glittering in the mist.

"Mama." Barton's word was as a sigh. He went to the grave, peered at the inscription, and petted the headstone. He leaned upon it, whispering, "I wish you would come back. I miss you."

The headstone was the only tangible object he associated with his mother, Charlotte Angelina Barre. His family all said she had died when Barton was almost six. One day, she was in the hospital smiling at him, and the next day, she was gone. Then Thérèse Pierrault came to live with them. He had always suspected that someone was lying to him. His mother had just gone away! After that, life was forever changed for him.

Weeping, he began to claw at the damp sod near the headstone; he pulled up handfuls of grass and clover. "Mama, come back!"

Frantically digging like a dog now, Bart, on his hands and knees, pawed and began stabbing through the wet earth with his pocket knife. "I gotta know!"

After some minutes, he felt something hard under his fingers and dug deeper. The object was wooden. Now afraid, his stomach gripped him like a snake with a mouse. It couldn't be a casket; he had dug down only a foot or two, but the dark wood glistened wetly as he peered into the small hole.

"I must be insane, but I gotta know!" He scrabbled through the earth and worked his way down, shifting the dirt away from the object.

"Mama, don't let it be you." He cried, barely able to see through his tears.

He pulled up the box, slicing away the entwined roots holding it. The heavy wooden box wasn't large, certainly not a coffin. Yet, as Bart rubbed away the dirt, there was a memory of this thing. He found a metal plate on the box lid and peered at it—the inscription was rusted away. He tried to open it, but there was no latch. Guiltily looking about, feeling as if a ghost or demon might spring out at him or maybe his friends would catch him, Barton hastily stood up and threw the box on the ground with terrible force. It cracked open, and he picked up a stone on the monument header and smashed the box.

"I have to know!"

He knelt beside the mess, picking through the moldering items—flowers, a crudely carved horse, an Indian head penny, a ring—but Bart was seized to stillness by the stone jar lying in the dirt. "No."

Barton picked it up, looked it over, and tried to pry off the lid, but it was sealed shut. He broke it open with the large rock. Fine silvery ash flowed from the jar, and chunky and glittering bits lay on the ground.

Barton let out a howl and flung himself upon the mess. "Mama!"

He wept inconsolably for what seemed a very long time.

◆ ◆

"What are you doin', boy?" Louis growled and kicked at him.

Bart was suddenly jerked upright. "No! I don't wanna go!" he sobbed. "It's my mama!"

"Oh, for the love of—" Garrett hauled the belligerent Barton into his arms.

"No! I can't leave her there!"

Louis tugged on his arm. "You idiot! What have you done?!"

Bart struggled to get loose, and then, all of a sudden, he saw stars and collapsed.

Garrett shook out his hand after striking Bart. "Come on, little buddy. Let's go play somewhere else." He gathered up his young friend.

Louis stooped to pluck two objects from the ground; he tucked one into Bart's hand and pocketed the other. Looking about the dismal area, he gave a shudder. "Yeah, I've had my fun here, let's scram."

Garrett stepped up the pace. With a moaning and hiccupping Barton under his arm, he commented, "Yeah, let's split this Dullsville scene! We need to find some women! This was a stupid idea, Louis." He kicked his brother in the ass.

The remaining night passed into eerie darkness on the empty road as Louis drove them through the countryside, to the Neches River, and then back into town. After stealing a loaf of bread and some cheese left by the dairyman in front of a darkened house, they drove away to the city park to eat and drink more whiskey.

They all discussed grand plans of what to do with their lives, or at least Barton did, and then, one by one, each man fell asleep.

◆ ◆

Monday, May 24, 1943

Bart roused roughly from his sleep, blinked blearily up and around at the sunlight-filled car, and smiled up at Louis. "Hey, am I home?"

"Nope. We got business to do today, so get your butt in gear." Louis hauled Barton out of the backseat of his car. Draping an arm about his shoulders, he and Garrett guided Barton into the doorway ahead of them.

Barton glanced around, noting two men ahead in line, and asked, "What are we doing?"

"Something important." Louis nudged him in front while tucking Bart's shirttail into his pants.

Barton rubbed his head. "Oh, man, I got a headache." He smacked his lips. "And I think a skunk took a hike through my mouth. What did we eat for supper?"

"Chili," Garrett answered.

Barton burped and asked, "What did we have for breakfast?"

"Nuthin' yet." Louis prodded Barton ahead. "You're next, buddy."

"What am I doin'?"

The man at the table before him wore a uniform and smiled at the trio unctuously. "Good morning. You are here to sign up? We just opened, and we need eager men like you."

Barton turned back to Louis. "Sign what?"

"Yes, sir, we are eager." Louis stepped up and signed his name. The man handed him a packet of papers, and Louis shoved Barton in his place. "Do it, buddy."

Barton sneezed and signed his name. "What am I doing?" Then, digging through his pocket for his handkerchief, his hand felt an odd object. He pulled it out and saw a petrified, pale yellow rabbit's foot and rusted chain. "Where …?" Still puzzled by the mysterious object, he was pressed aside by Garrett.

Garrett hastily signed, and the young men were directed to another room where, along with others, they sat down on the folding chairs lining the room.

Fidgeting, Bart stuffed the hairy foot back in his pants pocket. He looked about at the yawning and uneasy men in the room. Glancing at his watch, Bart noticed it was broken—the face cracked and stopped at 1:22—his clothes and hands were filthy. He whispered to Garrett. "I look like a bum. So what are we doing now? I wanna go home. I stink."

"Something important for your country, man."

"I don't care about my country," Bart hissed back and started to get up. "Look here, I got stuff to do."

"No, ya don't—at least nuthin' important like this," Louis commented as he paged through the leaflets.

"I'm looking for a job."

"Got one yet?" Garrett asked idly as he gazed about the room.

"No." Barton looked away with chagrin, hearing his stomach growl.

"This will do it." Garrett sat back with a sigh and combed his frowsy dark hair into place. "Look, we will all be together. How much more fun will that be, huh?" He ran the comb through Bart's bright red cockscomb, patting the wild curls into some order, and then passed the comb to his brother.

Louis elbowed Bart. "Yeah, be a pal for once. Yer such a sad sack lately." He quickly smoothed his dark hair and tucked the comb away in his jacket.

A tall, imposing man stepped onto the dais at the front of the room. He rapped a pointer on the podium to garner the attention of the men assembled.

"Who is that?" Barton asked, eying the olive and tan uniform with suspicion. "Oh dang, did we get arrested? What did we do last night?"

"No. That's Sergeant Raines; you know him from church. He's the recruiter here." Louis said mildly.

Barton felt his guts churn. "Recruiter?"

"Yeah, we're joining the army, just like we agreed last night." Grinning, Louis made a fist and popped Bart in the shoulder. "We're gonna go kill us some Japs and Jerries and make our mamas proud."

Barton's ears began ringing. "I don't want to kill anyone." He cast a menacing look at the brothers. "Except for you guys!"

"Sh!" Several hisses followed by indignant stares from men about them quieted Bart for a moment.

Garrett nudged Bart and whispered, "Do it for your mom."

He gulped, feeling tears rise. "I can't … she … she's dead."

Garrett looked at him strangely. "Well, then, do it for your dad and little sisters. Or your chicken-shit brothers! I still can't believe Paul backed out of joining the Navy." He shook his head. "Somebody in your family has got to have some balls and get on the bandwagon here."

"I don't care about them."

"Then do it for all the pretty girls. BettyAnn Sanders—she's still smitten. Maybe she can be your pen pal or sweetheart while you are away." Garrett snickered but sobered when the sergeant cast his eyes their way.

"Not BettyAnn!" Barton groaned. "She got me into this mess!"

Louis whispered, "Yeah, we had to get you out of your funk there, boy. Old Sanders gettin' you arrested just put you in Blues Town, man. But this should do it! You'll show him! Hell, we'll all show the old poop we got guts! We got balls!" He giggled and elbowed Bart in the ribs. However, he caught Sergeant Raines's frown and motioned for Bart to be quiet.

Barton rubbed his ribs, which felt nearly bruised, but he mechanically went through the motions of the morning, still very confused and nursing an upset stomach.

At the end of it all, Louis pushed Bart and Garrett along the aisle before him. "We are in like Flynn, boys."

"I think I'm gonna be sick." Barton scrambled out of the aisle, stepping on men as he went. Then he raced out through the front office to puke at the curbside.

Sergeant Raines stood at the doorway with a smirk, watching Barton as the men filed out. "It happens to the best of us! Good luck, men!"

Garrett and Louis collected their sick friend, but Barton choked on his words. "I still hate you guys!"

"Aw, no, you don't. It's just the rot-gut talkin'."

"You'll be happy. All the girls will think you are a big hero," Louis chuckled.

"Yeah, BettyAnn and Marcia will just die when they see us all in uniform. You know how Marcia gets all atwitter when she sees Alistair's chest full of medals." Garrett puffed up. "I'm gonna look mighty fine, too!"

"I hate BettyAnn!" Barton moaned.

"Come on; be a man, Bart. Yer in the army now!" Garrett laughed, and the trio headed to Louis's DeSoto.

◆ ◆

Over an early supper that evening, Barton dropped the bomb with his announcement that he had volunteered for the army. He fiddled with his fork, looking at the uneaten scrambled eggs and diced tomatoes with a roiling belly, feeling as if he might vomit again. Whether it was the hangover or having to divulge his news, he did not feel well.

Richard, upon hearing his son's news, slammed down his fork and knife and stamped upstairs without a word.

Cecily glanced at Barton and whispered, "Um, I think Daddy is upset."

Nancy made a face and rolled her hazel eyes. "No kidding, dummy." She turned to Barton. "You know, since you came home from college, everything has just been a big mess around here. By the way, you look like a hobo."

Camellia set aside her fork and leaned toward Bart, whispering harshly. "Yeah, Bart the Bum. First, you cheated us on getting to see you graduate. Don't you know how important that was to Daddy and Mom? I mean, all of us wanted to see it—you are the first one in this family to graduate college! Nancy and I think you are very selfish."

He shook his head and let out a heavy sigh. "I know how they feel. I got yelled at plenty enough for just showing up here."

Thérese, Bart's stepmother, was at the sink, turned about, and wiped her hands on a towel as she listened to the children. She brushed back a lock of brunette hair and came over. "Barton, I am sure you think enlisting was important; however, I thought you had other plans for your life."

His head jerked up, and he was quick to retort. "I did have other plans! I wanted to get a job, but there is nothing here in Beaumont!"

"Oh, please. Do we have to hear it all again?" Nancy groaned. Her tone was strident as she jabbed a finger in Bart's direction. "Then you should just go out and find a darn job somewhere else, and let us have some peace for once!"

Thérese gasped. "Nancy Annette! Don't speak to him like that!"

"Well, I am sorry, but Camellia is right! Everything has been a mess—you and Dad yelling at Barton about not graduating, then that BettyAnn thing last week—"

"I did, too, graduate! I got the diploma certificate to show for it," Barton yelled but then backed down. "Well, I will … when they send it to me." He glared at his half-sisters.

"Look, I didn't want all that folderol of marching around, wearing a stupid gown, and looking like a dope just to get my diploma while you guys are—"

Thérese sought to end the discussion. "Enough. We all know your reasons were selfish, and you didn't want us to make a big deal about it."

"Yeah, I didn't. Besides, you all can't afford to travel and stay in hotels, so I was being considerate." He looked at the dubious faces of his family—three pairs of hazel eyes and one of brown glaring at him as he continued. "I still graduated with an outstanding degree." He sneered at the girls. "I thought I would get a head start in getting a job before all the other graduates come looking for work. I gotta get a great job that makes lots of money. I'm not gonna be some little trained dog kissing up to a slave-driver boss's whims and getting paid peanuts for it. You will see my job will be terrific!"

"Oh yeah, so you say. But first, you are going to be marching to a different drummer, this time in the army! You won't like it, and you'll be lucky to come home alive!" Camellia stated acerbically. She stood up and swatted Barton on the head with her napkin as she went by. "You really stepped in it this time, dogface!"

Barton gaped as Camellia tossed her brunette curls and rushed from the kitchen, heading upstairs. "Who put arsenic in her supper? Sheesh!"

Thérese returned to the table to sit across from Barton. "Girls, finish your meal. In spite of our calamity, you still have school exams to study for today. I think you should go to the library tonight; you have a couple of hours left before they close."

"I don't feel like eating anymore." Cecily quickly dropped her dishes in the sink and ran after her sister upstairs.

Nancy picked up her toast and dutifully took her dishes to the sink, but then came to Barton. "I am sorry I chewed on you, but really, Bartie, you gotta stop acting so selfish. Grow up! Maybe you will get better by being in the army." She kissed his cheek. "I still love you even if you are the biggest troublemaker on the planet. Who do you think you are, Lex Luthor? Golly!" She dashed away upstairs before Barton could reply.

Thérese refilled Bart's cup with the last of the weak coffee and then sat back, eyeing him with worry. "Well, there you have it, Son; from out of the mouths of babes come words of wisdom and concern." She sipped her water, waiting for him to say something else. "By the way, you looked dreadful this morning when you crawled in. I guess your party with the Guillot boys was a smash, as indicated by your bruised face and the filthy clothes that you slept in all day."

Barton grimaced, barely recalling the night before, but he was now caught in the disaster of the morning. "Yeah, I suppose so." He shifted uncomfortably on the chair. "So … what about Dad? I guess he is giving me the silent treatment tonight."

Thérese nodded. "I think you shocked him. We are very worried, Son, and after the last escapade with BettyAnn, well … and this? What are we to do with you?"

"Look, I told you none of it was my fault. Even this army thing—the Guillots roped me in."

"Yes, they usually do pull you into some kind of mischief. I would think you'd be immune to their pranks by now. But then again, maybe this time it is not so bad."

"I think it is."

Thérese let out a small breath of aggravation. Her fine eyebrows were drawn with concern as she spoke. "Perhaps Nancy is correct that the army just might do you some good. Barton, you have often been a source of great pride and affection in this family because you are so intelligent and have done so much. But now this thing … well, it does frighten me. I thought perhaps after you saw all that Paul went through in nearly joining the Navy after Pearl Harbor and your family's reaction to it, it might have put you in a different mindset. However—"

Bart slammed a fist on the table. "Ha! You think that I am just a stupid kid, huh? Well, I am not. I will go. I damned near signed my life away on the dotted line, and it won't be to please anyone but me!" He scooted back his chair and stood. "I am a free-thinking man, and I will show you all! At least I am honorable and not cowards like Jacques and Paul! I'll be an outstanding soldier!"

Thérese took in a shocked breath. "You are just acting prideful; don't be foolish! You only need to be a grown-up, not a petulant child, Bart. As your mother, I think—"

"I am not petulant, and I don't need your advice, Thérese, because I never asked for it!" He stared down at her accusingly. His pale gray eyes were chips of ice. "You always come off so saintly, and yet, I know, and you know that you are not! I've got your number, Thérese, and you won't fool me any longer. You aren't my mother, so just stay the hell out of my life!" Barton stamped out of the kitchen and the house, leaving behind shattered nerves.

As she cleared the supper dishes, Thérese moved with a calmness she did not feel, wanting to fall apart and cry. She handed out the girls' school bags and kissed them as they left for the library. She was glad to have them gone in case Richard and Barton went head-to-head in an argument.

Feeling ready to burst into tears, she went upstairs to find Richard at his desk in their bedroom. She wound her arms around his shoulders and leaned to rest her head against his, suddenly noting the tiny silver threads glittering in his dark-brown hair. Barton was giving them all gray hair!

"Well, I believe we have finally lost Bartie," she said with a sigh.

Richard stiffened against her touch. "Not yet, I haven't."

"You hardly touched your supper. I know it wasn't much. Are you still hungry?"

He shrugged away, annoyed. "No. At this moment, I feel much like Barton looked, all beat up and worn out. My heart hurts, Thérese. I am trying not to overthink this or get angry. Besides, if I yell and tell him this is a stupid thing he has done, Barton won't listen. In fact, I am sure he'll make it worse!"

"I think he got quite an earful just now from his sisters and me. Right now, he is back to hating me."

Richard turned to look at his wife and said mildly, "Oh, you must have laid him low then."

"A little, but for some reason he is …" she let out a sigh and shook her head. "Forget it. I can never keep that boy on an even keel. Just the other day, Bart was full of praise for the roast chicken at supper and hugging me for baking raisin tarts. But then, today, I am again the evil stepmother. Maybe it is better that he goes away. I told Bart perhaps the army just might do him some—"

Richard set Thérese aside and stood up; his dark eyes were full of anger. "How could you say that? He is my son! I don't want to send him away—he needs my guidance! He has barely scraped through this last fiasco. I thought perhaps that Barton would be good again. Damn, those Guillot boys!"

Thérese sat on the bed and dabbed her eyes and nose with a hankie. "Unfortunately, he is not a broken clock and easily repaired, dear. There is something amiss in that boy. He continues to drive me crazy; one moment, I love and admire him, and the next, I am entirely disgusted by his callous and capricious behavior. What are we to do?"

Richard sat down again at his desk, this time leaning back in his chair and stretching his long legs before him. "I know I should be proud that he wants to serve our country. But we have lost so many boys to this terrible war. I cannot lose him, Thérese!" He swiped a hand across his teary eyes.

"Are you implying that you would risk your other sons rather than Bart?"

Richard gaped at his wife's remark but then shook his head. "I don't want to lose anyone, but especially not Bart. I shouldn't need to remind you why." He then picked up the telephone receiver and stated grimly, "I know just the medicine he needs."

"Do you think Dr. Nick can help him?" Thérese asked with worry.

"Non. Pépé and Mémé."

◆ ◆

The evening was hot and muggy. Swiping sweat from his face, Barton felt some respite from the shade of the elms and magnolias along the block.

He had really blown it this time—he'd lost his temper and given Thérese an earful. He left the house not only angry but also embarrassed by what he had said to her. It was very hurtful, and he had no idea where it all came from. So far, everything today has been a disaster.

He could not believe he had gullibly enlisted with his so-called friends, Louis and Garrett Guillot. Damn them! He did not want to be in the military; he had plans for a different life.

His mechanical engineering professor, Maxwell Canfield, had sent him home with a rosy letter of recommendation that should have gotten Barton a great job. Yet, he had not found one here in Beaumont. If he had the chance, he would have gone to Houston or maybe up to Dallas in the next week looking for work.

He wasn't sure exactly what type of job he wanted, but there had to be something better than being a grease monkey at a garage or working down at the shipyards. His brother, Paul, besides working in the family carpentry business, also worked nights at the Plymouth shipyards. He had gotten Barton an interview his first week home, but the job as a welder or riveter was not something Bart wanted to do. And certainly, not a vocation he might be stuck with for years or based upon his engineering and petrology degrees—he was better than that. His brother had worked there for nearly two years yet wasn't even at journeyman level. Paul made a pittance for his little family, which included his expectant wife, Amy, and their cat.

Bart kicked a rock and watched irritably as it sailed off and hit a parked car's wheel. Yeah, his life was out of control; maybe his stepmother and half-sisters were correct. He felt grimly that they were just nosy, busybody females picking on him again.

He impulsively felt as if he should gather up his pitiful few boxes and suitcase of his possessions and hit the trail—get on a train or the bus and get out of Beaumont! He could still feel the darkness from last night and last week's depression egging him on to get lost for good. His father most likely would not be silent about this latest mistake Barton had made. There would probably be a big fight later.

But for all of his protestations and stupid swaggering in trying to justify his actions, Barton realized he did feel foolish. He perhaps had ruined everything that might have been good just by reconnecting with his disreputable friends. He should have stayed far away, but the brothers showed up at his house that first night and dragged him off for a fun blind date … well, he had just let loose and had some fun. The cost for fun was now an expensive price, a bad memory of BettyAnn Sanders, and a really crappy weekend. Now, this awful mess. Damn!

Bart knew he must face his father and just go the round with him, taking the punishment or comeuppance. Thérèse's words that he should not act like a petulant child still hurt, and so did Nancy's remark comparing him to Lex Luthor. Bart shrugged back his broad shoulders, hiked up his pants, and put on a determined look. He raked his fingers through his mussed red hair, took the next turn at the end of the block, and headed for home. There was some fast talking to do, even if it was for something he didn't believe in or wanted to do. Bart didn't want to look a fool in his father's eyes.

◆ ◆

Barton entered the house full of bravado, yet his heart beat wildly in his chest as if expecting his family to all be there to pounce on him. However, the living room was empty, the kitchen clean and quiet, the house silent, and so he escaped up to his borrowed former bedroom.

He lay down on his bed, hoping everyone would leave him alone and that he might get some peaceful sleep when he realized he should change his clothes. Yawning widely, he shed his shirt and pants and kicked off his shoes, still wondering how he was so filthy. His bitten nails were grimed with black, and his palms and knees stung with dirty abrasions. "Must've taken a tumble," he mumbled and fell into bed in his underwear. Thinking he would take a shower in the morning after some shut-eye, he rolled over as he searched for a cool spot among the linens and his pillow.

At last, the languorous tendrils of sleep found him winding about in his fevered brain, stroking his weary muscles, and Bart succumbed to its therapeutic effects.

◆ ◆

The telephone was a distant annoyance dragging him from sleep, yet darkness still hovered about him. Barton had to push it all away, not caring for this clinging, ugly dream. He rolled over in bed but then heard a knock on the door. He didn't want to acknowledge it and put his head under his pillow, seeking the charms of sleep and a better dream. However, the knock turned into pounding, and Barton yelled, "Leave me alone! I am sleeping!"

"There's a phone call for you!" Richard's grim voice carried through the closed door.

"I don't care," Barton grumbled, wanting to ignore it. "Who is it?"

"Get your lazy butt downstairs and answer it!" Richard gave one more hit on Bart's door as he left and slammed his own door.

Barton sat up feeling groggy, but he hollered back, "Hang up! I don't want to talk to those Guillot idiots!" He glanced at the clock to see that barely an hour had passed since he'd fallen asleep. It was still the shank of the evening, and the room was awash in sundown's rosy glow.

"Dang it!" He grabbed the robe hanging at the end of the bed and struggled to put his arms in as he stumbled down the stairs to the phone alcove. He hoped that whoever was on the line had grown tired of waiting and hung up. But then, with a spark of hope, he grabbed up the receiver, thinking the call could be a prospective employer!

"This is Barton Barre," he responded crisply.

"*C'est bien*. I did get the right number, after all. I am glad you still know who you are. Took you long enough to answer. Time's are a-wastin' and costin' me money here while you dawdle along, boy."

"*Pépé!*" Barton smiled now and dismissed the odd salutation. "What?" He coughed. "Why are you calling?"

"Oh, we have missed you and thought perhaps you might enjoy coming to see us before you get too busy this summer. I could use your help on a few projects here."

Barton glanced around at the dim, empty alcove and then upstairs, wondering if Richard was listening in. "That would be swell. I think Dad is sick of me already. Yeah, I will come. When?" He listened and jotted the information down on the notepad near the phone. "Oh, I'd like that. See you in the morning." He hung up and then scrambled up the stairs.

Barton stopped at his father's closed bedroom door, listened for a second, and then knocked. He peeked in to see Richard alone at his desk. "Can I come in?"

Richard nodded. "You may." He responded but did not look up from his book.

Barton nearly tiptoed in but did not go before his father, instead hovering and remaining ready to make a run for it. "Um, I guess you know that was *Pépé*, huh?"

"Of course. What is your decision?"

"About what?" He scratched his head, feeling odd and again childlike before his stern father. "Oh … yeah. I will go see Grandpa and Grandma. They want me and need me."

"That is fine. Behave. I don't want to hear you've been trouble."

Barton nearly blurted out a retort but then clamped his lips tight. He nodded and headed to the door but stopped. "So you don't mind I am going?"

"Why should I mind what you do? You are twenty and insist you are a grown man, Bart," he replied tersely. "*Adieu.* Have a nice time with them, and mind your manners, Son. Just remember you have committed to a national obligation; see that you don't mess that up, too. The army won't be so lenient if you fail to show up on time, boy." Richard added darkly.

Barton shut the door, wondering why he felt so empty. All the former bravado of facing his father was gone, and so were the witty remarks he might have said regarding his latest fiasco. It was an anticlimactic end to an argument that never came. Standing in the hall, he called to his father, "So, can I get a ride to the train station? My train leaves at ten-fifteen." He waited and then heard his father come to the door.

He looked up at his father's face to see it was far too impassive.

"No. I have work. You have a train to catch, so I suggest you get busy." Richard closed the door behind him and trotted down the stairs.

Bart felt the air deflate in his lungs, shocked by the indifferent reaction. He spun around and slammed his door, now more determined to get ready for his trip. "Obviously, no one, not even Dad, wants me here!"

◆ ◆

A dark void surrounded Barton. Empty of sound and with nothing but loneliness, he could feel only a chill wind. He looked about, knowing he was lost, not just in the abyss but also perhaps in purgatory, and he wondered why. As if in answer to the question in his mind, he could smell raw earth, fresh and pungent, and sneezed.

Suddenly, there was an earthen hole before him. He knelt to peer into it, wondering how he could see it in the gloom, yet it was there. The edges of the hole began to expand, clumps of dirt falling inward, and he began to slide toward the hole. With a loud groan, the gaping maw swallowed him. He fell, clawing and grabbing at roots, and then bones jutted out. Afraid, his hands slipped from the aged, broken bones, and he plummeted downward.

Looking up, he spied the stars above, moving in a circular pattern as if the earth was rotating faster or he was spinning as he used to do as a child until he fell down. He continued to fall.

Why? He wondered. His stomach rose, and he felt he might be ill, yet he continued to move downward, flailing with futility. Heat rose as if a furnace was suddenly ignited; he could feel the waves suffusing his limbs and body.

"Repent!" A booming voice echoed amid the darkness of the abyss.

"I've done nothing!" Barton cried aloud. His voice did not echo—it was muffled in the abysmal channel.

"Repent!"

Black things flew at him out of the darkness, hitting his body, sharp talons striking his face and arms as he continued to fall. It was the damn raven from his childhood trying to kill him again, and this time it was an entire flock of them!

He tried to protect his face or roll into a ball, yet he was unable to control his limbs other than to flap his arms uselessly. Still, those black things fluttered about him, striking and pecking. Their ebony eyes glittered maliciously as the ravens' cries were shrill and deafening in his ears.

"Repent. Repent! Repent!"

Feeling tortured, he felt the flames arise to singe him. In a strangled cry, Barton yelled, "I repent! It wasn't my fault!"

His body ignited into crimson flames. As if born on the air currents of the furnace below, he felt afire and flew upward, still in the darkness. He continued up and then burst free into the Stygian dark and cold air above.

He felt burned to ash, his soul rising, but then, all of a sudden, pain surged through him, and he emerged a man again—burned black like ebony. The heavens wept, and a gentle rain washed him clean.

◆ ◆

Barton awoke lying on the floor beside the bed. With confusion, he looked about the room to find it aglow with dawn's feeble pearly light. Feeling exhausted, yet oddly, no longer in pain, he rose and sat on his bed, realizing that he wasn't in his bedroom in Beaumont but on the Barre plantation in Louisiana.

"Oh God, what was that?" he moaned, rubbing his face and head. He still felt gritty and was soaked with sweat. He glanced at the bedside clock and decided a bath just might purge that nightmare. He had been plagued by nearly the same *cauchemar* each night and did not understand it. Each time, he burned, and then sometimes, he was renewed. In one dream, he was sure he had died. That night, giant ravens carried him away and dropped him in a muddy swamp, where he was sucked under in the foulness.

"I have no idea what the hell I did to dream this crud. I must be insane. Damn you, Dad, for sending me here. It's probably all the old ghosts living here coming to haunt me now." Bart grumbled as he headed for his bath. "It's stupid to believe in spooks! I'm not the Cowardly Lion!"

◆ ◆

Barre Plantation, Louisiana
Wednesday, May 26, 1943

At *petite dejeuner* that morning, Barton hurriedly ate his meal as if starving. His grandmother, Annette, glanced at him with worry.

"*Mon p'tit fils, lentement.*" She cautioned him to slow down.

"Sorry. I don't know why I am so hungry this morning," Bart mumbled between bites of food.

Grandfather François bit into a warm brioche, then commented, "I have been wondering if your family is too poor to feed you."

Barton scraped up the last of the fried egg and potatoes, shoveled it into his mouth, chewed, and swallowed. "Why do you say that, *Pépé?*"

"Since you came here, you seem to be eating us out of the house. I did not think I was working you so hard. Am I?"

Barton grinned. "Not really. I am fine." He smiled at his grandparents. "Maybe I have been missing *Mémé's* wonderful cooking. It has been a really long time since I was here."

"*Merci.*" Annette beamed a dimpled smile at her grandson as she continued *en Français*. "We are glad to have you here. You are usually too busy with work and school to come see us anymore. I am sorry that we had more work needing to be done than we had time to sit and chat with you. Your father mentioned that you graduated, so that is a wonderful accomplishment—and ahead of time, too."

"Yes, what was it you were studying?" François asked as he sliced his eggs.

"Mechanical engineering. I also got a minor in petrology." He noted the puzzled quirk of his grandfather's eyebrow. "Um, that's the study of oil," Barton replied. He sat back, feeling good again.

François pursed his lips and nodded before he began to speak, also in French. "Impressive. Well, you were always good with mechanical things. When you were a boy, we had a difficult time keeping you from taking everything apart. You had such great curiosity and always too many questions."

Barton blushed. "I know I was sort of a pest and a brat."

Annette smiled. *"C'est vrais, mon guenon.* I think you are very much like Richard when he was young. He so loved to build things with his father. That is why François recommended him to Herr Kindle. If not for that wise move, I have no idea what Richard might have done with his life."

François patted his wife's hand. *"Maman,* that is old news." He turned to Barton. "So, Son, what do you say we head out to the apiaries in the apple orchard? Annette wants some fresh honey for her baking since sugar seems to be in short supply these days."

Barton gulped nervously—bees were not his favorite creature on the plantation. He recalled upsetting a hive box when he was six, and he had been badly stung for his curiosity. "Can I wear the bee gear?"

"Sure, you can drive the wagon too. Let's go harness up old Tinkle; she needs the exercise, and I need to save the gas for the tractor," François answered as he bounded up from the table.

Barton quickly rose, feeling some relief at working with his grandfather; perhaps the shadows of his *cauchemar* would fade if he kept busy. The only part of collecting the honey he enjoyed was working in the honey house, cranking the centrifuges to spin out the honey and then filtering it. When a child, Barton, and his siblings and cousins used to beg for bits of the honeycomb. Perhaps he would get such a treat today; his mouth was already watering.

"Yes, that sounds good." Barton took up his cutlery and plate and followed his grandparents to the sink. "I guess I should be glad that Dad didn't mind me coming here. At least the food is great!"

He kissed Annette as she began the dishes, and he left with François.

◆ ◆

The morning working with François went well, and Bart had a few jars of dark honey to take home. François sold the lighter and filtered honey to local stores. Then, before lunch, Bart spent an hour in the French garden weeding with his grandmother, a tradition with her and Bart. It was like being with the queen as she chatted, and he enjoyed hearing her sing as she worked. That afternoon, Barton and his grandfather leisurely fished in the nearby bayou while lazily floating in a pirogue. As the day progressed, Barton began to feel relief from the shadows of his dream. Time with his grandparents was just what he needed. He was feeling rejuvenated from his past weeks' escapades; even his cuts and bruises were fading.

However, at dinner, Barton had a surprise discussion, which he was not ready for.

After *grâce à Dieu* was said by François and the meal had begun, Annette commented casually, "Barton dear, you have yet to speak of your enlistment in the army. Are you going to talk about it, or have you changed your mind about going?"

Barton nearly choked on his first bite of fried catfish. "Um, are you sure you aren't going to yell at me too?"

He smelled a rat now. Coming here was nothing more than a conspiracy to get Barton out of Texas. Now, he was facing the same censure as at home.

"Now, why should we? I think you are courageous, yet Papa and I are both surprised you chose to go. Richard had indicated you were avidly seeking a job."

Bart anxiously mashed the food on his plate. "Dad's a blabbermouth. I do want a job, but I haven't found anything worthy yet, at least not in Beaumont." He sat back, feeling his ire rise. *Now, I will have a blowout with my grandparents, too. Damn! Dad just has to ruin everything!*

"Remember, Papa, how upset you were that Richard wanted to go fight in Europe, too? You and he nearly came to fisticuffs," Annette commented pointedly.

François's cheeks turned ruddy, and he coughed. "Uh, yes, I remember. However, Barton is different; he is older. Richard was barely eighteen and ready to go be a man." He turned his dark eyes upon Barton. "Do you feel the same—that you must prove yourself to your father?"

Barton fidgeted uncomfortably under the dark-eyed scrutiny of them both, noting neither smiled at him. He became startled when his grandfather patted his hand and squashed it painfully.

"Well, boy?"

Bart replied, feeling ridiculous for his simple but true answer. "Oh, maybe I do, although I hadn't planned on joining. I was roped into doing it. My friends and I enlisted together."

"I see. Well then, you do what you must think is your patriotic duty." François nodded. "So what is this I hear about a girl named BettyAnn Sanders?"

Barton reacted far too angrily as he threw down his napkin and knocked over his water. He leaped up as the water ran off the table. "I'll clean it up!"

Annette rushed over with her napkin. "No, it is fine." She hastily wiped up the spill and retreated to the kitchen.

François leaned over to Bart. "Boy, you can be honest with me. Did you rape that girl or not?"

"No!" He sat, put his hands over his face, and rubbed his hot cheeks. Barton then glanced at his grandfather. "No, it was just all a big misunderstanding. Her father accused me of having sex with her, but I didn't. He had me arrested, too."

"So, did you learn anything from that experience?"

"What's to learn? All I know is this—I hate BettyAnn for telling her father lies about us and lying to me, too. It was a mess. Thank God she is still a virgin. We didn't do it."

François, savoring a mouthful of herbed greens, then replied, "You do not sound repentant at all."

Bart's head shot up. "Repent?! Me?" He gulped and scooted back from the table. "Excuse me. I am no longer hungry. Tell *Mémé* I am sorry." He dashed from the room and headed upstairs.

François shook his head and shouted in French. "You should be sorrier about the girl! Fool! Peeshwank!"

Annette returned to sit at the table, noting that François was grumbling nasty remarks. "I see you have chased Barton away, too." She put a fresh napkin on her lap. "Don't be too hard on him like you were with Richard."

"Someone has to knock some sense into that boy."

"Ah, well, he is a third son like Richard and you," Annette commented.

"Yes, and we are all rock-headed mules. Sometimes, you have to beat us until we understand."

Annette leaned in and kissed François's grizzled cheek. "*Cheri*, you may be rock-headed, but you are also steady. I no longer must worry over you or our son Richard."

She ate a few bites and then spoke again. "I think we are all that poor boy has. Thérese says he doesn't have many friends and usually keeps to himself. Perhaps he needs a refuge from the world. I do not wish to cleave him from us by angering him. And now that he is soon to leave for the army, I think you know what we must do. *Oui?*"

François nodded but then caught Barton sneaking down the stairs wearing his knapsack. "Running away somewhere?" he called to the retreating youth.

"Um … just for a walk." Barton slammed the front door.

"You see? He is very much like Richard was at his age—he has too much restless anger in him. And from what Thérese and Richard say, I think we must all be very concerned for him to do what is right. I am afraid, too—of him volunteering to be in the army." Annette let out a worried sigh.

"*Moi aussi.* Richard and Thérese will be coming with the rest of the family for the week. We shall do it then," François announced as he motioned for the porcelain butter jar.

"What? Talk with the boy?"

"*Non* … the other thing. It is time, and for whatever reason, it seems to help our young men grow up just a little faster." François let out a slight cough. "It did wonders for our Francis and Richard's boy Paul."

Annette nodded. "Until then, give Barton a little respect and space to work this all out on his own."

"I agree. The boy just needs some hard work. There are irrigation channels to be cleared and dug. He'll feel better." François took up his knife and a dab of butter. "Now, if we can just eat in peace here before everything is cold, I shall be happy." He began to mangle his bread while fiercely spreading the butter on it. "No more discussion, Annette. *Non un plus mot.*"

◆ ◆

Barton walked in the twilight through the alfalfa field, feeling the dewy coolness of the tall grasses touching him. The day had been hot, and now there was a refreshing breeze off the Mississippi and the nearby overgrown irrigation ditch. He wandered along, caught in troubled thoughts, wanting to be alone, yet a pair of Catahoula hunting dogs paced alongside him.

He was probably acting like a stubborn fool. He truly did not want to go into the army; he wanted a job and a way to get away from his family. While he cared for them and had, at times, missed the family when he was in college, those years away had been good for Barton. He had learned to be his own man. It had been a long time since he had made such critical mistakes in judgment.

But since returning home to Beaumont and reconnecting with friends and family, Barton felt his careful restraint slide away, and his life spin out of control. He had made two very grave errors in the weeks past and wondered now about both his grandfather's words about repenting and his evil dreams. Yet the outcomes of his mistakes he felt were not his fault … although, perhaps the mistake with BettyAnn Sanders had led him to the result that he was now a soldier. *Oh, God!*

He could now recall that night. It was supposed to be fun too …

◆ ◆

Just weeks ago, in order to celebrate Bart's return home from college, his friends Louis and Garrett Guillot had fixed him up with BettyAnn Sanders; she was the sister of Garrett's girl, Marcia. They all went out for an evening picnic and fun along the Neches River.

After supper, Louis and Garrett disappeared into the bushes with their girlfriends. Barton, left alone with BettyAnn, had tried to fill the spaces with a witty conversation between the giggles and lusty sighs from the bushes, but he felt that BettyAnn probably thought him only a bore. He had no ideas for a safe topic to converse with the girl. She did not seem bright. BettyAnn just sat there, fidgeting and giggling at Bart's poor attempts at humor. She even yawned in the awkward silence.

BettyAnn was a pretty girl, slim-boned yet buxom, blonde-haired and blue-eyed. She reminded Bart of a former college girlfriend, Felicity Flannery. She wore a sleeveless yellow dotted Swiss dress and white sandals with red painted toes. Bart despised the color yellow, painted nails, and sandals. But he overlooked it all as she kept sending him coquettish glances, her pretty eyes downcast when she did speak and her dark lashes feathering her apple-pink cheeks.

At one point, she coyly put a hand on his thigh, laughing at something he said. That started it. Barton leaned over and kissed her on the cheek. Surprised, she pulled her head away, looking at him squarely. Her eyes darted to his mouth, and he repeated the kiss more forcefully on her lips.

He was gentlemanly with her. She kissed him back. BettyAnn took his hand and put it on her breast, and that was all the invitation he had needed. Barton gathered her up, and they reclined on the blanket where they had eaten their picnic supper. He poured a paper cup of cheap, fruity wine, and they drank it together between kisses. They lay down on the blanket, and she stroked him while kissing him eagerly.

Barton excitedly began to push up her dress, feeling her smooth thighs, but she jerked them together suddenly. He lifted his head, looked down into her wild blue eyes, and asked her if it was okay to continue. She closed her eyes and nodded yes. Bart planted tiny kisses, trailing them down her cheeks to her neck and then following a path over her rounded breasts. He tried to be romantic, as he had learned most girls enjoyed. She sighed and let him touch her in the secret place as he held her gently. He unfastened his pants and was feeling for her, even feeling her hand stroke him, when all of a sudden, she blanched white and screeched in his ear.

Horrified, Bart put his hand over her mouth to still her. He would have pulled away, except BettyAnn wriggled and moaned under him. Her hand gripped him so hard that he suddenly lost himself, wetting his clothes and hers but not making the connection. It was a terrible misfire. He frantically held her close and kissed her to stop her cries so he could stop shuddering from the fast sex.

"Sh! Betty! I am done. You're fine," Barton said nervously after a minute, afraid that the others would show up, wondering about the noise. He rose quickly and knelt over her, pulling his pants closed and tucking in his shirt. He pulled her skirt down over her legs and picked up a napkin, attempting to wipe the wet mess off her dress and his clothes.

BettyAnn whimpered, her blue eyes large and tear-filled as she watched him. He pulled her up into a sitting position and sat beside her.

"So, why pull the cold fish? I thought you wanted to do it." Barton looked around to see if anyone had heard them. They were alone. He did not need witnesses to his mistake.

BettyAnn said hesitantly, "I did … I mean, I do want to." She laid a shy hand on his arm.

Barton looked at the hand in distaste. "Well, you sure acted like you didn't! Why'd you scream in my ear?" He shook his head, his ear still ringing.

BettyAnn, seeing his harsh gaze, withdrew her hand and sobbed brokenly into her hands as if ashamed of her actions. "I want to go home," she mumbled through her hands.

"Fine, let's go."

The ride toward Beaumont was a quiet one but full of remorse and unspoken hurts. Barton glanced at BettyAnn once; she was staring out the window at the darkened scenery passing by, hiccupping softly with a hankie pressed to her mouth. He felt bad. The evening had started out swell: the picnic food the sisters provided was good, wading in the river shallows was fun, and everyone chatting and walking along the beach and under the trees at sunset had been great. The conversation with BettyAnn had not been exactly engaging, but the romantic moments leading up to the disaster had been exciting. He felt he needed to say something, make it right, or the stupid girl might say he raped her!

Bart cleared his throat and asked her, "If I stop the car, will you talk to me without hysterics?" He glanced at her and met her frightened eyes in the reflected glass of the passenger window. She was so small, hugging the door like a frightened rabbit. She nodded. He slowed the car, turned off at the easement, and shut off the engine.

He turned to her and took her hand, noticing it was cold. He could feel the nervous tremor running through her. Her slim hand felt fragile now, whereas a half hour before, it had been boldly touching and pawing him, even holding him for a while. Bart winced; perhaps that had scared her—holding his *zi-zi*.

"Please talk to me, Betty." He urged, pressing her hand. "I want to understand how you can turn away from me so quickly. Did I do something wrong?"

"What do you want me to say? That I am sorry?" BettyAnn retorted, stifling her sobs.

"No, that's not what I want." He waited for her to say something. Then he thought of something that had been bothering him all night.

"How old are you?"

"Eighteen. I told you that!" She spat out the words.

"Are you really eighteen? Because Marcia is supposed to be eighteen, and you are not twins," he queried logically and waited.

"Bart, she's nineteen." As if noting Bart's reproving look, she hurried to reply, "So what if I am not what I said! I'm almost seventeen, though." She sighed heavily, caught in her deceit and her confession. "At least I will be this next week." She turned a bit to him to ask shyly, "Y'all wanna come to my party?" Her smile was tremulous.

"Seventeen?" he echoed and gulped. "And you are still a … um, a virgin?"

She did not answer but nodded miserably and let out a shuddering sigh. "Well, I was until a while ago!"

He let go of her hand and struck the steering wheel, cursing under his breath.

BettyAnn cringed away, frightened. "I guess I am ruined now, aren't I?" She wailed anew, sniffling loudly against her hankie. She fearfully looked up at Barton.

He glared at her for a moment. He had to tell her the truth, even if it was embarrassing. Touching her cheek with a finger stroking the hot skin, he murmured, "You are still a virgin, *chérie*. You can take that to your marriage bed. It won't be me who ruined you."

Her cheeks inflamed and eyes wide, she gasped. "B-but we … and you did … and there was … the …" BettyAnn gestured at her soiled dress.

Barton shook his head. "I did. You did not. We did not make the connection. Believe me; you would have known if we had." He chuckled, but then, thinking of another retort, he laughed. "If we had done the dirty little deed, we would probably still be there doing it! I didn't exactly have much fun either." Bart regretfully smoothed the lump in his pants, still feeling sore from BettyAnn's firm grip.

"I guess I am the one who needs to apologize for messing up your dress," he said soberly, waiting for her to stop the waterworks.

BettyAnn laughed hoarsely and then said, "Oh God, Daddy is really gonna kill me now. My sister Marcia told him we were going to the movies after a supper picnic in the park, but I will be coming home without her. He's gonna wonder why I am … you know, messy!"

They both laughed.

BettyAnn seemed endeared by Barton's caring manner, and suddenly emboldened, she leaned over and kissed him lightly on the lips. "You're sweet. Thank you."

Barton was surprised at the kiss. "Don't start that again. I had better get you home before I really do take advantage of you!" He grinned wolfishly.

"Fix yourself up, comb your hair, wipe your face, and put on your lipstick. Your folks will never know," he said assuredly.

He started the car, and with a glance in the mirror, he pulled out onto the road and drove slowly through the dark country lanes, across the bridge, and into town, down silent, lamp-lit streets. He whistled softly and tunelessly to fill in the gaps in conversation as BettyAnn made her makeup repairs and gave him directions.

He pulled up at her house and left the motor running, expecting to talk some more. But BettyAnn swiftly kissed him and got out of the car. Her skirts swished as she happily walked to her door. She gave him a tiny wave. "Call me …" she called before she walked into the house.

He left quietly, glad he didn't need to walk her home, yet thinking that he might have to visit her in a few years. She was going to drive men crazy. He had almost taken a bite out of that forbidden fruit.

"Shit!" He grumbled. "Seventeen! She seemed older. I thought she knew what she was doing." Until she had screamed, that is. His ear still tingled from that. He went home and went to bed, thinking he had done the right thing after all.

◆ ◆

The next morning, Bart awoke to the telephone ringing in the downstairs hallway. A few minutes later, his door opened, and the surly face of his father peeked in. "Barton, get up now!" he demanded in a rough voice.

Barton got up and pulled on pants and a shirt, not bothering with his shoes. He went downstairs and peeked into the living room, where his father and stepmother were waiting for him.

"Sit," Richard commanded.

He sat.

"We just got a call from a Martin Sanders. He said you took out his sixteen-year-old daughter BettyAnn last night. Is this true?" He glowered at Barton.

"Y-yes, sir. I did. But I didn't know she was sixteen."

"Liar! He says she told you she was sixteen." Richard thundered.

Barton jumped up angrily, already defensive. He hated being called a liar. "She did not tell me that fact until afterward. I mean, until the end of the evening. I took her home right away when I found out!" he shouted back. "Besides, she'll be seventeen this week, so it doesn't—"

Thérese interrupted. "Afterward? After … what? Oh, Barton, tell me you didn't!" Thérese implored him with angry shock showing on her normally gentle face.

"Oh, *Merde* and damnation!" his father rasped, rubbing his unshaven cheek.

Barton recalled feeling tiny as Richard crowded over him.

"Don't tell me there'll be a shotgun wedding soon! Martin is furious, and he is too upset to say exactly what happened to her! She came back smelling of wine and sex, her dress dirtied and her hair mussed. Her sister came in later, crying that BettyAnn had gone missing. Evidently, he got a convoluted, outlandish story out of the two girls. The girl's reputation is now sullied. This is tantamount to rape!" Richard threw his hands in the air.

Trying to reassure his parents, Bart implored them to listen. "I took care of her when I found out she was so inexperienced—I mean, young. Oh, damn! I'm in trouble, aren't I?" He sat, suddenly putting his head in his hands, and let out an exasperated sigh. "She is still a virgin, by the way. I didn't hurt her in that way," he said to the rug.

Looking up, he hoped that fact would save him but saw Richard pacing the floor. Thérese sat with her head bent in quiet thought, absently picking at the fabric of the couch.

Richard turned suddenly to Bart. "She's a virgin, you say?"

"So she says. I certainly wasn't in the mood to check for myself! I can tell you that we didn't, um … make the connection!" Barton spread his hands in a silent plea.

"Stop acting like Alibi Ike with your ridiculous excuses—come clean, boy! I need to know so I don't feel a fool when I talk to Sanders again," Richard demanded as he towered over him, making Bart feel wormlike.

Barton told them what happened, except he left out the part about his little misfire. He just explained that they were heavily engaged in kissing and petting.

"So, how did you meet her?" Thérese asked quietly.

"Garrett's girl, Marcia, is BettyAnn's sister; we were all out on a picnic date. They fixed me up with BettyAnn."

"I might have known! You should have known that anything Garrett and Louis are into is usually not respectable. Those two are nothing but a pack of trouble! This always happens when you get around those older boys! You never seem to learn. Why do you think Jacques and Paul no longer have anything to do with them?" Richard said hotly before pacing away to stare out the bay window.

"I don't know if I can get you out of this, Barton. You were stupid and irresponsible to be involved with a young girl like that." Richard's voice was tremulous and weary. He shook his head before turning back to him.

"B-but, Dad, how was I—" Barton was once again cut off.

"You should not be taking advantage of any girls, regardless of their age. Shame … on … you, Barton Carl Barre!" Thérese shook her finger in Bart's face, emphasizing each word before angrily spinning away and stamping down the hallway. The kitchen door slammed after her.

Bart sat stunned. He looked sheepishly at his father. "So what am I to do, Dad? I can go apologize to Mr. Sanders if you want."

"If *I* want?" Richard bellowed indignantly. "It's what *you* should want, you little misogynistic ingrate! Don't you understand how damaging this is to a young girl and her family? People are going to talk about this, you know. I don't know how you can be so callous about other people's feelings. You should know better. I thought I brought you up to be a gentleman. Oh, what will Father Matthew have to say about this?" He spun on Barton. "That's it! We are going to confession. Right now!"

Barton was not comfortable discussing his personal life, and having to tell his father or a priest about the mess made it even worse, not to mention the fact that having pre-marital sex was considered a grave sin!

"Look, Dad, if I had not been a gentleman, I would not have stopped. And when I asked her, she said yes! Then, when she screamed—"

"Well, that should have been a warning to you!" Richard eyed his son nastily.

"Look here! I was careful. I still had to reassure her that just kissing did not take away her virginity. I could not do that to her. I am not that much of a shit-heel!" Barton theorized hotly. "So whatever she told her parents is a lie. She's probably afraid her parents will know she came willingly on a date with an older man. I am innocent. I do not need that kind of sexual experience!"

"Ha! You only think yourself a man, yet you are an irresponsible kid!" Richard shouted, but then, seeing the contrite and nearly ingenuous look on Bart's pale, freckled face, he amended his harsh words. "Fine. I hear your words, Son, and I hope that you are telling me the truth. But can you say all that to BettyAnn's parents, face-to-face?"

"I could, and I will. But I don't think Betty's parents are going to hear what I have to say once they know their little girl was wantonly encouraging me and had lied to me, do you?" Barton replied angrily.

"I suppose not." Richard already felt the defeat, as did Barton. "Martin seemed to think you put BettyAnn up to sneaking out last night."

Bart gaped. "Me? I had never met her before last night at the river! She came with Garrett and Marcia. It's a damned lie!"

"I think you have some chores to be done. Get to it while I think about this mess." Barton's father had dismissed him as if he were a child.

◆ ◆

Barton continued to feel the shame and anguish as he remembered the sheriff coming to the house that afternoon. He had handcuffed Barton and taken him straight to jail. There was no trial, and no one would hear his pleas of innocence or listen to his story. He sat in the cold, filthy cell with only a metal pot to piss in, a tin cup of water, and a chunk of bread, surrounded by filthy drunks for two days. He was miserable and knew that these had been his darkest moments. No one, friend or family, had visited him. He did not even have a Bible or rosary to pray with or to reassure him of salvation from his sins.

The deputy came early Monday morning, opening the cell to let out Barton and the drunks. The sheriff was waiting for him outside and roughly pushed Bart into the backseat of the car. They sped down the streets of the town with the siren wailing and people staring at the screaming black vehicle, and then they pulled up in front of BettyAnn's house.

There was a flick of the curtains at the window on the main floor. People came out of their homes and stood about, wondering what was going on as Barton was taken from the car in handcuffs. The sheriff shoved him down the walkway toward the front door. It was the longest walk of his life.

The front door opened, and then Marcia and her parents came out and stood on the porch. Marcia and her mother, both wearing pin-curls and robes, held each other. There was no sign of BettyAnn. Mr. Sanders, balding and stout in his undershirt and suspendered pants, held out a sheet of paper to Barton and spoke harshly. "Read it out loud!" His blue eyes glittered dangerously as he glared at Bart.

Barton glanced at the paper—an admission of his guilt. He gulped and looked around. People in robes and pajamas were now crowded on the sidewalk, all staring and whispering among themselves.

Glowering at the sheriff, Bart hissed, "This is a bum rap. It's a lie."

The sheriff cuffed his head hard. "Read it!" He commanded.

With watering eyes, Bart began. "I … Barton Barre, do hereby swear that I knowingly and disgracefully took advantage of a minor to ruin her good reputation. I regret my actions, and I hereby apologize to the Sanders family, to the girl I seduced, to the neighborhood, and to the town of Beaumont, Texas. I hereby swear to be a gentleman from now on, and as I have served my time in jail, I am now pardoned for my crime of passion."

He read it loudly, his guts cramping; he wanted to vomit as he spoke the harsh and archaic confession. He did not feel guilty of anything and was angry that he must submit to the allegations.

As he handed back the paper to Mr. Sanders, he said, "I am truly sorry if your daughter's reputation was hurt. I hope she will forgive me. You didn't have to bust my chops, sir. Betty lied to me about her age. I did nothing wrong." He offered his cuffed hand to shake, but Sanders looked at him repugnantly.

He spat in Bart's face. "Filth!" He then turned away brusquely, pushing his weepy family inside the house and closing the door behind him.

"What a fathead!" Bart groused.

He looked at the windows of the house, hoping to catch a glimpse of BettyAnn. There was a curtain moving on the second floor and the shadow of someone behind it. He raised a hand in a silent wave and then grimly turned away. The sheriff released his hands from the cuffs and headed back to the car. Barton wiped his face on his shirttail and then skipped a step or two to catch up with the sheriff, making a move to get back in the car.

The sheriff slammed the door as he growled, "Justice has been served. I have no more responsibility for you, Barre." The surly man got in the car, and with gravel spitting in all directions, he sped away.

The crowd backed away, talking in hushed tones, and with suspect glances at Bart, they began to disassemble to their homes.

Bart had a protracted and painful long walk home. He went silently to his room, not letting anyone know he had returned from jail or what had transpired after his release, and sadly realized his parents already knew what had happened. He felt branded—as if he should wear a big A on his forehead for an *abuser* or an F emblazoned on his breast for a *fornicator*. That day—his life should be over. Barton avoided all glances, and he talked to no one. He was incredibly embarrassed to talk about it with his sisters and hoped they knew nothing of his mistake.

He had moodily gone about his chores and ate his meals alone and felt as if he was invisible, for no one spoke to him. For those days, Barton was miserable. He vowed to stay away from women—they all lied. It was a nightmare.

Then, later in the week, his so-called friends, the Guillot brothers, abducted him with the sole purpose of cheering him up with a rowdy night on the town. They got him in trouble again; they joined the army the following day.

He still could not recall everything that had happened during that drunken night of debauchery and mess. So perhaps that night was the cause of his recent nightmares since he'd been staying with his grandparents.

Barton sighed wearily. For the sake of his penance for his own foibles and misdemeanors, he was going to assume his next duty—that of a soldier.

$$\cdot \blacklozenge \cdot$$

CHAPTER 2

A Letter To My Son

Barre Plantation
Francis Ville, Louisiana
Thursday, May 27, 1943

There was a brown, paper-wrapped parcel tied with twine lying on the quilt of his bed when he returned from a tiring day's work in the fields. He would not have noticed it save for the fact that it was lumpy under his hip as he sat down on the bed to pull off his boots.

Holding a booted foot in one hand, he fished out the package from under his rump. Oddly, there were no postage stamps on it. There was an envelope under the tied string. It read:

For Barton, Read First!

He recognized the tiny flowery scrawl of his father's cursive hand. He slid out the envelope and found it contained a thick sheaf of the fragile onion-skinned writing paper that his father favored. *Merde!* It looked like a book. His father could be rather verbose when writing and owned a more formal style of speech than his usual cultured Louisiana drawl. Barton looked at the letter with distaste, wondering when it had come.

Now what? He wondered.

He glanced at the clock on the bedside table, noting there was over an hour before dinner. He sniffed at himself, and with a grunt of disgust, he dropped the letter onto the bed by the package. He continued to pull off his boots, pants, and undershorts, kicking them aside. He tugged the worn, smelly chambray work shirt off and added it to the pile. He stood for a moment, enjoying the pleasant feel of nakedness as he idly scratched the private spots that were impolite in public to scratch during the day. Resolved to read the letter after his bath, he went into the adjacent bathroom to run a warm tub with some Epsom salts added to ease his achy parts from digging irrigation ditches.

Much refreshed from his toilette, Bart returned to the bedroom with a towel wrapped around his waist. Not caring he was still damp, he plopped onto the bed and retrieved the package and letter. Bart switched on the bedside lamp and settled back against the pillows, carefully taking the pages from the envelope to read his father's missive. He found it odd that the letter was dated today. He was suspect of some calculated preparation on his father's part. His fingers stuck to the delicate pages.

May 27, 1943

To my son, Barton,

Number three has sometimes been my lucky number. I was born March 30, 1900, as you know. I am the lucky third son of a third son. I have been married three times and have six children that I know of. Three of those are sons by my second wife, Charlotte (your mother), and three daughters by my third wife, Thérèse. I will probably never know if there were children from my first wife, as we were married only mere days before I had to leave her.

Barton was already feeling heady by the words scrawled across the page. He was stunned by the fact that his father had been married three times. This seemed to signify the weight of the letter. His father enjoyed telling stories. Papa's Parables, as Bart called them, always had a moral lesson or reason behind the tale. He sighed and continued to scan the letter.

The number three has guided or perhaps swept me along the river of my own destiny. It is because of this that I take time now to talk to you about the importance of such things, not that I am prone to superstition. It is because I have been formed by these numerical occurrences like molten metal in a crucible with the impurities burned away and poured out into a new mold.

I have been dead three times. No, that is not entirely correct, but I was nearly dead, and in each of those times, I reformed and became another man. When the number three was a present omen, something significant happened. You know they say cats have nine lives; I have had three. Perhaps I shall be lucky to live a long life and see all nine. I do hope they will be better ones! They also say old dogs do not learn new tricks. Well, Son, I tell you they do—I did. You will see this truth in my words.

So, while I have spent much of my life filled with my cares and concerns for family and business, I have had to push hard to keep what was just, genuine, and noble held like a dangling carrot in front of me so that I would not stray from the path.

Son, it is difficult to do this, but it is for the greater good. And for us remarkable La Barre men (the third son of a third son), we share a curse or perhaps a legacy for which we must always be mindful. It is a portentous legacy. In you, much is expected. Maybe the La Barre Curse might end with you—that is, if you live your life right!

The blessings God gives us, and indeed, what He gave to me, are a price above rubies and should never be wasted. It is better than all wealth, the knowledge that, as a man, I have done what was important, what has made a difference in the lives of others, especially my family. I am not a hero or a grand man or deserving of much. Nevertheless, I am honest about my life. I have tried to live as an example of these values of faith and honor: bearing humble pride, never forgetting the importance of family and hard work, and making one's life accountable not only to others and yourself but to God. These things I hoped my children would have learned.

"You are as humble as a stinging bee! Yeah, Dad, you taught us so much!" Bart grumbled as he read, annoyed by his father's pious tone and sanctimonious claptrap. He gritted his teeth to read.

I say these things to you, Barton because I am worried about you. I see in you much of myself from when I was young, and I was not the man I am now. I know I was foolish then.

Although you and I have not always had smooth paths or agreements, what I say to you is important. You must understand how you were made and how you may be able to redeem yourself when you have a dire need.

The quote "no man is an island" is true. He is the conglomeration of all the surrounding elements. As he is of the earth, his soul is like a well, drawing up the essences to strengthen him. Because of this, you must remember to be part of the earth and the life that is around you.

I see you try to isolate yourself from deeper emotions, from the people who care for you, and from the things that should be important to you. Conversely, I see you straying toward bright, shiny promises like a crow; these things have no merit.

"Oh great, so not only does the man call me a fool, but now I am an unfeeling, meritless crow!" Barton set aside the letter for a moment to stare at it. The cursive letters squirmed across the page accusingly. "I really gotta leave; there seems no way to please this man!"

Barton's father always said he loved him. Yet, it was always conditional. It was like fencing with his father. At first, Richard often parried with pleasant words, throwing Barton off, but then he would lunge and thrust to the heart, wounding with stinging words!

Reluctantly, Bart picked up the stack of papers, shuffled the previously read pages to the back, and, with an audible groan, continued to read.

I do see in you such incredible strength and courage, a search for all things just. Yet you revolt against anything that would threaten to hold you. This streak of rebellion and lawlessness that young men often enter will become burdensome to you. You will lose your cherished freedom if you continue down this destructive path. At this moment, I shall not go over your most recent trials, as you and I have already aired our opinions most heartily. I believe you will not repeat these offenses.

Barton sat up abruptly and clawed the paper, wadding it up, not wanting to see those remarks from his father. None of it was his fault! BettyAnn Sanders had lied and gotten him in trouble—so had his best friends. He sat for a moment, grinding his teeth and wishing ills on his father. The man could let nothing go. He was a bulldog who constantly worried and chivied Barton over past mistakes.

Now Bart was distraught. He smoothed out the paper to see the other things his father might say about him. Damn! If the man wanted a fight, Barton would give him a royal one, and all within the days before he was to leave for the army.

"*Petomane!* The rotten old fart! Let's just burn all the bridges to hell." Bart fumed and scrunched down to continue reading the vile missive; however, his eyebrows rose as he read.

I try to have confidence in you, Son, that you should prevail, but know this: you will be passing painfully through your trials by fire. At this moment, perhaps you see in yourself a warrior fueled by patriotism, filled with the lust to do battle. You are a young animal ready for its first kill and taste of blood. Therefore, you must go to war. It is not my war. You come from many generations of legendary men who fought for what they believed were liberty and justice, and many just for vain pride and their misguided honor.

But, Son, war is hell. I have been in one, lived, and nearly died for the cause of it. I pray you will not be killed and that your soul will not die morally eaten away by the horror that is war.

You never met your Great-Great-Uncle Albert Barton Philippe. Some say he went insane from what he experienced during the Civil War. He never was an easy man after that war, plagued by demons and the cauchemars of his battles. Another of our ancestors decided to fight the war in his own way; Armand Du Barre used his two ships for exports and trade between the Indies and the States and for transferring supplies, military equipment, men, and horses. He survived most of the war until he was handed over to the Union for conspiracy and gunrunning. He was hung from the yardarm of one of his own scuttled ships in Mobile Bay, Alabama. He was a fated third son, too, gaining much and losing everything.

I quote Leo Tolstoy, for it seems apt. "War and Peace" was your mother's favorite book, and I do recall you reading it. "It seems as though mankind has forgotten the laws of its divine Savior, who preached love and forgiveness of injuries—and that men attribute the greatest merit to skill in killing one another."

Stay safe. Pray daily, hourly, pray for yourself, your men, and your enemy. When you look upon your enemy, knowing that you must kill him, also know that he is just like you, a man, and you are depriving him of all that he has worked for—family, love, freedom, and life.

You will soon find out the life of a foot soldier is filthy, harsh, degrading, and dehumanizing. I believe war is the ugliest side of humanity, for there really is no beauty or true victory in war. It is an illusion, and everyone loses at all costs. In my opinion, there are few heroes. You should know that most of them are men who just stepped in at a moment in time, fully loaded with the possibilities of fate. There is no vanity or glory in the killing of a man; however, it is done. Yet you must be honorable in all that you do. You have accepted a grave commission, Son.

Please know that we, your family, will be praying for you and always that if this mad war should end, you will be returned to us alive and whole.

Now, here are some things that I freely must tell you, hoping they will help you, and some I will ask for myself.

Barton let out the breath he had held, expecting another rasher of crap. Instead, this heartfelt jolt of heroic blather and sentiment smoothed his brow and calmed him for the moment so he could continue reading. He never knew his father had been a soldier.

When I was a youth, my father saw my growing interest in young women. Knowing that I was handsome, and I had misused my charms in the abuse (deflowering and the ravaging) of our local blossoms (girls), sometimes causing a scandal, he sat me down to make some course corrections in my life's direction. Does this sound familiar?

As the third son, I had no immediate inheritance of business or property to come to me. My older brothers Francis and Paul would get those first when the time came. Father had money, but you do not give foolish kids money. He knew I needed some way to make a living for a future wife and family, and my academic skills were not job worthy of much to survive. He gave me the choice of working fishing boats out on the Gulf, working the docks, or working for his friend, a German carpenter near Weiss. By sending me away, Dad also took the fox out of the henhouse, thus protecting the girls. A wise man!

I was sixteen when my father sent me to be an apprentice in Herr Kindle's carpentry shop. I was there for a year and a half. I first learned to make doors and cabinetry, and soon, I had a flair and skill for making furniture.

When the Great War came, the lust for adventure rose in me, perhaps partly fueled by the lack of women in my life. I could not wait to enlist. I knew I needed to assuage the yearnings. As I know now, I was a stupid kid, and I put my life in jeopardy to prove a point to my old man. I made my parents ill with worry. I was ready to fight for something greater than my petty concerns. Yet when the war was before me, I felt great fear and thought perhaps I had chosen wrongly, but I was too prideful to tell my parents.

You might find these comments shocking coming from me. I've never been a coward. Yet, sometimes, there is nothing wrong with seeking peace. Remember, there is also nothing wrong with fear, but you must put it in the proper perspective and not let it make you a coward.

Every man in my unit was afraid, but when the battle came, we knew we had to do our best to fight. Daily, I prayed to be brave and to be honorable to my comrades and myself. I had to look with fresh eyes and a clean soul toward the war, knowing that I could die at any second. You must do the same. Make your peace before and after the battles.

Here is a time still imprinted on my mind …

Our Third Division had been on the move by trucks and on foot for well over twenty-four hours. We were coming from Laferté-sur-Aube on our way to the Marne bridges and Château-Thierry. For days, we marched through winding mazes of trenches, along dusty roads, over hills, and through blasted bloody countrysides, villages, and haunted, empty farms.

I will never forget the cow we found at a burned-out farm. The area had been eerily silent as we came through the woods and onto the farm, but then we heard a pitiful lowing for several minutes before we found her. Her horns and a foot caught in the barbed wire, she had an ugly hole blasted in her side; her bloodied flanks heaved and jerked against the swarm of flies. At her feet was a dead calf. Seeing us, she was renewed in strength and let out several loud bellows. Some of us thought to free her from the fence. Seeing her wounds were most likely mortal, we were hesitant to act. However, Private Angelo took swift aim and shot her before anyone could move out of the line, saying that she was annoyingly loud.

It was startling and brutal because she did not die quickly, thrashing about and bellowing to her last breath. The farm boys were appalled and thought she deserved a swifter, less painful fate. But the cow and Private Angelo had given away our position, and within moments, we were fired upon and shelled. Running for our lives, we retreated from the farm, taking a circuitous detour through the Belleau Woods before finally getting behind the pickets and into the trenches along the defensive line.

We left five dead men at that farm beside the dead cow. Angelo took a beating that night. Private Angelo did not live out the week; shot by a sniper while pissing. For many of us, it seemed an omen and a fitting demise, including the strict lesson for us to be watchful and never fire without an order. I felt more sorry for the cow than for Angelo. She was an innocent victim of the war.

We were in battle nearly every day and often took heavy casualties. After one long day of fighting, we arrived at our division rally point, feeling overheated from the forced march and battle. Our boots were soggy and heavily laden with mud, and our coats were coldly burdensome with a moldy damp from the past drizzle. Weary, we sat about in the trenches, waiting for the next muster. I remember it was June 7; we were resting and preparing for battle. The Germans were mostly quiet that day. We found out the next day they had been nearby, amassing for a major assault and push toward Château-Thierry.

I shared a tin cup of hot water with a drop of wine with my buddy, Corporal Stovall. We had no more coffee or tea, only water to heat. Some of the food and supply trucks had broken down along the way, and many of the trucks in the forced march had run out of petrol. We were feeling lucky to have our weak drink and a bit of hard biscuit from our kit.

I sat trying to corral my thoughts, hoping to take refuge in my mind. I wanted to assuage the anger I felt toward Private Angelo for killing the cow days before. Yet I found it difficult to find peace within the midst of hundreds of stinking, noisy men, their voices gruff and coarse, and to find ease on the cold, muddy ground. My belly groaned with hunger.

Then Stovall says to me, "Hey! Rich! This'll take yer mind off yer belly!" He tossed me a packet of printed cards. On the backs were written enticing messages in French.

I turned the cards over and beheld French nudie cards! I was shocked, and I gaped at the partially clad beauties. Bare butts like ripe peaches, full breasts like apples with cherry nipples; they pouted and smiled coquettishly, wearing little lacy corsets, stockings, and garters.

Son, I had hardly thought of a woman in many months, and to have these beautiful ladies in my hands, I felt the heat come on. They were like pieces of fruit to be eaten and savored. At that moment, I had the worst case of "tent pole" ever.

Now, you are probably offended, thinking your old man is a lecher! Hell, I have been married three times, and it was not for good luck, mind you. Nevertheless, I feel I can say these things to you, as I know you to be a well-loved young man, and you should understand.

Even as I tossed the cards onto Stovall's lap, my eyes were still riveted on them. I had to turn away. I remember yelling at him: "Shit, Stovall, what'd you do that for? I don't want to look at those! Mon Dieu!" I got up and walked away, anywhere to be free of those cards and the men's laughter! I think I must have traversed half of France back and forth through the trenches that night.

I was miserable. I wanted and needed that kind of forbidden fruit! Yet I had to put those wicked thoughts out of my mind. I found another place to sit and spent some time with my Bible, opening it at random; I was still plagued with images as I read.

"Then Naomi took the child and laid him in her bosom …"

"If my heart was enticed by a woman …"

I was guilty as a sin for drooling over Stovall's nudie cards! Then, the worst verse of them all struck me!

"And he shall destroy the wicked, and the sinners together: and they that have forsaken the Lord shall be consumed."

Oh, Son, I felt so wicked in those moments and knew that God had placed those biblical texts before my eyes to test me and show me the path of my downfall. I felt easily perverted by such carnality. I knew I was in the military to escape my lustful needs. I decided then that I would not think of or look at a woman again in that way save for her to be my wife. I was lucky that night roaming about, for while I was gone, my unit was gassed. Stovall was severely burned. A few others died in the attack. Perhaps God did save me!

A week went by, and we were marched back and forth along the lines. Often, we got to a place only to be told we must retreat—how futile it seems. Evidence of such things happening to others came down the line when we heard the report of the Second Division troops who dug in along a defensive line just north of the village of Lucy-le-Bocage. Marine Captain Williams, when advised to withdraw, had replied, "Retreat? Hell! We just got here!" Captain Williams did not survive the ensuing battle.

Most of the time, we dumb lugs did not know where we were. Another week went by, and our division split. We came into a small village on the edge of Soissons, and we made camp there. The AEF took over a few empty houses and a little hotel. We had been involved in heavy combat for several weeks and needed the time to recoup and regroup before heading back into the Château area.

It felt good to be in civilization again. We had the chance to bathe in fresh, hot water! After a few days, we heard that there was a girlie house in the area, and the soldiers were welcome. At the edge of town, there was a little bar with a blue sign over the door: "Le Lapin D'Or." It was easy to find—it had a gold rabbit on the sign and no words.

I trailed along one day with a clutch of men, myself not really into pursuing fleshly delights, but I heard they served beer and felt badly in need of a drink.

The long, dark mahogany bar had a white marble counter with a glittering mirror behind it. Little cut-crystal gas lamps glowed charmingly, and candles sparkled on the tables. It was an incongruous delight to be somewhere pleasant amid the war. Growing up speaking proper French from my Nice-born Maman, I was ahead of the other fellows who spoke little to no French. I was served first.

The matron there was a once-lovely older woman (perhaps in her forties). She wore a white gown and a white curled wig (resembling Marie Antoinette). She wore large gemstone rings on many of her chubby fingers and a beauty spot in the shape of a heart near her upper lip. This was Madam Lapin. She was short but very buxom and constantly smoked Gauloises and a tiny little pipe that lent fragrant musky incense to the air. She had four girls to offer the men "entertainment."

There was a sweet sparrow of a serving girl; she was dark-eyed, dark-haired with pearl earbobs, and a tight dress that showed her blooming décolletage. I ordered another beer, and between the cold, bitter taste and the sight of the French barmaid, I nearly swooned—I was in heaven! I went back to that bar enchanted by the barmaid, and after several visits, I asked to marry her. I was only jesting, so I was surprised that she swiftly said yes.

Barton breathed out a weary sigh. This letter was outrageous! How could Richard have done such things? Worried now, he shuffled to the next page, hoping that there wouldn't be more disheartening and lurid information. Yet, he felt caught in the tale as he read on.

The weekend came, and I met Lisette behind Lapin D'Or. She had a saddled horse and a bag of clothes for me to change—I was a soldier and did not want to be recognized. We rode into Soissons, went inside a chapel, and asked for the priest. He was a frowzy-looking old man wearing a decrepit patched black alb. He smiled at us and married us quickly, not even opening his worship book. I figured he had committed the service to memory, but he stammered and slurred in a few places with some "ers" here and there. I suspected he was drunk.

I gave Lisette the gold crucifix I wore (a gift from my mother on my first Communion), as I did not have a ring. Lisette gave me a small molded brass piece with a blue ribbon sandwiched between the two halves of metal—it had a figure of a rabbit on one side and on the other an old-fashioned skeleton key with a stamped Roman numeral three below it. There seemed something odd about the whole thing, but I figured it was just me, the new nervous groom. I was giddy at the prospect of being married.

We rode toward Lisette's village with me behind her on the horse's rump, and as we neared a forest glade, she guided the horse off the road and took us into the woods. We found a quiet spot within a cool, shady refuge with a sparkling rivulet of water, whereby Lisette set out a picnic with an old quilt, a bottle of wine, baguette, pears, and a chunk of brie. We toasted each other, the new Mrs. Richard Barre and me, the lucky groom. We enjoyed our bits of food and made sweet love in our private Eden beneath the watchful eyes of cooing doves and twittering birds in the trees. It was pretty romantic, and I can now wax poetic.

Yet, when I think of that time, I am astounded to know we were lucky to have lived the day; the Germans were less than a mile away in that wood.

As the evening approached, I knew I had to get back to my battalion, so we made plans to see each other as soon as possible, hoping we could make some other living arrangements. I thought quickly of deserting the Marines, but I knew the punishment would be severe. Perhaps Lisette could follow along, maybe be a washerwoman or a cook. I wanted her and needed her to be safe.

The next day, I made an official visit to the bar to look for my wife. Lisette was not present, but I was told Madame wanted to speak to me. I climbed the backstairs with a lump in my throat. I quickly found the Salon Rouge. Lisette was sitting on a cassock, weeping, winding and twisting a mouchoir repeatedly through her fingers.

Madame nodded to a chair for me to sit. "S'assesoir. S'il te plâit." She asked me in French if I spoke the language. I said I did. Taking a moment to gaze at me then at Lisette, with a frown, Madame Lapin launched into her tirade.

Did I know what I had done?

What was she going to do with her daughter now that she had been defiled?

She demanded that I pay her for the discourtesy and the evil deed done to her daughter.

I glanced at Lisette, who had stopped crying and had a most odd look on her face—her large eyes unwavering in intensity. And when she responded flatly, it hurt me.

"We are married, Maman. Richard is my husband now, and I am going to have his child."

I stood up suddenly, knocking over a crystal vase on the rug, and quickly regretted it as spots dizzily spun before my eyes when I tried to pick up the flowers. I sat again.

"What? How can ... what? You can't be pregnant, Lisette; we only had the one time after our wedding yesterday! You said you were a virgin!"

She hissed like a cat. "I am, and it is yours!" She gripped my arm fiercely.

For such a tiny girl, she was strong!

Madame Lapin, seeing there was nothing to move her daughter, a little too quickly said to me, "Well then, Monsieur, you shall pay her dowry. Or you take her away now in disgrace."

"I cannot. I am a soldier, and I have no place to take her," I gabbled stupidly.

"Then pay you must!" With that exclamation, Madame Lapin held out her ringed fingers and worn palm.

Sadly, I pulled out my coin purse and emptied its contents into her outstretched hand. The woman looked crossly at the coins; it was only a franc, a few centimes, two American pennies, two silver dollars, a lost tooth, and bits of lint. I then felt bad for all the money I had spent in the bar downstairs so I might flirt with Lisette!

Looking up at me with a look of disgust, Madame asked me, "So this is your bride's price?"

"I only have my heart left," I said in English and then finished in French, "Je regrette ... Oui c'est tout!" I hoped my face would show her my earnestness.

Madame closed her palm and said through gritted teeth, "You do not deserve her, you pitiful American cur. You are all dogs who sniff around and steal the best morsels from us! Leave now. Lisette will have nothing further to do with you. Filth!" She spat upon me.

Barton felt his guts clench reading the harsh words. *Oh, God … both he and Richard had been called filth.* Tearfully, he continued to read.

When I looked at them, the eyes of mother and daughter held the same haughty, cold aspect, as if distastefully viewing me like a cockroach to be crushed. It was then that I felt the icy fingers of fear creeping along my spine, pain seizing me in the nether regions of my heart, gut, and balls. I was lost.

"Lisette, please …" I begged. But Madame shoved me forcibly out the door, slamming it in my face.

For the next three days, I neither slept nor ate. I took on extra guard duty as my own silent penance. I composed many half-written and scratched-out pages of poems, letters, and petitions to Lisette, leaving them daily at the bar. Then, finally arriving at a worthy poem and a desperate missive, which I wrapped in a piece of red ribbon, I took it to Le Lapin D'Or, hoping she would see me. The door and her heart were closed to me.

On the fourth day, our troops broke camp, and we marched out at 0600. I kept looking along the way, wishing to see Lisette on the street. Then, for at least the next hour, I often peeked back toward the town, expecting I would see a slim figure upon her steed chasing after the troops. My heart ached for the possibility of a timely reunion—what Lisette's kisses would mean and what they would feel like. However, as the miles passed, my heart, like my feet, became weighed down by the mud on the road. I realized I had truly lost her. That day, we engaged those Germans who had hidden in the woods on my wedding day.

Within three weeks, I came down with typhoid fever like so many others in our regiment.

On one horrendous night, roaring artillery and gunfire thundered in my aching ears and painfully reverberated in my fevered brain. Not able to stand the din anymore, I flung myself over the top of a trench and ran toward the enemy line in a last effort to kill myself. I could no longer live with a broken heart and an empty future or the fever burning in my brain.

I screamed, "Kill me! Shoot me, you cretins! Tuez-moi! Je veux morir!"

Someone threw a gas canister.

Holding my breath, I ran blindly forward. A man lurched upright out of the darkness; surprised at my advance and startled, I bashed him with my rifle and then ripped him with the bayonet. I ran across the field, bashing and slashing as I went. I realized I was on the wrong side of the war when I felt bullets zinging past me. I dropped to my belly and crawled like a worm, slithering headfirst into a foxhole. I had the distinct feeling that I had been hit; there was an overall burning somewhere down below. My carbine was a broken ruin—I had never fired a shot!

Three days later, I awoke in a hospital with a cool cloth pressed on my forehead. I was under clean, crisp white linens. There were the subtle sounds of hushed voices and the mélange aromas of alcohol, soap, and onions. I pulled off the rag, and my eyes blurred. I saw a pleasant, chubby blonde nurse beside the bed holding a tray with a bowl of broth. Her eyes showed surprise, and she smiled at me.

"Oh! Corporal Barre, you are awake. That is good. Would you like some soup?" she asked me in accented English.

I felt empty, bereft of food, life sapped, energy gone because of the fever, my heart dead. My disappointment burned deeply that I was still alive. I said yes, and despite the dirty look from the soldier in the other bed, she turned and sat at my side and fed me spoonful-by-spoonful of rich, onion-flavored broth. I realized that perhaps the soup was meant for the other man when the nurse called the orderly for more soup.

"They tell me you are a hero, Corporal Barre. You very nearly died in your valiant effort," she said engagingly as she wiped a dribble of broth from my chin like a doting mother.

I also enjoyed hearing my last name pronounced correctly in French. The men in my unit pronounced my name Bar-ray, Barry, or Bear.

"Me? Surely, you have it wrong. Besides, I am only a First-Class Private." I gulped another spoonful, wondering.

"Non, non. They say you killed deux canardeurs, and it was because of you that your men were able to take a squad of the enemy by surprise. I think they are all dead," the nurse said with awe.

"*My men? All dead?*" *I asked, suddenly afraid I really had done something stupid and caused the death of my own men.*

"*Non, silly, les Allemands!*" *She chortled like a little hen, her eyes sparkling with humor. The little nurse fed me the last of the soup, gently wiped my burned face, patted down the covers, winked, and left me to my own thoughts.*

I barely remembered the battle except for the noise. I still had a constant chirring in my head and ears. I closed my eyes to remember. There were ghostly faces in the night amid horrible screams, and I shuddered, not knowing what they were or to whom they had belonged. There was a potent dread in that darkness of my mind, and I opened my eyes quickly to gaze out the sunny window and flee that evil.

The pain was still with me. I pulled back the covers with my bandaged hands, suddenly afraid of what I might not find. I found my leg splinted and thickly bandaged around my thigh. I pressed wary fingers there—my leg was intact. I breathed a gasp of joy at the thought of wholeness.

According to the doctors, the bullet had gone through my thigh and lodged in the femur, breaking it. I was lucky they had not amputated my leg! I had also suffered a severe concussion from falling on my head in the foxhole. I was lucky to have not broken my neck! And maybe luckier still to have survived the mustard gas attack with mild burns and the deadly typhoid fever, which, during the spring and summer, killed thousands of men on both war fronts.

With my thoughts lightened, I had survived it all; I snuggled into the covers and took stock of my existence to date.

Then, with a sad heart, I thought of my marriage to Lisette. I realized it had not only been a mistake, but I sagely knew it had been a ruse. I thought of the little brass medallion—Lisette told me to present "La Clef d'Or" at the bar when I wanted her. I truly wanted her! I had been a too-willing and gullible boy lured by the promise of love for sex. She was most certainly one of Madame Lapin's prostitutes, and the number three was her designation. The momentary, sweet thought of our time together after the wedding caused a grip in my guts, and I silently wished them both a life of hell. I was a poor sport.

I felt sick to my stomach, and the onion broth bubbled up accusingly in my throat. I tried to rationalize the event. All the talk and embarrassing thoughts of having defiled the beautiful Lisette were nothing but a lie. Was she pregnant, and had this scheme been a quick way to provide for her and the baby, who was clearly not my baby?

Thinking about the speedy marriage and the rumpled, doddering old priest, the ready horse, and Lisette pregnant with my baby, it all rang solemnly like a great bell of doom in my head.

I had given up my reputation over a hotsy-totsy. I lost my cherished crucifix to the greedy hands of the Lapin women, not to mention the last of my money in the world. Last sad point, I had idiotically run into battle suicidal with my broken heart.

I grimly knew I had fallen badly. I had not been faithful to myself, Lisette, or even honorable in the sight of God. I asked myself if I was courageous or only an accidental hero. I was none of that; I was a stupid, blundering idiot. I was a weak coward. My father and heroic ancestors would die of shame knowing what I had done. I made a silent prayer to God at that moment and promised to be an honorable man and to not listen to the "demanding things in my pants" or my foolish heart but to be cognitive and wary for my own sake.

As a half note on this story, Son, I was advanced in rank to corporal and awarded a medal for bravery. My compatriots had seen my charge onto the field as a daring feat, and inspired, many had followed. They had not heard my demented cries over the roar of the gunfire. I was mortified to carry such a weighty piece of metal over my heart, for over the summer, thousands of courageous men died during the Battle for Château-Thierry. I did not deserve it.

I later gave my medal to my father, who, not knowing the truth of how I got it, was pleased as punch. I kept the rabbit medallion and my Purple Heart medal for myself, thinking of La Clef d'Or as a perpetual warning against thieves of the heart and the spirit.

Now, here are the things I ask of you, Barton. Please accept the Bible that I kept with me while in France. Although it is a bit ragged, the words are still valid. Read it daily. Thérèse believes it should go with you too, that perhaps it was my fateful charm to survive. I also give to you La Clef d'Or. Carry it with you as a reminder not to be stupid or false in love.

When you are in France, and if you see the sign of Le Lapin d'Or, I challenge you to stop in and present them with La Clef. If you should meet up with Madame Lapin (though she is most likely dead by now) or her daughter Lisette, remember me to them. And, Son, if possible, see if you can get back my crucifix, wear it, and put it on as your armor against the evils of greed and lust.

Barton let out an expressive breath, feeling as if he had been running a race. "Holy crud! Dad!" He shuffled to the next page.

Here is the last thing I will ask of you. You are invited to the Summer Dance in Brusly. There, you will find some real flowers in the community. Be a gentleman. Dance with a few young ladies and then pick one to dance and talk with for the rest of the evening. Ask if you can write to her and if she will write back. Give her one chaste kiss at the end of the evening, and then come home and go to bed by yourself.

You are asking now, "What the heck is this fool talking about?"

Well, Son, I mean that you should have a friend back home who will write to you while you are away. (I do not believe you have many.) She will hopefully brighten the dark days and give you a sense of home. As she is not your sweetheart, you won't have an ardent desire to know everything she does, nor will you care enough to worry over her. I hope that this will keep you from making a foolish mistake like I did when marrying the first girl I laid hands on.

So, what do you think of your crazy old man, eh? Perhaps you are asking yourself if Mom knows about my shaded past love life. Yes. I have shared my story with both of them, Charlotte and Thérèse, but the other kids don't know. I didn't feel they needed to know. By the way, Thérèse gave me the idea for you to have a girl pen pal; it will keep you out of trouble. I agree with her.

I am sending you away a young, untried colt, and you will hopefully return to us a valiant steed! My ever-loving prayers and thoughts will be with you, my son.

Father,

Richard Barton Carlisle Barre

P.S. Do not forget to kiss your mother and sisters goodbye.

With a weighty exhalation, Barton set aside the letter and ripped open the parcel. There was a tiny tissue-wrapped piece, and he saw it was *Le Clef D'Or* with the blue grosgrain ribbon faded and frayed. It was so small, but it felt heavy in his hand; a weight of conscience bore down upon it. He set it aside with a bit of distaste.

The venerable black, crackled leather 1898 French Bible was well-used, the pages crinkled and musty from past dampness. There were bits of frayed ribbon and paper bookmarks wedged between the pages. He opened the front cover and found an envelope with a single, large, age-browned piece of paper, clearly old and many times folded.

Curious, Bart pulled out the paper and found that it held the names of his Barre ancestry dating back to the late 1690s to Avignon and St. Remy, France. Barton had not realized the family had gone back that far. He knew a few stories; the Barres were overly proud of their French heritage.

The La Barre side of the family, once granted land by King Louis XIV in Upper Canada, had been living in the French colonies of Acadia. Bart knew the story of an Acadian descendant, Clement La Barre, who had been prosperous in the northern colonies and was a man of great pride and honor in his community. After the English routed the French from that province in the 1750s, the stubborn family of La Barres refused to ship with the refugee families to return to France. Instead, Clement took his family, a few loyal friends (investors), and servants and bought a *barque, Le Poisson,* packing away all the petite ship could carry. Stopping in ports along the way down the coast of North America, he and his friends bought, sold, and traded goods. By the time they arrived in the French colony of Louisiana on the Gulf Coast, they had amassed a small amount of wealth. Clement was able immediately to buy land and a home in the rugged town of New Orleans to secure his family. Using his newly gained ship, he plied his trade. The La Barre family and their friends and investors prospered, with Clement finally settling along the Mississippi River, where he purchased nearly twenty square miles of land.

For almost three generations, there were several prosperous plantations owned by the La Barre family. The families of La Barre adapted themselves to the new land, despite the constant changes in the foreign sovereign rule of the Louisiana Territory, and then finally became part of the American colonies.

During the early days, the La Barre families owned slaves; their crops of indigo, rice, sugarcane, beans, honey, lumber, and cattle made for lucrative trade along the Mississippi River. Many of the crops were exported to the Indies and Europe using the fleet of La Barre ships.

Then, the War Between the States came, and the La Barres lost much of their land, their homes, and their slaves, as well as their trade business. Many of the younger men went to war; most did not return. Losing so much was not a total devastation to the La Barre family, for they miraculously gathered their resources to live more compactly on the remaining properties.

Following the Civil War, some of the Barres sold their land and left Louisiana, settling in Texas, Colorado, and Wyoming, where they bought land for cattle ranches and farms. The stoic family figured the money was money; they could always make more. Times and their fortunes changed, and La Barres had always optimistically met the challenges of the past ages.

One strong person was Barton's great-grandfather, Carl Barre. He kept some of his slaves and field hands after their manumission. Carl was a liberalist for slave reform, and during the war years, he did not always share his opinions in public; that would have indeed led him to ruin. But he knew that his manumitted slaves, and a few indentured servants would have no safe place to go; they were an endangered commodity in the war-ravaged Southern states. He had never been one for the whip, like other slave owners or even his father. People were not animals. For that simple kindness, many of his workers remained, knowing their families were safe and respected.

A man of the changing times, Carl wisely knew he could not take a chance in hiring new, reliable people. Carl allowed the "new" servants, cooks, maids, a dozen field hands, and their families to build their new homes, each using an acre of land to grow their own food. He provided the tools and the supplies they would need to live. The aged and decrepit slave quarters were torn down for materials, and the rest was burned. It was a day of jubilation for some, while others shed tears of worry as a new age descended upon the La Barre family and plantation. He changed out some of the more laborious crops for fruit and nut orchards, another legacy of his ownership.

Carl also built a schoolhouse on the estate, and all the children (of the manor and servants) were required to get their education at least to the sixth grade. Richard was the last Barre child to go to that elementary school. During the antebellum days, slaves could not read or write, and Carl had always thought that law idiotic. He felt everyone would be better served if his workers had an education; they could make a better life on either the plantation or somewhere else. That was the legacy of Carl Barre.

Barton's grandfather, François, was very much the same as Carl, an insightful, kind, generous, capable, and hard-working boss and family man. Barton loved and respected *Grand-Père* François.

Bart knew some of those old servant row houses, and at the time they were built, they were probably generous and pleasant. A few homes were still there near the sassafras, pecan, and hickory groves. Some of the descendant generations of former slave families continued to live and work at the old plantation, but now as salaried free men and women. Bart's childhood friend Mike Shaw lived in a row house; his mother worked as a picker in the orchards and sometimes as an extra housemaid during the holidays.

With a sudden thought, he felt badly that Mike had enlisted in the Navy last year. Barton would miss him this time. He had a sudden pang in his gut, hoping that they both made it through the war and could go fishing again as reunited old friends!

Barton's mind turned again to his heritage. Their Colonial French family was accented with only a few English and German wives in the past thirty years to add to their French blood. He knew that the pride of their French heritage had kept the La Barre family speaking the pure Colonial and European French rather than the Cajun and Creole patois that evolved in the community through the centuries. Yet many of the family members, as a joke, could all break into vulgar patois when prompted, especially his father, who loved to slur his speech in the mix of Cajun and English when telling jokes. Proud *Grand-mère* Annette would giggle for a moment, but then, if there were guests present, she would give Richard a serious glower to remind him they were of French aristocratic blood!

To this day, Carl Barre's second plantation house remains a proud reminder of better days. Despite the ill fates and family breaking up in the past fifty years, the current plantation was the last working entity still belonging to the La Barre family.

Richard had made sure Barton and his siblings knew what it was like to be born into such a family and to learn the responsibilities of home and farm. Richard had loved growing up in the old house, so he wanted his children to spend as much time as possible there. Barton knew the plantation of his grandfather François well, having spent many summers here. In his youth, Bart and his brothers helped to bring in crops and work the fields, just as he'd done today. He felt the labors today, though, of digging and threshing, for it had been a couple of years since his last visit.

Barton had fond memories of many hours spent with his brothers, cousins, and friends exploring the vast plantation or gliding by rowboat on the cooled river waters and bayous during the summer evenings. They had fished, dug for clams, and netted frogs, crawfish, and crabs. The river and bayous were adventurous places for young boys. As a youth, Barton had learned to hunt fowl in the swamp and shot his first deer at sixteen.

Reflecting again upon the family tree, Barton traced his finger along the family lines, noting where the name changed from La Barre to Du Barre to Barrie and, finally, to Barre. Some of the spelling changes had occurred from poor spelling or misread deeds and documents. He knew of at least two of his ancestors who had changed their names to avoid scandals and the hangman's noose. The family tree did not show all the names of the children of each generation, just the number of children (three to nine), and farther back, only the names of the ones that traced down to his father. Barton noticed his name was added under his parents' names at the bottom edge of the page. There were tiny marks beside many of the men's names, and he had to surmise that it showed the fated third sons—his grandfather's, his father's, and his were marked. There were many gaps between some of the marked names, so he surmised the family continued to believe in the curse.

Barton reflected upon the letter he had just read; perhaps this was another of his father's silent messages to him. "You must understand how you are made and how you may be able to redeem yourself when you have a dire need."

This scrap of paper showed him the paths of his ancestors and the potential life that could be his because of his heritage and the superstition of the La Barre family curse regarding the third sons. He wasn't sure if he wanted to believe in the curse.

Family legend had it that L'Egyptienne, a gypsy witch, once cursed all third sons of the La Barre family with innate charm and luck, yet they could easily fall to destruction if they chose selfishly. Barton smiled as he ruefully recalled his father telling him the story a very long time ago. That first cursed son had ruined a girl, too, and later died in prison a destroyed and broken man. As the current last generation of three successive third sons, if he lived a good life, then the curse would be broken. If he chose poorly, then he might be doomed, and the curse may continue to his sons and perhaps beyond. Was he cursed? Lately, it felt like it.

Feeling an onerous sense of familial duty, with the haunting shadows of those on the family tree long gone, Bart folded the paper and tucked it in the envelope with the letter from his father.

He looked about the room now again at the moment and sighed with contentment for the familiarity of the venerable house. This bedroom was always his when the family stayed with his grandparents, so Barton hoped his box would still be there. It had been some years since he had looked. Barton knelt and felt under the bed; tucked up under the bed frame was his secret cache. He pulled out a very dusty pasteboard cigar box (his old treasure box). He smiled fondly at the thing, put in the letter and medallion, and then put the box in his knapsack along with the Bible.

He wandered through the room, touching things with fond remembrance: the quilted bedspread, the white painted scrolled iron bed frame, the whitewashed wicker washstand with the crockery painted with green leaves, the oak highboy dresser with the narrow oval mirror. He was finally tall enough to stand and see his reflection in the mirror. The watercolor painting of a shepherd and flock always reminded him of something from the Bible.

He glanced up at the aged, green, ivy-patterned wallpaper and smiled. Every summer, he would count the giant leaves as he lay in bed. Sometimes, he would make it a game, crawling under or moving furniture about to find hidden leaves. He recalled the total—729. Once, he had divided the count for different colored leaves, yet after successive visits, the total count remained the same.

He headed to the tall, narrow window and noted that the thick, forest-green velvet winter curtains tied back with a sash were the same, but the white eyelet summer curtains were newer. They caught the breeze, which aided in circulating the air in the narrow, hot room. As a child, Barton always pulled the bed under the windows so he could catch the breeze and watch the flaming sunsets and fireflies in the trees. He would fall asleep under the moon's eye and the spinning stars, dreaming the fireflies were Tinkerbell's fairy friends.

At this moment, he felt exhausted by Richard's epistle, wishing he could lie down and sleep as an innocent child.

Bart recalled some of the previous shock and family arguments when his brother Paul wanted to enlist in the Navy after eloping with Amy Wendell. Richard had been brokenhearted and angry as hell.

For some odd reason, Richard initially kept his silence when Barton announced the stupid thing he had done by volunteering. Instead, Barton received a verbose letter from his father. He wasn't sure if it was meant as a punishment or if Richard was resigned to the fact that Bart stubbornly stuck to his guns. As his father always said, "It's your mess, boy; you clean it up!"

Well, yeah, it was a mess, and Bart hoped to hell that he wouldn't buy the farm! He sadly knew some of his former classmates who had joined up out of high school or in college and never came home from the war. He did not want to be one of those unlucky statistics.

Floundering among his thoughts, Barton found he still stood at the bedroom window, absently watching the golden haze creep upon the land and house as the twilight mixed with the damp steam rising from the river. The hot day was cooling now with a gentle, fragrant breeze from the water and freshly mowed lawn, bringing the sounds of fishing birds, hunting frogs, and a general thrum of the myriad of insects—crickets, mosquitoes, midges, and cicadas. The rooster had gathered his harem of hens to the coops, and Bart could hear their suppertime murmuring as someone put out their feed.

This place had always made him feel connected with something stronger than himself or the family. Definitely, it was a mix of God's creation and a product of man's hands. He loved this countryside and wished he could stay here.

However, there were too many people here—the people who would not let him forget his foibles or his past or even let him choose his own future without a fight. *Grand-père's* house and the more recently built houses out on the county road had his Uncle Francis and most of his brood living here, assorted cousins, grandchildren, and such. It was too busy a place for Barton. He had stubbornly chosen a different path, not in Beaumont or here. Then, one damaging night, everything he had worked for was ruined.

Stupid Louis and his brother Garrett Guillot had gotten him into this mess, Barton angrily reflected; they were just bored big boys! The Guillot brothers had no plans for their lives, but he'd certainly had plans; now Bart was stuck, shit out of luck. He was going to kick both of them in the pants before getting on the bus to camp. That trip would be a painful one for everybody!

Bart resigned to his fate and, hearing his grandfather shout for him, *"À Table!"* got dressed for supper.

◆ ◆

There was surprising news during supper. Tomorrow, Bart's Beaumont family was coming for a week, taking an early and quick vacation before the heat of the summer took over. He almost complained, jealously knowing that his time with his grandparents was now limited, for they would be busy with a house full of guests.

Barton ate his supper in silence, still reeling from his father's letter, yet wanting to confirm the stories Richard had written. As he sat toying with the creamed *epinards*, not caring for them, he wondered how to broach the subject of the heady letter. But supper was soon over, and there were Aunt Patrice, Uncle Francis, and his cousins,

Carl Louis, Thomas, and Anna, at the door, all ready for dessert and games of canasta and pan. Barton had lost his chance and his quiet evening.

He took his dishes to the kitchen and then headed for the stables, thinking that the company of the horses or goats might be preferable to his obnoxious aunt and her dull-witted and boring children.

◆ ◆

May 28, 1943

The following day, Barton stood by as his Beaumont family was welcomed by the plantation Barres, and before he could talk with his father about the letter, the house was full of people, and he lost his nerve.

Soon, there were more people crowded around the luncheon table, all talking excitedly and catching up with each other. He hurriedly ate and excused himself, afraid someone would make a comment about Barton's latest foray into idiocy and cause a caustic and bad argument, including an indigestible meal. Grabbing up a handful of bread, he retreated outside for a long walk, this time with a pack of Catahoulas and Brittanys following him along.

He munched on the bread, sometimes crumbling off pieces and dropping them to the dogs, and realized he missed a simple life like this. He had been working feverishly through high school and college for so many years in order to graduate early, yet he'd missed the idleness and fun of his youth—those days were gone. Barton did feel rebellious; he wanted to recapture some youthful fun but then stoically realized he should suck it up, settle into his new life, and forget everything, including his hard-earned college degree.

Maybe Thérese and the others were right. Perhaps he did belong in the army, for he no longer held a place here among his family. Embittered, he angrily tossed the last of the bread into the weeds along the road and watched the dogs scramble for it. Leaving them to their feast, he headed back to the crowded house, ready to be brave for just one more night. It was rumored there was to be a family gathering tomorrow night. At least he looked forward to the food.

The women of the Barre family were exceptional cooks, and when they all gathered, a feast was prepared, often savory and rich, traditional French food or favored Creole cuisine. He trotted up the steps. For now, he had chores and supposed that he might be lucky enough to spend some time with his brothers as they worked. He laughed at the irony. Vacations here on the plantation were primarily working ones, or at least they were now that he was a young man. As a child, he had lots of fun—sadly, those carefree and idyllic days were in the past.

◆ ◆

Saturday, May 29, 1943

Glancing at the clock, Bart realized he had twenty minutes to get ready for the special dinner. He knew he had better be early and look his best. *Belle-mère* Thérese had asked him to be present as the guests came in tonight. He truly did not enjoy big parties, but he would put on a brave face.

He went to the closet and took out his best suit, the dark blue serge (formerly Jacques's suit), a crisply ironed white shirt, and a blue striped necktie and matching braces borrowed from *Grand-père*. He buffed his black wing-tip shoes, pleased that they still took a shine. He dressed himself carefully, combed his curly rust-colored hair with a bit of lavender water, and smoothed his brows and pencil-thin mustache.

He smiled at his reflection and commented, "You look sharp, Bart! Too bad tonight is only dinner. I'd slay those dolls at the dance!"

He noted the pile of his muddy work clothes on the floor and quickly kicked them into the closet. He shut off the light and trotted down the stairs in time to see Thérese floating by in her pale blue organdy dress.

Her face lit up as she saw him coming down the stairs, and he accepted her kiss on the cheek in welcome.

"You look so handsome, Son."

Thérese sighed with relief. "The evening will be a success," she commented, taking his arm and leading Barton into the parlor. "I am glad you are finally in a good mood!"

◆ ◆

Later that night, Barton stood by the French doors on the terrace, breathing in the cool evening air scented with dewy, freshly mowed grass, verbena, honeysuckle, gardenia, lilacs, and roses. The night birds and crickets were noisily in concert. He sipped his after-dinner cognac, enjoying the warm sensation coursing down his throat.

He reflected on the delicious dinner he had enjoyed a while earlier. His favorite fish course—chilled shrimp and spicy tomato aspic, followed by baked game hens, roasted eggplant and tomatoes, and wild rice with wild mushrooms and garlic. The salad consisted of sliced pears with walnuts and homemade Roquefort cheese. The dessert made by Aunt Patrice was now his favorite and something new to the family, Bananas Foster.

But the highlight had been when Thérese and Patrice came out carefully balancing a towering *Sainte Honoré*—little puff pastry balls filled with creamy custard stacked almost two feet high with orange-flavored syrup drizzled down over the tower. He remembered it from Thérese and Richard's wedding years ago. Annette had made it instead of the traditional wedding cake. He thanked Thérese with an appreciative hug and warm kisses, as he knew she had made it in his honor. It felt good to be treated like a king and much better than when he'd left home last week like an unlucky, flea-bitten dog!

Bart knew it would be a very long time before he would eat a feast like that again. From what he had heard, the food in the army would be a lot of canned things, mashed potatoes, boiled beef, powdered milk, and God knew what else. Oh, and SOS—shit on a shingle! Barton's stomach flopped uncomfortably. He drank a large gulp of the cognac to dislodge the mental taste of such culinary glop. He smiled to himself as he realized he really was a bit of a gourmand and snob and very lucky that his family appreciated good French food.

Tonight's dinner party, held at his grandfather's plantation house near Francis Ville, was a big deal. The house had been decorated with tall urns of flowers, and they'd used their best heirloom china and silver. It would probably be the last time he would see *Grand-père* François and *Grand-mère* Annette; they were getting old and frail.

The entire family had come together for a brief reunion and surprise party in Barton's honor. His older twin brothers, Jack and Paul, were there with their wives, Celeste and Amy. Amy, huge with pregnancy, was also the talk of the party, as she and Paul eagerly expected their first child. She had miscarried once before.

Barton did not mind sharing the limelight; in fact, he was glad to do it. He would rather be a remote part of the festivities, not caring for the rowdy attention, yet remain watching from the sidelines. Doing so now, Bart scanned the faces of his Barre family, aunts, uncles, and cousins, as well as old family friends and devoted workers, committing them to memory. He knew he should remember them all here as a happy, noisy, and loving community.

He sometimes felt jealous of his family in that he did not always feel joy or interest in the minor events that occurred daily in a large family such as his. He knew the women thrived on such things. The men, while they talked of their own manly subjects, still enjoyed the thrills of new babies, engagements, marriages, and the like. The family reunions were also a time when they could come together to speak their ancestral French and enjoy rich, fabulous food and drink aged wines.

Barton knew from experience that his father loved to sit amid his large family with a drink in hand, a child on his knee, the flowers of his women fluttering about him, and the pride of his sons glowing in his dark-brown eyes. These simple, homely times that his father loved were the same ones that Barton drew away from, feeling uncomfortable with demonstrative love.

He hated having to make small talk, especially with people whom he had rarely seen or barely knew. He also despised the teasing of older siblings and cousins and joshing about as the butt of family pranks.

When he was young, the constant pinching of his cheeks, rubbing of his head, and general squishing and squashing of his childish body had led him to escape to a place where he could watch from afar but still be a remote part of the family, only to pop up when something good or exciting happened. When small, he hid under the settee in the parlor, then later under his grandmother's grand piano, and later still on the terraced patio off the main dining room where he was now.

As a small boy, he had often thought he was catlike, for cats liked attention but on their own terms. He knew that was why he enjoyed cats more than dogs. Dogs generally liked anyone who would pet them, talk to them, or feed them! However, a cat chose his companions and friends carefully, much the way Barton himself did.

He wondered briefly, *Where are the cats tonight?* He had seen none while he'd been out working or when he'd come in the house. No doubt, they had taken refuge somewhere away from the general chaos of the day and bright lights in the house tonight. A vast rural place such as this was a haven for cats; there were colonies of them here! There were mice and rats in the barns and fields, frogs and lizards in the swamps and grasses, and bugs and birds just about everywhere; it was a cat's paradise. Even the Barres' house cats led pampered lives here with fresh milk and cream from the dairy cows and goats, tidbits from the kitchen, and a multitude of people who would take a moment to pet them wherever they were in the house.

He hoped he would find one tonight and take it to bed with him. Barton slept better when there was a relaxing, rumbling purr from the foot of the bed, the soft paws gently kneading his legs and feet, and the feeling of a warm, silky body curled near him. It was bliss for him. He had missed having a cat while he was in college, too. He had long given up sleeping with his old, ragged toy dog Tou-Tou as a child, but a cat was another matter.

He heard his name at the edge of his musings and turned into the doorway, eyes searching the room for the speaker. He felt a tug on his jacket sleeve and found short

Amy looking up at him, her hazel eyes aglow. She could not stand close to him without pressing her large belly against him.

"I have a little present for you, Bart, but you gotta come inside." She smiled coquettishly as she handed him a small package and wrapped a hand around his wrist to pull him inside.

His cheeks glowing with the heat of the drink and embarrassment, he took the gift. "Should I open it now or wait?" he queried as he followed Amy back into the house, hoping to open it later. "You know I hate surprises."

"Please now!" Amy bounced on her toes. Just then, Paul came up and put his arm around her, pressing Amy to his side. They both wore wide, toothy grins and bumped each other affectionately.

"Actually, it is from all of us," Paul said and then gave a short, shrill whistle. The room quieted. "Hey! Bart's opening his present now," Paul announced to the room. People crowded around quickly, and then he urged Bart with a nod. "Get on with the unveiling, kid."

Now, with cheeks flaming, Bart tore off the paper and found a small, flat, black velvet box. *Some kind of jewelry*, he thought. With a swift glance at his brother, he opened the lid.

Nestled inside was a gold medallion and chain. It bore the embossed family crest of a flaming phoenix rising above a fiery cloud; on the reverse side, the inscription read *"Nous sommes contre les ventes."*, with a *fleur-de-lis* in the middle. It was the American version of the old La Barre crest from France—*"S'Elancer Sur Les Ventes,"* "Fly on the winds." The "new" motto (still over two hundred years old), "We are [fly] against the winds," Barton felt was appropriate for the Barre family. They had indeed prospered despite the winds of change and endured many wars and hardships. He felt a sudden shadow pass over him.

Bart looked up, surprised by the tears in his eyes and his choked feeling. This was his rite of passage as a man—that he was given the family crest. While in college, he had missed his twin brothers' rites when they turned twenty-one. He now looked around the crowded room and caught his father gazing at him with dewy, dark eyes. Richard raised his glass in a silent toast to him. Bart felt as though he had been forgiven for everything that had happened recently. The medallion represented he was a respected and beloved man. He held up the box to the crowd while everyone jostled for a closer look and oohed in appreciation.

Jack made his way through the crowd. As he arrived next to Paul, together, they grabbed up a struggling Barton, undid his necktie, and unbuttoned his shirt partway. Barton was stunned to silence as they put the necklace over his head. The pair opened their own shirts, revealing hairy chests and showing off their medallions. They each wore a prideful, wide grin.

"*Nous sommes les frères La Barre!*" the brothers roared and grabbed Bart in a brotherly trio hug.

With a bit of arm punching and wrestling about, the twins each gave Bart kisses on his cheeks, French-style, before releasing him. There was much laughter and many surly comments from elders about the supposedly officious moment overtaken by the brothers' silliness. More of the family and friends surged forward to kiss and pat Barton, acknowledging this special family moment. A few of the other Barre men, including François, displayed their medallions over their neckties. All of a sudden, Bart proudly felt as if he were part of an inclusive club.

He spent the rest of the evening being passed around the room, each person admiring the gold medallion that lay upon his tanned chest amid the cinnamon-colored hair. He felt so exposed, nearly naked before them, but left his shirt partly open, noting his brothers and father and a few other men did the same, each proudly displaying their La Barre medallions. Even though it was all embarrassing, Bart was glad there wasn't a more emotional or formal introduction with speeches and old stories from the elders of the family, as he had witnessed as a child.

He wearily answered the myriad of questions about his recent schooling, graduation, and upcoming enlistment, as well as the age-old questions: "Is there a special girl?" and "When are you getting married?" He listened to a few familiar Civil War and Spanish War stories from older friends and family and many anecdotes or warnings about being in the military. Not caring to hear about it all, his eyes glazed over as others droned on about their children's or grandchildren's achievements. He was glad when the last of the guests finally left, and the rest of the household began to make their way to the upstairs bedrooms or out to the kitchen to clean up the mess.

Finally, Bart escaped to the terrace and sat on the marble balustrade, swinging his legs out over the rose bushes and enjoying the cold stone under his rump. He pulled off his suit jacket, draping it neatly over the balustrade, and unbuttoned his shirt the rest of the way. The fragrant night breeze stroked his fevered, sweaty skin.

He reached up and touched the medallion, feeling the raised crest as he traced the words under his fingers. "*Nous sommes contre les ventes.*" Yes, he seemed always to fly on his own, to make his own way. With a sense of selfish pride, he was unique, just like the beautiful phoenix on the medallion.

He had chosen his own path, whereas his brothers had taken up work within their father's furniture business. Paul worked alongside Richard in the shop designing and making the furniture, while Jack managed the retail furniture store and custom construction jobs. The brothers were both married, they had homes of their own, and with Paul's first child on the way, the brothers had everything they always wanted.

Yet Barton was alone, a restless entity. His dreams were not fully realized, and he owned nothing. *Not even a cat,* he thought ruefully.

He looked up at the indigo depths of the sky, tracing the pinpoints of light and trying to identify the various constellations. *Was there a star for him, one that would guide him?* His father had written that he had one. *Where was Bart's star? For that matter, where in the hell was he headed?*

When he was finishing up at university, Barton had some job interviews and some ideas about a career. With a mechanical engineering degree, he really wanted to design something unique, something important. Barton always liked to work with his hands, tearing apart motors, gears, and cams, and he was fascinated by the inner workings of things. He also enjoyed making other things out of the pieces once disassembled, creating a new use for the same parts. Bart felt that this was where his destiny lay. He did not want to be a mechanic, though, but wanted to create something with a purpose. But where to go … And what to do?

His minor in petrology just might get him a job in that field, yet Barton could not envision himself chained to a life on oil rigs as a driller. Drilling for oil was a dangerous and dirty job that he had done one summer. It was only a job to get him work experience and make a bunch of money. But not the type of career he really wanted.

Barton Barre felt lost.

Now, the blasted war was like a dangerous pothole on his life's highway. He searched the sky for a moment, seeking perhaps a divine answer. Seeing none, he closed his eyes to see if he could forecast his future and see himself doing something. He searched ahead. Would he get married and have a family? That seemed a vague prospect. He hoped he would someday find a perfect, pretty wife like Jack's Celeste.

There was something else lying in wait for him; he felt it writhing darkly in the future like a hidden snake. He quickly hoped it was not death. Thinking perhaps that was why he could not imagine himself beyond the moment, he boldly questioned if he would die in the war. He quickly crossed himself and kissed the medallion, hoping that the gesture would somehow bless him to a better fate.

Suddenly, Bart felt a fan of air and heard a grunt beside him. He opened his eyes and found his father sitting beside him on the marble balustrade.

"*Compter les étoiles?*" Richard queried, looking up at the star-spangled sky.

"How did you know?" Bart asked wonderingly.

"I know that look. I've worn it myself." His father laughed dryly.

"Um, yes, I was wondering where my star was," Barton replied, trying to hide his emotion.

Richard's dark eyes gazed at Bart for a moment. He replied loftily, "Second star to the right and straight on till morning."

Barton cast a skeptical silver eye at his dad. "Are you sure? That sounds like something I've heard before."

"Uh-huh. It's from *Peter Pan*. Remember it? I used to read it to you. It was your favorite book as a child." Smiling, Richard patted Bart's knee.

A frown wrinkled Bart's brow, and then it quickly disappeared as he remembered something. Turning to Richard, he brightly asked, "Didn't we used to have sword fights while jumping on the beds? You were Captain Hook, Paul was Smee, Jack was Michael, and I was once Peter. I remember we all leaped on Paul's bed, and it went crashing to the floor!"

"Oh, aye, that we did, matey, to be sure!" Richard growled in his best pirate accent and laughed heartily.

Barton continued energetically. "Oh! Oh! I remember Mama came running into the room with her umbrella, thinking robbers were attacking us. She screeched at us when she saw the broken bed and all of us fighting and rassling about and hitting each other with pillows and our wooden swords." Bart laughed, and wiping tears from his eyes, he said, "I never could figure out what she was going to do with the umbrella. Did you?"

Richard nodded and continued. "Well, as I remember it, she was going to bash a robber with it, but in the end, she used it to smack each of you boys on the ass until it broke. Then she ran out of the room in a fury, came back with the warming pan from our bed, and smacked me with it! That pan still has a dent in it to this day!"

They laughed together at the amusing memory.

"God, I miss my mother," Barton said softly.

"So do I," Richard said soberly. Looking up at the sky, he reached out, took his son's hand in his, and squeezed it.

Looking back up at the sky, Bart asked, "Those were good times, weren't they, Dad?" He felt his father nod. "I wish I could go back in time."

"Tonight was a good time too—remember it, Son," Richard stated quietly.

A few minutes passed as they sat contentedly side by side on the balustrade, both enjoying the charms of the night and their recent recollections.

"You read it."

It was a statement, not a question. Barton felt that he and his father were deeply connected and somehow aware of each other's silent thoughts.

"It was … quite a story, Dad. I never knew all of that about you. It's not one of your little parables, is it? I wanted to believe it was true."

"It is part of your legacy, too, that you should know the secrets of your family. Perhaps knowing these things will make you a bit more patient and tolerant of the rest of us. I just could not let you go away ignorant of the fate of the men who came before you. I hope you understand. It is because I love you; you are special," Richard said to the rose bushes beneath him.

Barton could see that his father was trying not to make waves but to smooth the way for Bart's departure—baring his soul, such as it was.

"Yeah, I do. Thanks," he said stiffly and then added, "And thanks for my medallion. I love you too, Dad." Bart turned to his father, searching his stern profile in the dark.

Richard sighed. "Well, that's a good thing then, isn't it? If you didn't love me, then I'd have to kick your sorry little ass!" The solemn moment gone, Richard snorted a laugh and grappled with Bart. They wrestled playfully, then, suddenly, Barton fell off the balustrade and into the rose bushes below, nearly taking Richard with him.

There was a muffled "Ow!" and "Oh! *Merde!* Someone fertilized the roses today! Phew! *Putant!*" Barton noisily crawled out of the bushes. "You are gonna get it now!" he yelled as he ran back up onto the terrace. Brushing off his clothes angrily, Bart was just in time to see his father's brawny six-three form unfold and tower over his shorter, stockier five-nine.

"Still got some fight in you, boy?" Richard asked, coldly aggressive now.

"No, sir." Barton breathed in raggedly, seeing the dangerous glint in his father's eye.

"Good. Keep it for the war. I only want peace between us now; we shall fight no more." Richard confirmed. Stretching his long arms out and shrugging away achy shoulders, he said, "Well, it has been a long day. I have to help Papa with the tractor tomorrow. He says the throttle is sticking. Maybe you ought to look at it, seeing as how you're the mechanical engineer."

"Sure. I'll see you in the morning." Bart put out his hand shakily, showing his acquiescence. His father gripped it tightly and then pulled him into a warm, hard embrace.

"*Bonne nuit, Papa,*" he said as he released his father, feeling emotion welling up and noting the tears in his father's eyes.

"*Fait beaux rêves, mon fils.*"

Barton heard the soft reply as the French door clicked shut between them.

Those traditional sweet words his mother Charlotte would say to him after she kissed him good night. "Make beautiful dreams, my son." Bart stood quietly for a few minutes, not wanting to break the fragile thread strung between himself and his father, realizing how few those times had been. He wanted to be that favored son again.

It had been a good evening, and if he had not been enjoying himself, it was his own fault. He sighed, knowing that he was very unsure of himself at that moment and equally unsure of his future. However, he felt assured that his family probably loved him.

Somewhere out there was his fate, his joy lying in wait to be found. Perhaps he would soon see an end to the restless chaos within his soul.

At this hour, he needed the quiet abandon of sleep. As if in answer to his quest, he felt a gentle touch on his leg. Bart looked down to see one of *Grand-mère's* prized house cats, Annabelle, winding about his leg. She looked up at him, her large eyes glowing like topaz jewels. Seeing his response, she chirped once.

He scooped her up and said, "Let's go to bed, *ma p'tite.*"

Snuggling her purring body to his chest, they bid the stars, the dark night, the rose bushes, the crickets, and his destiny *Une bonne nuit.*

+◆+

CHAPTER 3

A Family Matters

Bart heard the rooster and chickens in conversation on the lawn below his window. The morning sun stabbed brutal fingers in his eyes as he blearily gazed about the sunny room, now sorry he had been too tired to shut the dark drapes last night. He had a residual headache from too much wine and cognac and too little sleep and felt his way to the alarm clock; pulling it to him, he saw it was after six thirty in the morning.

"Merde!"

His father would have been up nearly two hours before; they were probably already in the barn trying to fix the tractor. He sat up brusquely and met with a "Mrrup!" and an evil cat eye as he disturbed Annabelle's sleep. He reached out to pet her, and she touched his hand with a barely sheathed claw, a clear warning that she was not getting up yet.

"Yeah, yeah, go back to sleep, you lazy thing—wish I could be like you." Barton got up and padded to the bathroom. He briskly scratched his scalp as he tried to release the muzzy feeling in his head while he peed. Bart filled the sink and shoved his head into it, grimacing at the cold shock. He rose out of the sink, dripping like a wet beast, and roughly wiped his face and head dry with the towel. He brushed his teeth, raked his fingers through the springy curls of his hair, and left the bathroom.

Bart rummaged in the dresser drawers, pulled out a pair of dungarees, a short-sleeved shirt, and socks, and then retrieved his boots from the pile of dirty clothes in the closet. He dressed quickly. He pulled back the covers on the bed, trying not to disturb Annabelle, and left her to the morning sunshine that streamed through the bedroom window.

Squinting one golden eye at Barton's departure and then rolling her head upside down as if boneless, the Chartreux cat resumed her nap.

He smelled coffee as he went down the stairs. His stomach growled in eager anticipation of a breakfast he hoped he had not missed. He rounded the corner of the staircase and bumped into his youngest sister, eight-year-old Cecily; they did a momentary dance in the hall along with brisk greetings of "morning." She giggled and then ran around the corner and pounded up the stairs, her brunette beribboned braids bouncing. She gave him a headache with all that energy!

Bart continued down the hall to the kitchen. On mornings like this, the immediate family usually ate in the kitchen, where there was a round-robin sort of breakfast as everyone got up at different times. His boots announced his arrival on the linoleum floor, and Thérèse spun around, surprised.

"Oh, I thought you would sleep in this morning." She held up the coffee pot in silent query.

He nodded silently as he looked about to see what was left to eat. "I did." He sat and grabbed a still-warm beignet, a surprising morning treat, and stuffed it into his mouth as he watched Thérèse pour steaming chicory-laced coffee into his cup. "Dad asked me to take a look at *Grand-père's* tractor this morning."

"Yes, he did say something about that. I think they have already gone down to the shed. Francis is there, too. Jack's car would not start this morning. Maybe you could fix that too before we go to church."

"Church? We're still going?" Bart choked as he swallowed the beignet.

"Don't be a lazy heathen; of course, we'll go, but to the late service. So you need to hurry up here if you plan on fixing everything." Thérèse took out a plate with sausages and bacon, warm from the oven, and set it before Barton. "You are the last one to breakfast. Can you eat all of those?" she asked, nodding toward the remaining meat.

"Sure. I am starved! What else is there?" He snagged a piece of bacon and chomped it noisily.

"Want some scrambled eggs? Cecily found some big brown ones this morning."

At his nod, she wrapped her apron around her hand and carefully pulled out a skillet from the oven; it was hot and ready to cook. She deftly cracked a few eggs in a bowl, whisked them, dropped a pad of butter in the skillet, and cooked up the eggs.

"Isn't it nice to eat proper food again?" Bart asked while sipping the bitter coffee. "I mean all the fresh meat and real butter! I hate oleo—it might as well be colored lard." Barton noted Thérèse nod as he admired her expertise in the kitchen.

"Yes," she sighed, "this war has been a strain on all of us. I am so thankful we have our gardens and hen house; otherwise, we might starve."

Bart grunted in reply. "Yeah, I was getting pretty tired of eggs, though. But I like your cooking, and Grandma's the best. When I was in school, the food was lousy last semester." He ate another piece of bacon with relish.

Bart asked, "Did you know *Mémé* now employs a cook here at the plantation house? *Mémé* thinks she is too old and tired to fuss with making bread and rolls every day. Often, Aunt Patrice cooks, and her family eats with the old folks; they're sort of mooches, I think. I was glad when you came because *Mémé* allowed you to take over the kitchen. I am not so keen on Aunt Patrice's chow, although her dessert last night was really swell."

"Yes, I met Sallie. She helped us yesterday and is a capable cook." Thérese scraped the eggs onto his plate of meat, quickly cleaned the skillet, oiled it, and returned it to the oven.

She brought over the fruit basket, plopped it in front of Bart, and then sat down next to him. She searched in the basket for a ripe peach and sat peeling it as he voraciously ate the hot, tasty breakfast.

In between mouthfuls, Bart thanked her again for the delicious dinner party. He rolled his eyes ecstatically and grinned at Thérese. "Thanks for the delicious *Sainte Honoré,* too; that was the best surprise. I forgot you could make those. I wish Aunt Lorraine could've come. I miss those orange *gâteau* things she makes."

"By the way, our dessert was actually a *croquembouche*. But tell that to Patrice." She rolled her eyes and added, "Lorraine and Titus send their love to you. Perhaps you can see them before you leave town next week." She fed Barton a wedge of peeled peach.

"Yeah. Well, it was nice last night. Thanks."

"I am glad you appreciated our efforts." Thérese blushed. "It was my pleasure, *mon fils.* You deserved it since we did not do anything for your graduation." She was pensively silent for a moment as she held the dripping peach.

He could tell she wanted to say something and thought about his last words to Thérese earlier in the week. "I was kinda rough last Monday. I was having an awful day." Bart nudged her as he bit into another beignet. "What now?" he asked, expecting her to respond to his apology.

"Barton, you will be careful, won't you? I am so afraid for you to go to war; it is so far away, and you will be alone. Do you know where they will send you?" Her dark eyes were anxious and moist with unshed tears.

Surprised by her comment yet still feeling remorse, Bart put his hand on hers and held it.

"I don't know. Maybe I won't be sent abroad; some soldiers stay here in America to train others and to do administrative types of things. Uncle Francis thinks that will be what I'll get since I am a college graduate." He shrugged. "Who knows? Pop seems to think I am going to France; he gave me his *Lapin D'Or* doohickey, you know." He grimaced. "Oops."

"I know he did. He does tell me most things; we have no secrets," Thérese said, understanding his embarrassment. "Bart, please write to us straight away when you get to your training camp. Write a little each night and then mail it to us when you have a page or two. We don't care what the subject matter is; just let us know you are doing well." Thérese gave him the peeled fruit, wiped her hands, got up, and went to the oak sideboard. She opened a drawer, pulled out a packet, and gave it to him, saying, "I hope this will help." She kissed him on the temple and left the kitchen.

Bart opened the blue tissue paper packet. There was a compact, thin brown leather folder with his initials *BCB* gold embossed on the cover; inside, there were pads of writing paper, a pocket with a fountain pen, pencils, a tiny pencil sharpener, a new pink eraser, a rubber-banded stack of envelopes, and some postage stamps. Hiding in another pocket was a small, sealed envelope. He pulled it out. Inside was a handwritten card:

Congratulations! This is for you, my son. Do not forget us in your new life.

With love, Maman.

Then he noticed the paper had a little crinkled spot as if Thérese had shed a tear. He wondered now if perhaps the writing set was intended as a graduation gift, another thing he had ruined with his ill timing. He also found a paper bookmark with the Lord's Prayer printed on it tucked away in another pocket.

He put everything back inside the case and closed it; he held it close, sniffing the new leather and Thérese's lingering rose-scented soap. She must have kept this for a while in her dresser drawer. He was touched. He had not expected all the gracious outpouring of love and good wishes at his leaving. Most times, his family seemed to ignore him or spend more time arguing and bent upon annoying him. Or maybe it was just that *he* remembered it that way.

He scraped the remaining food into his mouth, gulped the last drop of coffee, and dumped his dishes in the sink. He ran up the stairs to his room and put the leather folder in his canvas knapsack with the other gifts his family had given him—hankies, neckties, and a dictionary.

He patted the cat and ran back down the stairs and out the front door in search of his father and grandfather.

◆ ◆

The day was already warm and steamy, and the lawn was still spongy and damp with the night's dew as Bart walked the long way out to the barns. He could hear someone banging metal on metal and cursing in French.

"Salaud Chien! C'est une bête diabolique!" (Dirty dog! It's a hellish beast!)

Whereby the loud voices of his grandfather and brother, Jack engaged in suggestions were heard.

"Maybe you should try something else … but not a hammer!"

"Arrête! Aiee! Mon dieu!"

"Don't hit it so hard; you're gonna break it!"

"J'm'en fous!" (I don't give a damn!) The angry retort came from under the hood. "Leave me alone! I am the mechanic here!"

Barton came around the wide doorway of the barn and found Uncle Francis wearing grease-smudged coveralls headfirst in the engine compartment of Jack's maroon 1939 Oldsmobile. His brother and grandfather were leaning in on the opposite side of the fender, coaching the mechanical banging. Noting Bart's arrival on the scene, Jack rose, smiling in relief.

"Hey! Uncle! Bartie is here. Let him have a go at it." Jack backed away from the car, giving Bart his spot. Eycing his brother with an anxious look, he murmured, "Do something quick before he ruins everything!"

Bart leaned in and watched Uncle Francis vigorously hammering on the wrench, the machinery making metallic groans, yet not giving up the stuck bolt. He assessed the situation before calmly asking, "So, is it the carburetor, do you think?"

His uncle rounded with the hammer, looking for the new voice; his glower changed to a momentary look of chagrin. He backed out and stood up, wiping the hammer with a greasy rag; a gimlet eye remained upon the monstrous machine. He flicked away the soggy cigarette clamped in his lips before answering. "Hmm, it could be the carburetor or maybe the timing or a fouled fuel line. I can't get the carburetor head off the stupid, idiotic machination of hell," he growled in French.

The four men stood looking at the engine as if something extraordinary was about to happen or the beastly thing would start all of a sudden.

"A piece of crap—that's what it is. I told you not to buy this clunker. You should have listened to me, boy." Francis loudly admonished Jack with a menacing wave of the hammer. "Only buy Fords."

"Well, *you* sold it to me!" Jack, taken aback, yelped angrily.

Bart stayed Jack with a hand on his arm and said instead, "Oh, so is that why you own a Chevrolet, Uncle?" Bart snorted a laugh and bent to the engine well. "So it doesn't start, eh? Is there any particular noise or thing that happens when you try to start it?" he asked Jack.

"Uh, it didn't make any noise at all, just the clicking of the key when I tried to turn it over," Jack said, bending over the car's fender to look at the engine with Bart. "It's a mystery."

"Sounds like an electrical problem to me. Let me look." Bart leaned in farther over the engine and began checking wiring connections.

Jack and his grandfather looked at each other knowingly.

Francis chewed his lip and the tail of his mustache in aggravation. "Huh! I didn't think about the possibility of an electrical problem."

"Someone get me a five-eighths crescent wrench and a wire brush," Bart demanded like a surgeon, still headfirst in the depths of the engine.

Jack swooped down and rummaged in the toolbox, found the items requested, and deftly handed them off to his brother.

A bit of clunking, the rasping sound of the brush, and a moment later, "Rag." Bart demanded again. Francis handed him the greasy rag. Without looking, Bart took it with a backward hand. After a few more minutes of activity in the depths of the engine, Bart rose out and stood looking thoughtfully at the car for a moment, wiping the grease from his hands on the rag.

"Jack, try starting the car. Let's see if that worked," Barton told his brother.

Jack eagerly dashed around to the driver's side, wrenched open the door, and settled his tall frame in the car. Looking hopefully under the raised hood of the car at his brother's face, he turned the key. The starter clicked and cranked over, and then, with a deep, throaty roar, the engine came to life. A bit of gassy exhaust popped from the tailpipe before the engine resumed in a content, voluminous purr.

The men all cheered, save for Francis. Barton endured the hearty claps on his back from his brother and grandfather and a rough shove from Francis.

"So it wasn't the carburetor after all." A grinning Jack nudged his uncle.

Uncle Francis, who in turn looked down his long, aquiline nose at his nephew, sniffed and, with a typically Gallic shrug, murmured, "It might have been. *Je t'emmerde á en toi voiture!*" (You and your car can go to hell!) "See if I help you again!" Francis tossed the hammer noisily into the toolbox. He swiftly walked away, his shoulders hunched, and a stormy look appeared on his face as he lit up another cigarette.

The cloud of smoke trailing in Francis's wake reminded Bart of an angry old hissing dragon.

"Oops! I guess he's pissed." Jack said as he and Barton looked at each other sheepishly.

François patted Barton on the shoulder and whispered in his ear. "Perhaps the tractor can be your next patient, eh?" Looking in Francis's direction, he said, "I'll take care of *mon fils.*" With a wink, he left the young men and chased after the stormy man.

"So what was it, a connection or what?" Jack looked in the engine compartment, searching for the newly repaired machinery. "I knew it wasn't the carburetor, but try telling that to Uncle."

"Ah, it was simple. The battery terminals were heavily corroded, and one of the cables slipped off. See here? I cleaned them and re-tightened the bolts and clamps." Bart pointed out the repaired battery. "You might want to get a new battery soon; it looks kinda old. When it gets all clogged up like that, either brush it off or pour a *Coca-Cola* on it—that melts the corrosion right off."

"What? Don't be stupid!" Jack looked agape at Bart and gave him a little shove.

Bart shrugged. "Hey, it works."

Jack nodded and replied suspiciously. "Well, I hope that was the real problem then. Knowing my luck, it will conk out again on the way to church. Better not waste any more gas." Jack reached into the car and switched off the key, and the engine died with a thump. He slammed the door and then put down the hood of the sedan.

"Do you know where the tractor is?" Bart asked, glancing about the barn for the tractor.

"Yeah, it's over in the peanut field, G'père was cultivating a patch for some squash for G'mère yesterday. The throttle stuck, and Paul and I had to come out and stop it. We pulled the fuel line to get it to stop. It was just running wild!" He raked back a handful of wavy brown hair that fell over his eyes. Smoothing his sweaty brow, he eyed Bart. "I think you should work on the tractor. Don't let Uncle near it!" he said in a hushed tone.

"Why didn't you just turn it off?" Barton glibly asked his brother, who responded with a shrug and rolled eyes.

Bart was wondering about the Barre men. They could not be so mechanically inept, could they? Or were they just finding things for him to do to make Barton feel he would be missed? On another yet more insulting thought, perhaps they were testing Bart with ridiculous tasks that anybody could fix.

Sullenly agreeing to the new task, Barton picked up the rag and toolbox, and then the two men headed to the field. He felt uneasy since he accidentally upstaged his uncle. Uncle Francis was the eldest brother and a prideful, tough goat who was stubborn to boot. He would not take another embarrassing moment from Barton without a fight.

"I hope *Grand-père* took Uncle to do something else," Bart said, continuing on the thought.

"Yeah, did you see his face? I thought he was going to implode or something! I don't care if he owns a garage; he stinks as a mechanic!" Jack said excitedly.

The two young men walked together, amicably catching up about the events on the farm. They were only three years apart in age; Jack and Bart were still close.

Even though Paul and Jacques were fraternal twins, they were far apart in temperaments and interests. Paul was always the bossy autocrat, the instigator of vicious pranks, yet the wide-eyed, innocent voice in the crowd, easily avoiding punishment. He had continued to be aloof from Bart.

Jack was always the fun older brother who had often taken young Bart into confidence, sagely unveiling the mysteries of their childish universe and sharing secrets. Frequently, they made plots of revenge against Paul's pranks and often sided with each other on things of importance.

Paul brooded and was overly cynical like his Uncle Francis. Jack was a blithe, heartfelt fellow, much like their grandfather, François. Barton was stuck somewhere in between pragmatic and somber in temperament, often quickly taken to slights of his character and made the butt of family jokes and derision. He had learned early to wear thick skin and try not to overreact, but his family knew how to get him riled. Bart had too often been the gullible, wide-eyed believer of tall tales and pranks. Therefore, in his own defense, he usually chose to ignore his family, especially Paul and his father. Recently, he was sly enough to keep ahead.

Bart also tried to escape from the pestering of his younger half-sisters, Camellia, Nancy, and Cecily, although he was fond of Nancy, the middle of the three girls. For a time, he had been a proud big brother to them all until the girls had developed their own tastes for dollhouse soap opera stories, girly adventures, and silly intrigues.

He got along well with G'père François, who felt empathy for Barton, himself being the third son and a sometimes forgotten middle child. That was why when Bart stayed at the plantation, he sought activities with his grandparents and avoided the boisterous and rousing twins, sisters, and many of his cousins. He enjoyed the arcane wisdom of his grandfather, who rarely seemed to get upset about anything and always had an endless supply of solutions for any problem.

A couple of François's liver and white Brittanys came loping out of the nearby cornfield and gamboled happily around the two young men as they walked. Both dogs kept up the pace alongside Jack, eagerly enjoying his attention. Bart looked away from the boisterous pair, feeling sad about their former murdered old Brittany, Katie.

Bart thought even his siblings' choices of duties on the plantation bespoke their differences. As children, Paul and Jack enjoyed herding cattle and gregariously annoying the chickens, ducks, and geese, leaving the collecting of eggs and hatchlings to the quiet child, Barton. Barton had preferred the company of the quietly munching rabbits, goats, and milk cows. He enjoyed the soft lowing of the cows and nattering of the nannies as he milked them, their breath sweet and warm on him as he tended them. The twins were employed with the dangerous chores dealing with the colony of bees, ruthlessly enjoying smoking them and collecting their golden hoard of honey. The twins preferred the bouncy, rambunctious hunting hounds and Barton, the serenity of the farm cats.

The girls enjoyed the various fowl and searching out their eggs, as well as feeding the rabbits, and as the sisters grew up, they joined Barton in the milking of the goats. In the past few years, when he was away at university, his cousins and sisters took up some of his chores during the summers. Brothers Richard and Francis held to the belief that their children should learn and enjoy the chores of the plantation, helping wherever the grandparents needed them. Bart's cousins, Carl Louis and Thomas, sometimes joined their father, Francis, on daily chores around the place.

Richard's other elder brother Paul and his family no longer visited the plantation, with the excuse they were too busy. Bart knew it was because of the private feud Francis and Paul still had from years before. After the stock market crashed in 1929, financially ruined and desperate, Paul brought his family to live on the plantation. After a few years of their constant arguments, Paul recovered from the disaster enough to return to Baltimore. He was again very wealthy and happily living far from his elder brother's curmudgeonly influence.

Barton was abruptly caught in his musings when Jack repeated a question and gave him a nudge in the ribs.

"Say what?" Barton queried, startled.

"I asked you, what are you going to do when you get back from the army? You know, for a job?"

"Um, I am not sure. Right now, I cannot think much beyond the next month or so. Who knows if I'll even come back," Bart morosely retorted.

"You mean you might stay in Europe or wherever they send you?"

Bart glared at Jack; he did not quite catch on. "Don't be a dope."

But then Jack continued enthusiastically. "I know; you'll end up being some kind of big hero. You'll knock the crap out of *les Japanois* or *les Allemands!*" he said and then clapped Bart on the back heartily.

"Yeah, something like that, although I have doubts about the hero part." He shrugged off his brother's hand and moodily scrunched into himself.

Jack picked up a stick and tossed it away. Both dogs charged away in search of the new toy. Moments later, they found it, and both grabbed opposite ends of the stick and awkwardly galloped in a tandem return. With the dogs grinning and drooling for more of the game, Jack threw the stick even farther out into the field. The two eager dogs sped away.

"You are so lucky. You have bigger balls than a bull. I sometimes wish I could go. I would give the Germans a fight. But I have duties and a wife." Jack slicked back a handful of hair and then continued excitedly. "Oh, did I tell you we think Celeste might be preggers? Paul and Amy aren't the only lucky ones around here," Jack said a bit smugly on the words *wife* and *preggers*. "Yeah, it is early. We don't want a lot of people to know just yet in case she miscarries again like the last two."

"Lucky you." Barton eyed his brother with a bit of contempt. "I guess I have nothing and no one to keep me here, so I am the one to go," he muttered.

"I am envious. You have a grand adventure ahead of you, little Brother." Jack rubbed Bart's curly head roughly.

Angrily shying away, Bart was facetious and surly in his own answer, giving a vigorous Gallic jerk of his thumb as he echoed his uncle's sour attitude. *"Superb! Fantastique! Je t'emmerde!"* he growled and said nothing more for the rest of their trek through the field.

They found their father and a neighbor puttering with the tractor and mostly standing about, smoking their pipes and telling jokes. After a bit of twiddling about,

Bart found the problem: a cotter pin was missing in the throttle assembly. Bart repaired that, and the fuel line was torn. After they gave it more gasoline, the tractor started up and was once again work-ready.

Dismissing himself from the entourage, Bart left the field. One of the hunting dogs, a caramel-colored Brittany named Amber, rambled over and greeted Barton with a lick on his hand. The spaniel, with her nose to the ground, ran back and forth in front of and around Barton in excited, tight circles as she explored the delicious scents of the earth. Catching her enthusiasm, Barton decided to adjust his morose mood.

He found a log and sat down on it to watch the ebb and flow of the river water on the sandy bank. Amber flopped down at his feet, smiling and panting happily. He slipped down, relaxing against the log. He breathed deeply the steamy heat, savoring the salty odors of the marsh and river water, wet dog, and his own sweat. Surprised that the dog would choose to stay, Bart gently massaged her silky ears and muzzle. She turned her beautiful, liquid-gold eyes on him in grateful ecstasy before melting in near-boneless relaxation on the ground. Even though Barton enjoyed the quiet of cats, he found there was immense pleasure in sharing the company of grateful animals. He sniffed away an emotional tug, fondly recalling his first dog, Katie, who was poisoned and died tragically at the hands of a despicable fiend.

Bart had only the rest of the week to spend with his family, and he was trying to be carefree and pleasant. He was trying hard not to argue or get in a snit with these people, yet sometimes his family just annoyed the hell out of him!

He felt the niggling sense of urgency in packing everything—every experience, every moment, every bit of love—tightly around him and burying it in his heart. He hoped it would be enough to sustain him for what he felt he might experience while away.

Bart remembered that dark, unknown entity he had glimpsed in his mind last night as he searched for his future. Despite the heated morning, his skin prickled at the thought. There was something ominous in his future—what, he did not know. He wanted to feel some confidence and to feel brave enough to join the army and go off to war, but the truth was he was getting more afraid as the days passed. He wished he could just run away.

He would love to grab a boat and hide out in one of the shady little bayous, fishing to his heart's content. He would ignore the rest of the world—let it all just explode and go to hell in the wink of an eye. But that was not feasible; he would be found sooner than he would like.

His father's letter had been a shock to him. He had not expected that kind of soul-baring, and it was almost embarrassing. He and his father had never talked too deeply about their feelings, their heart's desire, or much about sex.

His brothers had told him the facts of life, except that theirs had been the bull-and-cow story. He had seen animals mating; he'd grown up around it, as had the other siblings. But the art of it, the caring for another in the act of sex, he did not understand.

His first experience was thanks in part to his brother Paul and, again, the Guillot brothers, who arranged a blind date for him. Then Bart had had sex with several girls over the years. While in college, he came to find that sex could be a habit-forming drug. It had made him power-hungry, lustful, and animalistic in his yearnings, and eventually, Bart cared little if the girl had a good time so long as his own sexual craze was fulfilled. He had too many arguments with girls because they had nothing in common, and Bart had yet to find one who fed him what he really wanted. Going steady with a girl meant nothing to him except that he might enjoy sexual fun, and unfortunately, he had left broken girls in his wake.

He felt a bit of remorse at that thought, but not much. After his discovery that sex made him crazy following a failed romance with his roommate's sister, Felicity Flannery, Bart kept himself away from any attachments. He could then focus on his studies and not on female beguilements. As a result, he excelled in his studies and then graduated early. And now, at this time in his life, Bart had no one significant and had not had sex in a few weeks. The thought brought him pain again as he remembered the BettyAnn incident.

However, in his father's letter to him, Richard seemed to have forgiven him, and with a brightened countenance, he now remembered that his father had told him about the dance in Brusly. Barton was to have fun but not to get involved with anyone. He was sure to do that! No one would know what had happened in his own hometown of Beaumont, Texas.

Feeling better, Barton got to his feet, ready to make the rest of the day pleasant and to be nice to everyone despite his gloomy mood. It was time to get ready for church, anyway. Little Amber sprang to her feet and accompanied him home. They parted at the horse barn, where she ran for a drink of water at the trough.

◆ ◆

After church and a few chores, Barton was hungry once again. He impatiently came up to the back door of the kitchen and met with the aroma of cooking onions and meat. He went to the outdoor pump to wash before going into the kitchen where *Grand-mère*, *Tante* Patrice, and Thérese were setting up for Sunday dinner.

"So, where are the girls? Why aren't they helping out?" Bart grumbled as Patrice shoved a knife and loaves of bread at him.

Thérese laughed, "They were more hindrance than help, so they are with Richard and François in the goat barn playing with Lily's new kids. She had them while we were in church."

"Ah, rats, I missed it!" Bart kissed the women fondly, and without his usual complaint about doing kitchen chores, he quietly set to the task of slicing the freshly baked bread Patrice had put before him. His mouth watered at the aroma of the yeasty bread; combined with the tang of the sauteed onions and beef pot roast with potatoes and caramelized carrots, his stomach had extra reason to complain.

Later, he swiped the cloves of mashed garlic around the large wooden salad bowl before tossing in the shredded greens and then proudly *fatigué le salade*, carefully turning the greens in the vinaigrette so they were coated in the spicy, tart dressing. He snatched a bit and savored the crunch of butter lettuce but not the bitter dandelion greens—*pis-en-lits*. He felt proud to help, enjoying the murmured comments of the women, even kissing Thérese's cheek when she voiced surprise that Barton was capable in the kitchen.

"Of course, I learned something from you!" Bart laughed.

Loaded with stacks of dishes and silverware, he went out of the kitchen to the dining room on a mission to set the table. He did it, artfully placing the napkins and tableware correctly as the women liked. He went out to the garden, snipped a small multicolored bouquet of fragrant roses and honeysuckle, and placed them in a water glass on the table. Barton stood back, pleased that he could do this small thing. Annette came out with the basket of bread and the porcelain jar of butter and exclaimed delightedly at his presentation. She hugged him and sent him out to call the family to the table.

He passed the parlor and announced, "Dinner!" to his loafing cousins and then went to the porch and rang the large bell, calling *"À Table! À Table!"* He heard shouts from the barns and fields and thudding feet as people ran toward the house in eager anticipation of a hearty repast.

Soon after, he sat with his extended family and several favored work hands at the table as they bowed their heads in prayer, all solemnly making the sign of the cross, and then his grandfather said grace. Barton opened an eye and glanced at his grandfather when he asked a special blessing on Barton for exciting travels and a safe return. They all said amen and eagerly tucked into the feast before them.

Barton said a silent prayer to come home in one piece.

◆ ◆

The rest of the week flew by with many projects to do. Barton fulfilled his duty, working companionably with his cousins, brothers, father, and grandfather. He put up with the spur-of-the-moment hugs and sudden tears from the women, and he knew they were already missing him. Yet, good meals, jokes, hugs, and kisses helped them all to bear up to what would soon happen. He was keen that everyone about him was trying to stay in good humor, pretending as if everything was fine, and yet, they all knew that by the end of the week, Bart would be gone from them, perhaps forever.

•◆•

CHAPTER 4

Debutante Flowers

Friday, June 4, 1943

Barton came downstairs dressed in his blue suit again and ready to go, expecting to use his father's car for the night. He went to find him to ask for the keys; instead, he saw the family all 'dressed to the nines' and waiting eagerly for him in the living room and parlor. He dumbly looked around the crowded rooms.

Sister Cecily popped up by his elbow and said, "Surprise! We are all going with you! Isn't it just going to be so much fun?" She hugged his arm enthusiastically. "I have never been to an actual dance before!" she giggled shrilly.

"I see that." Bart gulped, feeling glum again. He had been looking forward to an adult evening with lovely young women and genteel fellows, not his father, mother, little sisters, and, dang it, the entire family! "I see we haven't left anyone out. Are the dogs and cats coming too?" He joked with a conciliatory smile and put his arm around Cecily.

"Gee, whiz no! Silly!" She bubbled and pulled him toward the front door as the rest of the family laughed and made their way out of the house.

Getting to the dance in Brusly that night was nearly a fiasco, but humor and finely campaigned planning came to the rescue. It took three cars with lots of people sitting squashed together and the girls on each man's lap to get to the dance. Barton was peeved to find that Jack's car battery had finally given up the ghost; otherwise, they would have gone in his big car. He was secretly glad, though, that his diagnosis had proven true—it was only a bad battery.

Barton was relieved that Amy sat on Paul's lap because he looked uncomfortable. Although he kept tickling Amy and making her laugh, she was giving him little slaps and telling him he would make her tinkle. Barton smiled at the endearing horseplay of his brother and pregnant sister-in-law.

An unconcerned Jacques was smooching in the opposite corner of the car with his wife, Celeste. They seemed happy. Bart was envious of their happiness. *Grand-père* and *Grand-mère* were singing an old French folk song and waving their hands in time even though *Grand-père* was driving.

Barton knew the song, but he had never been comfortable singing, and he only mumbled the chorus. Cecily was on his lap and singing the chorus loudly, too, a little off-key, but she was enjoying herself. Soon, everyone caught the singing bug, and he had to sing along as well; otherwise, Cecily would tickle him.

◆ ◆

The dance was a fundraiser for the war effort. The hall was decorated with patriotic banners and floating silver and white stars. A five-piece band accompanied a trio of beautiful women singers dressed in sequined red, white, and blue dresses.

Bart was surprised that Richard and François had tickets for the sold-out event. As Richard passed out the tickets, Bart began to be more suspicious about the family's presence this week and that odd letter. Cecily then talked to Anna about something they had seen earlier in the week and revealed Richard's secret by saying that they had come on Thursday, spending a day as tourists around Baton Rouge and staying in a fancy hotel. The little blabber-puss then yipped, "I'm so excited! This dance will be the best thing on our trip!"

Yes, Richard had once again controlled the problematic situation between himself and Barton; nothing had been left to chance. Bart swallowed his hurt ego as he looked about the dance floor at the lovely women present. "Maybe it was worth it all." He hiked up his drooping pants, slicked the sweat from his brow, and merged into the crowded room.

In attendance, there were many servicemen in their uniforms, looking impressive and heroic.

Barton hovered, listening to a few men. Some of the men were home on furlough from the Pacific and regaling their daring feats to an enraptured audience of teen boys and girls. Others were down from the Alexandria Air Base. Many were fighter pilots in training. Barton enviously noted their shiny wings and medals and the admiring looks they received from others nearby. A few were in training at the army base in New Orleans and ready to go fight. He would soon be one of them, and that gave him both a sense of pride and a pang of nervous fear.

Barton was appointed to spend the first set of dances with his sisters and Cousin Anna. Cecily, the youngest, was boisterous like a puppy, popping up and down, and he had to grab her around the waist and hold her to him so he could keep from stepping on her, the little rascal.

Tall Nancy was more sedate, like Barton, and they took a couple of waltzes seriously. Yet, she was lively in her conversation and devoted to him, and Barton matched her shorter steps. At the end of the last waltz, he playfully made a courtly bow and kissed her fingers, whereby she turned red and skipped off to get a cup of punch and cake. Bart laughed after her. He liked to dance, but he would rather dance with someone a little older—at least he was having fun. It had been years since he'd spent much time with his sisters.

Camellia tapped him on the shoulder and asked for her turn. She had just finished dancing with Richard, who was now sitting out with François; both were smoking pipes. Barton led her away. She was blushing, and while pretending not to flirt, he caught her peeking at a young man dancing with a blonde.

Barton felt a bit slighted, but he knew girls nearly fourteen were often fickle. Looking down at her flushed, pretty face, he asked, "Would you like to change partners, C?"

She looked startled and then said no and paid attention to her brother.

They finished the number, and then Bart led her to the young man and said, "My sister is a terrific dancer. Please enjoy her with my compliments." He left her with the young man. He glanced back to note that both of them stood looking elsewhere and red-faced. Oh well, he'd tried. Later, he saw them together.

Barton lasted only half a dance with his least favorite cousin, chubby Anna. After stepping on her foot, she limped away, eyeing him with reproach and calling him a clumsy plow horse. Barton had sneered back that she danced like a waddling cow.

He then cruised along the outskirts of the dance floor, sipping a cup of watered-down, tepid punch, nibbling on bits of tasteless pastries and greasy donuts, and watching the dancers. He felt like a shark trolling the waters for a pretty girl.

There were many girls to choose from, all in colorful and festive dresses, looking like twirling flowers out on the dance floor. He recalled his father's letter and hoped he could find just one 'special gal.' Yet, with the addition of the uniformed soldiers, many of the girls were swarming to them like bees to nectar.

He observed Uncle Francis stepping near a large potted palmetto and sneaking a drink from his flask. Bart wished he could get a snort, too, but decided it wasn't a good idea; he always got too rowdy.

He watched his father and stepmother dancing closely; his father bent near as he whispered in her ear, and she blushed. He wondered what Dad had said. He saw they were still handsome people and were garnering appreciative looks from other couples near them. When Bart thought about Thérèse as a woman and not his stepmother, it was to concede she was charming, lovely, petite, and delicate-looking. Yet, he knew she had a dedicated, generous heart and fierce loyalty to Richard and her children. Barton heard Thérèse's light laugh as they whirled by him, and Richard winked back at him as they passed. Barton shook his head, feeling like the outsider of an inside joke.

A woman at the microphone began to croon another sappy patriotic love song, "Comin' in on a Wing and a Prayer." Bart felt he needed some air, so he followed some others outside to the terrace garden. He stood breathing in the cooler yet humid breeze of the night. Feeling hot in his suit, Bart loosened his collar and necktie to breathe and pried away the phoenix medallion stuck to his sweaty chest. He caught snippets of conversations, murmurings in the garden below, and trilling laughter. Watching as couples strolled arm in arm, sometimes kissing, and wishing to be that demonstrative with a woman in public. He was always embarrassed, and he never knew what to say when it came to intimate small talk with a girl.

Barton caught a new scent of flowers, and his attention drew away from the couples below in the garden. He turned around and searched the terrace, wondering about the intoxicating aroma. A pair of lovely young women passed by, one tall, willowy, and dark-haired and the other short, golden-haired, and full-figured; they were engaged in a private conversation. He watched them and noted they were graceful, and he studied the dainty swing of their skirts and their sleek, lovely legs. He felt a familiar pull and suddenly wanted to follow them, but he did not.

The taller girl was wearing a sapphire-blue dress, modestly cut at the neckline, emphasizing her long, slim neck and slender shoulders; it was sleeveless with a little chiffon rosette at each shoulder. She was wearing a short string of pearls. Her glossy black hair swirled elegantly into a braided twist with rhinestone and pearl pins and a sweep of curly bangs over her brow. She was exquisite. The other girl was wearing a frothy butter-yellow dress with a wide bow at the back, her hair in ringlets bound in a large yellow bow. He preferred the look of the exotic dark one.

He watched the girls mingling with the other revelers, and then his eyes followed them through the maze of the low privet hedges in the formal garden. They disappeared under an arbor, and he waited for them to appear beyond—they did not. Searching and feeling anxious, he didn't quite understand the intense feeling. With one more glance toward the pattern of the maze, he stepped off the terrace and walked swiftly through the paths, listening for conversations as he rounded each corner.

He heard indistinct murmurs beyond the hedge and came upon the young women sitting in a narrow nook under the dripping wisteria arbor. The short blonde was crying with her face buried in her hands; the other held her, rocking her slightly. She looked up suddenly as he came upon them. He blushed and felt at a loss for a second and nearly turned away.

Bart hated seeing women cry, specifically, beautiful ones. Then, observing that the blonde girl looked miserable, he was compelled to say something. He was a sucker.

He knelt at her feet and offered his clean handkerchief. "You've ruined your mascara." He was rewarded by the girl's wet smile and a laugh. "How can anyone be unhappy on such a pretty night?"

"Please … leave us." The dark one held the other one protectively.

"Aw … I was just trying to be … you know … nice." Bart stood up and put his hankie in his jacket. "Anyone up for a dance with me?"

"Elaine found out tonight her beau came with someone else." The dark-haired young woman said in a whisper to Barton. "She saw them dancing together." She patted the other young woman's shoulder in consolation. "In answer to your question … no, she does not want to dance. So, go away … please."

Barton ignored the dismissal and held his hand out to the gal in the yellow dress. "I see. That is his loss, then. Perhaps you would do me the honor of dancing with me?"

She looked up at him with wonder and waved her hankie coyly at him. "Be still, my heart! But there are still gentlemen around. I feared I wouldn't find one tonight." She placed a feeble hand on her breast as if she might faint.

The taller girl groaned.

He looked down at the blonde and smiled charmingly. "Come on, before you expire from neglect. Let's make someone jealous, shall we?" He took her hand and then pulled the other dark girl up, tucking each girl's hand under an arm; Barton led them back to the dance.

He felt proud as he now had two lovely young women to dance with tonight.

The ensemble was playing a slow Tennessee-style waltz again, his favorite, so he asked the blonde girl, "Do you waltz?"

She nodded, and he twirled her out onto the dance floor, leaving behind the other girl at the chairs. He confidently drew her back into his embrace, and they spun around the floor.

Barton was enjoying the admiring looks of other dancers as he guided the lovely smiling girl, spinning and promenading through the couples. The dance ended, and with a glance at Elaine's flushed, cheerful face, he asked for another. She nodded, and they danced a slow fox-trot. Barton made sure he was overt in his moves and actually saw a young man glowering at him over the shoulder of an attractive blonde. "That must be your ex-beau," he commented and pulled Elaine closer. With his most charming smile, he quipped, "Your beau looks like he swallowed a bug." He made her laugh.

She was wearing a dazed expression by the last measures, and when the dance ended, Bart walked her to the chairs along the side of the dance floor. Squeezing her shoulder, he said he would be back. After downing two cups of punch to quench his thirst, Bart filled another two cups with the refreshing iced lemon punch and brought them to the young ladies.

Elaine was standing happily in conversation with the other young woman. Barton enjoyed seeing the two heads together—one dark and one light, a lovely contrast. He noticed the dark one seemed to follow every move that he had made on the dance floor, even when she danced with another young man. He would ask her to dance next.

"Elaine, you have not introduced me to your friend here." He nodded at the dark-haired girl.

"Oh my, I didn't?" She fluttered her eyelashes and then grasped the girl's arm. "This is my sister Elise. We are from Baton Rouge. We are visiting some friends here. Although Peter Starkey was supposed to take me to the dance tonight, he canceled, and my sister and I came together. That's when I saw *him* with *her*." Elaine glowered at the couple across the room and then hastily gulped down the two punch cups.

Barton noticed the beau was looking back at them, so he decided to make the kid jealous. He bent to Elaine, took her hand, and planted a tiny kiss on her fingers. *"Merci mademoiselle, je suis enchanté."* Then, standing up, he smiled back at the man. Bart saw the dolt grip a fist and send daggers across the dance floor at him. Good.

Another dance was starting, so he held out his hand to Elise. "Let's take a spin."

She was surprised and blushing as she timidly put her hand on his. He danced her out to the floor. Elise seemed unsure of her steps at first, but Barton liked the feel of her in his arms. She was tall, just inches shorter than he was, and he did not have to bend to her as he had with the petite Elaine.

In silence, they danced companionably, and Bart leaned to sniff her hair. He wanted to ask the name of the scent, finding it familiar, but thought it might be presumptuous. Barton smiled at her. "Are you having fun?" He nearly missed his next step as she shook her head.

"No, I am not," Elise said absently over his shoulder.

"Why? Do you not like to dance?" He worriedly looked at her, waiting for an answer, and loosened his grip at her waist. "Or are you not enjoying my company?" Barton was now feeling coldness from her.

"No," Elise said quietly. Then he felt her breath warm against his ear as she whispered, "My feet are killing me."

He drew back and looked her squarely in the face, surprised at the candid response. "Is that all?"

"Yes. But would you mind if I take my shoes off or if we sit the rest of this number out?" She smiled wanly at him, her face guarded. "I know I am being impolite—"

"Sure, whatever you want to do." Barton hastily led her off the floor back to their chairs. He noticed Elaine was missing. Looking about, Bart saw her with another girl; she and her girlfriend were definitely flirting with a pair of flyboys. He chuckled, thinking Elaine was already moving on. Her broken heart suddenly was on the mend—typical fickle female. *Dang it!*

He wasn't used to this debutante stuff or the *froufrou* manners of society people. It was embarrassing. He had gladly missed all that by going off to college early. He came from a poor family. They couldn't afford to have dancing classes, music lessons, or debutante debuts for his sisters. Thérese had been their tutor in most of the social graces while they were growing up. He just liked to dance and wanted a girl who would enjoy the same. He would go looking again.

He stood staring around the room to spot perhaps another eager girl because this one turned out to be a lovely wallflower but a dud.

Just then, he felt a delicate hand on his arm, and he looked back to see Elise slipping off her shoes. She stepped down onto the floor in her stocking feet. Bart thought she might be rich enough to own silk stockings. Thérese couldn't afford them and went bare-legged often. His sisters still wore bobby socks or went bare-legged, like tonight.

She smiled up at him. She was only an inch shorter now, still tall, and he saw she was happy, smiling with relief.

"I'm so sorry. I did not have any heels that matched my dress, so I borrowed Elaine's. Now I am sorry I did." She sighed. "Do you mind dancing with me in my bare feet? And please don't tell my mother; she would simply have kittens!" Her smile was engaging, and the absent look had vanished. She was willing to return to the dance floor with Barton.

Surprised by her, Bart suddenly sat down and pulled her down to the chair next to him. "Let's sit this one out and just talk. Do you mind?" He took her hand. "I have not introduced myself. I am Bar—"

Suddenly, a gregarious soldier dashed up. "Come on, toots; let's do the Boogaloo!" He grabbed Elise from her chair and, with an arm about her, whisked her away to the dance floor.

Barton gaped at the audacity of the man as a sudden heat came on him.

As the beat changed for a new song, the drummer began a complex bass rhythm, and then the trumpets and trombones joined in a raucous jitterbug tune. The lights came up, and nearly all the young women, soldiers, and men joined in the dance. Bart noted his sisters Camellia and Nancy were out on the dance floor as well. He stood up to see over the crowd as the wild dancers flung themselves in gyrating movements about the floor. Some guys were flinging the girls between each other or swinging them under their legs or overhead. Bart wished he were out there now with Elise. She looked frightened as the soldier flung her aside and then yanked her back, actually stepping on her foot. She limped through the fast steps.

Barton's hand reflexively gripped tightly, wanting to clobber the stomping oaf. He didn't care for the way the fellow leered at her or held the girl so closely with his leg between her thighs and then tossed her about like a rag doll. Elise's skirt flew up as the man threw her overhead, and Bart could see her lacy panties.

Barton saw red.

Shoving his way through the crowd and on a turning move, he tapped the soldier on the shoulder. He grabbed Elise's hand. "Beat it, buster! This one is mine!" He twirled Elise away from the astonished man.

Another soldier came up and pulled the angry young man off the floor as he made to go after Bart.

"Sorry, sucker!" Barton just grinned and finished the dance. A less boisterous song came up, and he kept Elise tight in his arms.

"Will you let go of me? I can't breathe!" Elise shoved against Barton's chest.

He released Elise slightly. "You still wanna dance with that guy? You are lucky to only get stubbed toes from him," he said tersely.

"Well, who do you think you are anyway? You are bumptious and rude!"

"No, I am Barton Barre, and that pissant was rude to just steal you away like that while we were talking."

"I see. So you stole me from the soldier? Does that make it equitable or better?"

"I thought so."

Elise studied Barton for a moment and then let out a small sigh. "Still, it was boorish. And you are just as impertinent as that fellow … who, by the way, smelled of booze and too much hair oil."

"I haven't had a drop, so I'm stone sober. I know it was rude, but who cares. At least I am not letting the room see your bloomers by tossing you around now, am I?" He grinned cheekily and winked at her.

Her dark eyes flared for a second, and then she bit her lip. "You saw my—"

"Mmm hmm, they are pretty panties with blue lace—" He winked.

Bart suffered the slap and let her go with a laugh. He pursued Elise as she pushed her way through the crowd of dancers toward the punch table.

"Buy you a drink?" He held up a cup.

"No. Besides, it is free." She sniffed and turned about to ignore him. "Go away!"

He sidled closer. "Aw, come on, honey." He batted his long eyelashes at her.

"Don't call me that! You don't know me."

"Come on, Elise. I just saved you from that toe-stomping jackass." He winked at her. "I almost got clobbered for it, too."

"Ha! So what do you want for a reward for your gallant deed? My life? My hand? What?" She flapped the hankie tied on her wrist. "A token of my esteem?" She sneered.

"Only your time. Let's go sit the next one out. I think you need to rest your toes and cool your hot attitude." Bart pulled her along to a group of chairs near the potted palms.

He fed her punch and cake, chatted, and made casual joking comments about the surrounding people. He waited while she went to the restroom, coming back with her stockings in her purse. It was some time before he realized he had done all the talking, and they were not dancing. Bart invited the girl back out to the floor. She seemed reluctant at first.

This time, Elise matched his steps. By the second song, Elise was more at ease. Barton realized she had been encumbered by wearing her sister's shoes; they had looked too small for her narrow, graceful feet.

As they danced, he felt Elise come alive, and she engaged him in increasingly cheerful conversation and seemed assured in following his lead. Barton felt a swell of pride as he paraded them around the floor. She matched him in every dance style, and he never once stepped on her!

He sensed she was unique, and he was compelled to stay with her through the evening. Elise brought out good feelings from deep within him. He was surprised to feel so comfortable and so able to talk with her. Bart brought her another large piece of cake, and they shared it during a band break. He was surprised she would eat so much! He liked her. She was not a flirty or wilting flower like her sister, Elaine. Elise, although graceful and sweet, had spunk and tart wit.

Once again, on the dance floor, Elise, minus the new stockings, was sprightly and gay.

"You are a surprising dancer. Did you go to dancing school?" she asked coyly as Barton twirled her under his arm.

He broke into laughter. "Uh, no. But thanks. My stepmother will be happy to know her lessons were not in vain." He grinned down at Elise. "She said that was one of many charms a young man should have because girls like to dance. My other girls have never complained." He shrugged at the comment. "You are pretty good too."

"I should be. Half my life, I have had ballet, social dancing, and comportment classes." She retorted as Barton held her a little closer. "But I think my years of dancing were wasted upon other girls and homely, chubby boys."

Barton grinned impishly. "I hope that doesn't include me."

"No, sir."

Elise's laughter was like tinkling crystal—delightful—and Barton ate it all up, wanting only more time with her. This time, he kept hold of Elise. As other men tried to cut in or asked her to dance, Bart sent them on their way with surly growls or looks. He would not share his prize. He even ignored Elise's reproof.

"You do not have to stick around on my behalf, you know. I can take care of myself. I do not mind."

"I know. Unless you really want to let those bowser hounds and flyboys chase you around?"

"Are you not doing the same?" she asked with a bit of pique.

"Nope. I like what I got right here. Why do you want to run away?" Bart squeezed her gently in his arms; he was rewarded with Elise's dimpled smile.

After many songs, the pair went out onto the terrace for some air while the singers took another break.

◆ ◆

"Richard, tell me what I am seeing over there." Thérese turned Richard's face toward the open French doors.

He caught Barton holding hands with a tall girl walking out the door to the terrace. Richard and Thérese stood by, watching the young couple as they swayed at the balustrade, leaning toward each other in blithe, animated conversation.

"Is that something we should be worried about?" Thérese asked him. "Damn, that boy. He can be so charming; he gets girls everywhere he goes these days. This girl seems very young, and I am afraid of another repeat of last month's shameful episode. Surely, he would not do something stupid," Thérese commented with some heat in her voice.

"Well, it was your idea to let Bart have one final fling at the dance here." Richard, seeing the concern on his wife's face, took her arm and led her across the floor. "Okay, you win. Let's go break up the party and just see how serious it is."

Slowly, the couple strolled over to their son and the mysterious girl.

"Barton, you have not danced with your mother yet. I think she would like that," Richard said engagingly to the young couple as they stepped up. "Who is your charming companion?"

Barton, suddenly embarrassed, made the introductions. "My father, Richard Barre, and his wife, Thérese, may I present Miss … Elise … um, of Baton Rouge." He realized he had no last name for her.

Bart's parents were charmed by Elise, and they talked to her for a few minutes. Then Richard bent to Barton. "Go dance with your mother, Son."

Putting on a brave smile, Barton stiffly offered his arm to Thérese, and they went back inside to dance, but not without a worried look back at Elise, afraid to lose her.

◆ ◆

"Would you care to indulge an old man with a dance, Miss Elise?" Richard asked all of a sudden and bent in a courtly fashion, offering her his hand; she took it. Richard, hearing her trilling laugh, suddenly felt a ping go through him. Taking her arm, he steered her onto the dance floor, where they danced through two songs. Richard enjoyed her bantering conversations; she shyly flirted with him, and he flirted back, equally charmed by the young woman.

He was feeling young again. He thought—*they did not make women like this anymore— she was a rare jewel. I wish I were twenty years younger—and single. I would sweep Miss Elise off her feet! What a delightful coquette!*

He caught Barton and Thérèse looking across the floor at them. His wife wore an amused look on her face, but Barton's regard was stony cold. The song ended, and Richard started to lead Elise off the floor. He caught sight of Barton sliding his way through the crowd toward them, resembling a determined tiger ready to devour his prey. Suddenly, Richard perversely asked Elise for one more dance. She agreed, and he whirled her away, only to forget how many more dances he shared with Elise.

While they were dancing, he asked if she was of French lineage and if she spoke the language. He was delighted to hear her swift change to French; her accent was precise and much like his French mother and not the local Creole patois. He engaged her in conversation *en Français*, and they talked effortlessly. Her family was like the Barre family, with over a hundred years of colonial French ancestry. Yet, in it all, she divulged no family information, or their surname, or where she grew up.

So it was that Richard found himself not even listening to the actual words anymore, just enthralled by the young woman's silky voice and her enthusiasm for dancing. He oddly felt as if Elise belonged in his arms; she was such a delight! Richard had to take a deep breath and break his hold when handing the beautiful young woman back to an anxious Barton after noticing the music had ended. He returned to the terrace to clear his head.

"Well, that was an interesting little display, Richard. Maybe I am the one who should be worried now. I will forget about Bart." Thérèse stood at his elbow, staring at his handsome, sweat-dampened profile in the moonlight as he blotted his face.

Pocketing his hankie, Richard put his arm around her shoulder and pulled her to his side. "You have no worries from me. I am in love with you, and that says more than a simple flirtation, Thérèse." He bent and kissed her ardently. Seeing her surprised face, he released his wife and said, "You know the Barre men; we can't resist the attentions of beautiful women." He leaned back on the balustrade, pulling Thérèse into his arms as he looked back to the dance floor.

They silently watched Barton and Elise walking off the dance floor toward the refreshment alcove.

"I think we have a dangerous little woman there. She is but a young siren. For now, I think Barton is just having fun. It is good he goes home tomorrow; otherwise, we would have more to worry about," Richard commented sourly.

He peeked at his watch, noting it was close to midnight. He was feeling his age as the long workday in the field and his broken desire of earlier came washing over him. He wanted to go home and make love to his pretty wife.

"Are you tired, *ma chérie?*" he asked, hugging Thérese to his side. She nodded yes. Richard suggested, "Let's go get Paul and Amy and the girls and go home. I am worried Amy might drop that baby out on the dance floor if she stays any longer. I also think we should relieve the other dancers from Paul's obnoxious displays and knocking into people. I thought you taught him how to dance properly!"

They laughed at the idea and started to go inside, but Richard could not resist lighting the flame of desire as he patted Thérese on her behind, saying he needed her to tell him something naughty. She giggled and then whispered her naughty secrets in his ear as they walked arm-in-arm back into the ballroom.

They noted Richard's brother Francis and his wife, Patrice, looking like young lovers on the dance floor. Francis kissed his giddy wife, and they wove about through the other dancers as if punch-drunk. Richard stepped by to announce they were leaving, and Francis only waved him on and amorously snuggled into the neck of his wife.

Richard fanned his face with a hand, smelling the strong alcohol fumes emanating from Francis. "Phew! Good thing Carl Louis drove. He'll need to put that pair in the rumble seat! I predict someone will be sick as a dog on the way home—he's had too much spiked-punch!" Richard laughed with his wife.

"I saw he smuggled in a flask." Thérese giggled. "Maybe Paul had some of that, too, and that's why he dances like a drunken stork!"

"That is being kind, my dear! Paul, unfortunately, did not get Charlotte's dancing talent, unlike our Barton. I never thought the boy would be a decent dancer."

Thérese swatted Richard's arm. "Indeed! Are you impugning my teaching abilities?"

"Not at all. Bart's latent talent is just a surprise to me."

"Well, he has the charm of being the third son, just like his father." Thérese hugged Richard close.

Laughing at their jokes, Richard and Thérese then found Barton and Elise sitting on the side, chatting away and holding hands. Richard keenly watched them for a moment but then stepped forward to thank Elise for the dances.

"We're going home, taking Paul, Amy, and the girls, and you should follow soon—it is getting *late*. Remember, you have a big day tomorrow." He emphasized the word *late* and was relieved to see that Barton had caught his meaning and made no argument. Bart swiftly kissed Thérese good night and nodded his farewells to Richard. Richard and Thérese left in search of their other children.

◆ ◆

Barton reached into his jacket pocket and pulled out a fountain pen and a pad of paper. He wrote his two addresses, one in Texas and one for the plantation, and folded the paper into a neat square. Then he put it in Elise's hand, closing her fingers around the note as he kissed her hand.

"Will you write to me, Elise?" he asked her eagerly.

She blushed and looked at him with a concerned gaze. "Why do you want me to write to you? You hardly know me," she asked him plainly. "Besides, this was only a dance. We are not dating. Would you prefer my number? You can call me sometime."

"No, I cannot. I am going home tomorrow and leaving for the army on Monday. But I would be honored if you would choose to write to me while I am away," he said earnestly.

"But that is so silly."

"Please?" he begged.

◆ ◆

Elise noticed Barton had yet to release her hand. She could feel a tremor in his warm, firm grip. Suddenly, eager to kiss him while watching Barton, his smile was tremulous, and his water-pale eyes were searching her face. Despite feeling as if she was too bold, Elise squeezed his hand in response and leaned ever so slightly toward Barton to kiss him.

Elaine bustled up exuberantly, like a warm, fizzing soda pop, as she threw herself into the chair next to the pair and started to chatter away.

Elise knew Barton felt the intimate moment burst like a bubble, and they reluctantly fell back to earth. Bart's eyes were chips of ice as he glared at Elaine.

"Are you listening, Elise? I said we need to go." Elaine nudged her. "The dance is over! I don't want to miss our ride. Look, the band is already packing it in. *Vite!*"

"Barton is leaving tomorrow for the US Army. He wants me to write to him," Elise said flatly, still looking at him. She pulled her hand away, keeping it tightly closed around the paper in her palm.

"Uh, yes. If I may have your address," Barton countered with a tremulous smile.

"Oh! Isn't that just swell? You are the fourth fella who gave me his address tonight. This is such a novel thing, writing to soldiers. I don't know why I never did it before!"

Suddenly interested, Elaine hung on Barton's shoulder and printed her name and address on the pad of paper he gave her. Tearing it off, she then folded it and kissed it, leaving a red lip print on the paper, and handed it all back to him. "That should give you some sweet dreams," she said conceitedly and then murmured against his ear, "Thanks for dancing with me earlier. You are cute and a charming gentleman!"

Elise noticed Bart was blushing and saw him holding the paper while still staring at her.

"Elise, we have to go now. Where are my shoes? Why aren't you wearing them?" Elaine urged impatiently.

"I left them over there somewhere," she replied absently, still watching Barton. She felt her sister leave.

"I am sorry, Barton. I should not … my parents would not …" She held out the paper.

Barton took her hand, crushing the address in it. "I insist. I wish I had more time to spend with you … I'd take you out properly."

"Will you write to me too?" she asked softly.

"Yes, and I would rather this kiss be yours," Barton said as he looked at the lip-imprinted paper. He suddenly took her hand and kissed it fervently.

He had a sparkling tear in his eye, and he sniffled and gave a little embarrassed cough. He sat back up stiffly as Elaine came back with shoes.

Elise had a moment of clarity to say, "Those aren't your shoes, Elaine." She squeezed his hand again and let go.

"How about a proper kiss for luck? Or one for the road?" He grinned slyly and leaned in toward her.

Elaine tugged, and Elise rose to her feet abruptly. Barton fell on empty air.

"Thank you, Barton Barre, for a lovely evening. I will consider what you asked," Elise said primly as she took the shoes from her sister, who was already pulling her away. "Thanks for rescuing me from toe-stomping, drunk, and clumsy army men," she called as she looked back at him. "I will not forget—"

He watched her leave, the sapphire-blue skirt swinging daintily as she walked away barefooted. She did not put on her sister's shoes.

Barton drew a heavy sigh. "Couldn't even get one little kiss—what rotten timing! Damn!"

He reluctantly went to find the rest of his family so they could go home. All of a sudden, he turned back into the crowd, wanting to rush after Elise and ask her something. An important topic never came up in all of their conversations. Not finding Elise, he shrugged it away. It was now too late to ask. She was lost in the departing crowd. With his lousy luck, he would never see her again. However, on a new hope, he would ask in his first letter to Elise, "How old are you?"

◆◆◆

CHAPTER 5

Letters

July 24, 1943

Dear Son,

I hope this letter finds you well and safe. We have been hearing many reports of the war both in the newspaper and on the radio, and things do not sound good either in the Pacific or in Europe. I am hoping for your sake you will not be going abroad. Have they decided where you are going? Do you have a choice? Probably not. Wherever you go, do not be an arrogant fool and step up for some doomsday project for which no one will return. I am sorry. I do not mean to be so demanding and sour, but I would hate to lose you, Barton.

Barton grimaced at his father's words, thinking the man must have innate knowledge or a mental link to him. Richard always knew when he was up to something. Bart was nearly seven hundred miles away in Georgia, and his Father already knew something. Just that morning, he had volunteered to ship out with the Quartermasters once he took a crash course in officers' training and logistics for POL (Petroleum, Oil, and Lubrication supplies). Nevertheless, Bart was heading to England with the promise of a position as a company first sergeant and would have men under his command with the POL quartermasters. He shook his head, took a sip of his root beer, and continued to read his father's letter.

I should have written sooner, but things on the home front have been chaotic. I do have some good news and more bad.

Your sister-in-law, Amy, gave birth to a son on the evening of June 8. Paul and Amy named him Emile Oliver François. We arrived home from our trip just in time. The baby was a week late and big. Are not all the Barre babies overlarge? Little Amy had complications, as did Emile. However, I am happy to say that they have both recovered. And baby Emile, my first grandson, is a strapping, healthy boy. He drives his parents crazy, though; he cries a lot, just

93

as you did at his age.

Thérèse spent a week with them to help Amy after Emile came home. She was exhausted and was glad there were no more babies for a while. I was glad to have her home again; eating frozen leftovers and eggs got boring, as did Camellia's "modern" one-dish casserole. Lord, deliver me if I see another green bean noodle casserole or deviled egg rice delight. I will also be glad for this war to be over—maybe we will return to tasty food and real meat. There are days I wish we lived on the plantation where we always had lots of food. I think I need another vacation with Mom and Dad.

The county deputy came by after our vacation with grave news (sorry for the pun), but it seems there was vandalism in the Magnolia Cemetery in May. Some graves were desecrated, rude graffiti on some markers, headstones knocked down, and someone broke into your mother's grave. The wooden box was smashed open, including the stone jar of her ashes. We were surprised to find most everything still in the box, although Thérèse's old wedding ring was missing. I have no idea why this happened. It was horrible to think of a person robbing and desecrating graves. Thérèse and I reburied what remained, and I reset the headstone on top of it all to thwart further robbery. I am sorry. I almost did not want to tell you, but you are an adult and should know such evil things do occur in this sad and tormented world.

Barton felt darkness seep into his mind. *What kind of creep did such vile things?* Yet, he had a feeling that he knew it. He grabbed out his shoebox of stuff from home and dug through it to find the dirtied and pale yellow rabbit's foot. He knew his grandfather had given it to him after his favorite rabbit, Jocko, had died when he was only a little boy, yet Barton had missed that lucky rabbit's foot for a very long time. It mysteriously had been in his pocket the day he and the Guillot brothers volunteered. He pressed it against his head as if some memory would slip into his mind, yet it did not. *It could not be true. Was it me?*

Barton stuffed the foot in his pocket and picked up the last pages of his father's letter, settling again to read. He hoped that, in all of this, there would be some logical answer regarding what he sickly felt, yet he was disappointed.

Jacques and Celeste are saddened that she miscarried the baby last week. It seems unfair that they should be so cursed not to have a child yet while everyone around them is happy and bouncing new babies. They will keep trying.

Barton, the last news is the worst of all. I have lost the store and had a fire in my workshop. June 15th, a terrible riot began down at the Pennsylvania Shipyards. This was a racial issue that had severe implications for Beaumont. The Texas State Guard and the Rangers were called in to quell the riots and to keep the peace. Now, you may think it was the blacks rising against the whites, but you would be wrong.

A black man attacked the white wife of a worker at the shipyards. Hearing the story, the man's coworkers became enraged, and soon a mob formed. They went to get justice from the city and were not satisfied. They ran rampant through Beaumont, targeting many of the colored businesses and some neighborhoods. Now, this was not just a small group of men but escalated into the thousands. Unfortunately, the mobs went ransacking and burning along Pearl, Gladys, and Forsythe Streets, and some ventured down the side streets, too. The warehouse next door to mine was torched, and part of my workshop suffered burn and smoke damage.

I was working late on that evening on a custom order with Titus. Thérèse was visiting Paul (thank God), and the girls were with Lorraine. Titus smelled smoke. We went out in the alley and saw the flames from next door. Then, we witnessed people running along the alley and the main street—the entire block was an orange-red glow. I called the fire department and the police right away. They told me there was a riot going on! Titus stayed to help next door. I ran to the corner, and there I found my store and the hardware store next to it both engulfed in flames. I broke the windows and hauled out as many furniture pieces as I could, including some of my files and sales books, but that was it!

When I looked up the street, I could see other businesses on fire. I heard breaking glass and people yelling and fighting. Some were looting the shop fronts. It was a night right out of hell! I ran the few blocks to Jeff Parnell's bakery and saw it was already consumed by fire.

He had heard the noise of breaking glass downstairs, and thinking it was a robbery, he called the police and went to thwart the thieves. But when he came down the stairs, someone hit him as he came out onto the sidewalk. Jeff could only stand there with blood running down his face and watch his dreams burn up. We sat down on the sidewalk and cried.

I suffered some minor burns and cuts from trying to save my store. One fire extinguisher can against an inferno was like spitting on it. I also sustained a few wounds trying to stop men as they ran along, breaking windows and fighting with people. Thérese thought I was heroic but rash to get involved. I did not feel so because I saved no one and nothing.

That week, Jeff stayed with us. Titus stayed home with Lorraine in their guesthouse, both afraid to go to work. Both men were in harm's way as Negroes seemed to be personae non grata all of a sudden—tempers were high for days after.

Paul and Jacques have been at the workshop trying to clean up and make repairs with Thom Finnegan and Dan Porter over the last few weeks. If I can find another affordable place to work, I may move there. Our workshop holds bad memories now. This could be a sign of the times to make a change! We had a fire sale for the few things I rescued, which helped some. I still have cauchemars of watching my work go up in flames. I guess for me, the La Barre Prophecy and Curse still holds. What was the grave sin that my family or I be punished for?

However, three good things did occur because of the riot and disaster.

A former business partner of mine, Maitlin Verowen, was arrested as one of the inciters of the riot and for many of the severe damages and personal assaults on Negroes. He was going by an alias, John Stone, and working in the shipyards. It makes me nervous to know that he was so near, living in Port Arthur. One would think he would be far away from his crimes. Therefore, that part of my old court case with Calumet and Verowen's assault should end after so many years.

It is my thinking that the villain came back to hurt me again. I had thought the man had gone because the police never found him after my accident, just his abandoned car with my blood on it. It has been a mystery these years, not knowing if it was Maitlin Verowen who slaughtered our chickens or left poisoned apples on our porch, which killed dear Katie. So perhaps his bigotry also was for me because I fired him and because I am not prejudiced. I employ anyone with a skill without a thought of race or creed. There seems to be a lesson somewhere in that, but I have yet to find any real consolation.

After all these years, Titus, Lorraine, and Jeff left Beaumont and headed for Canada. Jeff knows now that he can have a successful bakery in a white neighborhood. It is best for Titus because they can now live properly as husband

and wife. Maybe you did not know this, but he and Lorraine were secretly married in the summer of '35 in Canada. But they have been living apart these eight years, except for Titus, who is living in Lorraine's guesthouse. Now, they can stop the secrecy and lies and be honest in their love. They are brave.

It is sad for us, though. I have lost a dear friend, my business partner in Titus, and a wonderful sister-in-law. I am unsure how my business will survive without him. Thérèse is, of course, both elated and crying for their loss. However, the couple is not getting any younger, and they want so much to be together and not to waste life waiting until society accepts their mixed relationship. It is no longer comfortable or feasible for them to remain here in Beaumont.

Thus, all of this has been hideous and has been a black mark on our town. There have been migrations of black businesses and families who have left the area, afraid for more of this in the future, all because of the crime of one fellow. It brought Titus and me to think back on our own lives with the nasty racism we experienced when my shop was burgled in '35. His brother, Isaiah, barely survived the incident. You may not remember it because you were only a child, but it was a blatant reminder for Titus. The sign of the times was flashing in neon lights for him and Lorraine. They left two weeks ago. The family misses them terribly.

I sold them my old shop truck, rattle-trap that it was, at a cheap price so they could move away easily. It was sad to see them leave a lifetime of belongings sitting on the curb with only a few essential items in the truck and the back of Lorraine's DeSoto. Titus sold his old Ford, as he did not think it would make the lengthy trip to Canada. We shall send Lorraine money once they are settled, for several people came by after seeing the pile of furniture and things in front of the house. We saved some items for Paul and Jacques, too, who are still technically newlyweds two years in and need much for their families. We were hoping to buy back Lorraine's house, perhaps for Paul, but the price is too steep for us, even at a deal from Lorraine. It is better to sell it and for her to receive the profit that they can use to build their lives again in Canada.

The streets in town look different now, with many of the burned-out and damaged buildings; some have already been razed and are barren lots. I think I have found another store to buy and am in negotiations to purchase it. I wish I was a wealthy man—I would take advantage of the new properties on the market!

I thank God we had insurance. I am in debate with the company as well; they do not want to pay, as rioters caused the destruction of my property. I hope this mess will all work in our favor.

We miss you. Please stay safe and write soon. Your mother and I always enjoy your letters. Your sisters send their love and will write soon.

With Love,

Father, Richard

Barton felt ill after reading the horrific news. He clenched his fist around the old rabbit's foot, which for some was a sign of good luck, and wished he had been there for them. Maybe he could have stopped the people who burned the family business or even ransacked the cemetery. How could such diabolical things happen in Beaumont?

But then, Bart thought about his old theory that everything in the Barre family's life had gone to hell when his father had taken in the colored Joseph brothers. Their lives were never the same, and year after year, things were really wracked with bad luck and hardship. It seemed more so than what their friends suffered during those hard times of the thirties. So perhaps it was a blessing in disguise that Titus was gone; maybe Bart's family would do better now. Phooey, on his father's theory that the bad times were a part of the family curse. Bart did not believe in curses but bad luck; yes, that seemed genuine enough, and he'd had his share of it.

Bart was squeamish about the bigotry aspect. He had been trying to understand the extreme prejudices he'd witnessed in the army, too. The colored men were segregated with their own barracks, units, mess halls, and latrines. In town, the Negroes could not go to some of the bars or cafés. In some, they had to sit in special sections or eat outside. Barton had tried to turn a blind eye and keep his opinion to himself, but to see the blatant disregard and exclusion of people was unjust in his mind. He wondered how he had never witnessed or paid attention to it while growing up, yet he knew the caste system was in effect in Texas as well. In 1935, innocent and deaf Isaiah Josephs had been nearly beaten to death just because of his color. It wasn't fair.

For the Barres, blacks held no particular or demoted class. Richard had taught his family to be color-blind. Perhaps Barton had just ignored whatever he had witnessed like everything else because he abhorred prejudice. Or maybe it was that he had been more enlightened than most and lived sheltered in a white society with a few privileged black friends.

Here in the training camp, he witnessed the swing of biases from men, who he would have thought were logical and intelligent, who changed quicksilver to hate and cruelty. Men who upheld their unbiased opinions on color or race or who allied with the wrong men were just as quickly targeted, suffering malicious treatment, pranks, and hatred. Barton kept his mouth shut and looked away when he could.

He saw that many of his comrades from the Deep South were this way, and some were easily incensed and always ready for a fight. It was similar to the schoolyard bullies trying to impress and have influence. It only got worse when there was a crowd because everyone took a swing. Bart had at one time been a bully himself, but it was mostly for self-preservation among his brothers and peers. Lately, he'd had his share of fights; when he could manage, he kept them verbal. He got plenty of harassment, too, as he somehow soared above and beyond his compatriots primarily for his aloof and impartial handling of such affairs, leaving many in the dust, including his buddies, the Guillot brothers, who loved to brawl for no reason.

Some prejudices also did not apply just to blacks but to American Indians, Asians, Italians, Polish, Irish, and even some of the Scandinavians and American Germans were at risk and lumped into the "enemy of the people" classification.

God, the entire world really was at war! And he did not understand how these men could find enmity among their peers and comrades rather than saving that hatred and physical violence for the war ahead of them. It was unfair and stupid. If he were biased toward anything, it would be stupidity!

Barton had not written to his father for some time because he was so busy lately with exhausting training. He decided to drop a quick line or two so Richard would not worry. After all the family had experienced recently, his Father deserved better, and that included words from his son.

As he wrote his own missive, he wondered what to say about Lorraine and Titus. He had been witness to their caring relationship for many years. When he was a teen, he found out about their secret marriage and said nothing to his family, leaving it a private matter between himself and his step-aunt. It was also because of his findings that Bart convinced Lorraine to build the guesthouse in her backyard. Titus lived there for many years—this way, they could keep their marriage hush-hush but be together in a prejudiced society. Titus was devoted to Lorraine and spent many weekends working on Lorraine's house, or sometimes they would disappear for a day or two on a weekend and come back looking extraordinarily cheerful. When Bart was younger, he had never thought much about them as a couple, and they had been friends for so long that he had just grown accustomed to seeing them together. After careful consideration, he thought he could extend good wishes to Lorraine and Titus, who were officially his aunt and uncle, now that they no longer had to hide their marriage!

As a youth, Barton had always been in awe of Titus Josephs. The man had been a college history professor and was able to recount any historical time. Bart could also thank equally talented Lorraine for getting him through school. The pair of ex-college professors had been his staunch supporters, helping him to advance grades, and then insisted he go farther than the local Lamar Junior College. He went on with a scholarship to the Texas Agriculture and Mechanical College. Lorraine and Titus also helped Barton to stay focused and committed, his eye on the Golden Fleece Prize—his sheepskin for mechanical engineering.

Perhaps they had also been his good luck charm, for without his degree, Barton might have been just another shlub, a latrine licker in this man's army. Or, as his father had been prone to call the lower echelons of the military—cannon fodder.

Barton could also thank Lorraine for getting him into baseball, a sport he loved. He had played in some of the local kids' clubs and through high school and college. If it had not been for Titus beaning him with a ball and giving Bart a concussion, and Lorraine's wise counsel, Barton might have ruined everything. He had been tempted to try out for a team in St. Louis when the recruiter was impressed by his skills. He had practiced and played hard to earn the right to play on a real team. He was an excellent shortstop and batter and had high stats. He felt prideful that even here in camp, in a simple game of softball among the men, he was made a star player! Bart thought maybe he had made the wiser choice after all by staying in school, even though he was now reluctantly heading for war!

◆ ◆

Amstead-on-Devon, England
December 27, 1943

After a long, grueling day, Barton flopped on his cot to relax for a short while with his mail. He was excited to receive more mail from the States, and he eagerly tore into it as if it were a Christmas gift!

December 2, 1943

My Dearest Barton,

Please forgive me for not writing to you sooner. I did not know where to write to you until a few weeks ago. I have been so worried for you. I expected to hear from you by now!

The envelope bore a sloppy but unfamiliar address. It was not one of the Boulanger girls' handwriting—Elise and Elaine were neat letter writers. He shuffled through the pages to see who was writing the letter. He noted there were several pages of yellow writing paper covered with big loopy script. The paper had been perfumed—an oily drop on the edge of one page smelled like roses.

"BettyAnn Sanders! Oh crap!" He groaned aloud.

Bart could not believe the girl was actually writing to him after the humiliation he'd had to suffer for her. He was in the army because of her!

He glanced at his wristwatch; he had another ten minutes before he had a meeting with his commanding officer. He resettled on his cot to finish reading the letter, hoping it would be something good at least.

My sister received a letter from Garrett. He mentioned you guys were stationed together in England. He gave my sister his address, so I am hoping this will find you as well.

Marcia has good news. We hope Garrett will be able to come home for the big event. She is expecting a baby in the early spring. Mama and Daddy are torn between happiness for a grandbaby and being angry that Marcia and Garrett weren't married or even engaged. I think it is all so very romantic!

Bart gaped at the letter, yelling, "Pregnant! Holy Crapola!" Shaking his head, he reclined again to read.

I am sorry for the trouble months ago. I still feel ashamed that everything went poorly, so you had to suffer Daddy's punishment. Well, I did not get off so lightly either. Daddy gave me the belt and restrictions for a month—no birthday party this year! Now, maybe I am glad we didn't do it all the way because of Marcia's big problem.

I wanted to see you again, and when Marcia said you had joined the army with Garrett and Louis, I was afraid I lost you.

I hope you do not hate me after what happened. I suppose I am too young for you, and you think I am just a Dumb Dora. But I really like you, Bart. You are just dreamy and sweet. I wanted to tell you that night. I will be honest; you were the first boy to kiss me, except that I do not count Todd Gary from the fourth grade. Silly me.

I did not know what would happen after a kiss. I know I must have seemed stupid not to know what was going on. My sister has since informed me of my folly and has explained the more delicate matters beyond a kiss. I think now that she and Garrett were doing a lot more than kissing in the bushes! She is now paying the price of being sick all the time and growing fat!

I am sorry I ruined your evening. Had I known more, I might have said yes. Tho, I still might have been afraid. Barton, dear, knowing all these things, I think much about you. I know we have something between us. I share my feelings with you now, hoping you might feel the same as me. Maybe you were afraid to tell me because of what my father did to you.

If you feel the same, please write to me. If you do not have feelings for me, please be nice and write to me to tell me so. I will not write you again. Until I hear from you, I will be hopeful. I will also think good thoughts for your safety.

Yours—Always

BettyAnn Sanders

P.S. If you see Louis and Garrett, tell them, Arnie and Alistair Montgomery say hello. Alistair is home on medical leave. He lost a hand and eye in the Philippines. Marcia sends her love. Say nothing to Garrett or Louis about the baby just yet. She wants to tell him! Oh, and can you send me a picture so I can kiss it every night? That way, you will know I still love you.

Stunned, Bart sat for a few minutes to absorb the letter. He was surprised by the girl's persistence and audacity in thinking that there was something more than a kiss between them. Evidently, her sister Marcia was leading her along or a hopeless romantic too and certainly in trouble!

He never wanted to think of or hear from BettyAnn again. The situation still rubbed him raw and rankled at his nerves. It had been a sore point between him and his family. Now, to get this letter plainly stating she had feelings for him was just too much. Bart snorted at the girl's description of him. He had never been called those adjectives before, and while some other man might take them as a favorable compliment, Bart did not. He was not sweet.

He felt sorry for his childhood friend Alistair, losing a hand and eye. The news just brought the war so much closer to home. Barton was lucky that he had not been in battle yet, just a few air raids and buzz bombings while in the pub in a nearby town, for which he could only take cover and hide like a frightened rabbit.

He angrily crumpled the letter, thinking of tossing it away. However, it was a link to home. Maybe when he had time, he would write as the girl asked and tell her to grow up. For now, he shoved the letter in his box in the footlocker and then neatened the covers on his cot, readying to go. With a final glance in the mirror to straighten his tie and smooth his newly shorn hair, he left the barracks.

◆ ◆

Thirty minutes later, Barton left the meeting with his CO, feeling a bit cocky. He had new orders—he was transferring. Soon, he would be the new supervisory sergeant in charge of the POL logistics depot at the US Army and British RAF *Whitcliff* base further east along the English coast. He loved this fast track and felt as if someone upstairs was looking down upon him and keeping him safe.

Sheltered in his coat, Barton pulled up the collar against the raw wind and tromped through the mud, disliking the squelching stuff. He went along to the mess hall and lined up to get his platter of glop. Actually, since he had been in England and on the army air base, the food had improved somewhat—at least, it mostly resembled food.

He liked the sausages they received occasionally; bangers and mash had become a favored meal. He noticed today they had fish again, and while he enjoyed fish, this was dried and salted scrod or dogfish, reconstituted into fried fishcakes. Barton was hungry, so he would eat it. Lately, he could not be choosy. He held his tray out for the server as the man dumped two cakes, a pile of boiled potatoes, and something looking suspiciously like green slime on his tray.

"Oh, lovely. Mushy Peas … again." He wrinkled his nose at the messy plate.

He grabbed up three slices of dense, dark bread, and munching on one slice, he dropped the rest on top of his meal. A new food shipment must have come in today. They had fresh tangerines and apples, a rare treat in the winter. He greedily grabbed a couple of each, hiding them in his coat pockets. He made his way through the mess, snagging a mug of burned coffee along the way. He found a seat at a long table and dug into his meal.

He had taken on the Brit's way of pouring malted vinegar onto his fish and did so along with copious amounts of ground pepper. Most of the food he had eaten so far was bland and boring, although the Brits did have a penchant for horseradish, mustards, and fruity, vinegary sauces called chutneys. Barton missed the tasty food from back home, both the French and the Louisianan Southern spicy cuisine. He even missed the Mexican food and savory barbeque from Texas. He could almost taste a bowl of chili con carne right now.

He ate through his meal quickly, dredging the last of the peas with his remaining slice of bread. Chewing, he looked around the hall and noticed it was less crowded than usual. "Must be another deployment going on," he muttered. Within a day or two, the base would be packed again with more troops for training exercises.

The air base not only trained fighter and bomber pilots but also had parachute training, which he had undergone. It was exhilarating to fly high above the earth, the land below looking like a patchwork quilt. He hated jumping out of the plane. The first seconds of free fall with no control scared the piss out of him. It was a bad thing to piss in your jumpsuit! But he had survived eight successful training jumps and was now qualified to be a jump leader, boldly leading his men into the wild blue yonder! He didn't enjoy the night jumps, though. It was difficult to gauge distances in the dark, and yet, to look out over the darkened sky, passing through misty clouds, and then to see the silver threads of the rivers or creeks winding like snakes below him was spectacular. So far, his luck had held. His team had also trained in packing crates for parachute supply drops. He was proud of his men and their successful efforts.

Something was going on; everyone felt it, so it wasn't all paranoia or gossip. The Brits said their Prime Minister Winston Churchill was meeting with the US superior officers and generals for some kind of coalition operation. Although, no one said when, where, or how—that was the way of things around here. No one below a commander or general knew anything until something happened. Barton was a first sergeant, and before this time, he rarely knew much until someone yelled or passed along orders.

However, in the army, men were the same the world over, as gossip and passed-on secrets still got around, even though they were theories or innuendos at best. Mostly, the men were left in the dark as to the latest plans. Barton found there was a lot of hurried preparation and waiting around in the military, and nobody could complain without a backlash from above. Anticipation was often a psychological killer, especially when the previous plans went bust.

He left the mess hall feeling full but not sated by the poor, tasteless fare. He buttoned up the collar of his wool coat as the night was cold and misty again and sheltered in its meager warmth. He looked up into the night sky and saw only a few pinpricks of stars; the moon hid its face behind the heavy clouds. He thought they just might have snow again tonight.

Living in steamy southern Texas and Louisiana, where it rained often, had not prepared him for the frigid rains of southern coastal England. The other morning, he had awoken to snow on the ground, and by midday, it was raining, and they had slush. The camp was muddy, and everything tasted and smelled of the damp. Barton slogged through the muddy track on his way back to the barracks, noticing the ground had firmed in some places, already icy mud.

He passed several flyboys, who were also bundled in their coats, and just nodded in passing him, not wanting to take their faces out from the warmth of their sheepskin collars. The airmen and their crews mostly stayed in their own groups—they were the elite of the camp around here, like the football heroes in school.

Bart returned to the camouflaged Nissen Building, which housed some of the Americans. After stomping off his muddy boots on the mat inside the door, he walked through the dimly lit barracks, noting there were still a dozen occupied beds. The men were reading, playing cards, writing letters, and talking in subdued tones. He nodded as he passed them. He received few smiles, some with eyes averted. This was the last group of men whom he had trained, and they seemed hesitant to talk or greet him. They all knew things were winding up—everyone felt it in the air. Friendships were formed and lost quickly around here. He went into his small room and office and closed the door behind him. As if on cue, the noise in the barracks rose.

Barton wondered if the men knew something he did not. However, he had learned that was the way. When he moved up in rank and command, he had left friends behind, and people were now reserved around him and on their best behavior. In some ways, Barton liked the special treatment; in other ways, he did not. His men and comrades no longer felt comfortable talking to him or cutting up in front of him. The men had also learned early on not to take advantage of Barton's good moods. He lost Garrett to the other side of the base, where he supplied fuel to the bombers and fighters. Garret had all new friends among the flight crews.

At this time, Bart had only one other man he could call a friend—MP Master Sergeant Schmidt.

Harlan Schmidt was also from Texas and a Houston man. Barton often felt they could speak the same language because he was from near home. The man was blond, blue-eyed, and homely as a mudpuppy. At six feet, Schmidt was lanky-limbed and stringy-muscled but a reliable and formidable man in a fight. He had a swift, hard punch that hurt like hell. The man knew where to hit a man, too; he could stop a brawl with one or two blows.

Bart and Schmidt had become buddies off the base; they often went to have a pint at a pub in nearby Amstead or at the base club. Barton was never much into American beer, but he liked the dark, bitter ale, and a good, thick-headed Guinness was always a welcome treat after a rough day. The men often talked over their pints, played darts, and ogled the lusty tavern wenches. For Bart, it was his only amusement since he joined the army.

Schmidt did not have any education beyond high school, as he had joined the army right after graduation. Harlan was four years older than Bart was. Sometimes, he audibly resented the fact that young Barre had arisen in rank so quickly.

Mostly, Barton succeeded because he wanted to be better than other men. Another rising factor was that Barton was college-educated and intelligent. Surprisingly, Barton never teased sourpuss Schmidt about his less-than-adequate education; Bart knew better.

Schmidt was not exactly brainy, speaking like a country bumpkin, but he had a brawny way of attacking things and problems. He had an intuitive knack for nosing out trouble—Schmidt was a slippery snake, lying and charming his way through the paperwork and red tape to get what he or Barton wanted. He always had eyes and ears in places that usually revealed noteworthy tidbits of information—often something lucrative to be used as blackmail, all for his betterment.

However, Barton felt Schmidt also failed to succeed or rise further because he was essentially lazy, often pushing off physical work on others who were sometimes recognized for their efforts. Barton was usually surprised the man had any rank above a corporal. Somewhere at some time, Schmidt must have impressed someone. There were traits that Barton liked about Schmidt; the big lug usually knew how and when to keep his mouth shut, took orders well, and owned a dark sense of humor.

Barton was pleased to know Schmidt was transferring with him to the new company. Their CO saw Bart and Schmidt work well together. For one thing, the thievery had all but stopped when Schmidt came on the scene. The MP quickly found the *bugs* within their company ranks. Reselling government-issued supplies was frowned upon, yet it happened all the time, especially in backwater bases like this. Schmidt would be an asset to Barton's new command.

Barton dropped a pair of coal nuggets on the hot embers in the potbellied stove. He sat at his desk, pulling out the leather-bound writing kit. He chose several sheets of paper and decided to write letters to his folks and the Boulanger girls, as it had been more than a month since he last wrote home. Christmas had been a bust with no gifts from home, and he had little news to write about.

◆ ◆

Beaumont, Texas
Wednesday, January 26, 1944

Thérese pulled her sweater tightly around her shoulders, feeling the chill of the windy day. She dashed back into the house from the mailbox with the stack of letters, having noticed one was from Barton. She called to Richard, who came down from his library (the twins' old bedroom), and together, they sat in the living room before the warm fireplace to read Barton's letter. The first thing they noticed was that the letter was written in French, in Barton's large, loopy, backhanded scrawl. They wondered at it as they translated it.

December 27, 1943

Dear Folks,

Things are fast-paced here; men and equipment are in and out before one can hardly count them. I have some good …

Oops! Air raid!

The letter ended abruptly with a splatter of ink and then continued afresh.

"How thrifty. Bart didn't waste any paper!" Richard commented with a smirk and received a swat from his wife. They resettled to read it.

January 6, 1944

Dear Family, (again)

Greetings of the New Year! I celebrated the New Year with a pint of bitters with some pals in a local pub that welcomes us Yanks. (That is what they call us over here. It's derogatory, if you ask me.) I was missing home that night for sure—the food and the company were poor in comparison. We had fish and chips for the celebration dinner. Although we did have some real scrambled eggs for New Year's Day, usually, it is some powdered mess they insultingly call "eggs." Mostly, we eat a lot of porridge and toast for breakfast. At least our base has coffee, as they have just installed a bakery and a coffee depot. Good bread and strong coffee can make a man feel human again.

Thanks for the box of things that I received this week. Please tell the girls thanks for the knitted socks, the crocheted hat, and the mittens. The wool items are welcome—it has been frigid here this winter, with a constant freezing drizzle that invades the bones. Thérese—I like the black wool sweater you crocheted for me. I am wearing it as I write this letter—our barracks are as cold as the North Pole tonight. Ha! Our barracks are nothing more than a glorified corrugated tin can lying on its side. No insulation and only a few centrally located coal stoves. I miss our roaring fireplace at home.

They call sweaters "jumpers" over here, and one of my mates was jealous of my new gift. He wanted to trade me several boxes of tea biscuits (stale) and cigarettes for it, but I chose not to—unfair trade there! These men are like boys with baseball cards, trading out their unappreciated items from home for something better!

Thank you, Dad, for sending the National Geographic and Life magazines. They are very welcome, and once read, they make good trades for other needed things. I also appreciate your letter. I am doing fine.

Richard chuckled. "I know about those types of trades. One man's discarded socks could be a lifesaver in a pinch! I once traded a too-small knitted hat and red socks for a pair of gloves and a tin of coffee—good deal there ... although I felt bad about it and never told Mom I traded them away!"

Thérese glanced at Richard. "Well, I guess we are lucky. Bart truly appreciated the gifts, and he actually said thank you, which he rarely does." She gripped Richard's arm. "So what else does he say here?"

I have enclosed a recent photo of me; however, it does not show my latest rank. I hope you will like it. We were at a party in the pub to celebrate a buddy's birthday and New Year's. I am just glad I wiped off the confetti before Joey took the picture! He said, "Send it to yer Mum with my love!" So there you go. Love from Joey Huggleston, our camp photographer and archivist.

Thérese took out the miniscule photo from the tissue paper packet and let out a groan to say tearfully, "What has happened to Bartie's hair? It is all shaved off! Oh dear, there is not a curl left!"

Richard squinted at the photo and began to chuckle. "Well, there's our monkey, *Grand-mère's guenon!* Look at those ears!"

Thérese grabbed back the photo, cradling it in her hands. "Oh, don't say that! I think he is still handsome." She kissed the picture.

Richard laughed anew. "Oh, sure he is if you like shaved orangutans. It's not a very good photo if I do say so. And look at that crazy smirk of his." Richard smoothed his own thick, dark mustache with a pair of fingers and then tapped the photo. "The kid is still trying to grow that silly caterpillar! It looks like he penciled it on his face for this picture!"

Thérese stood up and set the small picture on the mantelpiece, propping it alongside Barton's service photo and other family photographs. "Well, I am glad Bartie thought of us enough to send a picture. At least we know he is fine, but he looks scrawny. Maybe Bartie is not eating properly. What did he say about beer? He is probably being misled by those Guillot boys again!" She snarled with reproof. "I think I shall tell Arnelle Guillot."

Richard shook his head, waving his wife to him. "Forget it, Thérese. They are grown men. I am sure he is fine. Now sit, please, so we can finish reading Bart's letter." He pulled his wife down upon the couch and kissed her cheek, then took back the letter, holding it so they could both read it.

> *Even though England is at war, we have little in the way of battles here in our corner. Our flyboys go out from here to meet the Germans in the air over the Channel on a variety of sorties and attacks. We experience too many air raid drills to keep us on our toes. The claxons and sirens are frightening, and when they go off during the night, I feel I will have a heart attack!*

> *I have news of a promotion soon and will have a new supervisory command. I will not say where at this time. We are told to be very careful what we say and write to our friends and relatives. So please forgive me if I say little as to my actions or duties—we are at war! Loose lips sink ships!*

> *I am fine and mostly well (I do have a cold, but I will live)—I hope. I forgot to say the jar of Ovaltine, tea and peppermints, Christmas cards, and the letters from Cecily's classmates were a welcome treat, too. As I received many kids' letters, I have shared them with my crew. Even though they are written by schoolchildren, it made the men feel good—a sense of home for them.*

> *They try not to be sad thinking of home, especially on these holidays, but some men here cry silently at night, missing their families. And as we are soldiers, we do fear each day. However, we are thankful for each day that we survive. I feel fortunate that I have not yet gone into battle, only in exercise. I currently remain so far back on the administrative front, which is both good and bad, and others are sometimes resentful of my position.*

> *There are days I see the planes come back battle-torn, the pilots and*

airmen wounded, or we wait for planes that do not come back at all. It fills us with despair. We say, "That is too bad for John or such," and we say he was a good guy, and we move on. There is little else to do, you know. When that happens, most men want to get right back into it to fight and avenge their lost comrades. Then again, we want to just duck and find a deep enough hole to hide in until the war is over!

This war is a real mess. I am sorry. I was stupid to think I might have made a difference. And the situation to which these ends have brought me here still rankles me. I sit here on my thumbs, waiting for my turn to move forward, yet perversely hoping it will not be my day to die.

There is something no one ever tells you about war—it hurts the citizens more than it does the armies who fight. It isn't like an enormous battle on a football field where the winners, losers, and spectators go safely home afterward. England has taken some hard hits these past few years, and you can see the war on everyone's face. The countryside and many towns are empty after a blitz. It is a shock to drive through what had once been a bustling village only a month before but is now a burned-out ruin. People here have lost so much. I can only imagine the terrible damage we have caused to Germany as well. But maybe the Huns deserve it.

The Brits have a saying, "Keep Calm and Carry On." Man, it is hard to do it when the claxons are going. I wonder what will become of the generation of children who live through this conflict. What will life mean to them?

Sorry I sound maudlin, but the cold, dismal winter days creep into my veins and make me angry and sad. I admit I do miss Beaumont and my safe little room.

Please do not tell the girls that I write these things. They looked at me with admiring eyes, thinking of me as a hero. I am not one yet. So far, most of the heroes around here go home in wooden boxes. It is very much as you said it would be—war is hell!

Kiss the girls for me and punch the boys. Tell them their brother is still alive and kicking somebody's ass. It just isn't Jerry's yet. Love to Mémé and Pépé if you write or talk with them. I will write later when I get to my new post. Pray this all ends soon!

BB

Richard wiped a tear from his cheek. He took the letter from Thérese's icy fingers, noticing they were both shivering. He put an arm around her shoulders, hugging her close to him. After kissing her temple, they sat quietly for a few introspective minutes before he said anything. The fire in the grate crackled merrily and danced on the wind that suddenly blew down the flue. It was getting windy outside, raw and cold. A storm was moving in.

"Barton sounds good, doesn't he?" Richard tried to sound pleasant.

"Good? I thought he sounded miserable! I have never heard him speak so sadly or even so eloquently. He is scared." Thérese looked up at Richard's profile, trying to assess her husband's mood.

"Well, war is hell. You can't exactly have the boy spouting roses, rainbows, and poetry, every other word! So far, he is safe—he has yet to fight or actually be in the war. When that happens, then we shall find out how brave he is. He did say some good things, though. I like what he said about the war baby generation, didn't you?" Richard smiled and added, "I don't think he has ever been so appreciative of the small gifts we sent, either. It was worth the ration tickets."

Richard cocked a sly eye at his wife. "Bart is growing up. He rarely thinks of the consequences of things. I thought the boy was finally showing foresight and compassion. I could tell he wanted to crow about his promotion but was keeping it reined in. It makes me wonder if he really is up that high already and what Bartie has done to earn it."

Richard got up and stretched widely, his bones and muscles making satisfying pops and creaks, and then stepped over to the hearth. He poked up the fire and added another log to the grate, making hot, red sparks fly up the flue like fireworks. He glanced at Thérese, who was wiping tears away with her handkerchief.

"His letter made me feel the cold of England. You felt it too, didn't you, *ma p'tite?*"

Richard came back to the couch and pulled Thérese onto his lap, settling his arms around her to hold her close.

Richard continued. "I was surprised to find how emotional his letter sounded. Usually, it is all boastful gibberish or nothing at all that truly tells us how he is. I guess our son is finally growing up. Maybe being so far from all he knows has helped him to learn empathy and to find that he really does care for us and can be appreciative of what we have done for him. I am glad that all the money we paid for his college education has at least taught him to write well. He almost sounds like a poet."

"Bartie gets that from you, darling. You are always articulate and exuberant with your descriptions. You tell the best stories." Thérese kissed Richard's cheek. "I did feel the cold. Reading his letter and hearing the wind blowing outside made me feel for him even more. I am happy he finally sent us a picture. He looks so official in his uniform … so grown up." Thérese sighed heavily and leaned her head against Richard's shoulder.

They sat that way for some time, watching the fire, enjoying their close physical bond. They were content knowing that Barton was safe; at least, he had been three weeks ago.

Richard was getting an idea with Thérese on his lap. She was warm and snuggled next to him. He began to kiss her on the neck and ear; she smelled like vanilla and spice from baking apple crisp. Thérese started to purr in response, enjoying his kisses. She put her arms around him and kissed him back, running her hands through the dark waves of his hair. Suddenly, tears came, and soon she was choking on them.

"What are these tears for, *ma chérie*?" Richard cupped her face in his hand, wondering how the romantic moment had melted into tears. His dark eyes were worried as he looked at the lovely face of his wife.

"I am being silly, Richard, I know. I was just thinking about Barton and wondering if there is any chance that he might one day have a marriage like ours. He deserves to be loved. I could feel his loneliness in the letter. It made me sad for him. I am sorry, my love. Kiss me again, and I will forget about it." Thérese pressed her cheek against Richard's broad chest; she could feel his strong, steady beat and felt once more safe and content.

Richard stroked her arms and nuzzled her neck once more, trying to get back the sexy feeling when all of a sudden, he heard loud voices coming up the front walk and stamping on the porch. "Damn! The girls are home from school!"

"Too late!" He kissed Thérese quickly and slid her off his lap to land in a floppy heap next to him on the couch. He deftly snatched a pillow, putting it on his lap.

The front door crashed open on a gust of icy wind. Cecily came running into the front hall with her playground voice still turned up to full volume, shouting that she had won. But then she came to a skittering halt at the door of the living room when she saw her parents. Nancy slammed the front door and collided with Cecily as she struggled to wrench off her coat sleeves.

"Mom? Dad? What's going on? Why are you home already, Dad?" Nancy asked, surprised. She came into the living room and dropped her coat over the floral chintz-covered armchair.

"Why do you ask, nosey Nelly?" Richard laughed, nervously smoothing back his mussed hair.

"Yeah. Who died?" Cecily asked suspiciously as she leaned over the sofa arm, looking curiously at her parents.

"No one," Thérese said, embarrassed as she readjusted her skirt around her knees. She patted her brown waves back in place, tucking a hairpin back into her coiffure.

"Well, you both look weepy, pink, and kinda funny, and I don't mean ha-ha funny," Nancy stated, sagely taking another quick look at her parents.

"Oh, we were reading the mail. We got a letter from Barton today. I'll read it to you later," Thérese said as she got up amid the enthusiastic squeals from the girls about Barton's letter. Thérese swiftly planted a kiss on Richard's lips and scooted past him as he gave her an affectionate pat on the behind. She turned, smiling, and caught his catlike smirk.

"Girls, hang up your coats and put away your things, will you? I'll go get everyone some warm milk and crackers," she said as she went into the kitchen, leaving the noise behind.

She needed a few minutes to regain her calm composure! Drat that Richard and the girls' poor timing!

◆ ◆

Barton felt confused by the letters he received from the Boulanger girls. He could never tell who was who, as they both signed their letters with initials, usually EB. Occasionally, there was one who signed her letter EGB. She wrote in a neat, small, elegant script as if it were calligraphy on an invitation. Her words were usually more poignant and emotive, too. He often hoped those letters were from Elise rather than Elaine. Barton knew he should have written immediately to Elise so he could have distinguished the two sisters' writing styles. He felt ridiculous after these many months suddenly to write the girls, asking who was who.

Both the sisters were lovely—one dark, the other light—and their letters were also like night and day in their differences. He enjoyed getting something from home, but he often looked forward to EGB's letters. She talked about things other than the parties or the events around home and Baton Rouge. She spoke of feelings, although they were not always directed toward him. But she shared how she felt about the war and the world, and she described her simple days in pleasant prose.

Yet Barton found there were things she did not say; there was no mention of school names or college and her studies, and it always made Barton wonder. He had yet to know her age. She seemed older than the other sister did, yet she seemed more innocent and of a delicate nature. EGB did not seem to be interested in local gossip or celebrities, whereas the other sister often wrote about people Bart did not know and couldn't care less about.

Most often, he would receive two letters in a packet from their address in Baton Rouge, Louisiana. Sometimes, there would be several notes tucked in, each written on varying days. One girl, with the larger handwriting and gossipy letters, usually dabbed her paper with *Shalimar* perfume; the other girl did not, although the entire packet smelled of the perfume. He remembered the fragrance Elise had worn the night of the dance, which he later found out had been *Muguet des Bois*. It had suited her, and the scent had stayed a fragrant memory tucked in his mind whenever he thought of her. Aunt Lorraine sometimes wore that scent—a happy, sweet memory.

The girl with the big handwriting even made a mistake once, writing, "Dear Billy." Man! That had hurt his ego. Bart hoped that was from flirty and dippy Elaine and not Elise. He also wondered if he was the only soldier Elise wrote to, as evidenced by the incorrect salutation. It sort of chewed away at him, and he jealously hoped he was the only one.

However, today, he decided to be bold and write a personal letter only to Elise. She was the one who stayed in his mind after so much time. He would ask specific things, and perhaps she would answer his letter. He was concerned, though, about writing anything too personal, as he did not know if his letters might be shared between the sisters or with her family and friends. Yet, he remembered Elise seemed to be a private person, and he would hope not to make a fool of himself. He was lucky in a way, feeling as if he had not made that great an impression on the pair the night of the dance, yet after these many months, the Boulanger girls had been faithful in writing to him.

Barton sat for a moment to gather his thoughts and then boldly wrote to Elise Boulanger.

February 12, 1944

Dear Elise,

Thank you for your recent letters. When men here receive letters, it is always a thrill hearing their name called and knowing that someone back home cares. When I hear mine, it is as if a thread connects from my heart to home, and I can feel the gentle tug. I think whenever I read one of your letters, that I feel the tug more.

I would like to think I have a good memory of my evening with you at the dance last year, which is still alive in my mind. However, I would like to ask you a favor. I would like a photograph of you so that I might have you with me as a more tangible memory.

I was interested to read that your family owns a French import store and bakery. I am happy that you are of French ancestry. Of course, your surname is French, but you know there are French names all over Louisiana, and most people are a mix of everything.

My family has a long history of French ancestry, never marrying outside of their pure French heritage until my mother, who was German and French, and I have a Scottish aunt. We still speak French at home—it has been something our family has never wanted to lose.

Do you speak French? If you do, perhaps you might write to me. I do miss it, and a letter "en Français" from a lovely girl would be a delight in my day.

I am probably a fool to ask it, but would you put your perfume, Muguet des Bois, on your paper? I like that scent!

How are your classes?

I will end this letter for now. I am including my new post. I was promoted and transferred to another base and a new company. For now, things are hectic here all day and night. We all feel as if something big is coming soon. But I do not wish to worry you, and I just ask to hear from you.

I look forward to your letter.

My kind regards to your family and your sister, Elaine.

SSGT Barton Barre

Barton regretted sending his only recent picture to his parents—it was stupid because Elise should have had it. The only other picture he had was of him amid a crowd of faces graduating from their POL training in Georgia. He would ask Joey Huggleston to take another photo, but only after his aide sewed Bart's extra stripes and new emblems on his uniform. Elise would be surprised!

◆ ◆

Baton Rouge, Louisiana
Friday, March 3, 1944

Elise rushed home from school. She had forgotten her flute, so she needed to grab it and run to get to her extra lesson on time. Mrs. Flaubert would be upset if she was late. All the music students were practicing for an upcoming recital, and she had two pieces to work on.

She ran, thundering up the stairs to her bedroom, dropped her schoolbooks on the chair, picked up her flute case, snatched her music, and was ready to leave again. Still juggling the items in one arm, Elise stopped in front of her vanity for a moment. It was windy outside, so she ran a brush through her wild, dark curls and readjusted her barrette. She pinched her cheeks, although they were pink enough from the cold and running. Elise reapplied her lipstick and turned to leave.

It was then she found a letter from Barton Barre propped against her jewelry box; his large backhanded scrawl had become familiar. Elise picked it up and noticed it was addressed only to her.

Usually, he wrote one letter addressed to both her and Elaine. Now, this seemed different. She wanted to open it, but with a glance at her wristwatch, she'd be late if she tarried any longer. She looked around and across the hall to see if anyone was nearby; then, she hid the letter in her underwear drawer, wrapped in a pink scarf decorated with roses. As the letter was addressed only to her, she wanted to read it alone. She picked up her purse and bolted down the stairs but accidentally slammed the front door, causing her mother to shout after her.

Elise sprinted along the two blocks to her teacher's home, her long legs making the distance seem shorter. She breathlessly arrived at the front door just as two other students crowded the porch; she smiled at them, and they comically all squeezed through the front door, each trying not to be late.

◆ ◆

116

Madame Flaubert was waiting for them in the music parlor beside the grand piano with the other students who were already sitting and ready to play. She looked down her nose through her gold pince-nez glasses at her students as they filed in. Her white marcel-permed hair gleamed brightly in the lamplight, and her gaze, though stern, was hiding an indulgent smile as she watched her students ready themselves for the lesson.

Elise Boulanger was the tallest of the girls, even though not the oldest. She was usually the first ready; her flute was tuned, and her music was set, so she was prepared to play. Meanwhile, the other students were plinking, twanging, and burping their instruments to tune them or adjusting their seats and fidgeting. Elise caught Mrs. Flaubert's eye and smiled prettily, implying she was ready.

Edna Flaubert thought Elise was probably the loveliest girl she had ever known, and she was also very talented in the flute. She was proud of the girl; Elise was intellectual, sweet, honest, charming, and always punctual. However, her sister Elaine was another matter—she was late! Edna glanced at the watch brooch pinned on her dress and made a generous decision.

"Students, while we are waiting for our pianist, I have an announcement." She smiled, looking about the room to see her students' faces now turned attentively on her. "We have a special birthday. Elise turns fourteen today! Shall we give her a tune?" Edna raised her hands and directed the students as they sang the birthday song, *"Bonne Anniversaire à toi …"*

Elise blushed and ducked her head, smiling. "Thank you. My birthday is Sunday, madame, and I will be fifteen." Elise gently corrected.

Edna Flaubert waved the comment aside and handed her a small white package with a pink bow and ribbon tied around it. *"Bonne Anniversaire ma chérie!* You may open this later. I believe our pianist has arrived!"

Edna went to open the front door, admitting a flustered, windblown Elaine, who blushed and started to explain, but seeing the uncompromising look on Edna's face, she swallowed her excuse and rushed inside to sit at the piano. With a few deep breaths and much fumbling and fussing with the piano bench and noisy turning of music pages, she finally looked up at Edna, ready to play.

❖ ❖

Edna directed the ensemble in Pachelbel's *Canon,* with Elise as the featured instrument. The flute's notes swirled and floated, dancing arabesques in the air—it was Elise's favorite piece. She practiced diligently and was proud that she did not make any mistakes today. She would practice more tomorrow before the recital on Sunday. Elise glanced at her sister, who was missing notes and, in the end, crashed on a wrong chord, which made Mrs. Flaubert grimace.

At the end of the piece, while Mrs. Flaubert gave her critiques to the individuals, Elise whispered to Elaine. "You are late, and I am not talking about your tardiness in getting here. You came in late on the cue, and at measure forty-two, you were off like a racehorse, then came plodding in at the end. Didn't you practice?" she hissed at her sister.

"Miss Boulanger? Are you teaching this lesson?"

Elise turned pink and looked back at Mrs. Flaubert. "*Non, madame.* I apologize." Elise sat in her chair, embarrassed.

"Elaine, as your sister so astutely noted, you are late, your timing is lackadaisical, and your phrasing is pitiful. I also did not recognize the last chord you played. Are you sure you have practiced this piece?" She glared at Elaine to see her cringe and turn pink. "Well then. Let us see how well you play on our next piece, Mozart's *Rondo.* Do not disappoint us. Is everyone ready?"

Mrs. Flaubert changed the music on the wooden stand, looked up at her students, and held her hands at the ready, counting off the beat so the students would begin with a twitch of her baton.

◆ ◆

Elaine rolled her eyes and watched Mrs. Flaubert so she would come in on cue this time. She glanced at her sister, who was standing playing her flute and watching the teacher, not even looking at her music. She wondered how Elise could memorize music so quickly. Elaine, while proficient enough in playing piano, decided that Elise owned the true talent in the family. Elaine, the oldest by five years, always felt Elise was ahead of her, leading the way. Somewhere along the years, Elise had surpassed Elaine as the favored daughter. Elise was Miss Perfect in everything. What annoyed Elaine the most was that Elise's talents came naturally, while she had to work hard to come that close.

Thinking of that now annoyed her; her fingers stumbled, and again, she made several mistakes. She quickly caught back up with the ensemble. *Applesauce!* She thought to herself in frustration. *Mrs. Flaubert will skin me alive! I must practice this weekend, or I will just embarrass myself on Sunday at the recital.*

Elaine made a mental note to call Tommy and cancel their date for tomorrow. She would have gone out with him tonight, except that the family was celebrating Elise's birthday today rather than Sunday because of the recital. When finished, she sat down, nodding her head in agreement when Edna complained about her performance.

"*Oui, Madame.*" She agreed, subdued, feeling like a deflated balloon.

◆ ◆

After their recital practice, the girls walked home together in moody silence. Elaine was smarting from the harsh criticism she'd received from Mrs. Flaubert. She noticed Elise was silently dark and pensive. She wondered what was bugging her. Edna had only reprimanded her once; otherwise, Elise was once again Miss Perfect. Elaine gave her an elbow in the ribs to jostle Elise out of her thoughts; instead, her sister stepped ahead and suddenly broke into a run, dashing the last half a block to the house. Elaine saw her skim past the front hedge and gate only to bolt up the stairs into the house. Elise looked angry, and Elaine wondered about it.

She hurried home suspiciously, concerned that Elise was ready to tattle for something Elaine had done, so she bent into the raw wind and came in a minute after her sister. She heard her mother shout something from the kitchen, but she ignored it and went upstairs to find Elise. Their bedroom door was closed, and she opened it to see Elise lying on her bed, looking miserable. Elaine came in, shut the door, put her books down on her desk, and hung her coat in the closet. She sat on her bed and slipped off her shoes; all the while, she was casting surreptitious glances at the morose girl. Elise rolled over, burying her face in her pillow. Elaine had to know what was bugging her sister. She sat on the bed next to Elise and patted her back. "Sis? What's wrong?"

"Go away," Elise said miserably, shrugging away the touch.

Elaine thought Elise was crying. She pushed her over and saw she was. "What is wrong with you? You still sore at Mrs. Flaubert?"

"If I tell you, you can't tell Mom. Promise?"

Elaine held up her hand in a scout's oath and crossed her heart. "I promise. Now tell me."

"I am dying, Elaine," Elise blubbered.

Elaine fizzed and frowned. Laughing, she said, "If you are dying, Mom and Pop should know. What are you talking about?"

"Don't laugh at me. It's true. I am bleeding," Elise said hesitantly and sat up, sniffling.

"Where? I don't see anything." Elaine picked up her sister's arm and searched her face.

Elise jerked back her arm. "Not there! Down … you know … there." She nodded to her nether regions.

Elaine sat for a moment, her brow furrowed, and then it came to her. "Are you having a period?" she asked exuberantly.

"I don't know!" Elise snapped. "I feel terrible, Elaine. I think something is wrong! I fell in gym class when Donna Noonan tripped me. Then later, when I went to shower, I saw blood running down my leg. I washed it off, and then it was just sort of there again. I was scared to go to the nurse and miss my Italian class. Sister Clarice would have a hissy." Elise sniffled and wrapped her arms around her abdomen. "I think I am going to be sick."

Elise got up quickly, and Elaine followed her into the bathroom. Elise fell to her knees and retched into the toilet. She sat down on the cold tile floor and looked up at her sister with dark, woeful eyes. Elaine knelt beside her, now feeling compassion for Elise.

"Does your stomach hurt like you've been punched?"

Elise nodded miserably.

"Do you have a headache, honey?"

Again, she nodded. "Maybe you should call Mom; I think I need to go to the hospital," Elise said woefully.

Elaine interrupted and sagely confirmed her symptoms. "No, you just have your period and a bad case of the cramps, Elise. Don't you know how badly I feel when I have my monthly too?"

"Yes, I do, except that I just thought you have stomachaches. I didn't know it makes you bleed. Are you sure?" Elise whimpered.

Elaine caressed her sister's forehead, sweeping back the black silky hair from her sweat-dampened brow. She pulled down a washcloth and stood up to rinse it out in the sink. She laid the cold cloth on Elise's forehead. "I am sure. There, that will help. I will get you the hot water bottle and some aspirin and tell Mom to make you some mint tea. That always makes my stomach feel better when I have the queasies."

She looked down at the pitiful figure on the floor. "My little sis is finally a woman. Welcome to the club!" She kissed Elise. "Sorry, I have to go tell Mom. Get ready for her because she'll come tearing in here to help her baby." Elaine left Elise lying on the bathroom floor.

"You are a double-crosser, Elaine!" Elise shouted but then rested her head on the cold porcelain rim of the toilet, allowing it to soothe her headache. The astringent aroma of bleach caused her to sneeze explosively. After a minute, the pounding in her head subsided, except that she was seeing little spots like buzzing flies before her eyes. She closed her eyes and rested, trying to push the nausea down and not groan with every cramp. She heard excited voices and thumping up the stairs as her sister and mother came up and burst into the bathroom.

◆ ◆

Beatrice knelt beside Elise. "*O lá-lá, ma p'tite bébé!*" she exclaimed as she took in the pale, teary face of her daughter. "Do you still need to throw up?" She wiped Elise's brow with the cloth. Elise shook her head no.

Beatrice stood back up and pulled Elise up with her, holding her close. She looked round at Elaine, commanding, "Go make your sister some tea while we have some time here." She shut the door as Elaine left. Beatrice bent to the tub, patted in the rubber stopper, and ran warm water, sprinkling in some fragrant bath salts.

"Get undressed, baby; a nice, warm bath will make you feel much better." She helped Elise undress and step into the tub.

"Ow! It's too hot!" Elise sank down in the steaming water. "My skin is prickling." She bent forward, hugging herself with her arms around her knees as a cramp roiled in her belly.

Beatrice saw her wince. "I know it hurts." She gently bathed Elise's back and shoulders and then told her, "Lie flat in the tub; sitting in a ball does not help the muscles."

Elise gaped at her mother, who hovered over her. "Mom … ew! Can you turn around or something? I am naked here!" she said, embarrassed and glowering at her mother.

Beatrice gave a chortled laugh. "Oh, you think you have something different than I do? I brought you naked into this world; I know what you look like. Now relax as I told you, or you will not feel any better, Elise." Beatrice stood firmly planted, arms akimbo, and waited for Elise to unfold herself and lie in the water.

"Good." Beatrice stood looking at her daughter, realizing the tall girl no longer fit in the tub. She had very slender, shapely long legs and a curvaceous, slim figure. Elise had been wearing a brassiere for nearly two years, but Beatrice now noticed she had a lovely, full, round bosom. Under her schoolgirl uniform, Elise was still a girl, but lying naked was a woman—a beautiful young woman!

Beatrice suddenly turned away and found her hankie in her apron pocket; she wiped her eyes and nose, snuffling back a tiny sob. She just envisioned her worst dream possible, her baby daughter Elise, who had grown up—a beautiful woman who would soon leave her. Men would be after her like hounds on a rabbit. She and Édouard already had enough problems with Elaine and her many suitors. Her daughters were lovely, but Beatrice was not sure how to keep them safe other than by locking them away.

"Mama, are you crying?" Elise asked softly from the bathtub.

"Oh, I am just being silly. I cannot believe you are grown; you are a woman now." She bent by the tub, wiping her daughter's face as if she were three again.

"I am sorry that you have to experience pain, *ma fille*, but that is a woman's lot in life. You can thank Eve for that sin. As you grow older, you will get used to it; for now, I am sure you feel very sick. It will not last long. Elaine said it started this afternoon after gym class, yes?" she asked to see Elise nod her answer. "Well then, maybe a few more hours of cramps, then you will feel better," she said with assurance, handing Elise the washcloth and turning to pick up her clothes. "You'll have to wear your jumper tomorrow; your skirt is soiled."

"Mom, tomorrow is Saturday." She giggled.

Beatrice put a hand on her heart, exclaiming, "Oh dear! I forgot we are celebrating your birthday tonight, Elise. Do you want me to cancel? Are you feeling very poorly, baby?"

"If this is all it is, I think I will be okay. Don't cancel; I don't want to ruin everyone's fun. Besides, Grand-mama is coming all the way from Alexandria."

"But, Elise, what about *your* fun? If you don't feel well, we should cancel, and you should stay in bed like Elaine does. I will bring you some soup," her mother said pointedly with a quirked eyebrow.

Elise's face looked sober. "No, Mom, I want my party. I won't turn fifteen ever again, you know. You have gone to a great deal of trouble and preparation; I could not do that to you. Getting my period was perhaps just another birthday present, letting me know I am growing up and have to be responsible now." She stood up in the tub and reached for her towel, no longer ashamed to stand naked before her mother. She looked down upon her body and giggled. "I guess I am growing up because minutes ago, you were my towering pillar of comfort, and now I feel so tall and oddly like an adult."

"*Ma fille*, you are already too responsible, and I am very proud of you. But please be a girl for a while. I agree that you should have your party—we don't want to waste all my good food. Come out now, and let me tell you how to take care of yourself when you have your woman's time." She helped Elise from the tub.

Just then, there was scratching on the door. Beatrice opened the bathroom door a little and shouted to Elaine to get her feminine things, and little Chérie rushed in, yipping. Elise bent to scoop her up, but her mother gently footed the tiny poodle out as Elaine came back in. For the next ten minutes, Elaine, Beatrice, and Elise cloistered away in the bathroom as they instructed Elise in the subtle arts of feminine hygiene.

They all shrieked when there was a startlingly loud knock on the door, and they heard a male voice booming outside.

"What are you all doing in there? I have to go! I have been waiting forever while you hens are clucking away in there!" Édouard shouted, loudly knocking on the door once more. "The damned dog is out here too, making a fuss. What is going on?"

Beatrice opened the door a fraction, and looking through it, she caught her husband's eye and whispered, "Use the downstairs bathroom, can't you? We are busy in here." She closed the door and then opened it again. "I'll tell you later. Oh! And would you please turn off the burner on the stove? *Je t'aime Bébé.*" Beatrice cajoled and shut the door again before her husband could say anything else.

"*Vous rigolez! Merde!* I knew I should have had sons. A man can't take a decent shit in his *own* bathroom in his *own* house anymore with all these damn women. Always … it is a crisis of the hair or lipstick! Bah!" Édouard grumbled in French as he stomped down the staircase, leaving Chérie to whine and snuffle at the bathroom door.

All three women broke out laughing. Beatrice opened the bathroom door, and they scurried into the girls' bedroom with Elise bundled in her towel. They spent the next several minutes helping Elise get dressed in her robe, and they set her up in bed for a brief rest before dinner. Elaine brought the cooling mint tea. Beatrice had a hot water bottle wrapped in a towel, which she placed on Elise's belly. She tucked a colorful crocheted afghan around her daughter.

She kissed her forehead and said, "I had better see to your daddy before he makes a mess of things. Here is Chérie." She handed Elise her little poodle. "Rest for now, my darling girl."

She left the two girls and Chérie and went downstairs to tell her husband the bad news. There was another woman in the house!

◆ ◆

The evening was extraordinary and filled with nearly magical surprises for Elise. They had several bottles of wine, a delicious meal of vichyssoise, shrimp étouffée, scalloped leeks with tomatoes, and Elise's favorite salad with marinated artichokes and mushrooms, all served on their best Limoges china and crystal. The party included her girlfriends Millie, Winnie, and Rosalie; her maternal grandmother, Nanette Laforrêt; and a pair of Édouard's business associates and their wives. She received perfect, lovely gifts of jewelry, perfume, and books of poetry. The best surprise of all was her mother's antique silver flute—Elise knew it was a special gift and treasured heirloom.

She felt grown up as she wore her new ruby red dress with the chiffon red roses cascading down one hip from the sequined belt. Elise wore her new three-inch heeled red satin shoes, which she felt like a tall statue as she towered over Elaine and Mom. Elaine did Elise's hair in a grown-up French twist with pearled and red rhinestone hairpins and one red chiffon rose tucked in.

Elise was surprised when her father opened an expensive, huge Jeroboam bottle of Dom Pérignon champagne at the party. Everyone cheered when the cork popped explosively, and the family crowded around with their glasses to catch the bubbling fountain of wine. Édouard looked tenderly at his youngest daughter and made a toast.

"To my beautiful daughter Elise—today she is a new woman! I wish her a lifetime of love and joy. May she find her match one day, but not too soon, eh? *Bonne Santé!*" Édouard kissed her, and Elise flushed to know that her father knew she'd started menstruating today. Mom or Elaine was a busybody!

"*Merci, Papa.*" Elise blushed, kissing him back. In heels, she stood nearly as tall as her robust, handsome father did. Elise knew that she more closely resembled him, tall and ebony-haired, while Elaine resembled blonde, blue-eyed Beatrice with dark golden hair and a petite, voluptuous figure.

Everyone applauded and made their own toasts to Elise's health, good fortune, and turning fifteen. Grand-mère Nanette commanded attention by standing and toasting Elise in French. But then, as she kissed her cheek, she admonished Elise for being too pretty—it would only cause trouble! Elise could only solemnly nod and smile. But then, to break the dark spell cast by Nanette, the family broke away to get their share of the elegant chocolate cake Beatrice had made.

Elise cut and served out generous slices of the cake until everyone was served, and then she cut herself one and sat to eat it. She savored the rich *gâteau* with the dark chocolate fondant decorations. It was decadent and probably had cost her mother their entire monthly rations for chocolate, butter, sugar, and other expensive ingredients making up the delicious cake. Elise plucked off one hand-formed chocolate rose and set it aside so she could admire it before she ate it, wishing she could save one perfect rose as a remembrance of the day. Her mother was an artist with pastry. Elise was caught off guard in her thoughts when her father asked if she and Elaine would play for the party.

She humbly rose and went upstairs to retrieve her flute from school while Elaine sat boldly at the piano, trickling a little Bach piece to entertain the room full of family and friends. Amid it all, dainty Chérie went from person to person, pawing at a leg or foot, asking to be picked up. She finally found refuge in Nanette's lap. Chérie sat with her dark eyes twinkling and black button nose sniffling excitedly, watching the garrulous party. Elise kissed Grand-mère and stroked the tiny dog as she stepped by with her flute. She took up her place by the grand piano and whispered the Pachelbel piece to Elaine.

The two girls played perfectly and delightfully. Elise played two complex solo pieces, and then Elaine played two Mendelssohn etudes. Finally, they asked to sit down to rest from their musical labors to an appreciative and applauding audience, who asked for an encore.

Elise stood back up and said she would play her own composition, called *"Le Printemps de joie"* ("Spring Joy"). She took a deep, steadying breath, looked at her mother and her father, and then closed her eyes. The music flowed out of her flute in bright, rippling tones like a bubbling brook. For minutes, the notes danced on the musical breezes, swirling up as airy butterflies to float and hover above the plain of music, then rose higher on a breath, like God whispering, and floated down gracefully to land at the audience's feet in a tender, feathering caress. The audience was silent as Elise took a deep breath and opened her eyes. Then the spell dissipated, and her family cheered, wiping tears and blowing noses in emotional response to the delightful music.

Elise was elated but humble in her praise. She had not played her music for anyone before, not even Madame Flaubert; she had been hesitant to share her creation. Now she knew that the music was appropriate and deserving of being heard by others—it sounded beautiful to others, not just her ears. Elise had snuck into the school theater last week so she could practice the piece; it had given her goosebumps as the music swirled about the echoing acoustics of the theater. The drama teacher, Mr. Penn, had surprised her when he stood up out of the darkened orchestra section to applaud her efforts. Shocked, Elise had fled the stage, as she'd thought she was alone.

◆ ◆

The special birthday evening ended, and Elise kissed her departing friends with many a gracious thank you. Elaine stayed below to help clean up under the watchful eye of autocratic Nanette, who spent more time complaining about the Boulangers' lack of servants. Poor Daddy stoically let it go, saying he didn't want to ruin a perfect party and evening with petty arguments.

Elise carried her gifts and little Chérie upstairs with her, putting her on the bed. The little black dog circled, pawed at the chenille cover, and then curled up to watch silently while Elise put away her gifts and changed out of her party dress.

Elise caught her image in the mirror and stood for a moment, appreciating her figure in the dress. She did look grown-up and not like a gawky fourteen-year-old anymore—better than she had in the borrowed dress last summer. She made a few poses like a Hollywood picture starlet, and then, giggling at the silliness of it all, she unzipped and carefully hung up the expensive outfit.

Still, in her petticoat and slip, she went to the bathroom, cleaned up, brushed her teeth, and washed her face, removing the grown-up makeup. Elise padded back to her room, closing the door and feeling fourteen again. She sat at her vanity, taking out the rose and hairpins, letting her hair fall in soft, thick ebony waves and ringlets alongside her face and feathering her shoulders. Elise turned down the room lights and sat, studying herself, thinking she was pretty in the pink vanity light.

Everyone always told her she was pretty or beautiful; however, Elise just thought she was herself, nothing special. All of a sudden, she felt herself to be a woman again. She wondered if her birthday or the onset of her menses had made the changes she now saw reflected in the mirror.

Wide-set, nearly jet-black eyes sparkled back; her lips were ruby-colored, like wine, and plump. She smiled to see her small, even, white teeth. Her cheekbones were high and round, her face an oval shape with high, delicate wings for brows; her hair was seductively arrayed about her face. Someone once told her she looked like young Elizabeth Taylor, except taller. Then, one of her girlfriends said that she resembled Lana Turner or the Madonna statue in church. Elise thought she just looked like *herself*—Elise Marie Genevieve Boulanger.

She suddenly remembered Barton's letter and got up from the vanity. She opened the bedroom door a crack and listened for a moment to hear her family still loudly working in the kitchen and living room below. She took out the letter and laid it on her pillow. She finished undressing and put on her nightgown. Sliding in bed, she took up the letter once more. Little Chérie now came to lie by her side. Elise settled with Barton's letter, absently stroking the petite, petal-like ears of her pet while she read.

She read it twice. She could not believe that Barton was interested in her. He had written only to her and said to give his kind regards to her family and her sister, Elaine. Elise carefully refolded the letter, putting it back into the envelope, and then clutched it to her heart. His words did not say he was in love with her, but the letters meant something to him. He wanted her photograph to keep with him. That had to mean he thought her special. In fact, she had been nervous writing to him the first time, worried that Barton had probably forgotten her. Yet her letter and Elaine's had been forwarded to him, and he wrote back within two weeks to them both. She could not believe her fortune that a chance meeting at a dance could inspire or fuel a relationship with a brave young man like Barton Barre.

Elise, suddenly filled with emotion, kissed the envelope. Holding it close to her, she smelled the paper, wondering at the leathery scent. Was that Barton's cologne? He asked her next time to spritz her perfume on the letter. Elise could not believe he recognized her favorite perfume, *Muguet des Bois*; he said it was his favorite, too! She now heard footsteps coming up the stairs and hastily tucked the envelope in her pillowcase, picked up her bedside book, and lay back on her pillow to appear as if she was reading. Chérie gave her an odd look, and with a doggy grunt, she curled tighter and tucked her head under a paw to sleep.

Elise was reading when Elaine came in. She gave Elise a quizzical glance and then had to ask, "Reading, are you?"

"Mmm hmm," Elise said, staring at the book.

Elaine came over to the bed, plucked the book from Elise's hand, and turned it over onto her lap.

"What's up, Sis?" Elaine thumped down on the bed, looking at her sister. "You should be happy and not moody anymore."

Elise set her book aside on the bedside table. "Elaine, how do you know when you are in love?"

"My! My! Little sister is waking up and wanting to know all the secrets of the universe today! So not only do I have to tell you the facts of life, but I have to tell you about love now?" Elaine was quick to retort.

"Well, better you than someone else, right?"

"I suppose so." Elaine stood up to take her dress off. She unbuttoned the tiny pearl buttons that ran the length of the bodice, pulled the top off, and then shimmied out of the dress and carelessly tossed it onto the chair near her bed.

"Don't let Mom see you throw that dress there; you had better hang it up, Elaine." Elise chided her sister. She rolled over and lay on her side watching and cradled Chérie. "So, how do you know? Have you ever been in love, Elaine?"

Elaine hung up the dress and turned back from the closet, smiling. "Oh yes, many times."

"But isn't that just infatuation? If you are in love, isn't it supposed to be forever?" she asked, watching Elaine taking off the silk slip, wadding it, and stuffing it in her dresser drawer.

Elaine put a foot on the chair, unhooked the garters from her stocking, and rolled it down. "That is what everyone says, including all the poets you so love to read, Elise. I think you find love wherever you want to look. It's out there because everyone wants to be loved." She shrugged and undid the other garters, rolled her stockings into a ball, and put them in the dresser.

"Aren't you going to rinse those out? Your drawer will be smelly, Elaine."

Elaine shrugged. "That's why I have a sachet in the drawer. For heaven's sake! Stop picking on me; you would think it was your birthday or something!" Elaine said grumpily as she unfastened the garter belt and her brassiere, dropped them in the drawer, and closed it. She paraded nearly naked through the bedroom to take out a robe from the closet.

She made a final comment before she left the room. "If you want to know what love looks like, Elise, just look at Mom and Daddy—that is true love. Don't be a worrywart; you'll find love one day before you are an old maid." Giggling, Elaine closed the door behind her.

With a frown, Elise shot back. "I am not worried!" Irritated, she rolled back over in bed, taking Chérie with her, and turned off her bedside lamp. She snuggled into her pillow, hearing the paper crackle beneath her cheek. She sighed wistfully as she thought of Barton. She liked his letters, too. This last one Elise wanted to keep forever. She had one tiny revelation as her mind slipped into sleep: she had fallen in love with a man on her very first day of being a woman. She wondered if Barton was falling in love with her, too.

◆ ◆

Elise waited until Monday evening before she had private time to write her letter to Barton. The weekend had been busy with guests, church, her music recital, and family activities, and it flowed quickly into Monday. Tonight, Elaine was studying at the library with her friends. Her parents were listening to a radio show downstairs. She could smell her father's pipe tobacco, the aromatic cherry incense wafting up the stairs into her room. Elise closed her door, not wanting any distractions. Chérie was sleeping on Elise's bed, making tiny yips in doggy dreamland.

She sat looking at the blank papers before her. What should she say to Barton? Before tonight, Elise had not felt compromised in her thoughts, and she was able to write anything to Bart. She took out Barton's letter to study it; for one, he asked her to write to him in French. Elise grew up hearing French in their home, and she spoke it fluently enough, but even her penned French felt stilted as she began to write her greetings to Barton.

What do I call him? She silently wondered. *Dear? Friend? Or maybe Darling?* Instead, she simply wrote "Barton." Then, in French, she thanked him for his kind words and recent letter. Elise told him she was happy to hear that her letters were well received in that they cheered him. In the next paragraph, Elise wrote about her birthday and the recital. She talked about her composition *"Le Printemps de joie"* and that it was well-liked by her audience. Elise sat thinking about the other parts of Barton's letter—he wanted a photograph.

She glanced around the room, searching for a photo. Most of the items displayed belonged to Elaine—her beaus, movie stars, and pictures of the family on vacation. She had so few photos of herself that she was not sure what to send Barton. Elise took out her scrapbook, flipping through the stiff black pages as she searched for a picture. There were school photos, but she was in her black and white parochial dress or Girl Scout uniform or her girls' volleyball team skirt and blouse, not exactly photos a man might want to keep in his pocket. Elise paged through the book, and then she found two she thought might be best.

Elise and Elaine were standing together by the foot of the staircase in their friend's house on the night of the dance in Brusly last May. Elaine looked like a butter pastry in her lacy, fluffy dress. Elise stood stately and tall, towering over Elaine. She was always self-conscious of her height; this past year, she'd shot up over her sister, who remained short and petite. Elise looked grown-up in the borrowed sapphire blue dress; it flattered her tall figure. But noticed she was not smiling in the photograph. Elise was glad that she had gone to the dance. She might never have met Barton Barre if she had stayed in that night as she wanted. For that, perhaps, she could thank Elaine for dragging her along that evening.

She took the snapshot out from under the photo mounts, leaving the page empty. She wondered if she should cut off Elaine's side of the photo but then decided Barton might like to have a picture of Elaine too, as he had danced and talked with her that night. In fact, Elise had felt the thorns of jealousy when Barton had been so gallant with her sister in the arbor, and he danced well with her.

However, it was later, when Barton spent the evening talking with Elise, that she realized she liked him. He was witty and cute. Barton had bravely saved her from the boisterous boogie-woogie soldier and many other leering young men. She had no idea how old he was, but he had to be at least eighteen or more if he was enlisting to fight in the war. Ruefully, she thought Barton must be older since he was a sergeant.

Mother and Daddy still did not know about Barton or that she had spent most of an evening in his company while her sister was dancing with everything male. Elaine and Elise had fought about it on their way home that night. Elise told Elaine she would tell Daddy she was flirting with every boy there and even saw Elaine kiss a few! That had shut her up. The secret was still Elise's private fantasy of a memorable night of dancing with a handsome young man. It turned out better than any debutante ball she might go to—she met her *Prince Charmant* that night.

Now Barton was writing to her.

Elise studied the other photographs in the album, noting they were from the summer after she'd met Barton. She had gone swimming at the beach with a bunch of kids. There were a few of her in her navy blue and white polka-dotted bathing suit. She found one she liked; she was sitting on the beach blanket with her arms around her knees, and the wind was blowing her hair away from her face. She was smiling and laughing at a joke someone said just as her friend Rosalie took the picture. Elise thought she looked happy. She signed the edge of the photo: *For BB—Hi, from EB.* Elise took that picture out and tucked it inside the envelope with the other.

She again read the last page of her letter, wanting to write some more but unsure what to say. Elise heard her father coming up the stairs and quickly stuffed the stationary in her scrapbook and closed it. She sat waiting for her father to knock or come in, but he did not.

Breathing a gasp of relief, Elise took the letter out once more. She wrote a brief note, feeling this would be her last chance before being caught with the letter. She folded up the paper and almost put it away in the envelope before she remembered Barton asked for her perfume. She dotted the paper with *Muguet des Bois* on the corner of the last page, and then Elise kissed it before folding it away in the envelope. Elise hoped Barton would get her letter soon before the perfume wore away. She put the letter in her purse, planning to mail it in the morning on the way to school. She put away her writing things and shut off the desk lamp. Ready for bed now, she took Barton's letter once more and tucked it in her pillowcase. She curled up with Chérie to sleep and, perchance, to dream.

◆ ◆

East Whitcliff, England
April 18, 1944

Barton received a letter from Elise Boulanger along with one each from his father and brother Paul. It was a special day for him, as he rarely received letters, but once or twice a month—three in one day was a treat. He wondered if they were for his birthday that week. However, there was a busy, escalating mess happening around him, and he took all three letters and folded them in his pocket to read later at his leisure.

He was working on the broad side for nearly twenty-eight hours straight. Barton requested additional men to fill in since the last idiot had killed himself and his three buddies, one of them Bart's pal Joey Huggleston, in a convoy accident while training. What luck! The very week in March, General Bradley said there was to be a big push, the biggest ever—Barton lost four good men, one of them an ace mechanic. He was sorely shorthanded, and no one had replaced them yet.

It was the duty of the quartermaster's petroleum supply company to see that everyone was supplied with anything needed now and for the future of the planned attack. While Barton was not at the highest level and didn't sit in on the 'secret' talks, he knew in his bones that all the hype and frantic work lately was going to be realized soon for a planned invasion into France.

They were now training nearly every day for at least two to four hours—logistics reviews, combat exercises, and infantry instruction; again learning to parachute; participating in the dreaded agility course of brambles, hedgerows, bunkers, muck, and mire; and boring calisthenics, which Bart despised. Even the food in the mess hall had changed—it was worse. The air base resembled a chaotic anthill, busy every moment of the day and night.

Bart and his crews all heard many rumors about Rue de Calais, Caen, and Cherbourg and that there might be POL depots—dump sites set up there along the lodgment areas to get the boys going once on the other side of the English Channel. Once Cherbourg was secure, the engineers would build the pipelines from the coast into Paris. It would fuel the entire Northern European Theater with supply stations dotted

131

across Northern France and be easily accessible to the advancing Allies. There was so much to learn and remember.

Lately, Whitcliff's flyboys were hardly seen around the base mess, as they were also heavily involved in exercise, field and flight training, and flight operations. Daily before the sun lit up the land, for close to an hour, the drone and rumble of the B-17 and B-29 strategic bombers and the P-39 and P-51 escort fighters echoed across the base. Then, later in the afternoon, they returned, refueled, and restocked with armaments and ordnance before many were sent out again on short reconnaissance night missions.

Whitcliff's DH-98 Mosquitoes and the USAAC's P-39s, which Bart dubbed "the little dogs," went across the Channel daily to annoy and piss off the Dutch and Northern German territories with little raids on their airfields. Pissing on them with sprayed bullets, mischievously taking out grounded fighters, cargo planes, and fuel tankers, and generally shooting anything that moved in the sky, the fighters were effective. Soon, the Huns retaliated.

Nearly every day for the past two weeks, there was a Nazi buzz bomb or little speedy FW-190s and Messerschmitt BF-109s skittering overhead. Sometimes the Luftwaffe's screaming 290-Schwalbes ripped up the base's camouflaged Nissen huts and air pads and were generally annoying and scaring the shit out of everyone. The Krauts seemed to know when to hit, too—just as many of the planes were returning from missions on empty, barely armed, and most unable to take off for another fight without refueling. The squadrons had taken some heavy losses recently. The futuristic, fast Schwalbes looked like something from a Buck Rogers comic book. They were feisty sparrows and nasty fighters!

The surprise attacks caused the flight manager to change up their bomber schedules, making them more random. The previously serene little air base was always on alert now. Barton always felt a sense of nearly paranoid creepiness, jumping at every flyover or loud noise.

Since the beginning of March, the twenty-four-hour daily transfer and supply of cargo planes, convoys, tankers, and jeeps was no longer an exercise. It was coming up to the big day when Barton and his men had to be ready to fulfill the needs for the *big push*.

He spent time now reviewing the order lists for the petrol, oil, and lubrication supplies, POL as they called it, and was astonished by the high demand ordered. He suspected it was not only his base under the mass movement. But also dotted along the southern coast of England, there were scores more of such supply depots, and all were scrambling to make ready for the unknown day.

For the past two months, Barton had hardly breathed, eaten, slept, or thought of much else than POL as the wheels of war moved forward. No one had leave or time off; it was a grueling around-the-clock workday preparing for the next move.

At first, the men thought the newly appointed Staff Sergeant Barre was being a shit-heel and playing tough in not allowing the men any extra time or that the constant drudgery of each workday and repeated exercises were more of a punishment for their lack of faith in him. However, they soon learned it was bigger than their company was and more involved than their depot—it was the entire war coming to them!

At first, Barton had been tough on the men. Their CO, Colonel Stanley Ricker, had shared his opinion that sometimes men sitting far away on the back lines of the war had a tendency to lose focus, start cutting up, or not take the order seriously if it did not please them. Barton, knowing that the activity was beginning, had his company working in shifts of twenty-four hours each so that the men could build their stamina and be ready to do their jobs when the big day came. He would have no one whining that it was too hard or too much work! Everyone worked, and that included Staff Sergeant Barton Barre. The colonel was pleased.

◆ ◆

Finally, after his long shift was over and he was able to take his break for the next six hours, Barton went to the mess hall, again, a Quonset hut-type affair made of prefabricated metal. The noise of the dinner hour echoed about the room. He noted a group of flyboys across the hall being served plates of steaming meat and potatoes.

"Damn!" he exclaimed. "They'll be flying tonight!" He envied their exalted status and menu but not the heavy risk that was required of them.

He found little comfort in a very poor supper—some kind of stew with gristly bits of meat, a lonely piece of a parsnip, and two chunks of potato. At least it smelled like food. Barton grabbed up two heavy, doughy biscuits that looked American, not the traditional version of English biscuits, and dumped them onto his mess plate. "Thank God there's coffee!" Barton amended and sat at his usual table to eat.

Shoveling in the stew and chewing a rubbery piece of meat as he wondered if it was goat or mutton, Barton grimly surveyed the mess hall. Noticing some men must have recently come off shift or were on their ten-minute breaks, they looked worse than he felt. Men were weary and falling asleep in place; some just sat blear-eyed with faraway gazes as they ate or drank their coffee. He knew how they felt.

Barton could not afford them many luxuries, such as more days off, personal leaves, or furloughs. But he could now change the shifts to accommodate those coming off the long hours and give them more time to rest. That is until the Jerries took potshots at the base again, or the top brass decided it was *the big day!*

Bart had wanted to experience what extreme sleep deprivation could do to a man, and now he knew. Long study days and nights while in college were a cakewalk compared to prolonged physical labor. These few weeks had been nearly as arduous as his first boot camp training! The drill for his men was over; they had passed. Proudly, Barton thought the men were now conditioned and ready for action to be on twenty-four-hour duties if needed.

He finished his meal and was eager to order something special for the men. Like children, they needed little perquisites to keep them going, so a good meal or a cake would cheer them, along with his new depot schedule.

He dumped his mess tray and then snagged an apple and another cup of coffee as he went in search of Mess Sergeant Bindley in the kitchen. After a brief discussion, the cook agreed to come up with a surprise for the men. Barton left with a knowing smile on his weary face and looking forward to a treat, too. He walked through the mess, acknowledging the men by clapping a shoulder here or there, until he came to Specialist Parkington. Barton sat next to the man as he yawned and sipped a cup of dark tea.

"Parkington, report to me at 0600 for the new duty roster. You are off for the rest of the night. Before then, get some sleep, man!" Barton patted the short man's shoulder and left, secretly smiling as he saw the astonished looks of the men at the table with Parkington and heard hushed remarks. He loved to keep the men guessing.

With a spring in his step, Barton returned to his quarters, and with a desiring look at the bed, he wished he could go there and die for a week. However, there was a duty roster to reschedule. He shucked his jacket, hung it up, and wearily sat at his desk.

Every part of him ached; even the roots of his hair hurt. He raked his hands through his short, curly hair, rubbed his skull, and felt a renewed tingling stimulus.

He pulled out the roster to study it. Barton would be fair, and the men coming off tonight would have a half day tomorrow. He'd bring those on a brief break now and put them on the morning shift. The first day would be a little rough, but everybody had to do their part. Thus, satisfied with the schedules, he called his secretary, Corporal

Seagraves, to type it. The young man stifled his yawn, took the roster, and then swiftly left Bart's quarters.

He hoped his CO would not have any other orders that might cause Barton to redo the schedule again. He had cleared it earlier in the day, but still, with all this fractious activity about, who was to say that something would not start right up? Maybe the 'big day' would be an hour from now or tomorrow or the next day; no one was telling him. For now, his men would have a slight reprieve and a little reward before the war was in their faces!

Bart, having fulfilled his duty for the evening, took off his uniform, neatly set it aside, and reclined upon his bed to rest finally. He closed his eyes and tried mentally to mute the sounds from both inside and outside—the hissing camp stove, the shouting working men, and the obnoxious loud marching cadence song as men tramped past; the whine and thrum of the big engine diesel trucks, and the general noise of the around-the-clock supply depot. It was then he recalled he had more reading to do; there were letters in his blouse pocket. Bart reached over to pull the shirt from the chair, taking out the now-dampened, mashed envelopes. He had sweated all over them and worried he might not be able to read them. He pressed them on his mattress, smoothing out the wrinkles and folds, and decided to open his brother's first.

Scanning the letter from Paul, Bart found it was only bits and pieces of family daily news that was nothing exciting. There was a photograph of Paul, Amy, and baby Emile. Barton thought they looked happy. The baby was dark-haired like Paul and had light eyes like Amy. Emile was almost one year old. Barton recalled his sister-in-law, who was hugely pregnant with Emile last summer and now laughed to see the kid finally nearly a year later. The child looked to be a handful as he squirmed off Amy's lap. Bart noted Paul's hand discreetly hanging onto the boy's leg while the family posed for the photo. The kid had a mischievous smile as if looking to commit some kind of faux pas, like pee on Amy or go running off! Amused, Barton set the letter aside and took out his father's letter.

He tore it open and read for a bit. There was nothing much at first in the letter, mostly family news, something about the girls' school, and Nancy would be in the Easter pageant at church. Richard's daily observances about the furniture business in his new store and their latest foray into making baby furniture caused Barton to laugh as he read Richard's comment: "There is a boundless future in the making of baby furniture—there will always be a need unless people stop having sex!"

Barton sobered as he turned to the next page. There was a newspaper article glued on the third sheet of paper that shocked him. He felt his throat close as he read.

LOCAL Son dies a war hero

March 12, 1944

US Army Tech Cpl. Louis Guillot of Beaumont, Texas, came home to his family after eleven months abroad; instead of cheers, it was to tears.

Cpl. Louis Guillot, age 23, suffered nearly mortal wounds after a blast that killed most of his unit in Sorrento, Italy, on February 28. Wounded, Guillot valiantly saved two men of his unit, getting them to medics. However, as he returned to the destroyed building for another man, picking up PFC Allen Silas, they were caught in a sniper's sight, and both were shot dead.

Capt. P. Frobisher said of Louis Guillot, "He was a good man, he was a funny man, but he took his life and work seriously when it came to helping his comrades fight. His men will now have him 'up there' as an angel." He wrote to the Guillot family in a letter.

Another brother, Second Cpl. Garrett Guillot is serving in the US Army somewhere in England.

Memorial services will be held:

Our Lady of Tears Mortuary Chapel,

March 18 at 2:00 p.m.

Interment at Magnolia Cemetery, Beaumont

Barton now felt the war come home to him. His good friend Louis was dead. Barton rubbed his head, feeling as if he could not understand the clipping. How could this come to him from around the world and tell him his friend was dead? He felt sorry for Garrett and wondered if he knew yet. A month had passed since the news clipping had been written.

He fondly remembered Louis as the jokester of the bunch throughout school and in boot camp. After training, the men had hoped to stay together; however, Barton had gone on to the school for officers' training and logistics in the POL Quartermasters Unit. At the end of boot camp, Louis had wanted to get into the war and was trained for reconnaissance and sent off somewhere, at the time, they did not know. Garrett, wishing to stay with Barton, signed up for the Quartermaster's Unit as well. In this last move in March, Garrett was transferred for special training at Slapton Sands Beach for a secret mission—*Exercise Tiger.* Barton was promoted and sent on to East Whitcliff.

With a rueful, teary smile, Barton thought Louis corporeally ended up in Italy. He was sad. Bart would miss his friend and coconspirator in many pranks. He still did not want to forgive him for getting them into the army, but he conceded Louis went out doing something worthwhile—finally. Now, he wondered why Paul had said nothing about Louis; they had once been best friends and classmates.

Bart continued reading his father's letter, which stated Richard was sorry for Bart's friend. Moreover, he and Thérèse had gone to the funeral service; it was beautiful but very emotional, and the Guillot family suffered their loss, the mother and sisters inconsolable.

Thérèse wrote that she and Richard had brought food to the family and had made a special fundraiser in their neighborhood and church to raise some money to help give Louis a fancy burial with many flowers and a large headstone. Some neighbors did not have money, but they donated some of their sugar, flour, butter, and chocolate rations so the Guillots could make a chocolate cake in honor of Louis because it was his favorite. The army gave him a hero's farewell, and Louis's mother, Arnelle Guillot, was presented with an American flag at the gravesite next to Louis's father and grandfather's graves, who were both veterans of past wars.

Thérèse also wrote …

> *A piece of cloth is a poor substitute for a son in your arms. Please be careful, Barton. You are loved, and we would miss you so much if something so dreadful were to happen. We are also thankful that you did not leave behind a wife and a new baby like Louis did. Marcia (Sanders) was devastated as she took her folded flag for their son, Lance. Paul and Jacques are heartbroken, too.*

Barton could tell that his stepmother was upset as she wrote, for her lovely script was a wandering, shaky thing.

He felt remorse and anger, too, for Marcia. Bart never knew she and Louis had been married. He thought Marcia was Garrett's girlfriend—oh, cripes, now there was a kid too! Like many other guys Bart knew, the couple probably eloped at the last second. Or maybe Garrett was a creep and refused to marry her, and Louis, always the hero of the bunch, married Marcia. Yet Louis or Garrett never said a word. A tangled mess was sordidly revealed upon Louis's death. BettyAnn hadn't lied!

His father resumed the letter to say that he missed him, and they prayed daily for Bart's safety. On another note, Richard mentioned Barton's friend, BettyAnn, had stopped by the house a couple of days after Louis's funeral, wanting to know if Barton was safe. She had not heard from him since her last letter in December. Richard stated his son was a busy soldier, and it was not easy for him to write.

> *I thought I would let you off the hook, Son, since BettyAnn seemed so desperate to reach you. If you wanted to write to her, you would have. You do not need her causing you further worry while you are fighting over there. I do not need to remind you of the past. Do I?*

Barton felt his face flush hotly, again embarrassed.

"No, you do not. Thanks, Dad." Finished with the letter, Bart put it back in the envelope. "Man, did I dodge a bullet there!" He let out a slight exhalation of relief. "It might have been me with a kid on the way with BettyAnn wailing about it."

Sniffling back a feeling of loss for Louis, Barton also felt sorry for his family to be at home and plagued with the war even there. His stepmom had her victory garden. Actually, she always had a garden, but after the war came, she renamed it with a little sign. They planted all roses and vegetables in the front yard instead of grass so they could save on water and food bills. He had helped one summer to dig up the front yard to plant the thorny things. While making friendly visits with Richard, Thérese used the extra roses to give to families who had lost their sons in the war. Dad donated his push mower to the war effort for scrap metal. Barton wickedly thought that somewhere in the war, an enemy was wearing a piece of his dad's lawn mower as shrapnel!

Their furniture business continued to build camp cots, footlockers, and modular mobile cabinetry for the army. Even Grandfather François was working for the war effort. He'd sold a crop of his peanuts and soybeans to the military every season since Pearl Harbor happened. Grand-mère Annette and the girls all made crocheted or knitted hats, gloves, scarves, or socks to send to the men overseas. The women in Grandma's church got together once a month and packed up boxes of toiletries and items the soldiers could use, along with the knitted or crocheted items. Last Christmas, Barton had been the recipient of such largesse. Everyone was mindful of the war because the war was at home, too.

Barton felt sad and oddly a bit homesick. He set the letters aside and turned off the lamp. But when rolling over on the bed, he felt something crinkle under his leg and pulled out an envelope. There was one more letter to read. Barton turned on the lamp again and sat up, gently tore open the envelope, and shook out the sheets of paper. He caught a whiff of something floral; he sniffed the paper and knew it was Lily of the Valley perfume. Feeling a little thrill rush through him, Barton unfolded the letter and found two photographs.

There she was, his Elise—the beautiful, dark-haired one in the lovely dress. Even though the photo was monochrome black and white, Barton remembered Elise's dress as a deep shade of blue, like a jewel. Looking at the picture of the two sisters, he now recalled their differences; Elaine was bright, bubbly, and fickle. He quickly discovered that night she was a big flirt. Elise had loyally stayed with him. He conceitedly knew Elise did not dance with anyone but him after he rescued her from the annoying soldier. She had seemed at first reserved and unsociable, yet as the evening progressed, he felt from her a tantalizing thrum of sensuousness and easy, gentle compatibility.

Looking at the photo, Bart saw she was not smiling and wondered why. The other picture showed Elise in a bathing suit at the beach. She was lovely, with a cheery smile. He almost wanted to kiss her. He stroked the photograph fondly, stupidly wishing her here, then not. Shaking his head from the rush of sentimental whimsy, Barton read her letter.

She wrote in French as he had asked, and she talked of her birthday, her flute recital, and her family. She spoke briefly about the gifts she received. Elise wrote of her toy poodle Chérie.

Barton now wanted to compare the writing, for this letter seemed different, both in her handwriting and in her formal and stilted language. He hoped Elise was still the girl whose letters he enjoyed reading. He took out his shoebox of letters, opened the girls' last letter, and compared the writing. Elise was his gal, after all! Nevertheless, he wondered about the changes; perhaps Elise had run out of things to say to him.

Now Barton wondered something else. Did Elise say how old she'd turned on her birthday? He reread the letter and found she had not. Damn! He would feel like a bumbling idiot to ask. He had forgotten to ask what college she went to or from what high school she had graduated. Next time, he would flush her out with more specific questions. Barton was sharp! He would love to write to her now, but he had to get some shut-eye. Reluctantly, Bart put the photos and letter back into the envelope and then slipped it into his pillowcase. He turned off the light and lay down to sleep with the delectable, dainty scent of Elise in his nose.

CHAPTER 6

Normandy Invasion

Months before the actual Normandy invasion, there were deceptive actions and intelligence ops such as Operation Fortitude and Operation Bodyguard to trick the enemy regarding the exact place and date of the invasion. Pas de Calais was offered as a landing site, as it was so close to the English coast. A fictitious camp was set up with decoy tanks, trucks, tents, and supplies on the southeast coast of England just across from Calais as if readying for the invasion.

Lt. Gen. George S. Patton, who earlier in the year had led the Americans to victory in the fight over Sicily, had been sitting on the sidelines anxiously awaiting his turn in the upcoming operations. For brutally slapping a disgruntled soldier and professing him a coward, Patton was removed from duty. He was reinstated to oversee this diversionary tactic, yet he felt the command was an insulting slap in the face.

With radio bases in Scotland providing fake messages of a northern plan to attack Norway, the Germans now had two areas of concern. Double agent subterfuge, radio reports, and aerial photography showed a build-up to invade these targets in France and Norway. The Allies hoped to lure the Germans away from their valid target— Cherbourg and along the Normandy beaches of France. While others 'accidentally leaked' or obtained intelligence regarding code names of the beaches, their operations took the German High Command by surprise. Adolph Hitler held to the belief that what their intelligence discovered were only rumored ploys. The logical place for an invasion would be in the Rue de Calais area. Hitler was convinced General Patton would lead that attack—he wanted personally to defeat the audacious Patton, as they had both fought in World War I. The Führer wanted to humiliate the Americans' top generals to prove that Germany was the superior power.

In the days just before the Normandy invasion, German officers also theorized that any immediate invasion would be postponed due to the inclement weather that had shrouded the coast for the past month. Rumors of beach landings or invasions at Caen or Cherbourg, a deep sea port, were dismissed for the time. No one would risk coming in on anything but a high tide and clear skies. Prideful German commanders felt these places were also zealously guarded since they were easily accessible from England.

Relieved, officers left the field for war games in Rennes, giving many of their men time off. Field Marshall Rommel left his post for his wife's birthday in Berlin and, hoping to solicit more Panzer tanks from Hitler. During the days of confusing subterfuge, the commanders would also not commit to a solitary plan of defense offered among their generals—each believing *his* plan the best solution. However, the order within the high command eroded. The Führer stepped in with a strategy of his own to fortify Calais with a million troops.

◆ ◆

France
June 2–5, 1944

The preliminary invasion began a few days before Operation Overlord, which involved cunning British and Allied intelligence, surveillance, and many armed deceptive "attacks."

To continue the deception, Operation Cover was engaged; using the Eighth Air Force, four bombing missions pelted the Pas de Calais area, striking coastal German defenses, inland transportation, and airfields, thus stirring up the anthill.

The night before the Normandy invasion, in Operation Taxable, dummy paratroopers, among real ones, were dropped between Le Havre and Isgny. On the coast, Operation Glimmer had the RAF dropping 'windows' (foil pieces) into the ocean and small crafts towing in barrage balloons, which to the German radar seemed as if a vast naval convoy was on its way to Cap D'Antifer south of Le Havre.

The deception was complete.

◆ ◆

In a letter to the Allied Troops, Supreme Commander Gen. Dwight D. Eisenhower wrote:

> **You are about to embark upon the Great Crusade, toward which we have striven these many months. The eyes of the world are upon you. The hopes and prayers of liberty-loving people everywhere march with you. In company with our brave Allies and brothers-in-arms on other Fronts, you will bring about the destruction of the German war machine, the elimination of Nazi tyranny**

**over the oppressed peoples of Europe, and security for ourselves
in a free world.**

◆ ◆

Using the advantages of a fractionalized and confused German defense from the deceptions in the days previous, the Allies were ready to go. Taking the risk of not waiting any longer due to the poor weather or allowing the enemy to discover their ruse, Eisenhower and the Allied commanders pressed the Allied forces into attack mode.

During the night of June 5, 1944, through the following day, massive Allied air strikes, glider landings, and parachute invasions from the 101st Airborne Division on the mainland of Normandy were employed. These attacks were to break any enemy communications and allow Allied forces the ability to seize roads, railways, or bridges and eliminate a German counterattack. From behind enemy lines, the Allies would clear the area to allow safe egress from the beachheads. From the English Channel, Allied naval ships kept up a bombardment on the coast, hoping to drive the enemy from the beaches and break the outposts. American and British submarines prowled the Channels' waters as silent guardians for the maneuvers during the night.

Using Mother Nature's gifts with beaches brightly lit by the full moon and seasonal spring low tides, early that morning of June 6, in historically the largest amphibious assault ever, Western Allied troops invaded northern France. Under the guise of Operation Neptune to invade France via the English Channel and Operation Overlord to build lodgment areas for the invading troops, Canadians, Free French Forces, the United Kingdom, Australia, and the United States joined in the assault.

In the Channel and above in the air, the forces of the Royal Norwegian Navy, British ships, the Brits' RAF, the Royal Australian Air Force, and the United States sought to beat the enemy into submission, or at least divert attention away from the amphibious landings.

Each beach had a code name—Omaha, Gold, Sword, Utah, and Juno. Most of the amphibious invasions coming from Portsmouth, England, were landed along them. Some forces from Devon were deployed, despite the failed Operation Tiger on April 28, whereby nearly every team was lost during the exercise to prepare for D-Day, either killed by friendly fire or sunk by German E-boats.

◆ ◆

The morning was chilly and foggy, and the sea was heavy and restless. Many of the troop and equipment transports floundered under the rough waves, and men bailed out water and vomited, praying not to sink. Some landing craft did not make the targeted beaches that morning, sunk by the sea, woefully off-course, or stranded on sandbars.

In the early hours of the morning, the Germans stationed along the Normandy coastline knew finally that something had gone terribly wrong. There were many phone reports from outlying posts and citizens to headquarters during the night about sighting paratroopers, ships, and fighter planes, not to mention bombing runs. Yet the German commanders at first only scoffed at the news and did not take the sightings seriously. They believed an invasion would only happen around Calais since many of their troops had been deployed there. It was a case of nervous fools engaged in gossip or diversionary ploys by the enemy at best. There was no plan for counterattacks.

Then, some of their phone lines went dead, and communication between the outposts and headquarters was silent. The individual commanders at the beach sites and in towns along the way began to take control to prepare for the seemingly imminent invasion. It was almost too late now, for the strength and frequencies of the upcoming Allied attacks would prove cunning, incisive, and deadly, ultimately breaking the German outposts.

At the eastern end, Juno Beach was heavily fortified, nearly as much as Omaha, with German defenses of pit machine guns, pillboxes, concrete walls, and a high chalk seawall. Despite the heavy defense, the Canadian troops fought through the defensive lines and were off the beach within a few hours and heading inland. Each invading force had an objective to reach a principal town or village, drive back the enemy, and take control.

The western side of the long, 5-mile stretch of Omaha Beach was guarded that morning by parts of the German 352nd Infantry Division, mainly composed of teenagers, untrained in battle and supported by a contingency of experienced men of the 91st, who had fought on the Russian front the previous winter. Many of them were recruited from Poland, Mongolia, and Russia. Lieutenant General Dietrich Kraiss, hearing odd reports through the night and feeling in his gut that something was amiss, went early that morning to a beachside bunker. He witnessed the incoming ships through the mist as dawn lit the sea and sky. He put out the call to arms.

The beach itself was dangerous—some parts inaccessible with sand bars and stretches of deep water near the shoreline and high chalk cliffs. Omaha took the heaviest casualties that morning, for along her beaches were fortresses and bunkers with heavy German guns, hedgerows fortified with land mines, defensive pit trench lines of armament, and men ready for a fight.

Due to the rough seas, each of the six landings at Omaha was off target. Americans coming off the LSTs (landing boats) or swimming into shore from stranded or sunken transports were caught in the crossfire. Many men floundered in the wet sands only to step on a land mine that took out many of their nearby comrades.

The Allied commanders, seeing their troops in grave trouble at Omaha, sought to recall them. Britain's Prime Minister Winston Churchill was perhaps more concerned, recalling his failed Gallipoli amphibious invasion of 1918. However, within a few hours, some units had infiltrated and moved past the German defense and were able to spread out, providing a safer route for more deployments further along the beachhead. There were many brave dead men left behind on the cold beach.

Gold Beach took heavy casualties as well when the British 50th Infantry Division met with a small village on the beach filled with German troops. However, they were able to meet their objective, fighting valiantly to invade past the beach and on the road to Bayeux, a pivotal town. Their intention was that with the villages liberated, in a few days, they would be able to begin Operation PLUTO (pipelines under the ocean) for oil transport rather than relying on oil tankers out at sea.

Sword Beach, swarmed by British troops, found less resistance. By day's end, Allied forces had advanced nearly five miles inland, yet they had not made their goal for the day—Caen. There was heavy German defense surrounding the town.

At Point du Hoc, the farthest end of Omaha Beach, German defenses had heavy artillery and bunkers to be captured and neutralized because they could jeopardize the other beach landings, but to get to them required scaling ocean cliff walls. The US 2nd Ranger Battalion lost many men that first day (and in the days after) to take out those fortifications. However, their sacrifice would protect the rest of the invasion forces in the days ahead.

Utah Beach had fewer casualties, and some of that was due to the US 4th Infantry arriving off-target farther southeast than planned. This westernmost beach had less resistance from the enemy because many of its defensive troops had been deployed elsewhere in the days before. By the afternoon, the invading forces were off the beach and moving inland to meet up with the 101st Airborne Division.

Over 130,000 troops, half of them American forces, invaded the beaches that morning via troop transport ships, miscellaneous naval ships, and merchant ships. LCTs/LSTs (landing crafts for tanks, trucks, equipment, and artillery and landing crafts for troops) brought them farther toward the beachheads.

While the enemy was surprised at the attack, the Germans held hard to their conquered French prize when it all began. Despite their fortitude of mined beaches, barbed wire maze fences, pit guns, *Rommelspargel* (Rommel's asparagus—embedded stakes to prevent planes from landing on the beach), bunkers, and massive guns, the Germans could not contain or repel the constant assault of the vast army, naval, and air offensive of the Allied forces. Operations Neptune and Overlord were too aggressive and too concise; with months of planning, the many subset plans were in place to work through nearly any surprise counterattack or difficulty. The surprised Germans could not adequately push back or retreat in time. Their defenses were too scattered, with many of their tank commands and troops fighting in the Netherlands, Belgium, and other parts of France or waiting for the expected Allied invasion in Calais. They could not gather quickly enough, nor had the orders to repel the enemy. Prideful Hitler's own plans jeopardized them all.

◆ ◆

RAF Base
East Whitcliff, England
June 6, 1944

Barton dashed to his office, relaxing for some minutes to write in his journal. He was excited and inked again over the initial entry:

> *We did it!*
>
> *Today Is the Big Day!*
>
> *Operation Overlord Is in Effect!*
>
> *We got word at 0630 this morning when the whole maneuver began. RAF Brigadier General Eliot Campton and Colonel Ricker called a halt to all work, gathering the entire base together for the announcement. On a large map, they outlined the Allied attack planned for Operation Neptune and Overlord.*
>
> *The Germans occupying many of the seaside towns are holding the beachheads along the coast of Northern France in what Hitler calls his Atlantic Wall-Defense 51. With enemy gunships patrolling the seas of the English Channel, it should prove to be a rough haul. But the colonel has confidence in the bold move of the US and Allied Armed Forces' leaders. There were preemptive airstrike raids along the French coast last night and this morning to push the German defense back from the beaches. One such foray went out from this very*

base only last night. However, three B-17s, six Mustangs, and eleven Spitfires out of thirty planes have yet to return. We can only hope that the men will be parachuted out safely and that they can get back to the Allies.

Thousands of men are prepared for their invasive foray onto French soil; they are going over with preloaded tankers and trucks. The mechanized armies of the US and the Allied forces will be well supplied. This is the best way to get tons of fuel and supplies over there, as airdrops are too risky and cannot drop fast enough to do the job.

Historically, nearly every army or navy of the civilized world has tried to attack either England or France from the Channel. There are scores of ships lying at the bottom of the sea from failed attempts at the perilous crossing. Now to do this with the vigorous defense of Hitler's armies along that dangerous coast of France is indeed aggressive and bold, but it is a needed thing to do if we are to push into France and Germany and win this damned war.

A few men nearly incited a riot as they shouted, "Yeah! Yeah! We will go!" and "Down with the Huns! Death to the Nazi bastards!" The colonel had a hard time getting everyone to quiet down.

I, too, wish I could be there to see it all happen. Perhaps a bird's-eye view would be exciting and out of harm's way! Yet, my men and I will not go in this first move, but later. Everyone thinks that the invasion will be an impressive battle for the history books and wishes they were involved too, just to have their names in it. According to Campton, he told us, "You should all be proud today. For these many months, you have played an integral part in this grand operation by providing trained troops and POL supplies to the invading armies. On this day, we shall be victorious through our preemptive hard work!"

Earlier this morning, we were already on the move, loading up POL supplies and filling the tanker trucks and the C-47 cargo planes before the actual "word" came. After the fifteen-minute briefing, the depot was bustling again. I am proud to admit that there is little difference in the work of the men except that they now know everything we did was for real. These past months were not an exercise in futility. There is a general sense of high-spirited eagerness in the men's tasks and extra professionalism displayed. My company is running like a well-oiled machine.

We can only hope that our invasion will soon mean the terminus of the war.

After recording the event, Barton put away the diary and turned away from his inner ruminations. He left his office to go out among the hustle and bustle of the depot, feeling the energizing thrum and zeal of the men at work. He dove into his work, this time with patriotic enthusiasm.

◆ ◆

The US Navy left American Liberty ships (Corn Cobs) scuttled to form a breakwater off Omaha Beach's sandbars, making it easier to land more troops in the days after D-Day. DD Tanks swam ashore on the first day's invasion. Then, treadway bridges and concrete Mulberry harbors were added to allow smoother approaches for vehicles, troops, and materiel. Each landing site served as a mere stepping stone as the soldiers came in, providing less enemy resistance and hazards as the days went by.

In the days following D-Day, the assault on France's shores continued with massive deployments and brilliant assaults. By the end of June, over 850,000 troops, nearly 150,000 vehicles, and over 570,000 tons of supplies had been landed on the various beachheads. Conversely, the initial loss of life was lower than expected, approximately 10,000 during the first day's invasion, which still was a high price to pay for all the effort.

In the days and weeks after, as the Allies began to take hold, it was a daily battle against cunning Rommel's German Panzer teams. Original plans of striking at Caen and taking over the strategic towns of St. Lô and Bayeux on the first day proved difficult and costly for the British. Gen. Eisenhower believed they would soon be victorious; now that the US troops had landed and rallied, they began pushing out the enemy along the coast, taking small towns and German-fortified holdings. Meanwhile, British Gen. Montgomery stubbornly pounded away at the German resistance in Caen and Cherbourg.

◆

CHAPTER 7

Broken Hope

Baton Rouge, Louisiana
Friday, June 9, 1944

Elise grabbed up the stack of letters from the hall table, hoping there was mail from Barton. He had not written in months, not since she'd sent him her picture. For the first month, she anxiously waited for his letter, wanting to know what he thought of her pictures and hoping for more kind words. She had been in a state of nervous semi-flight for nearly two weeks, floating on her own cloud nine as she thought of his words and her memories of Bart at the dance.

She had written again to tell him she had written a letter accompanied by photos, but it had come back a month later! It really was a long time ago, and so much had happened in between that time. After his special letter, Elise felt connected again to Barton and half in love with him. Then, when she did not hear from him, she began to worry that Barton saw she was too young for him. She did not remember if she had written how old she was, but certainly, he could tell from her photos. That thought upset Elise for a few weeks.

Then, as her school volleyball tournaments, choral concerts, recitals, semester exams, and the promise of a summer of freedom passed through the months, Elise had to put Barton to the back of her mind. The lack of a letter from him after so many months led her to believe one of two things: Barton was no longer interested in her, or he was dead!

Maybe he went over on D-Day or something! She shuddered to think of Barton dead. The news on the radio and in newspapers was grim: so many men had died just a few days ago as the beaches of France were invaded. No, she must be positive and think only good thoughts of Barton.

She dumped the stack of mail back in the basket and went upstairs to practice her flute. Chérie, sleeping in the wicker basket in the bedroom, looked up when she came in. She uncurled her petite body and yawned widely, her shiny dark eyes following Elise, waiting for an opportunity to get some attention.

However, Elise flopped on her bed, still feeling a pang of dejection, and decided she could practice later. She felt the bedspread pull a bit and looked over her shoulder. "What!" Elise snapped. She heard a yip. Chérie wanted up, so she scooped up the dog. Chérie licked Elise's cheek and hands in greeting and snuggled under her arm to lie with her mistress as she read a pair of glamor magazines. Chérie was soon tired of watching her turn the shiny pages, and she snuggled next to Elise's hip for another snooze.

Elise wistfully looked at the magazine to see beautiful, curvaceous, proud-looking women with big, dark, long-lashed eyes, full red lips, and sultry looks. She wished she wasn't such a tall thing. Yes, she had a pretty face, but these were women with their broad shoulders, wasp-narrow waists, perky ample bosoms, and shapely legs, were like purebred horses, the best that nature made! They sported designer fashions, not like Elise's bland home-sewn creations. She got up off the bed, bouncing small Chérie, who irritably grunted and went to lie upon Elise's pillow.

She stood before her vanity mirror, where she held up a magazine and posed like Lana Turner, only to realize she was not curvy and sexy like the starlet. Elise took the other, flipped the pages, and posed like Katherine Hepburn with her head tilted and her hand held just so near her cheek. Elise dropped the magazine on the floor and pulled her hair up into a twist, mashing her ebony curly locks to look like Katherine's hair.

"Nope! I am not that kind of beauty." Elise bent to retrieve the magazine and sat at her vanity, where she paged through it some more, wanting to find a star's image that spoke to her.

She saw a model who wore a broad-shouldered dress; she wore a tall, fez-styled hat that had a crepe de chine drape that swept down and around her broad shoulders— that was a swell look! Elise grabbed her silk kimono and draped it over her head and around her shoulders like in the photo and put on her best pouting starlet moue; she batted her eyes as she posed like the model in the picture.

"Ah, nuts!"

Disgusted, Elise shoved the magazines off the vanity into the wastebasket below but then regretted her wasteful action. She retrieved them to give to her girlfriend, Millie Layton.

"Forget it! I will never be a great beauty. People probably lied, wanting to appease me because Elaine is so lovely. I am nothing but a tall, gangly goose girl with knobby knees and elbows!"

Elise critically searched her face, thinking her dark eyes were too large and her cheekbones too high. When she smiled, her eyes crinkled and got small. She opened the vanity drawer and took out Elaine's makeup kit. After applying a rich berry-red lipstick, she practiced several smiles, wanting to look pretty and alluring like the models. She needed eye makeup. Using the expensive French mascara and the tiny brush, she spit on the black cake and swirled the brush around to make a thick paste. She brushed the mascara on her eyelashes and noticed they looked better. She added more, brushing them up and out, letting them sweep in long feathers to the outer corners. She put on a little eyeliner and batted her eyes; they looked great! However, they felt so thick and gloppy, and then she saw a little smear under an eye. When she attempted to wipe it away, she smeared the entire mess underneath and on her finger!

"How in the heck does Elaine do this?" Elise grabbed a tissue and the cold cream and wiped it all off. She cleaned the brush and put everything back in the drawer. Just in time, too—she heard Elaine running up the stairs and then burst into their bedroom. She glanced at her in the mirror just as she took a last swipe of the greasy smear on her face, pocketing the tissue.

"What's got you all excited?" Elise queried, annoyed that she was nearly caught.

"Oh, me? It is just the best news ever, that's what!" Elaine said, breathing fast and shallow. She was taking off her clothes and tossing them on the floor of her closet.

"Got a hot date then?" Elise asked now and knelt on her bed to watch the show.

Elaine raced about the room, ransacking the closet, opening drawers, sorting through clothes, and making a mess in their once neat room with her discarded choices.

"Hot date?" Elaine rolled her eyes. "No one says that. I've got a date with a dreamy and sexy Superman," she cooed as she patted on bath powder and spritzed perfume on her neck and wrists.

"So, who is the boy?" Elise drawled, rolling her eyes with feigned interest. She picked up little Chérie, who was sniffing nervously at Elaine.

"Not a boy—a man, Elise!" Elaine grinned as she slipped into a fresh petticoat. "Terrence Dillard! What a dreamboat … every girl at college says so! I'm so lucky!"

Elise was now interested. "Football or basketball?" she queried, knowing Elaine's penchant for the sporty hero types.

Elaine was fastening her garters and stockings. "No, tennis. In fact, we are going to Terrence's tennis awards banquet tonight. That is why I have to hurry."

"That is rather short notice."

"Maybe. But I can be ready in two shakes." She giggled, smoothing the seamed stockings over her calf. "He is lucky I am a natural beauty and don't need much prep."

"Where did you meet him?" Elise asked, giving in with a sigh.

"Outside my English class this afternoon, I opened the door, and boom—we knocked each other over!" she commented briskly as she pulled on a pink ruffled dress.

Elise got up and went to her sister, pulling her long amber hair out of the way to zip up the dress. "So, how does that make you a guest at his banquet tonight?" She spread Elaine's hair back over her shoulders and smoothed the organza ruffles, arranging them neatly.

"Oh, he picked me up," Elaine giggled as she adjusted her breasts in the low-necked dress. "You know ... he picked me up. Get it?" She shook her head at Elise's obtuse look. "Afterward, we went and had a cream soda at the student union, and then he invited me to his banquet tonight. It was all so sudden, but I said yes!"

Elise noted her sister's enthusiasm bubbling over, seeming happy to be going out again on a Friday night. Since her second breakup a month ago with Tommy Vance, Elaine had been a grumpy witch!

Elise shook her head, continuing to watch as her sister bustled about. Elaine tried on earrings and necklaces and finally decided on a short string of pearls and a pair of pearl bauble earrings accented with brilliant rhinestones. She swept her hair up and held the golden curls.

"Elise, come give me a hand here. Use the pearl hairpins. He'll just love it this way." Elaine stood before the vanity mirror and held her hair up how she wanted it.

Elise helped to style the hair by using the pearl-headed hairpins she had used for her birthday hairstyle.

"Have you told Mom and Daddy yet that you are smitten by this male god?" Elise asked. "I am surprised they're going to let you go." She felt Elaine grow tense under her hands.

"Um ... I haven't in that way. But I am a grown-up. I don't have to get their permissions for dates."

"Maybe that is true, but you don't know anything about this boy, do you?"

Elaine glared at Elise in the mirror. "Man, Elise ... man. I know enough." She continued loftily. "He is handsome, he is on the tennis team, he is wealthy, and his family belongs to the Country Huntsman's Club. He is a popular guy on campus, and nearly everyone knows and likes him. So what else do I need to know?" She glanced at Elise's reflection in the mirror and frowned. "You look like Daddy. Stop it. I don't need your worried looks and prudish attitude." Elaine pulled away and patted her hair impatiently. "That is fine. I have to do my makeup. Buff my shoes, please ... the cream patent leather T-straps." She turned away to apply her makeup.

Elise grimaced, wondering if Elaine would be able to tell she had used her mascara! She searched for the shoes and found them in the jumbled mess on the floor of the closet. She buffed the patent leather heels until they were shiny and looked like new.

Elaine did not notice that the mascara was damp; she was brushing it on, anyway. Elise caught up with how her sister did the seemingly simple task and put it in her mental memo about how *not* to do it the next time. Elaine hurriedly applied her rouge and lipstick, using a finger to mark Cupid's bow, then wiping off the excess deep red on her upper lip and carefully blotting her lipstick on a tissue. Suddenly, Elaine sprang up and made a little turn with her arms held out.

"Well, how do I look?" Elaine asked briskly.

"Like a piece of pink cotton candy."

Elaine frowned slightly and glanced in the mirror. "Do I really look like candy?" She glanced back at Elise, who was frowning, and she quickly kissed her on the cheek. "Don't worry about me; he will think I look great. Not bad for twenty minutes, eh?"

Elise wiped off the lip print, rolled her eyes, and asked, "When is he picking you up?"

"Oh, he is already waiting downstairs."

"You have got to be kidding me."

"I told you it was a spur-of-the-moment thing. He wasn't even going to go tonight until … um, we bumped into each other." Elaine grabbed her matching pink wrap with the ruffled trim and dyed marabou feathers. She stuffed a hankie, compact, and lipstick in her pearled evening purse. "I had better go rescue poor Terrence before Daddy says something embarrassing!"

Grinning, Elaine went out and carefully stepped down the stairs to make her grand entrance, pausing halfway on the stairs to pose just so she would be seen at an attractive angle from the front room or parlor.

Elise shook her head, disgusted. Everything with Elaine was a big show, and everything had to be something it was not. She followed her sister down, waiting as Elaine made her entrance like a spoiled debutante. She heard everyone exclaim her sister's beauty and then a sharp male wolf whistle. She scurried into the parlor to take a secluded spot by the potted fern and palm to watch the show. Her mother and father were chatting with a tall, slim young man who affectionately greeted Elaine.

He wore a dapper, trim mustache and had large jewel-blue eyes and long, dark eyelashes; his wavy dark-brown hair with sandy-blond streaks was neatly coiffed. He wore a stylish, fitted navy blue suit that accentuated his broad shoulders and long legs. Elise could smell lavender. Wasn't that Daddy's toilet water?

Elise thought it odd. *What did he do, go to school in a dress suit?* She heard her name, and Elise stepped out from behind the leafy fern, hearing a chuckle.

"This is our daughter Elise … Elaine's younger sister." Beatrice pulled Elise out to shake hands with Terrence.

"This is Elaine's date, Terrence Dillard." Beatrice made the polite introduction and pushed Elise to straighten up from her slouch.

"This is another little beauty." Terrence took Elise's hand and gallantly kissed it. "Hello, darlin'!" He smiled at Elise with perfect white, even teeth and ogled her for a moment too long.

Elaine possessively grabbed the man's arm. "Well, we should be going! Yes, Terrence?" She glared at Elise, who put her kissed hand in her jumper pocket.

He broke the spell and looked down at Elaine with a wry smile. "Hungry, are you?"

"No, but isn't it time we go, Terry dear?" Elaine said poignantly.

"Oh, right you are!" he said with a glance at his wristwatch. "Well, nice to meet y'all. And you too, Elise!" Terry winked at her.

Elise stood back as the couple sailed out the door on a waft of lavender water and *Shalimar.* She wiped her hand off and felt a shudder go through her.

"My younger brother Clarence is going to like Elise!" Terrence's comments echoed as they walked away.

"What a nice young man!" Beatrice commented. She sighed, watching the pair from the parlor window. Terrence put Elaine in the miniscule foreign car at the curb.

Édouard harrumphed as he sat again in his chair; he put his feet up on the hassock and rattled his newspaper, trying to fold it into something resembling a newspaper again. He suddenly dropped it on the floor and stood up; he then went to the window and watched as the little maroon MG roadster zipped away. "I don't like it," he grumbled, sounding like thunder.

"Like what, dear?" Beatrice asked as she picked up the glasses of lemonade on the table.

"Him. He is too slick! Can you imagine going into a complete stranger's home and asking to change your clothes in their bathroom? Ha! He is nothing but rude and a young, pandering snot! Elaine will be lucky to get home in one piece!"

"Dad!" Elise said, shocked.

Surprised, Édouard looked around at his daughter. He came to stand over her and waggled a finger in her face. "Don't you dare bring home a … a shiny, conceited piece of work like that! You deserve better."

"But you let Elaine go out with him!" Elise accused.

Beatrice replied with an exasperated sigh. "Yes, you did. You worry too much, Édouard. If you did not like him, then you should have said something beforehand. I liked him. He seems charming and quite well off—"

Édouard glared at his sighing and wistful wife, not allowing her to finish her thought. "I don't care if he is wealthy or not! This will be the first and last date. How can Elaine continue to embarrass us like that? That kind of boy is only looking for one thing!" he whispered sternly.

Elise waited to hear what the one thing was, but her father left the living room and followed his wife into the kitchen. She could hear them arguing in hushed tones in French and knew she should not interfere or even listen in.

True, she had not liked it when Terrence kissed her hand. He was handsome enough to be in the movie pictures and resembled Errol Flynn. Yet kissing her with a bold and gallant panache had made Elise very uncomfortable.

She decided to go back up to her bedroom to wait for dinner while her folks had their discussion. She hoped it wouldn't be too much longer—the chiming hall clock had already rung for six! She went upstairs and flopped moodily on her bed with Chérie.

She wondered just what Daddy was talking about—*that kind of boy*. She all of a sudden realized she had never felt repulsed when she was with Barton Barre. He had been a gentleman. He held her hand and kissed it, too. Perhaps it was love at first sight that made a difference!

◆ ◆

Elaine was upset that Terrence had somehow gotten the wrong message during the evening. She just thought it was a dinner date, which also had a dance following the awards banquet. That was fine because she loved to dance.

During the meal, Terry slipped out a few times with an excuse that he had to get some fresh air or use the restroom. However, when he sat back in his chair next to her at the table, Elaine smelled liquor.

As the evening progressed, Terrence became bolder, holding her hand a few times or putting his arm over the back of her chair. Once, his hand came down possessively and fondled the pearls on her neck, even slipping lower to dangle above her breast. He daringly breathed in her ear after a few of those missing-in-action moments, and Elaine began to worry.

She sat nearly silent during much of the main course and then ate the strawberry shortcake and weak coffee with a pink face and feeling hot. Terrence put his hand on her knee a few times, and she felt his hand sliding higher along her thigh, once under her dress, even while he was talking with his friends. Embarrassed, she could not shout at him to take his hand out from under her dress skirt, not in front of everybody, but she pushed his hand away and moved her chair a few inches away from him.

Regardless of her discomfort, Elaine tried to be conciliatory when Terrence received his trophy and plaque for the top player in his league. He gave her such an exuberant kiss afterward that her head hurt. She was embarrassed by the whoops of laughter that rang about their table, teasing them. Terrence seemed to take it all in as a joke and grinned like a jackal, keeping her close under his arm like a prize.

After the ceremony, she asked him to take her home.

"You really want to go home? Maybe we can go park somewhere." Terrence's eyes sparkled with mischief.

"I want to go home now. This was all a bad idea—"

"What? You are telling me I have to leave all of this so early? My friends are going to want to know why." Terrence looked angry.

"Tell them I have a headache. You could always come back here afterward."

He put his arm around her waist, drawing her close to him. His liquor-laden breath fanned her face. "I just couldn't do that. Besides, I don't think you want the rumors to go around that our date ended early, do you? What would people think, Elaine? I mean, I am a popular guy. I could have asked anyone to go to this thing tonight. You don't want to ruin my good reputation, do you?"

"No. You did ask *me*, though. Perhaps it might be better if you did take me home, and then the rumor would be that you are a gentleman." Elaine looked up at him with a somber expression. "Please, I think I have had enough, and so have you. If you are enjoying your time with me so much, then why keep running out and drinking? Hmm?" Elaine cringed, thinking she sounded just like Beatrice!

Terrence stood up taller and brushed back the lock of hair that had fallen over his brow; he gave a little laugh. "Oh, that … you noticed, did you?" he asked huskily.

"Don't be a fool. Of course, I did, and so did everyone else at our table. Your friend Charlie even followed you out just in case you were sick." Elaine bent to pick up her handbag and unhook her wrap from her chair. "So if you are not too drunk to drive me home, then let's go, please." She cocked her head at him, waiting for Terrence to answer. "Perhaps I should call my father to pick me up. I don't think he would be too impressed with you then."

Terrence shook his head. "Oh no, there's no need for that! My dates don't end with daddies picking up their tearful little girls!"

"I am not in tears!" she said hotly and swung away from him.

He suddenly cornered her between a table and the empty chairs. "I want to dance with you." He lifted his head and gave a quick scan around the room before looking back at Elaine, his electric-blue eyes intense upon her face. "Look. Everyone is on the floor! Come on, dance with me. I promise I will be a gentleman."

He pulled her closer to his body. "Just a few, then we can leave, and I will take you wherever you want to go as long as it isn't farther than fifteen miles. I don't have enough gasoline for that." He leered down at her. "You want to get lost and run out of gas with me, hmm?"

Elaine blanched. "Uh, no. A few dance numbers will be fine. Then you can take me home, Terrence."

"Good. And call me Terry." He kissed her cheek lightly, tossed the handbag and wrap on their chairs, and pulled Elaine onto the dance floor.

They danced a couple numbers, and Elaine relaxed as she found him to be, as he said, gentlemanly. He held her lightly and guided her around the floor.

"You know why I had a few snorts, don't you?"

She shook her head. Terrence leaned down, his words soft in her ear. "I needed the courage. You are the prettiest girl here tonight."

Elaine stumbled back from Terry, surprised by his admission. Then suddenly, she felt something was wrong with her shoe and begged him to stop at their table. She sat and found her heel was loose. Terrence suggested she dance in her stockings, but they were new and her last good pair, so Elaine went to the ladies' room to remove them. When she exited, she found him anxiously waiting for her by the door. He humorously swept her along, dancing between the tables until they came to their table; he tossed her purse on her chair and danced Elaine out to the middle. Elaine began to have fun, noting other girls dancing barelegged. Nobody dared ruin precious stockings!

Terrence was lively and attentive and danced well during the first few songs. Every so often, he drew her close after a spin or turn and would hold her tightly until Elaine pushed him away to keep some breathing space between them. After so many of those sneaky maneuvers, she gave up and let Terrence hold her close.

Then there was the mirror ball dance—with the band music beguiling and the female singer sultry, the floor was dark with only the glittering ball casting diamonds around the room. Terrence drew her in, his body immodestly pressed to hers.

She could sense everything—feel his taut muscles, smell the lavender water, feel his bourbon-laden breath, warm, humming in her ear. Fate would have it that there were three slow songs in a row. Elaine even protested a sore ankle, but instead, Terrence held her tighter, nearly lifting her off her feet as he bent to wrap himself around her petite figure.

He began to touch her neck and ear with butterfly-light kisses, and Elaine's body betrayed her as she swooned slightly, allowing Terrence to continue. She had felt him grow hard against her, and while it was not the first time that evening, or Elaine's first experience to feel such a thing from a man, she pushed him away, again asking him to take her home. She'd had enough!

Terrence finished the slow fox-trot with her and then escorted Elaine off the floor to their table. He helped her with her wrap. With his hand on her waist, he ushered her outside.

In her flushed and nervous excitement, she left her shoes under the table.

A few miles away from the club, he pulled over on a dark, tree-lined street. Terrence glanced at her and gave her a charmingly white smile that disarmed Elaine, making her forget her previous resolve.

"I know we don't really know each other, having only met today, but I want to see you again, Elaine. I really like you. I think it was destiny that we met today." He turned off the engine and put on the parking brake. He turned in his seat to her. "May I see you again? Please?"

Elaine found his nearness discomforting and beguiling, so she sat looking at her hands in her lap. "Perhaps … I don't know, Terrence. This evening was not what I expected."

"Me either." He lifted her chin to see Elaine's face, asking softly, "You do like me, don't you? Or did I get my signals crossed?"

"I do, but—"

"I thought we had a good time tonight; we danced well together. You are a little angel on your feet. It is no wonder you are so popular."

"Thank you. I have to tell you something, though, Terrence."

"Terry. Call me Terry. I like the way you say it—you roll the *R*s, sounding so proper. I love it when you speak French!"

Elaine gave a little laugh and blushed. She felt a finger trace down her cheek and around her ear as he fondled the pearl earring.

"You are lovely, Elaine. I would be proud to have you be my girl. You are what I need in my life." His hand snaked around her neck, drawing her closer.

Terry's lips before her were smiling and inviting and waiting to be kissed. She wanted to be kissed. She closed her eyes as he leaned toward her; his lips barely touched hers.

"Mmm … you still taste like strawberries. More," Terry murmured.

He pulled her head closer again and dipped his head, tasting and kissing her slowly, gently, and Elaine let herself fall into his hands. An arm went around her, and soon, he pulled her into his lap, kissing her. Her legs were in the passenger's seat, the gearshift uncomfortably between them.

Elaine tried to relax and enjoy the heady experience of Terry's expert kisses. His hands were light on her body, gently tracing the contours of her ribs, bust, shoulders, and neck; his lips moved over her face in small kisses and then trailed along her neck. He slid the neckline of her dress off one shoulder and kissed the dewy skin there.

Elaine sat up and pulled her dress back up. She cradled his cheek, hoping to control Terrence so that he would not wander again. "Terry," she murmured against his lips. "Terry … I think …"

He captured her lips again, kissed her harder, and gathered her body close, his arms now a prison.

Elaine wanted out. "Terry, please." She pushed feebly against him, mumbling against his hard-pressed lips.

"You want me, don't you?" he said hotly against her skin as he kissed the exposed décolletage. "Oh, you are so sexy, Elaine. My God, you are driving me insane!"

Elaine felt his hand slide up her leg and under her dress, and she pushed at it, now scared and frantic. "Stop it, Terrence! I don't want you like that!"

Her words were stopped as his tongue rushed into her mouth, kissing her deeply, sucking away her breath and tongue. She battled for a few seconds with her own tongue pressed against his to stop the invasion. She pulled a hand free and slapped him hard on the arm and then his face.

"Ow! Oh, you like it rough, do you?" He shook her a little and tickled her ribs hard, capturing the slippery Elaine, only to devour her again. "I'll teach you … give you a love bite you won't forget!" His hands were harsh and demanding on her now.

He grabbed her hair and held her head so she was trapped between the door, the steering wheel, and his body, the space tight in the little car.

If she had half a mind, she would knee or punch him and crawl out over the door, but Elaine hoped to keep the situation from escalating while maintaining some dignity.

Terry enjoyed kissing and sucking while his hands roamed freely on her body. When he touched her between the thighs, she stiffly slammed them tight. He gave a small, wicked-sounding laugh under his breath as he kissed her for a few moments before Elaine began to cry and went limp in his arms.

The onslaught went on for longer than she wanted.

Terrence stopped and raised his head to stare at her. "What's wrong? Why aren't you kissing me back? You are crying …"

She looked up at him in the dark, crying with accusation. "I am not enjoying myself. You are a brute! *Laisse-moi!* Please take me home now." She tried to sit up, grabbing onto the steering wheel. Terry put a hand behind her and pushed her up. She scrambled back into her seat, which was an ungraceful maneuver. She landed with a fluffy flop, the ruffled skirt nested around her waist.

Giving Terrence a nasty look, she lifted her hips and yanked her dress skirt back down around her knees. Letting out an exasperated sigh, she looked back at him. "Why are you just sitting there, you big, horny, mauling ape? Take me home now!"

Suddenly, Terrence laughed; he clutched his belly and gave her a side look before bursting into riotous laughter.

"It's not funny. That's it, I'll walk!" Elaine grabbed up her wrap and purse and looked down on the floorboard. "My shoes! I left them at the dance!" She slapped Terrence on the arm, and he feinted to protect himself, now nearly choking with laughter. "Stop it! It isn't funny! We have to get my shoes!" She turned around and glared out at the dark night.

"God, but you really take the cake, you know it? I don't think I have ever had such a date!" Terrence pulled out his handkerchief, wiped his eyes, blew his nose, and pocketed it. "Do you know how funny you look?"

Elaine glared at him. "Me? A few minutes ago, you were proclaiming my beauty."

"Here, let me." He reached a hand to her face.

She leaned away but snapped her teeth at the fingers, almost touching her face. "Don't touch me."

"Don't bite me; I am only trying to help you." Terrence wiped a thumb across her cheek and showed it to her.

Elaine gasped; dark red lipstick colored Terry's thumb. She fumbled in her purse for her compact mirror. When she looked at herself, she screeched to see lipstick smeared all over her cheeks, nose, and chin.

"Oh, my Lord! Look what you did! And you look like a clown, too!" She grabbed out her hankie and began scrubbing her face.

"You are making it worse. Give it here, Elaine." His voice was softer now, and he snapped his fingers at her, waiting for the hankie.

Looking up at him, she said snottily, "Haven't you done enough?"

Now he sobered. "No, I haven't." Terrence snatched the hankie and put a hand behind her head, holding her as if she were a small, petulant child, then methodically wiped her face like a patient parent. He even did a bit of spit polish and then sat back to regard Elaine. "I think you need soap," he said drily.

"Oh, you are incorrigible!" She smacked him on the arm.

He handed back the hankie. "I am sorry. Oh boy, do you know how to kiss! You had me going there!" He leaned to her and gently kissed her cheek.

She sunk her head between her shoulders, deflecting any further demonstrations. She glanced in the mirror again; her mouth looked better, but her mascara and hair were a mess.

"What made you attack me like I was a piece of meat?"

Terrence leaned back in his seat and cast a blue-eyed, sad look at her angry face. "You are not meat. You are candy, so sweet, and I can't get enough of you. I think I am addicted now. You have to see me again." He let out a small, embarrassed laugh and fidgeted with his pants crotch. "I might die if you don't."

Disgusted, Elaine shook back her hair and pulled her wrap closely about her. "I don't think that would be a good idea, Mr. Dillard."

"What's with the formality? You seemed to have a good enough time. You kissed me back, and I seem to remember your hands touching me, and it felt very nice."

Elaine's eyes went wide. "Touch you?! Well, if I did, it would have been an accident! You put my hand on your … your … *zi-zi* … dingus! I would never …" She turned away in embarrassment.

He leaned dangerously close as he laughed. "But you did touch me and admit it—you enjoyed my attentions." He rubbed his cheek. "Although I didn't care much for the slap in the face, I thought you were playing rough. I kind of like fighting with you, after all. You were exciting, like—"

"So I noticed. However, I did not like it one bit. I was trying to get you to stop. You were positively acting like a wild animal." She gave him a heated stare and looked away again.

"I *am* an animal, so are you … my little vixen."

"Don't say that. I am not your anything!" She spat.

"Sorry. So, Elaine, will you please go out with me again? I promise I will be better behaved." He looked at Elaine with a slight pout and batted his long eyelashes at her. "Come on, you know you like me."

"I don't like being mauled. You hurt me, you big oaf!"

Terrence put a hand to his chest in mock hurt, drawling, "Oh, you sorely wound me, *mademoiselle*, because no one has ever called me such names before."

Elaine looked darkly at him but could not keep the hard edge anymore, and she smiled reluctantly.

Terrence swooped in and planted a light kiss on her lips. "Good. I am glad you forgive me. Now, when shall we meet again?"

"That depends on you. I think we should stick to daytime dates. I am not sure I can trust you. I might still have to walk home tonight, and if I do that, my father won't let me see you ever again, no matter what you say."

"I see. How old are you anyway?"

"I'll be twenty this summer. Why? How old are you?" she replied stiffly.

Terrence rubbed his face and jaw, now looking a bit sheepish. "I'll be twenty-two in October myself, and if you did not know it already, I will be a senior this fall."

"I'll be in the junior class."

"I guess we really don't know each other much, do we?"

"Not really." Elaine rolled her eyes at the inane remark.

"I would like to start over here. I think I got the wrong impression of you."

"Why would that be?" she questioned.

Terrence sighed and took a deep breath. "It's just that I have seen you in the company of so many guys on campus, and you are always so flirty and smiling. You looked like a fun girl."

"I am a fun girl, but not like you want." Elaine sniffed and haughtily looked away, now upset that there might be rumors about that she was a loose, good-times girl.

Terrence reached out a hand to stroke her cheek. "I know you are fun. I have had fun tonight. But you are more … you are still a virgin, aren't you?"

Elaine let out a shriek. "Oh! Oh, now you are just a plain downright … *salaud! Je ne suis pas une salope! Mon père, il aurais ta peau!*" (Dirty dog! I am not a whore! My father, he will have your skin!) "I have never …" She batted at the door handle as she tried to leave the car, but Terrence pulled her back.

"I don't know about the French parts, but I think I can agree that you have never done it before. Maybe that is why I like you—you are special." Terrence smiled and tried to take Elaine's hand. She swatted him away.

He won and held her hand firmly. "I promise I won't take advantage of that fact again. As I said, I was mistaken and a bit drunken by your charms." He kissed her hand. "Please, I would be very hurt if you couldn't trust little ole' me. Please, baby?" His blue eyes glittered dangerously in the dark.

"I doubt that I should. This entire night—everything that has happened so far— has been against my better judgment." Elaine tossed back gravely.

"Then why did you say yes when I asked you today?" Terrence sounded angry and sat back in his seat.

Elaine leveled teary eyes on him. "Because I thought you were a considerate man. I thought you might have been special too, someone I should know." Choking on a sob, she continued, "I thought you were a gentleman and liked me for me, not because you thought I was a floozy." She flapped a hand before her face, feeling tears come on. "I am just a stupid girl, I know. But I was flattered that you should ask me to do something nice on our first date!" She gave a little cry. "I thought it meant something!"

Terrence moved closer but was inhibited by the gearshift and the console and groaned. "Settle down before you have the vapors." He put his arm around her shoulder. "I am nice," he said huskily. "I am someone who you should know. You are a wonderful girl."

He hesitated for a moment. "I have a confession to make … I made sure I was there to meet you outside of your English comp class. I followed you there today. I wanted to ask you out for a date, but then my mouth ran off and suggested the banquet tonight."

"So you planned the entire mess … knocking me down? And that was your idea of the proper way to ask me for a date? Now I really have heard everything! *Un mot de plus et je sors!*" (One more word, and I leave!) Elaine glared at him wide-eyed, looking shocked.

Terry smiled wanly and passed a hand over his brow. "Well, not the falling down part. I was going to just step up and ask you, you know … like a normal person." He shook his head. "Look, honey, it was an unavoidable accident." He gave a weak little laugh. "I did try to make amends … I bought you a chocolate soda. So, may I have another chance? Please?"

"We had cream sodas, you jerk." Elaine quickly corrected him, staring. After a moment, she gave a little tinkling laugh. "How can I say anything but yes to that rambling, ridiculous story? I hope that you are being truthful and I am not making another insidious mistake." She pointed an admonishing finger at him. "But I get to pick when and where for the next date, and if I say stop it, you stop."

"Yes'm. Anything you say." Terry looked abashed as he fluttered his dark lashes at her.

"Okay. Now, please take me home."

"Just like that, huh?" He looked sad but then gave her a broad smile. "How about a couple good night kisses?"

"Oh, I think you have had more than your share of them already." She looked away with haughty indifference.

"Oh, well, you plant one right here, and we'll go. C'mon …" Terry offered a puffed cheek.

She gave him a peck, and laughing, Terrence started the car.

When they arrived in front of her house, she brushed aside his invading hands. "Let's not start anything again, please. Thank you for an interesting night, Terrence. Let's just forget it."

"Call me tomorrow, honey."

Elaine turned to leave, but he snatched at her wrap and put his calling card in her hand.

"See? There's my number. Make it soon. Don't forget … a guy like me is a good catch, and you have certainly snared me in your net, little mermaid. Tell me something sweet in French, and then you can go." He laughed, trying to snag her hand too.

Elaine evaded his wandering hands. "*Tout doux! Dans cette guerre lasse j'ai fini par accepter ton offre.*" (Gently! This is a lost war—I am done accepting your offer.) She swatted his hand away with her insult. She climbed out of the low-slung roadster with as much grace and dignity as she could muster, all the while wishing she could run home and slam the front door in his cheeky face!

She tiptoed onto the porch with a quick glance back at Terrence, finding he waited at the curb in his car. He gave her a wave, watched her enter the house, and then sped away.

"What a conceited rat," she grumbled, "he didn't even walk me to the door!"

Elaine peeked around the corner of the parlor to see if anyone was there and was relieved when she didn't see anyone. She turned off the hall light and scooted, shoeless, up the stairs to her room, dumped her wrap and purse, grabbed her bathrobe, and headed to the bathroom. Elaine was relieved that everyone seemed to be asleep; she did not need any confrontations after the night she'd had! Her father would have pulverized Terrence for being a boor and not walking her to the door.

She turned on the bathroom light to survey the damage. Her cheeks were red, her mascara left dark rivers down them, and her hair had come down in rattail lengths all around. "Oh yes! I am so *Beautiful!*" She snarled at her reflection as she yanked out the last of the pearled hairpins—two were missing; she figured they must still be in Terrence's car. Elaine scrubbed her face, removing the makeup, not caring if she dripped on the bodice of her dress; she would not wear it again in a million years. Her mother was right—the neckline was too low and provocative. She was sorry to have begged for the summer frock.

Elaine fumed as she thought of her ill-treatment tonight—what a mess. She brushed her teeth and rinsed her mouth with *Listerine*, burning the taste of Terrence's bourbon-laden breath and tongue from her own. No boy dared to do that to her, shove his tongue halfway down her throat! She felt an overwhelming shudder rise and shook herself. She had slapped him for it, too. That had not gone over well, and Elaine suddenly realized how big Terrence was. Perhaps she'd gotten off lightly and had been lucky not to be raped!

She trembled as she reached to unzip the dress and yank it off her body. She looked down and saw a dark bruise on one breast and then looked up at her reflection and saw two more bruises on her neck. Horrified, she knew she was in trouble. Her family would ask about the bruises on her neck. She'd have to wear a scarf for a week, and it was summer too!

Groaning, Elaine stripped off the crinoline petticoats and satin slip, garter belt, and panties. She took off her bra and gently touched the purple bruise. Angrier now than when it happened. She did not know Terrence would make marks on her like this! She ran the hot water and scrubbed her body, wanting to erase the scent of him and his marks—"love bites," he had laughingly called them. She was sorry now that she had ever flirted with Terry, or any boy, ever!

Elaine had certainly felt excited by his kisses and his touches, but it had also scared her half to death. However, after thinking the entire evening over, she decided to sleep on Terry's request to see her again. He certainly was the most exciting, wealthiest, and most handsome fellow she'd had for years.

She was planning to be a virgin when she married—that was the proper way to do things. Besides, she didn't need Daddy to break Terrence into confetti-sized pieces for ruining her. She hoped that if she did go out with Terrence again, he would not act as he had done. She just might give him another chance; he had seemed genuinely repentant for his brutish behavior. Perhaps he really was crazy about her.

Elaine finished her ablutions, daubing witch hazel on her raw lips and bruises. She gathered up her things, and shutting off the bathroom light, she crept to her room and closed the door softly. Then Elaine tossed the clothes on her chair and found her bed with the linens already pulled back. She got into bed and laid her head on her pillow with a sigh as she closed her eyes.

"Did you have a good time, Elaine?"

"Yes. Thank you, Elise." Elaine pushed her face into the pillow, afraid she might cry.

"I hope that the boy was nice to you. Daddy thought he might be a scoundrel, but Mother said no. She thought Terry was a gentleman."

Elaine's heart thudded in her chest. Daddy always knew.

"Go to sleep, Elise."

"Bonne nuit et je t'aime, Elaine."

"Love you too," Elaine echoed. She had hopes that Terry was her destiny—she had fallen for him earlier in the day. He was beautiful but a scoundrel. Now, he was a tempting sin. Elaine felt pain all the way into her wicked and guilty little soul.

◆

CHAPTER 8

Je Suis Un Soldat

East Whitcliff, England
June 1944

Each day melded into night into the next day until Barton had nearly lost track of time in passing. Despite the D-Day invasion earlier in the month, their work on the air base had not lessened. The days were hectic and fully charged with things to do; continuous field training, the need to write work orders and fill requisitions, people and schedules to be managed, and the constant parade of vehicles and tankers coming and going. Often, Barton found himself in a surreal twilight of sleeping and wakefulness. He dreamed of oil; he could smell petrol on his skin and clothes; could taste it on the air and in his food; and he, like the rest of his men, was beyond bone weary of POL! However, their workload would not improve for Barton or his men.

It was nearly the end of June, and there were rumors he would transfer again, this time to France, going over with parts of the 5th Infantry and the 5th Quartermasters Company. It was planned that they would take up posts along the northern coast of France at strategically placed dump stations to resume the distribution of the supplies that had already gone over the Channel in the earlier deployments.

As the units began deploying from the air base, Barton took his leave of the freshly trained men, wishing them well and offering them good tips on keeping safe and whole. Well, at least he thought they were good ideas as he stoically bade them adieu.

One evening, after seeing a unit off, Barton made up a knapsack with a snack, took out his writing case, and addressed two envelopes, one to his parents and the other to Elise Boulanger. Then, he escaped for a walk along the chalk cliffs. This might be his last chance for privacy and time to write. The move was on, and he did not exactly know when he was to go or if he would because plans changed as often as the intermittent rainy weather.

On the path along the chalk cliffs, Bart found a white coiled shell, a part sheared away to reveal the swirled chambers inside, perfectly detailed. He pocketed the fossilized treasure, hoping it was a good omen for his upcoming pilgrimage to France. He hiked to

166

a windswept tree, parked his butt between the exposed roots, and, to be on the higher side of caution, braced his feet on the roots against the sneaky winds. Bart planned to write a quick note home before it was too dark.

However, inspired by the beauty of the drooping sun over the western cliffs of white, now tinged with orange and pink, he let his mind and pen wander.

June 21, 1944

Dear Family,

This is it. I sit here at the farthest edge of England's chalk cliffs, dangling over the dark, gray, stormy English Channel. The sun is aflame as it dies in the west, and the wind oddly blows warmth. The big day has arrived, and I feel my life is about to change; whether that is for the good or the bad, I do not know. I hope for the good. I may get to our homeland after all. I am excited that another member of the Barre Family will return to his ancestral land of France. I shall say hello, Dad! See, I was listening, and I remember your cautionary letter.

I need to tell you some things in case something happens to me. I have a bank deposit box in the Beaumont Savings and Trust, Box 132. I have some war bonds and oil shares, each from Spindletop, Hughes, and one from Rabbit Hill Wells, where I worked a few summers ago. They are probably worth something by now; use them for the girls' schooling.

I also would like it if you could contact a friend, Elise Boulanger, in Baton Rouge, Louisiana, if I should die. We have been pen pals, as you once suggested, and she might want to know. If I should die, please bury me next to my Mother, Charlotte. There should be enough money in my deposit box for a proper headstone, just not a pink or yellow stone, please!

I hate to think of these things, but I guess I have to. I could die tomorrow, and no one would know what to do. Please give my collection of baseball cards and memorabilia to Paul for baby Emile when he grows up. To Jack, give him my collection of National Geographic Magazines, because he likes the pictures. Whatever else there is, throw it away or give it to the charity box at church. I have nothing for my sisters but good thoughts. As for you and Thérèse, I hope that my body will end up back home and you will get a flag like the one Arnelle Guillot received for Louis.

By the way, thanks for sending the clipping about Louis. It saddened me, but I would have never known anyway until I got home. I have lost track of Garrett—he did not transfer with me the last time. I think he has already gone over (FR). Well, I have another letter to write in this brief time that I have. Thanks for your letters and good thoughts.

BB

◆ ◆

English Channel
Sunday, July 9, 1944

Barton's 5th Quartermaster's company, amid thousands of other men as part of the overarching 7th Engineer Combat Company Battalion that included the 5th Army Infantry, left England destined for Normandy. The crossing was terrible, although Barton couldn't gauge what a good crossing might be!

On shipboard, amid the haranguing jokes of men nearby, he heard others moaning and losing their breakfast. Even his buddy, Schmidt, looked green. Barton was unsure if people were seasick or afraid, but he knew he could not take the rolling ship and puked up his meager breakfast. The fear and anxiety of the landing and future battle was something else for him.

He yawned away the lateness of the two previous nights as he had been preparing for the crossing. Roll call, then pack up his gear, muster again, and then ride during the night in a cold, crowded troop transport for two hours. Muster again and march out to command barracks for their briefing. Get kitted out, clean and check armaments, eat, shit, chat, muster, and then crowd again into trucks. One hour later, after a bumpy ride on the western road to the coast, they were boarding a ship and again underway within another two hours, packed like sardines in a can. He already missed the Spartan comforts of Whitcliff Air Base.

The seas at this early hour were heavy, the spray cold and invigorating as he wiped away spittle, hoping he wouldn't vomit again. The skies were still dark to the west, with the flaring, glimmering line to the east like a match just struck. He leaned his head against the bulwark and closed his eyes.

He wasn't sure if he should pray; others were. If he could quickly get to his Bible in his duffle bag, he would, but he gave up on that idea—too much work. Besides, what would he look for there in the Bible? Would he find words of comfort to allay his fear? Or contrition for what he was about to do—take people's lives?

While his father was a man of abiding Christian faith, Barton had never put much stock in religion. However, he did touch the phoenix medallion and dog tags on his chest through his shirt. The family crest might protect him as well as any words, saintly medal, or crucifix. He was a Barre, a man from which legendary heroes sprang. This morning might finally be his chance to show his skills as a sergeant to lead his men and be a valiant warrior and an intelligent and crafty man to survive the ensuing battle. Then again, he might never make it off the ship as he ducked from the explosive spray of water from a nearby shell. Their boat was under fire from the French coast.

He looked across at a man with his head in his hands, quaking and praying. Yeah, this was no way to die—blown up before we could arrive on shore.

Somehow, they made it to a point of rally among other ships.

All the men were nervously filled with excitement and adrenaline, ready to do battle as they left the troop ship. He lost two men, one who had broken an arm trying to climb down the netting into the LST and one who fell into the sea and was crushed between the ship and LST. Already, the day seemed doomed.

The ride in the LST was harrowing, with waves crashing over them, soaking them at every turn. Some men repeatedly called upon God and Jesus, afraid they would sink! Some held each other or clutched their rifles and grinned sickly, trying to be brave.

Bart yelled to his men, "Hey! It's like a roller coaster!" He hoped to offer some levity even though he was afraid, too. The seawater around their feet mixed with the vomitus of frightened and seasick soldiers, yet the men dutifully scrambled from the transport, ready for a fight. Many men were dizzy, affected by the heavy surf, falling down and wading in the deep water to shore. There was no great glory in their arrival! Some conquering heroes!

Barton, too, was nearly run over in the excited rush of men, and he fell into the choppy water. Cursing, he sprang up, unsteady and burdened by his field pack and wet uniform, only to slog through the receding wave dragging at him, his feet buried in wet, soggy sand for every step. The wind whistled through his ears, and the rising sun was in his eyes as he looked up the beach. Damn! The glare was so acute he could barely see the other LSTs and men rushing headlong onto the shores. No one would be able to see or hear the enemy! He wondered where his friend Schmidt had ended up.

Wanting to appear undaunted after falling down, he returned to the ramp and hollered out to the men as they came. "Come on, boys. Make yer mamas proud! Move it, turtles! You're damned targets!" He fell in, taking up the rear as the last of his men came off, goading them along through the surf and beach like a barking sheepdog.

They landed at Utah Beach without much resistance, and he never fired his rifle. He was sickened to see the broken-vehicle-littered, pitted beach. It was blackened in places, with some holes bearing gruesome remains from previous battles. After unloading the vehicles from the LCTs, they were ready to go in the preloaded trucks, carrying all manner of supplies destined for General Omar Bradley's 1st Army and Major General Stafford LeRoy Irwin.

By the late afternoon, with all of them rallied and briefed, the men deployed by the waiting trucks, and some headed inland on foot. Bart was destined for a tiny burg near La Madelaine with a dozen men.

As they drove along, he could smell acrid smoke—a black pall lay over the landscape, along with fiery auras wavering in the distance. "What the hell happened?"

The driver eyed Bart with a narrowed eye. "Shit, you can thank Montgomery for that. The Brits dumped bombs on the coast from Caen to Cherbourg and La Madelaine this morning. It was supposed to root out the Krauts, but they missed—didn't want to hit the troops coming in."

"That would have been us. Holy Crapola." Bart rubbed his face and looked about the devastated countryside.

"What a snafu, huh? They nearly destroyed the whole coast here. If I was a Kraut, I wouldn't want to stay. What's left?" Specialist Joe Frankel grunted as he lit up a cigarette and offered the pack to Barton. "Here ya go. It helps with the smell."

Barton lit up one. His eyes were bleary and watery from little sleep and encrusted with sea salt and sweat—he rubbed it all away. The dismal, hazy scene didn't change—most buildings were nothing but smoking rubble. People crawled through the ruins, searching and bringing out the dead.

"Shit, those aren't Jerries. Those are citizens and little kids! Someone's gonna pay for that one!" Bart stated gruffly and coughed. "Now, I am not so excited to be here. This is a disgusting mess."

"Yup. You can thank yer lucky stars that you are here now with me. Some of the others are heading straight into battle country. They already had a dust-up this morning with a bunch of Polacks wearing German uniforms."

"The Polish? I thought they were our allies!"

Frankel shrugged. "Not all, I guess."

The truck driver in the convoy hastily dumped Barton off at the POL depot before rumbling away with a wave. "See ya later, Sarge," he called out as he drove off.

❖ ❖

The depot looked like a scene straight out of hell. The chaotic activity, noise, and smell of petrol and diesel fumes made his head swim, especially after the rough crossing on the transport ship.

Now Barton swallowed a taste of bile again. He sidestepped a backing behemoth-sized truck loaded to the top rails. Then trudged through the greasy mud and slid a bit to a pair of men, asking them for directions to the CO's command tent. He found his way and reported to the man.

Lt. Col. George Hilliard was the man currently in charge of this depot, and the man before Barton was clearly not him. A very rumpled, oil-smudged Negro specialist sat at the cluttered field desk, a cigarette dangling from his lip, its ash threatening to fall. The man was busy shuffling through a mountain of requisitions.

"Goddamn … where the F is it?" he growled, dropping part of the sheaf of papers on the desk. He shuffled some more and then noticed Barton standing before him. He looked up with a grumpy expression on his dark face. "What the hell do you want?" He suddenly jumped to attention, seeing Barton's chevrons. "Sorry, Sergeant!"

Barton, with a slight wry twist of his lips, saw the colored man nervously twitching, still at attention as he waited for Barton to reply. Bart said in a firm voice, canceling the amusement, "Staff Sergeant Barre reporting for duty. I am looking for Lieutenant Colonel Hilliard. At ease, Corporal."

The man stood down. "Sorry, he ain't here."

Barton gave the man a steely-eyed look. "Where might I find him?"

The corporal took a couple of steps to the tent's doorway and pointed across the busy depot. "See that white tent with the red cross on it? You'll find him there."

"Is he sick?"

"Dead." The corporal said simply. "Shot himself yesterday evening, or so they say. Although, it coulda been a Kraut sniper, too. We still got a bunch of those around." He returned to the desk, shuffled through more papers, and then looked up only to growl. "Don't worry. Hilliard will go home to his wife with all the folderol and pomp of a war hero."

Barton stared. "You aren't joking?"

"No, sir. I don't joke about the dead ever," the corporal said grimly.

"Who *is* in charge around here … you?"

"No, I don't want that headache. That job will probably go to you now, if'n I'm a-thinkin' straight. You are the highest-ranking noncom for now. They seem to come and go a lot." He pulled out two requisitions, perused them for a second, and dumped the rest on the desk.

He went around a pile of crates and paused to say, "Although I never woulda thought Hilliard would take himself out of the picture so soon—been here less than a month." The corporal shook his head. "So I suppose you'll be needin' quarters and all? You can have the colonel's—it'll be cleaned out. The blood, you know."

The garrulous corporal stopped suddenly. He stood up straight, saying, "I forgot to introduce myself. SPC Sherman Feathers the Second; you can call me Squib, though, if'n you want." He saw Bart did not make a move. He juggled the papers in his hands as he headed again to the tent flap.

"You may call me Staff Sergeant Barre. I would appreciate it if you would show me to my quarters and my aides," Bart said stiffly.

"Well, as to your aide, that would be me, yes, siree." He thumbed his chest. "We don't get a lot of time to talk around here; things move mighty fast, so I can't keep the First Army waiting and all."

"You seem to be doing nothing but talking," Barton observed. "So, have you found what you were looking for there?"

The man had a puzzled look for a second and looked at the papers clutched in his hand. "This? Oh, they'll do."

"Then I suggest you get on with your duties. I will walk with you, and you can familiarize me with the depot's layout, my quarters, and who is who. Understood?"

The man grinned cheekily. "Yes, Sergeant! Follow me."

"May I stow my gear here for now?" Barton asked and dumped his duffel bag and field pack on the floor and briefcase on a chair.

"Yes, nobody else will bother it but me and you now." The corporal grinned and set out to lead Barton through the depot and camp.

The man definitely knew his business, Barton grimly acknowledged as he slogged along in the mud, taking mental notes. The special corporal was probably older by a decade than Barton was. However, the short, heavyset man scurried quickly, negotiating past moving vehicles as they deployed. He shouted orders to a few drivers and pointed out certain men who Barton would need to know for their skills. He talked briefly about schedules, oddly pronouncing the word like the British—shed-yule. A few men stopped their tasks, gawking with wide eyes as they passed and caught Bart's fresh chevrons on his sleeve and his air of authority only to mutter to each other.

He was secretly pleased. He actually liked it when men snapped to attention when he came around. Barton even perversely enjoyed the men's comments he overheard once and took it to heart. Barton was an "arrogant asshole with stripes," and yes, this asshole would have the disrespectful lot of latrine lickers cleaning the oil refuse barrels in a second flat if they crossed him.

Barton quietly assessed the men and the chaotic work, noting the messy array of supplies and wondering how they found anything. He was wondering, too, why the colonel had thought it imperative to commit suicide with so much going on around him. The colonel's death was a shock to everyone in the depot and a damned inconvenience, or so Specialist Feathers said.

Barton noticed there were many colored men here and was surprised; he had only encountered a few while in the army here in Europe, and they were usually British. He wondered where Specialist Feathers was from and what his story was; he had a Southern accent, placing him from Mississippi or Georgia.

Barton had an educated southeastern Texan accent colored with his French Louisianan family's patois and a bit of stuffiness from his recent stay with the Brits. His accent was now a muddled mélange, and he could easily fall into any one of them. He had discovered the longer he was in England, the more he sounded like his fellow Brits, including their word usage. Barton had always liked foreign languages and slang, and using the regional and societal vernacular, it said something about the person who spoke. Speaking that way had undoubtedly made it easier to get along with the locals! Daisy Duncan, the barmaid at the King's Garter Pub, had certainly enjoyed Barton's Texas drawl spiced with the Brits slang and his cooing *mots d'amour* of encouragement.

Damn! I never said goodbye to her!

Barton focused again on his aide.

Listening to the corporal, Bart was wondering just how educated his guide was. He knew coloreds were usually in their own units, but occasionally, they were mixed around, especially if they had needed skills. This specialist was definitely skilled in logistics and requisitions and was demanding and persistent. He was garrulous, almost to the point of annoyance. The corporal boastfully was a viable source for gossip; he kept eyes and ears open to everything said and done. Barton thought perhaps 'being in the know' made the man a better aide than most others. He was learning to like Feathers.

There was one major thing that Barton objected to while in the military, and that was to be kept in the dark and out of the loop; he wanted to be in on the up and up and the QT. Most of the time, he had to be resilient enough to make changes at a moment's notice, to swing full circle and accept whatever actions or consequences the ensuing orders would provide, whether Barton thought they were sound, just like waiting out his turn to come across the Channel, each day sitting on needles until the order came.

So far, many of his COs had been impressed by him with his shrewd, discerning manner and his ability to control his men and do their jobs lickety-split. Whether Bart himself felt like the COs assholes with stripes, he always got the job done. People took notice. With Hilliard gone, Barton was wondering if he would write his own ticket up the ranks again. People were often promoted to fill the gaps in wartime.

That night, Bart discovered through the conversations with Specialist Feathers that there were only a few *top brass* above him right now, here in the area, before Generals Bradley and Irwin. He took careful note and decided he would meet them all soon. Even though he was officially under Irwin, he had never met the man.

He also went over the duty rosters with the corporal, including his introduction to his shift teams that night at 2345 and the following day at 0600.

Yawning at the lateness of the day and his heavy, greasy K-Ration meal, he dismissed his aide to let him get two hours of sleep before his introduction. Barton was wondering if it was even worthwhile removing his uniform and decided not to, except for his muddy boots. He lay down on his new cot in his new tent; amid the roaring noise of engines and voices, he took a nap.

◆ ◆

POL Depot near Caumont, Normandy
Monday, July 24, 1944

The following weeks for Barton were a comedy of errors, military snafus, disappointment, and a royal mess, as discovered when the corporal and a French First Sergeant Dominic Flambeaux met with Barton. He felt as if his command was a joke, and someone, somewhere, was laughing at him! This was the first opportunity that Bart had to talk about what was going on, other than fulfilling requisition orders with nearly mindless haste.

During the weeks, he discovered that many of the colored men in the camp were parceled out from the original 4009th Negro unit that had landed first in Normandy to set up the beginnings of the depot sites. As Bart listened to Specialist Feathers, he could understand how the man knew so much, for he had been a part of Operation Overlord since its earliest beginnings.

Barton asked why the pipelines had not been put in, why everything was being ferried around in the five-gallon jerricans, which was in itself a waste of petrol, and why was so much of this stuff stockpiled and still sitting here?

The answers were simple: the original plans were sacked. The Allies were still fighting over Cherbourg and St. Lô and along many of the roads leading away from the coast. With the enemies still occupying the area, the initial pipeline designs had not been run and might never get done. The plan itself had been perhaps a wistful indulgence among the Allied high command with the over-eagerness and assurance that they could easily conquer or push the Germans from the coastal areas.

However, the Germans were still keeping the 1st Army and Allied Forces running back and forth. As of today, rumor along the front had General Bradley pounding the Jerries, seeking an opening from St. Lô. For now, it was easier to deploy what was required as requested with a convoy of trucks. They certainly had enough stockpiled.

"But I thought we were to have POL stations all along the northern coast from here to here by now," Barton fumed, jabbing a finger on the map of France. "I was led to believe we would be dispersing, fanning out, not sitting here with our thumbs up our wazoos. We have hardly moved anywhere! Most of the 5th Infantry has already moved out of the area." Barton glared at Feathers and Sergeant Flambeaux.

Flambeaux made a pinched moue face and rubbed his arched nose. Shrugging in the Gallic way, he spoke stiffly in heavily accented, broken English and French. "I am sorry. I am not familiar with a *wazoo*, and I am equally sorry that the war is not triumphantly moving forward as you like it. Perhaps you would like to speak with *le généralissme*, Le Clerc *ou peut-être* … General Irwin, or Bradley himself? Perhaps you have some secret military skill to bring success, *n'est-ce pas?*" The sergeant all but sneered at Barton.

Barton stifled a rude comment, rubbed his flushed face, and abruptly sat down in his chair. He looked at the two men before him, one frowsy-haired, dark man trying to hide a smirk and the other a light-skinned man with oiled blond hair, a long nose, hooded blue eyes, and wearing *un l'air d'hauteur.*

Barton spoke in his 'flawless French' to the snarky sergeant, surprising the man. "So what do we do? As Lieutenant Colonel Hilliard is no longer with us, and I as yet have no direct orders from anyone above my corporal here, what is the plan?" He did not want to look weak in front of his aide. "I don't want to be pigeon-holed and sitting idly by like a tinhorn ninny."

Squib continued to stifle a laugh.

The sergeant, responding in French, cattily pounced on the point. "Ah *oui*, poor Hilliard—such a waste. They say he received a … what do you say, *un Chèr Jean lettre* … from his mistress no less." The man glanced at Specialist Feathers, who nodded with a wink.

Barton suddenly swung on his aide. "*Dites-moi, est-ce que vous parlez Français?*" (Tell me, do you speak French?) He barked.

"*Oui, Sergeant, je parles tout bien!*" (Yes, Sergeant, I speak it well!) The corporal snapped back and grinned lopsidedly.

"*Merde!*" Barton groaned, and the men broke out laughing.

"Shit." Squib echoed, "You think they'd put an ignoramus out here to deal with these Franks?" he made a rude noise.

"Yes … indeed. *Merci* corporal." Flambeaux's smile was sly as he leaned down and rustled around in an olive-drab canvas bag at his feet, continuing to speak *en Français*. "So, are you of French heritage, Sergeant Barre, or did you just learn our language in school?" He brought out a dark green bottle of wine and set it on the desk before Barton. "Here, we confiscated this from the little group of *Allemands* we captured a few days ago. It should be a nice little wine." He peered at the label. "1937—should be good by now. You take it as my welcome to France, eh?"

Barton took the bottle and, studying it, had a gut-grinding sense of *déjà vu*. There was a red label with a sexy, buxom, dark-haired woman eating grapes with a picturesque view of a vineyard behind her. His family drank this brand. He looked up suddenly. "*Quoi?*"

"You speak French well enough, but it is different, not like these other thick-tongued mutts with their broken, upside-down grammar." He rolled his eyes to the corporal. The sergeant said *en Français* with a sneer and crossed his legs, tweaking at the crisp pleat in his spotless field trousers.

Barton, still staring at the wine bottle, came back to the conversation. "Oh! *Oui*. I am descended from French colonists in Louisiana. We have always spoken French in our home; it's a tradition," he said proudly in French.

The sergeant nodded, sniffing suddenly as if in distaste. "*Ah, les Creoles et les Cajuns!* King Louis's Louisiana. I wish to go there one day. I have heard the food is delicious and the women beautiful."

Barton now could turn the tables. "Ah yes, the food is delicious, as are our women. But we are a spicy and dangerous lot, just like our *saucisse andouille* and alligators, and not to be trifled with." He set the bottle down with a thump and gave the sergeant a steely look, wishing he could tell him to take a flying leap off the short end of a pier.

"*Oui je comprends.*" Flambeaux nodded, understanding and hearing Barton's implied warning. "So you asked what we are to do. For now, I shall let them know that you are in command here, *le maréchal des logis*, and that you will fulfill our requests as they come in. *Tu comprends?* If anything should change, I shall tell you, our little sergeant … how you say, what is up? *Oui?*"

Barton stood up; he put his hands on his hips. "*Oui, Sergeant*," he said stoically, taking the man's diminutive, cutting remarks, careful not to provoke a fight now.

The French sergeant casually remained sitting. He looked up at Barton and waved a hand at the wine. "So I bring you this gift, and after we open it and drink a toast to *our* newly formed *Alliance, I* shall tell you what *you* will give me," he said carefully, his sea-blue eyes coolly regarding Barton.

Barton, not to be easily manipulated but also to understand the possibilities of favors, said *en Français*, "As for the gift, I thank you, but I cannot drink with you. I am on duty. However, I shall save it for another time when you and I can speak more freely. If there is anything that you need and we have, then the corporal can order it up for you."

He glanced at his wristwatch, hiding a smirk because he could tell the man was miffed. Bart then said briskly, "If you will excuse me, I have some details to attend to at this time. Good day, Flambeaux." He spun on his heel, grabbed his helmet and clipboard on the way, and marched out of the tent. Barton did not give the man the honor of saluting or deferring to him; Flambeaux was beneath him. How dare he give orders like that and then ask for favors?—Especially after insulting him as if he were a big dummy or a child.

Barton skirted several pallets of crated new K-Rations and others of barrels of powdered milk and toilet paper being loaded onto trucks. There was something else bothering him, and he could not put his finger on it. The sergeant's attitude was so superior, and Barton hated that. He realized he probably should have been more congenial to the man. His army was in Flambeaux's homeland, fighting for them. Nevertheless, he found the first sergeant irritating, and his implied comments and bribes did not exactly sit well with Bart. Sure, he had done much of the same before at Amstead and Whitcliff to get what was required, but he had been in command then.

Here, he was in command of what—boxes of toilet paper, chocolate bars, field rations, tires, petrol, truck, and vehicle parts, with a bevy of trucks ready to deploy and feed the army or supply them with fuel. He was used to dealing with paperwork, scheduling, training men, and seeing work done. Barton now felt as if he were running an all-night store and gas station. Every order popped up—a sudden requirement to be expedited ASAP. He was tired of putting out all the petty fires of greed and needs.

Somehow, he felt his current command was all beneath him for his education and talents. From everything that he had seen thus far, Barton was a third thumb. His aide, Feathers, could run it all while Bart sat on his wazoo and whistled *The Yellow Rose of Texas!*

♦ ♦

That night, while off duty, Barton took time to reread some of his letters and magazines from home. He had one dog-eared and worn magazine he had not given away. He was reminded of Louisiana as he flipped the pages, looking at the serene photographs of a bayou with trees thick with dripping Spanish moss and slow, eddying currents that belied dangerous waters. Pictures of floating little pirogues and lazy houseboats made him wistful. He had saved the magazine because it was like home, or where he wished it was home—the Barre plantation.

Talking in French to the sergeant had reminded him of home. He only wrote home in French; he had not spoken it with anyone since he had been in the army except in private with Daisy Duncan.

Finding out the corporal spoke French had given him a great shock; even though it was colored with an American Southern accent, at least Feathers was intelligent and bold. Barton silently added another positive mark in the man's favor. That was probably another reason Squib was here—he could speak to the locals.

Barton had observed that the sergeant and corporal had a working relationship, and that pleased him, except that he felt a tiny curl of envy rise to think the men might be friends. He would have to ask Feathers later what Flambeaux ordered. Barton should have stayed and negotiated. What if the man abused his station and took more than was his due or was selling supplies back to his compatriots?

He knew that happened more often than one would expect. Bart's superiors had lectured him and his teams well until they were all sick to hear it. These countries were hurting; the people were losing their homes, their livelihoods, their towns destroyed, and their daily lives upset beyond endurance. They were starving for any handout from the armies as they passed through the cities. For the last year, he had been cautioned never to give away or sell to citizens what was needed for their troops.

Conversely, supplies were always under guard against hungry thieves. Taking a ride out into the country might give him a better perspective on how to deal with this clanking backwater military dump depot.

◆ ◆

Barton rested after supper to update his journal. Lately, he had been so busy that he had been remiss in writing in it or any letters home. He barely had time to fart or think before someone was complaining or bugging him like chattering monkeys.

Wednesday, July 26, 1944

We are finally hearing good news! Following a massive bombardment yesterday from the 8th and 94th USAAC, the 1st Army swept through St. Lô and, in a victorious move, pushed the Germans southeastward. Our 5th Infantry came through St. Lô, then attacked and captured Angers today. It is exciting— the word is we are soon to mobilize now that St. Lô is cleared.

I cannot wait to leave this shitty place. I feel like a chained dog here, unable to move or hardly bark out an order without Squib gawking at me cross- eyed. I want an official command. I'll be happy to leave Flambeaux behind, too; what a prissy smirk he wears—always demanding more than he should. I know we are here to fight for these folks, but sheesh! He's got a bad attitude—he gives us little and takes everything.

◆ ◆

Northern France
August 1, 1944

The First and Third Armies joined forces to create the US Twelfth Army Group and began their sweeping mobile campaign, driving the Germans out of Normandy and Brittany across France to cross the Seine and reclaim Nazi-occupied Paris.

The movements were exhaustive, combative, and costly. Now, under the demand by Pres. Franklin D. Roosevelt, newly reinstated Lt. Gen. George S. Patton Jr., took command of the Third Army, which was composed chiefly of infantry and armored tank battalions. This was a command for which Patton had solid experience once having control of an armored battalion during WWI and then spending years training troops and tank corps just for this day.

In their sweep from Brittany south into Le Mans, his battalions used up nearly 380,000 gallons of fuel per day. Using brilliant tactics of penetrating the German defense from four directions at once, Patton ripped a sizable hole in the French Western Front, thus bypassing the German Seventh Army, which earned Patton admiration and ridicule for his bold, expensive, but reckless plot. The Germans reluctantly retreated, once again scattering their beleaguered troops.

By August 7, the Third Army had exhausted all fuel supplies and sat waiting for more packaged fuel and provisions to come up from the rear. Feeling the invigorating effect of their victories, the Fifth Infantry Division, now a part of Patton's Third Army in the Twelfth, pushed north to capture Chartres on August 10. Using these ill-advised but bold tactics, Lt. Gen. Patton arrogantly continued to command other divisions in his swift, easterly drive across France for another three weeks. Assisted by the Seventh Armored Division, the Fifth Infantry captured Fontainebleau on August 18.

◆ ◆

Barton sat near a dripping fountain among a trampled rose garden. The stone horse was missing its head and one leg. Part of the stone basin was cracked. It had been beautiful until today. He whittled a sharper point on his pencil and then began an entry into his journal.

August 18, 1944

> *Fontainebleau is beautiful, better than any pictures in a history book. I had a little time to make some sketches. Gotta get me a camera—I don't think my drawings do Fontainebleau any justice. I have been somewhere Napoleon slept, kind of, like "George Washington Slept Here!" So much was destroyed, though—trees downed, the gardens trampled. The nearby towns really got clobbered. And I am sure the antiquities were looted already by the Germans. A few rooms I saw in the palace were empty save for the rubble left behind by the enemy. I am sad about the poor treatment, but the Red Devils are victorious today.*

◆ ◆

Dourdan, France
August 20, 1944

Finally, among a contingency of fresh recruits, Barton's Quartermaster Company rolled out to lead the supply convoys and deployments along the Seine River, following in the Fifth Infantry's wake with a small convoy from the Red Ball Express. He left behind his competent aide, Specialist Feathers, to train new men. The Fifth and Bart's quartermasters were initially to overtake Patton's army from the north and, with the Third Army aiding them, would force a small advance into the German territory near the Meuse River. There, Barton and his company, under the new command of Lt. Col. Lee Samuelson, would set up their strategic net of depots, ready to feed and fuel the massive Third Army when they passed through the area.

In a small and perhaps smug way, Barton finally felt he was heading where he should be as part of a new advisory panel to the lieutenant general. Yet, he knew his treatment was not above his men and certainly not above the lieutenant colonel, for they both did much of the grunt work as much as his men did on a daily routine. For that, Barton was glad because it kept him physically fit and prevented him from getting fat and soggy by sitting behind a desk all day, stamping requisitions, and filing inventory sheets. That's what he had staff clerks for, like PFC Peter Dion and young Corporal Billy Meadows.

Barton had another advantage over most of the other men in his company; he spoke fluent French despite Flambeaux's derogatory remarks about Barton's accent. Barton was often brought along to translate for the locals when the army needed supplies or information. He enjoyed scouting out supplies. Lieutenant Colonel Samuelson compared Barton to a truffle pig, able to "sniff out" the goods for the army, and he fondly nicknamed him *Le Cochon des Truffes*, a name Barton despised.

It was on some of the reconnaissance trips through the conquered villages and towns that Barton began to have compassion for the people of France. Even though often their villages were destroyed, the people, like ants after a drenching rain, swarmed around them, frequently welcoming the GIs after the nasty occupancy by the Nazis. Some folks brought baskets of cabbages and fruit and pulled from secret places bottles of wine or aged cheeses or sausages, offering them as rewards or in trade for other coveted things: petrol, cigarettes, or chocolate. Sometimes, women would kiss a GI and make much of them, hoping for extra extravagances, some as simple as lipstick, nylon stockings, and canned or powdered milk for their children.

Barton felt leery of such fickle passions. Recalling his father's letter and the warnings of the *Lapin D'Or* medallion, he steered clear of any such entanglements, preferring to deal only with the men and staying away from such bribery. Seeing how poor and desperate these people were for freedom and eager to recoup their bitter losses, Barton could not offer to help them more than was allowed. He could ill afford to feed the starving masses.

The Third Army was a powerful force to reckon with. And Barton, although he was not uncaring, he was, after all, *un soldat Américain.* Let *Le Croix-Rouge Française* help their people. He was here to do a job and keep Lieutenant General Patton's Army moving!

◆ ◆

August 25, 1944

I read reports that the First Army alone consumed over half a million gallons of petrol in one day for the push across the Seine on the 24th. Today, the Allied Forces entered Paris under the command of French Maj. Gen. Jacques Le Clerc, an action that has seriously annoyed Patton. I am sure it put a dent in his highly polished ego. Everyone is lying low and avoiding the man! God! I doubt the oil in the entire state of Texas could keep Patton's greedy machines fueled. I don't know how we will keep up; so much fuel was spent. It's a nightmare!

Barton stuffed his pencil and diary in his jacket pocket and surveyed the scenery through the dirty, bug-smeared windshield of the truck transport, groaning a bit as they hit another pothole. He was weary already of the daylong trek through the ruined farmland region. He closed his eyes to rest, knowing that as soon as the convoy stopped, he was on duty for another rough night of work.

◆ ◆

August 26, 1944

"At the present time, our chief difficulty is not the Germans but gasoline. If they would give me enough gas, I could go all the way to Berlin!" Lieutenant General Patton bitterly said of the dilemma that his Third Army suffered while he waited for petrol supplies to move forward. The Third Army now had possession of four fronts along the Seine River. Jubilant French citizens met them as the tanks rolled through the small towns following the rapid departure of the German Seventh Army.

Barton could only laugh at the candidness of the audacious general as word came down the line about the strategic victories and chained defeats of Patton's war machine. Yet, the general seemed selfishly oblivious to the needs of the many, still striking out with every division to continue his wild race across France with Germany's borders as the prize!

◆ ◆

Villaneau, France
Sunday, August 27, 1944

The grumbling, heavy cloud cover gave way to a steamy, cold, drenching rain during the night. Barton heard thunder and rolled over in his cot to look at the luminescent dots of his wristwatch propped against a case of toilet paper. He sighed wearily, finding it was after two in the morning, having been asleep for less than an hour. He wound his watch, afraid he might forget in the morning's rush of business. They had made camp hastily last evening, expecting the rain to deluge them at any second and flood out the already mud-mired roads, but it was coming now. He lay for a time, listening to the faraway sounds of straining truck engines and whining gears as the continuing convoy of trucks labored on the muddy roads, coming in to refuel and load before moving past the temporary depot camp.

Regardless of the bad weather, the POL convoy was still in motion, trucking petrol and supplies across northern France to the army divisions. The day had been long, humid, and hot after they crossed the Seine River with minor exchanges of fighting as the Fifth pushed northward. Barton's company was amid the division, so by the time they arrived on the scene, the fight was over, and the trucks rolled through the shattered areas.

He was off shift to sleep now but found himself curiously awake despite his fatigue of an eighteen-hour day. He rubbed his face as a cold drip hit him squarely on the forehead. He picked up a flashlight and shone it on the canvas tent above him.

"Damn, there's a leak!" He got up hastily and moved his cot away from the dripping spot. Suddenly, the rain sounded more like thunder as it hit the canvas tent, sending up a heavy mist and droplets from the ground. He shoved an empty honey bucket under the drip, which was increasing to a noisy pissing sound. Bart rolled back in the cot and pulled up the woolen blanket around his ears, trying to drown out the sound of the riotous rain and the lumbering trucks.

He felt a sense of loss and loneliness for an odd reason. He was nearly alone in the tent, as many of his comrades were on duty, yet hundreds of men in the camp surrounded him. The camp was on half duty—half of the crew resting, waiting for the rain to subside, while a freshly rested crew continued to work around the clock until the next shift. He was on in the morning at 0600. He sighed, thinking he might not fall asleep again, yet wishing he would. He wanted to sleep that dreamless oblivion, easing the aching, bone-tired weariness often imposed on him within moments of crash-landing in his cot.

Tonight seemed different. Barton lay searching the dark tent, wondering if he had forgotten to do something, yet Bart knew he had not. He explored his mind, and for brief seconds, he found fleeting images of people dashing like an elusive deer through the trees.

Elise! How could he have forgotten her? He searched the shadowed memories, seeing her at the dance, sparkling in her sapphire-blue dress, her dark eyes shining up at him, her adorable, mysterious Mona Lisa smile, her tinkling crystalline laugh, the way her slim body felt in his arms as they danced. The Lily of the Valley perfume was always something to remind him of her.

Their troops had passed a wooded field full of flowers some days ago, and the perfumed scent had driven Bart half-mad thinking of Elise Boulanger. He could instantly recall that heady aroma, and visions of her lovely face floated in his mind.

He wondered now why he had not heard from her. It had been months. He had a sudden thought perhaps she was no longer interested in him. Had she found someone else? Barton experienced an inward pull of his guts, feeling sick. Barton did not want to lose that tiny thread to home. The letter written in June probably sounded morose, and he had said goodbye, but that was in case he died! It was no wonder he felt a sense of loss; he had not had a letter in months—from anyone. Then Bart foolishly realized it was his own fault. He had never written back to anyone after the last letters in June. People probably thought he was dead!

His summer had flown by quickly, burned by the sun, drenched by rain, covered in mud and stinking petrol. His days flowed together with hardly a notice or a way to remind him of their passing other than his infrequently written journal and that he was painfully still alive. Once they were mobile, they had a few narrow escapes and skirmishes along the battle-torn roads. There were still snipers about and a few odd squads of the Germans who were reluctant to leave. Daily, as the convoys moved along the back roads of France, they were sitting ducks for potshots, and yet somehow, most of the trucks and the men survived. It was the long-distance guns and the *Luftwaffe* that harried them the most.

The trucks, though, were suffering. The constant running of the engines wore them out, and the requisitions for replacement parts and tires were nearly as exhaustive as the required petrol supplies. Yet the men kept plugging along. Some men, though, were sick of the long days and hours on the roads. Sometimes, just to take a break, weary drivers radioed ahead with news their truck was stuck in the mud or had mechanical problems.

Barton's company kept close records of maintenance while trying to keep their trucks running, and a few men had been punished for such lies. However, the lieutenant colonel was sometimes lenient because he understood the vagaries that befell them. But he, too, was a harsh taskmaster, pushing their company forward at a fast pace, gleaning and gathering what supplies they could as they went, all for the army and their victorious glory in their belabored march across France.

Barton did not care for lies and sneak thieves. From time to time, as they came through an area, the locals begged for anything they could use or eat, and when the convoys stopped, extra guards were put on to keep watch over the supply trucks. Some of the villages were sadly empty, and Barton now thought of them as his mind wandered over the past month of his travels through France from the landing at Utah Beach to the destroyed towns of La Madelaine and Caumont, then along the roads to Chartres and bypassing south away from Paris and into the Marne Valley.

He was starving after the long trek but for a different and spiritual food—the food of home and the love of someone special. Barton decided to write a letter to his family and Elise the next day. Even though he had said goodbye, he could not let the girl go that easily. Elise was in his blood.

Barton rolled over in his cot, the wood and canvas creaking under his weight, and tried to sleep. Fields of white flowers beckoned to him, and for a fleeting second, he could smell them … and her. He chased that dream to its end.

◆ ◆

Charly-sur-Marne, France
Sunday, August 27, 1944

Skirting that morning's battlefield, which lay smoldering with broken and blasted machinery, Barton viewed it all with a sick stomach. An overturned enemy supply truck, empty troop transports, and numerous lines of dead men lying in the mud as if on exhibit proved that the Americans had won. Battle-weary, smoking Sherman tanks sat like guard dogs on the road, their men loading on fresh ammunition and fuel and clearing out the muddied tank treads. They bypassed ranks of captured German infantry, marching along the road in defeat, guarded by US soldiers and trucks. Bart was not proud of his men as they jeered the enemy soldiers and threw things at them. It seemed like an inane and petty act to Bart, especially after viewing the battlefield carnage on what should have been a beautiful Sunday morning. His father's words twisted in his mind: "There is no beauty or genuine victory in war. It is an illusion ..."

After some hours, the convoy, led by a reconnaissance escort, swung northeast again, this time headed for the infamous town of Château-Thierry, where, in 1918, a horrible many months-long battle had ensued.

Barton glanced at the cloth map and grew excited. This was the area where his father had fought so gallantly with the AEF. In a way, he could not believe that his journey would actually take him there—maybe it was his fateful destiny. He pulled out a pencil and the journal from his jacket pocket, ready to jot down or sketch what he saw.

As it grew into the evening, Barton glanced about the countryside to see broad expanses of uncultivated and neglected fields bordered by thick, dark forests and broken fences. The few houses dotted along the land were destroyed and empty ruins. He spied dead cattle and horses in a few bombed-out places.

Barton sadly felt his father's story rise like a ghost from the past. He squinted against the bright, hazy sunlight lying low upon the horizon, capturing the image in his mind like a snapshot photo. Bart would never be able to describe what it was really like or paint the scene properly, but he thought the land was hauntingly beautiful. He breathed deeply the invigorating scents of cedars and pines, a cloying tang of perhaps old spoiled vineyards and fallen fruits, all peppered by the dust of destruction and the road—so much waste when many were starving, including him. Bart patted his growling belly and drank some stale canteen water to still it. He stuffed an already-chewed wad of gum in his mouth and tossed out the foil wrapper, thinking it would fool his stomach. After a few minutes, he found the gum was hard and rubbery with no flavor; he spat it out.

He made a couple of quick sketches of a ruined house as the convoy slowed and stopped for a minute but was dissatisfied with his efforts and put his notebook away. He watched as the men clambered back onto the trucks ahead after checking for survivors or enemies, wishing that he had gone. He needed to pee.

Barton relaxed against the hard seat of the Jeep and closed his eyes; the sun was harsher now as it began its descent over the low-lying hills and forest to the west. Even with his eyes closed, he sensed the slanted, fading red heat on his neck.

Then, after a time, the sensation passed as the road curved, and he felt a chill go through his body. Shuddering briefly, Barton pulled his jacket on as they passed a shaded pond, stirring up some geese and a swan pair. They passed through an avenue of tall, shadowy trees. The convoy's dusty wake sparkled in the last light of the dying sun, and he coughed, feeling bone-dry from the hours spent on the road behind lumbering vehicles.

He could definitely go for a cold drink, like a beer! However, as he looked about the dimming landscape, he knew there would be no chance of such a luxury. There was most likely not a town anywhere near for miles; he peered at the map and couldn't see much in the darkening twilight, just dots and snaking lines, which looked confusing from his point of view in the jouncing Willy Jeep. He could swear they had passed the same pond earlier.

Barton readjusted his helmet; it had been rocking on his skull and giving him a dreadful headache. He could smell himself and knew he stunk from travel weariness, worn-out adrenaline, and an unbathed body. He hated to stink; he hated feeling gritty and dirty—never had liked it much, even as a kid. He glanced at his hands, saw the dark line of grime rimming his short, bitten fingernails, and was repulsed.

How much longer would they be on this uncivilized donkey trail? He wondered if they were going anywhere close to Château-Thierry. Would he be able to see it, or would they pass through it in the night?

He passed a hand over his unshaven cheeks, rubbing his skin briskly to stay awake. They had been on the move for two days, making temporary camps along the way, and Barton's ears ached and rang from the incessant whine of the vehicles' engines around them. He tasted the dirty grit in his teeth and felt as if his kidneys and bladder might burst from the rough ride and the long hours with only a few ten-minute breaks interspersed throughout the day. Lieutenant Colonel Samuelson was driving them hard and fast. Bart thought Patton might have an enviable comrade in the terse and regimented colonel.

He glanced at the corporal who was driving; the man had a determined and grim look on his face as he tried to see the road ahead with the dim slits of light emanating from the Jeep's covered cat's-eye headlights. Ahead, Barton saw only a vague shape lumbering ahead, with tiny slits for taillights.

They were still in enemy lands and were essentially in a blackout mode of travel. Usually, the Red Ball convoys could run with full lights; it kept the accidents down, but they weren't following those orders tonight. The lieutenant colonel was sure they were all in grave danger. Looking behind him, Barton could see a shadowy truck with just the headlights covered, tiny slits made a weak beam of light, but he could see the dim glow of the dash instruments on the tense driver's face. Everyone looked dead tired, just as he felt.

He still needed to pee. Barton shifted uncomfortably on the hard seat. His aide, Private Dion, was curled asleep on the back seat as if nothing was going on. Next to Dion, Corporal Albert Rossini, leaning with his chin on a hand and resting against his M1 carbine, sleepily watched the dark countryside. Barton yawned and watched ahead and then broke the silence.

"Do you know how much longer we are to be going? Don't we need to stop soon to refuel?"

Cpl. Ed Danvers glanced at the gas gauge and then at Barton. "I don't know, Sergeant, but I hope it's soon. We got only an eighth of a tank left. Although I think we are getting close, we've been slowing down for some time now. It's hard to tell, though, with these damn cat eyes."

"Well, that's because it's dark now." Barton snorted. He glanced out at the wooded area. "I haven't seen a farm or town for miles now."

"Do you know where we are on the map?" Danvers asked.

Barton squinted at the folded map. "Uh, I did a while ago, but I can't see the damn thing now in this black void. It feels weird, like a spook house." He shuddered as he looked about the surreal dark forest landscape—everything loomed up large near the roadway while the rest of the trees were eerie-lurking monsters.

"Yes, sir, it does." The corporal nodded. "Real creepy-like. I never did like those dark tunnels or haunted houses at carnivals." Danvers shivered as he looked up a bit to the trees. "I keep thinking that some Kraut is going to jump out and shoot at us."

"Well, it could happen, although I think we wouldn't be the first ones they'd shoot. This convoy is half a mile long, and we are in the middle of it. I think we'd know by now if something like that happened." Bart gave a quick snort of a chuckle.

"Oh, yeah … that's right. Sorry, my mind is playing tricks, I guess. Every tree or bush looks like something!" Cpl. Danvers grinned sheepishly.

"That's all right. We always must be on guard, and the more eyes on the road, the better," Bart commented wisely and sighed.

"So, where were we headed the last time you saw the map?" Danvers asked as he jerkily maneuvered around a large pothole in the road. "I swear we are going in circles. But then, these trees all look the same."

"Well, it looked like Château-Thierry, but that was some time ago. We might have already bypassed it."

"But I didn't see a town." Corporal Rossini piped up. He yawned and sat up straight, wiping his face. "It's a big city, right?"

"Well, it certainly isn't like New York City!" Barton said snidely and shook his head. "I have no idea what it is except a famous place. My old man was there in the Great War."

Rossini leaned forward. "Oh … yeah? When was that?"

"The summer of 1918. My dad was with the AEF and fought here. It was a pivotal battle in the outcome of the war," Bart said with sage aplomb, proud now of his father's involvement.

Rossini nodded, looking impressed. "Wow. So, did he make it out alive?"

Barton glanced at the youth with wry disbelief. "Well, I think he did. I am proof that he made it home."

Dion, now awake, slapped Rossini on the back, scaring him. "You ignoramus! How would Sarge be here if his father died?"

Rossini shrugged. "I dunno. There are lots of kids that don't have fathers who got killed in the wars."

Barton grinned, amused at the naïve pair. "True, but I am not that old. I'm only twenty-one."

Dion nodded and sat back against the seat. "I told ya, Al. He's almost one of us, just a baby face!"

Rossini sat back, too. "Yeah, well, how'd he get so far up then?" he asked Dion, jeering.

Barton smiled to himself but answered for Dion. "I keep my ears and eyes open and followed orders—that's how. Now shut your traps, or you'll let the Germans know we are out here."

"Ha! With these noisy trucks, they gotta know anyway!" Rossini griped loudly.

"Stow it." Barton gritted. He turned about in his seat and sat for a time, eavesdropping on the whispered conversation between the younger men.

PFC Peter Dion was from Champlain, Illinois, and he reminisced about good restaurants and jazzy places to dance. Cpl. Albert Rossini, who called Chicago his home, talked about his family's restaurants and missing the food and his mother. They were both nineteen now, and Dion had joined up with aspirations that he would see the world and have exciting adventures. Barton nearly laughed at that remark but kept any derisive comment to himself.

Young Rossini said that he left home wanting to show up to his old man, who thought him a worthless, wimpy kid. Bart cast a quick look back to see that both of the men were small, skinny, and hardly looked their age. He wouldn't be surprised if they had both lied when they enlisted. Rossini still had acne, and his voice had a tendency to get squeaky, sometimes rising to a high falsetto when excited. If Barton didn't laugh at him, he only found the Mickey Mouse voice annoying after a time.

Peter Dion, conversely, was soft-spoken, sometimes shy and quiet, but he was obedient and so far had proven to be a decent and competent office aide to Barton. He was almost a pretty version of Rossini, with cherubic features and dark, large, liquid eyes and curly black hair. Unfortunately, Sergeant Schmidt got a look at the kid and dubbed him Pretty Dolly—the moniker stuck.

Rossini had thin lips, bad buckteeth, and a long Modigliani nose, which he had yet to grow into. The youths were buddies after they went through training together. They were sort of bookend friends—where one began, the other left off. Both had wry and silly wisecracking senses of humor; they seemed to like dirty practical jokes and tried to make a bad situation better by finding something funny about it. Barton thought, at times, they were like his brothers, the twins, always cutting up.

The first time Barton witnessed the Illinois pair in battle, he noticed Dion was an excellent shot, and the kid kept ribbing Rossini that "he must be cross-eyed and blind if he couldn't see the Krauts in the trees looking like baboons with targets on their asses." Rossini had been smug afterward and said that Dion was only there because he was his fairy godmother. That had gone on for a big laugh, but Barton had not entirely caught the joke. Still, he could tell they were devoted as friends.

Barton was too often reminded of his own brothers Paul and Jacques, who were once upon a time a wild and inseparable pair. Bart had a pang of longing for home and even missed that camaraderie with the mischievous Guillot brothers.

Barton now began to feel ill at ease, tired of the lumbering engine noise and the banter from the backseat, and he was now urgently hungry on top of really needing to pee! Angrily, he slid down in the seat and covered his eyes with the helmet brim, hoping to ease the pressures of it all and catch a few well-deserved Zs.

Some time passed, and Barton had drifted off to a somewhat quieter plane of existence when he was jolted awake and nearly slid off the seat. He grabbed the dash and sat up; pushing his helmet in place, he glanced about at the still-dark road and then glared at his driver.

"What in the hell are you doing? Give a man a warning, will you?"

Danvers put the vehicle in neutral with the brake on, the engine idling roughly. "Sorry, Sarge, but we have stopped. Do you want me to see what's going on?"

Barton stretched, easing his back and cramped leg muscles as he turned to get out. "No, I'll do it. You all stay here." He climbed out, walking stiffly, and crossed in front of the vehicle to go alongside the supply truck ahead.

"Hey! Bailey!" He called up to the driver. "Where are we?"

Corporal Skip Bailey looked down from the cab and peered into the dark. "Oh, Sarge, hey. Don't know, but I think we are stopping for the night. Somebody ahead said there's a roadblock or somethin'. Do you want me to radio up and find out?"

"No, stay put. I'll go." Barton patted the dusty door and stepped away. After a quick assessment of the area, he veered off into the shrubbery at the road's edge, glad for the stop so he could take a leak. Feeling much improved, Barton trotted along the convoy. The trucks began to shut down as he passed by, and he knew that something was up. He finally came even with Samuelson's vehicle and rapped on the door.

The colonel opened the door and let Barton step up on the running board to lean in.

"We are stopping here for the night. Colonel Rice's demands, not mine. I would rather continue," Samuelson explained. "We need to refuel and get some food, then let recon scout ahead before sunup." He shone a flashlight on his watch. "Hell, it's no wonder that my stomach's complaining—it's nearly midnight. Tell your men to shut down; we should be safe enough here for the time being. Sorry we didn't quite make it to somewhere civilized, but these roads have been more treacherous than we were led to believe. Tell everyone to stay in the black, no lights or fires, and to keep quiet—no radio chatter! There are still pockets of resistance ahead. The Armored Division had a fracas a couple of hours ago with some of the Krauts' Seventh. They sabotaged the road and took out some trees. We'll have to clear them in the morning when we can better see." Samuelson yawned widely and thumbed his watering eyes. "Excuse me … but go see to your men. Pass the word if you will."

Barton nodded. "Yes, sir. Anything else?"

"No, just try to get a little sleep if you all can. It might get ugly tomorrow morning if the Fifth Armored hasn't cleared the way for us, but I have confidence that Rice will rout out the rats. We are not that far from Reims, and I think we have just been damned lucky so far. Keep on the watch. Dismissed." He edged toward the door and gestured, shooing Barton away.

"Yes, sir." Barton made a brief salute and climbed down from the vehicle; he shut the door quietly and trotted back the way he came along the road, passing the word.

The men began to climb down off the trucks, and a few snagged Barton. "Sergeant, do we make camp here? Are we setting up a depot?"

"No. Stay with the trucks. Pull rations and make sure everyone gets fed in your unit. Nobody is to wander away; stay by the road. The trees have eyes and ears. We'll pull out at dawn. Pass the word."

The group began to mill about, yawning and clumsy from the long hours and lengthy drive, yet they warily went about their business.

Barton arrived at his Jeep and found Dion and Danvers lounging against the vehicle, sharing a cigarette.

Danvers popped up, trying to look alert in the face of a giant leonine yawn. "What's up, Sarge?" He finished and rubbed his eyes.

Barton pulled out his canteen and drank. "Keep close to the road and our vehicles." He said between long sips. "We'll sleep in the Jeep. Go ahead and heat up our dinner."

Dion ran off to a supply truck behind them but came back quickly bearing packages. He showed them to Barton. "These are chicken noodle soup, and this one is beef stew. Which one do you want?"

"I'll take the stew. Thanks." Barton followed Dion to the front of the Jeep while Danvers started the engine again. Dion yanked up the hood and propped it up with a stick. They put the cans on the engine manifold to melt the congealed grease. Barton pried open the tins of peaches and one of the biscuits. He ate one biscuit, swallowed it dryly, and then sipped his water. The men stood about the engine, waiting patiently for the food to heat. Barton glanced about and saw others doing the same in the front and rear trucks; some were eating their food cold, not caring that the food was greasy and lumpy.

"Where did Rossini get to?" Barton asked suspiciously.

Blowing his nose loudly, Dion finished and answered. "Oh, Sergeant Schmidt and Wells pulled him for night watch." He yawned. "I told them I slept some and could go, but Schmidt said no." He shrugged. "Don't make a diff with me." He sniffed the bubbling cans. "I think we can eat this stuff soon." He pulled a packet out of his jacket pocket. "Here, I got us some chocolate, too, and this can of milk. I thought we could have cocoa." He smiled up at the men.

Barton grinned at the thoughtfulness of the young aide. "See, things like that get you somewhere." He produced a silver flask from his jacket. "And I have a tot we can add to the mix before we sleep." He winked at the men, who were looking shocked. "Sh, only a drop—we still gotta be on our toes tonight."

Danvers and Dion nodded enthusiastically and crowded around, waiting to serve up their meal and get their drink.

"I think the Sergeant likes us," Danvers said to Dion when Barton walked away with a cup of soup for Rossini.

"Yeah, he isn't all that bad, sort of a big dog with a loud bark. But if you pet him the right way, he'll like you." Dion smiled into his metal cup of cocoa. "I like working for him even though he is usually a crabby crankpot."

Danvers loudly slurped his soup, sucking in a mouthful of rubbery noodles. He nodded. "Yep, Sarge can be right friendly at times. Most of the guys don't know him like we do; they think he is a big snotty blowhard."

Dion smiled again. "Yeah, and that's on his good days."

◆ ◆

August 28, 1944

The men put the canvas top up on the Jeep and curled up to sleep the few hours remaining of the night. All too soon, the sun poked intrusive fingers through the trees and awakened them to the tune of a warbling bird.

Barton stretched, coughed, and spat outside the vehicle. He looked about to see the dark shadows of the dense forest about them, although dust motes sparkled like tiny diamonds in the early pearl-pink glow along the roadway. Climbing down from the jeep, he stretched, feeling his bones and muscles snapping and complaining from the uncomfortable night spent sleeping in the Jeep seat. He stepped along the road and passed into some dark underbrush to do his morning constitutional, noting another man finishing his job. The guy sheepishly tossed Bart an almost empty roll of toilet paper as he exited the shrubbery nearby.

Bart felt better after the short walk and relieved his body. He climbed up the ditch to the road and set off for the lieutenant colonel's vehicle. Men along the way were rising, their voices muffled in the early dawn; some echoed slightly in the forest. It felt good to be out here this morning—the air was fresh, there was a delicate cool breeze, and he could hear a gurgling rivulet of water somewhere nearby. Birds were singing and flitting from the trees. He wished he could walk farther into the tranquil woods for some solitude, but duty and wariness called him back.

He found Samuelson up, drinking a mug of coffee while perusing his map and orders, already shaved and looking fresher than Bart felt. Leaning against his truck, he waved to Barton, smiling. "Ah, another early riser—glad to see it."

"Yes, sir." Barton winked and blinked, rubbing sleep from his eyes. "The coffee smells good."

193

Samuelson nodded. "It is. Have some. Come, I want to show you where we are," he stated, unfolding the map onto the bumper of the truck.

Barton poured out a steaming cup of the black brew and took a wary sip; it was as oily and harsh tasting as the motor oil they poured into the trucks' engines! He drank it anyway. He stepped back to look at the map.

"You see, we crossed that creek last night and took this turn. Then, about ten last night, we veered northwest about four kilometers, so we are now about here." He pointed to a curve on a map with a snaking dotted line.

Barton shook his head, silently noting that they had been going in circles last night, lost in the dark. "Hey, we did bypass Château-Thierry!" Barton said, surprised. "Dang it."

"Yes, there was a pocket of resistance. Colonel Rice radioed that we should either stop and wait for them to clear it or bypass it altogether."

"I wanted to see the town."

"Really." The lieutenant colonel eyed Barton curiously. "Are you a man of history? Interested in seeing the battlefields nearby?"

Barton nodded. "Yes. My father fought there in 1918. I wanted to see what it was like."

Samuelson smiled. "Ha! There is something we have in common! Both my father, the colonel, and my uncle, a captain, fought in France. Not quite sure where, though." He idly rubbed his pursed lip with a finger but then continued. "Well, it is pretty much like this. We are in the Belleau Woods and will come out on the road over here; that is after Armored has cleared the way." He pointed at the map.

Samuelson then gazed about the forest road. "It certainly is pretty, such a pity to have a war in a place like this. There was probably some good deer hunting around here before the war." He mused aloud. "Hear that? A woodpecker is already at work." He cocked his platinum-blond head in the direction of the tapping sound, then, hearing a raucous laugh from the road, he snickered. "So are the cuckoos."

"Yes, sir." Barton idly missed the joke and peered at the map. "Sir, I have a question."

"Proceed," Samuelson answered as he sipped his coffee.

"Is it possible that we might stop somewhere around Soissons?"

"Yes. I believe that is our objective today."

"Are we stopping or passing through?"

"A division of the Seventh is supposed to rendezvous with us near there. We'll stay a few days to take on extra provisions and then meet up again with the rest of the Fifth after they have cleared Reims."

Barton, nearly crowing with glee, said, "Oh, well, I am glad about that."

"Why is that?"

Barton sniffed, feeling remiss to say the truth of his personal quest, so he pressed on logically. "Um, well, I was thinking it would be a good place that we could get a little rest and maybe have a bath since we missed Château-Thierry."

The colonel laughed aloud now, clapping a hard hand on Bart's shoulder, "You are an unusual fellow, Barre. Yes, we might be able to do that. But before that, we have a bit of work this morning. Get your men up and ready for the day. I mean to be on the move soon by 0615; the day is wasting."

◆ ◆

By August 28, Patton's army was reined to a snail's pace after finding their fuel allocations fell short again by hundreds of thousands of gallons. The Red Ball Express, begun by the 4009th Quartermasters unit in the early days of the invasion, had become a nonstop convoy supply train of over six thousand trucks, linking the forward-moving armies with the supply depots in Normandy. However, the supply train was falling short and could not range far enough or fast enough to keep all Allied military forces and Lieutenant General Patton supplied simultaneously.

On August 31, Patton's powerful army came to a grinding halt, exhausting all supplies. Sitting just the other side of the Meuse River, Patton was angry about the halt now as General Eisenhower allowed for fuel to be deployed to the northernmost forces under the command of Gen. Montgomery, Gen. Omar Bradley, and Lt. Gen. Courtney Hodges, thus forcing Patton to sit on his thumbs while wanting to enter the Lorraine Valley first in his bold plan.

While waiting for fuel, Patton's division depleted their large-caliber artillery ammunition during several skirmishes with the enemy. This caused a shortage, which was not easily replaced. Hitler's forces seized the opportunity and sent more troops into the area, hoping to push Patton back or defeat him. For the following weeks, Patton fought long and hard in the Metz area; it would be some of the bloodiest months of the battles to date since the invasion on June 6th while still making insignificant advances into the German defense. Food rations, clothing, ammunition, and petrol were short while the Red Ball Express continued to serve the Allied Forces up north for a pincer-like attack, pushing the German defensive eastward, back over the Belgium and German borders.

Patton, a clever and brilliant strategist, discovered through his charge through France that much of the French Railroad west of the Seine River was still viable. Employing some rail lines, he was able to move supplies into areas previously unreachable by the convoys. He finagled and bartered with French businesses and industries to provide supplies and repairs for his machines of war. Then, using confiscated German supplies and munitions when they won a battle, Patton began to restock his depleted army's supplies. On some days, the Germans were bombarded by their own artillery. Using the Third Army as a base depot, Patton continued to amass whatever supplies, petrol, and munitions he could and made a battlefront from his almost stationary post. No one would stop the indomitable old blood-and-guts Patton from winning this war!

◆ ◆

By the end of August, the overarching plans of Operation Neptune and Overlord officially came to a halt. Most of the objectives were achieved earlier than expected during the ninety-day invasion operation, which initially was to push the Germans away from the coast and beyond the Seine River. By July 24, the Americans began Operation Cobra, which was to take command of Northern France from their breakout after the beach landings. By August 25, the liberation of Paris by Le Clerc and the Allies was achieved, and by August 30, the last German troops were pushed beyond the Seine River.

New plans were begun to push the Germans out of France and into Germany.

During these months, from D-Day to the middle of August, over 2 million Allied troops, hundreds of thousands of vehicles and trucks, and half a million tons of supplies landed on the beaches of Normandy. In all, losing troops and material was significant, with 209,672 casualties, 36,900 killed in action, 153,475 wounded, and over 19,000 missing. American troops alone lost nearly 21,000 lives, 90,000 wounded, and over 10,000 missing in action. Losing 4,101 airplanes and almost 17,000 airmen who were killed or lost during Operation Overlord. Over 4,000 tanks were destroyed during this operation.

The French lost many citizens in these actions during the preliminary bombings prior to the invasion and the breakout from Normandy, losing over 20,000 persons. Many of these lives were lost in the ill-fated Calvados region after Montgomery's Allied bombing on July 9 and the Falaise Pocket operations.

Of the German resistance in these areas, from D-Day to mid-August, nearly 500,000 lives were lost. In the push across the Seine, where the German Seventh

Army was encircled by Allies and US troops, they suffered 10,000 killed in action, with 50,000 troops taken prisoner. Overall, much of their western and northern forces had been decimated by aggressive plans and cunning Allied Generals, such as Eisenhower, Patton, Bradley, Montgomery, and Le Clerc. With a loss of so great a territory, too many lives lost, and armaments low, leaving the Germans a tenth of their Panzer tanks, the Third Reich suffered near defeat as they hightailed it east to the borders of Belgium and Luxembourg. Hitler quickly pulled troops from campaigns in Russia, Poland, and Italy to fill in the gaps.

❖

CHAPTER 9

My Far Away Home

Baton Rouge, Louisiana
Wednesday, July 12, 1944

There were industrious rustlings, thuds, shuffling noises, and an oddment of items chucked out from inside the closet. Curious about the noise, Beatrice approached the closet warily and ducked as a wad of clothing flew out and landed in a heap across the room. Chérie was on Elise's bed but not out of range from the flying objects, as evidenced by a shoe, several sweaters, and a muffler tossed on the bed. Chérie, always the opportunist, nestled in the muffler with a content smile on her petite muzzle. Beatrice patted the little dog and stepped toward the closet.

"What is this mess, Elise?" Beatrice demanded and pulled the string for the overhead closet light.

There was a short, muffled scream, and Elise rose out of the dark depths, clutching a jumble of things in her arms. "Mother! You scared the daylights out of me!" she accused and backed out of the closet.

Beatrice stood now, her arms akimbo. "So, to what occasion do we owe this enthusiastic activity?"

Elise dropped the armful of clothes on the bed and flopped on the edge, bouncing Chérie. The little dog complained with a grunt. "I cannot find something." She had worry lines over her slim eyebrows.

Beatrice sat on the edge of the bed beside her daughter, scooping up Chérie into her lap. "Well, can you tell me what it is? Perhaps I have seen it. Maybe I have washed it, or it could still be hanging on the clothesline outside." She logically suggested.

Elise fidgeted and looked down at her nervous fingers. "It is not clothes, Mother." She flung her hands at the closet and room. "I have looked everywhere, and while it shouldn't have been in there, I looked anyway." She let out a short, defeated breath. "It's lost, or Elaine has taken it." Her voice dropped, and she was muttering.

Beatrice thought her daughter looked too upset for something minor, even though everything these days was an emergency or an 'I-have-to-have-it or I'll die' kind of

198

situation with Elise and Elaine. However, she had to admit that Elaine was more prone to tantrums and theatrics than Elise was. Therefore, with those thoughts in mind, Beatrice felt this was something important. She put her arm around Elise's slim shoulders and pulled her nearer.

"Tell Mama what is missing. Maybe Chérie and I can help you find it. Why the mystery, hmm?" She scrunched Elise to her side and made her giggle.

Suddenly, a tear escaped down Elise's cheek.

Beatrice knew but asked, "Is this perhaps something to do with a boy?"

Elise jerked her head up, and with eyes wide, she wondered aloud. "How did you know? Did Elaine tell you something?"

"Now, what would Elaine have to tell me that you cannot?" Unclipping a dangling barrette, Beatrice smoothed back the wild ebony curls and tamed them with the barrette.

"It's just that I am missing a letter. I thought maybe Elaine might have taken it to spite me."

"Oh, spite now. Are you two quarreling again?"

Elise turned to her mother, now renewed in her minor troubles. "You see, we have been writing to a fellow who is fighting in Europe, and yesterday she accused me of stealing him and—"

Beatrice drew back, alarmed. "You have been writing to a soldier? Oh, Elise, *ma pauvre p'tite agneau.* You shouldn't pin your hopes on some heartbreaker like that. Oh, Papa will be disappointed in you."

"It's not like that, Mama! Besides, Elaine has three others she writes to all the time!" Elise stood up and began to pace as she spoke. "Remember last year when Elaine and I went to visit Nettie in Brusly? Well, her daughter Becky invited us to go to a cotillion. Actually, it was just a big dance to welcome in summer and get donations for the war. Elaine was excited to go because Peter Starkey was going. She wore her best dress too—you know … the yellow one with all the lace ruffles."

Beatrice gave a little laugh and sat back more comfortably on the bed, pushing aside the clothing. "What dress of Elaine's doesn't have ruffles?"

Elise continued to pace about the room, her hands fluttering as she explained. "True! Anyway, Elaine was upset because he came with another girl. Elaine was crying, and then there was a most handsome, very nice young gentleman who got her to stop crying, which you know for Elaine once she starts it is a—"

"Flood!" They both ended together with a laugh.

Elise giggled. "Yes. The young man was so charming and friendly that he nearly swept her off her feet. He took her dancing just to make Peter jealous. It worked, too."

"I see. Very interesting, so why am I only now hearing about this *ma fille*?" Beatrice asked in her best should-I-be-a-concerned-mother tone.

"Oh! Well … I agreed not to tell you and Daddy what Elaine did. I won't either." Elise gave a sly look at Beatrice. "It's not that bad, but we agreed."

"Hmm … I suppose this has to do with the young gentleman then. Was she seen kissing him or something?"

Elise looked shocked. "No! Oh, no! She dumped him on me and danced with positively everybody. She and Becky were positively big flirts, Mother! It was shameful!" She said emphatically and flopped on the bed beside her mother. Elise giggled, realizing what she'd done. "Oops, I just blabbed anyway."

"Isn't Elaine always a flirt?" Beatrice was glad to know it was nothing too serious.

Elise nodded. "Yes, but she was disgusting, and I think she was rude to Barton, who was kind to her. She did not speak to either of us the entire evening until the end of the dance."

"Oh … well, if that is all, why all the fuss and bother? She has had at least four or five beaus since last summer, and Tommy Vance twice renewed. Now there is this *charmant* one, Terrence. He might be a keeper, although Daddy doesn't like him much."

Elise nodded with some eye-rolling. "I know. She was going to tell you and Daddy that I was dancing with Barton and a very naughty soldier. But with the threat of my telling you about her indiscreet flirting, she clammed up." Elise shrugged. "I know it is blackmail, but it worked."

"Well, it is over now," Beatrice said with a calm tone she did not feel. The girls just might turn her hair white overnight with their antics.

Elise continued, now wringing her hands nervously. "It's not really over. The young man went into the army the very next day. He was happy to make my acquaintance, and he—"

Beatrice, alarmed now, said snippily, "Well, of course he would. You were lucky to have escaped with only a dance or two! That is it; you are not allowed to go out with Elaine! She is too old for you and drags you into bad situations. She does not take care of you as she should." Agitated, Beatrice stood up and replaced Chérie on the bed.

Elise stood again and stamped her foot, irritated. "But, Mother! I can take care of myself! And Barton is not like that! In fact, he was very kind. He introduced me to his family, too. They were all there. I danced with his father—ooh … a very tall and handsome fellow. All of his family are just beautiful—the men dark and handsome, and the women all very lovely. Did you know he has two brothers and three sisters?"

Beatrice began folding up some of the articles of clothing, not liking this conversation. "Really! Well, how could I know anything about them, as you have only mentioned them all?" Beatrice gave her emotional daughter a worried look. "It's all right, my dove, come here."

She gathered Elise and petted her, noticing that her daughter no longer fit comfortably within her arms and bosom. "You are a big girl, I know, and more responsible than even Elaine."

"That's not saying much, Mother." Elise quibbled with an affected sniffle.

Beatrice snuggled to breathe the warm, youthful scent of her daughter. "It is fine. So what of this Barry boy, then?"

"Barton," she murmured against Beatrice's shoulder. Elise sniffled. "We have been writing back and forth this past year." Elise looked up. "He wrote one just to me. I cannot find that letter."

"Was it something special, dear?"

"Yes, maybe. Barton said that he liked my letters very much and wanted me to write him in French and send him my photograph."

Beatrice only shrugged. "Not a problem then."

"Yes. But I think something may have happened. Or maybe he doesn't like me after all. I have not heard from him since spring." Elise began to cry. Sniffling, she asked, "Do you think something happened to him? I mean, he was most interested in writing to me. I wrote to him again, but the letter came back."

Beatrice understood now the concern. "I hope that you are not in love with him. He said he loves you?"

"No, not in so many words … but I think he liked me very much. He was special … I have been so worried."

"So he is French then and not an American?" Beatrice was puzzled by the rambling, disjointed story.

"No, he is like us. His family owns a plantation here in Louisiana, but he is from Texas. He told me he was visiting his family before he left for the army. I would just die if something happened to him." Elise hugged her mother hard.

"*O bébé*, don't cry. See, this is why you should not be involved with older people. A boy in the military is always a worry. You know how Mrs. Harrow goes on and on about her pilot son flying in China. She just has nightmares about him. We are lucky no one we love is fighting."

Elise looked startled at Beatrice, her face pale. "But what if I did love him, maybe a little? He was a friend, and we liked each other. Elaine writes to him too, but she thinks his letters are boring. I don't."

Beatrice sat with her daughter again on the bed. "You and your sister are so different; you cannot compare her feelings with yours, Elise. Besides, you have a smart, good, commonsense head on your shoulders. And your sister? Well, hers is full of fairy floss and starry hopes, I am afraid." She chuckled and was glad Elise did, too. "Even though Elaine is in college, she still is a twittering girl, and Daddy and I worry over her more than we should. Now you … you have much to be thankful for, and we are so proud of you."

"Thank you, Mama. I guess I just thought it nice that I had a handsome young man who liked me, not like the silly boys around here. He danced very nicely too and even kissed my hand goodbye, like a proper gentleman." Elise touched her hand reverently.

"What does this *Prince Charmant* look like? Is he tall, dark, and handsome too?"

"Oh, no. Just the opposite!"

"What? He is a short, fat toad?" Beatrice replied, looking shocked.

Elise laughed. "No. He is a bit … um, I don't know … different. He doesn't look like his family at all. He is a little taller than I am and quite strong. He has rust-red, very curly hair scattered with blond and a few little freckles on his cheeks; kinda cute, really. His eyes are like big, sparkly silver coins. And he has dimples. When he smiles … oh boy, I thought I might faint. He has them just like Daddy; you know how handsome he is when he smiles." Hugging her arms, she gave a little squeak of girlish glee.

Beatrice smiled, and her blue eyes sparkled with the thought of her winsome husband. "Oh, I do know. I guess you and I have more in common than you thought; we are both dimple adorers." She pushed a gentle finger into Elise's cheek to release her own dimple. "You have Papa's dimples, too, and when you were a baby with chubby cheeks, I used to poke you right here to make sure you would always have them." Beatrice kissed her daughter's cheek. "So, does this young man have a last name?"

"Yes, he is Sergeant Barton Barre from Beaumont, Texas," Elise stated dreamily.

"Barre … Barre? I know that name; Édouard's mechanic is a Barre. Maybe that is his son." She waved a hand, dismissing the idea. "But no, you said the boy was from Texas … probably not related after all. Although you did say his family has a plantation. There is the big La Barre plantation upriver out of Francis Ville … I wonder if that is it … It seems we do business with them. We get our honey and some of the produce and meat from them. Maybe Daddy knows him." She was thoughtful for a moment and let out a sigh. "As for your letter, Elise, where did you keep it?"

"In my pillowcase."

Beatrice smiled. "I know just where it is, honey." She patted Elise's hand.

Elise gaped. "You do? After all this, you tell me now?"

"Look in your jewelry case—I put it there yesterday when I did the laundry. It was in your bed linens when I changed them." She turned and watched Elise race across the room to search for the missing item. She smiled to see her daughter take out the letter and turn around with glistening eyes.

"This is it. Oh, thank you, Maman." She gave a low coo of pleasure.

"Not a big thing, that. Perhaps now that *Le Grand catastrophe* is over, I can tell you a bit of cheerful news. Oh, and do find a better place for that thing." Beatrice smiled to see Elise stop from slipping the letter under her pillow and turn away. "I put things like that in my lingerie drawer. Nobody looks in there," she said with a wink.

Elise giggled and put the letter under a stack of scarves.

"I just received a letter from Graciela. She says that the family wants to come down for a month or so before school starts. I thought we might take a long week or two at the lake house; it would be fun for all of us to get away for a bit. Then Rose will probably stay with us for the fall and winter terms to go to school. After I talk to your father and we square up the plans, I'll write Gracie a note saying yes. We have room, as always, for them. Won't it be nice to see little Rosie again? It has been some months."

Elise looked interested now. "Is Didier coming too? I missed him last summer when he didn't come with the family."

"I suppose. Let's see, Didi is about fifteen now, I think … oops, seventeen! My, where has the time gone?" Beatrice shook her head but continued. "Maybe he might like to come earlier and work in the store with us. I'll ask Papa. A teen boy is always in need of pocket money. Maybe Daddy and Rey can take Didi and fix up the lake house before we go. It is always such a dusty mess, and we end up spending most of the week just cleaning and repairing the place before we get to have fun and relax. You know how crazy Daddy gets when the Bontés visit us; everything must be perfect and spit-polished."

Beatrice clapped her hands as if everything was done and said, "Well, I need to keep busy; the day is wasting away while we chatter like jaybirds here." She stood up and smoothed down her apron front before heading to the bedroom door. "I do hope that you will tidy this up, yes?"

"Of course. Thank you, Mama, for saving my letter." Elise stepped to her mother and kissed her on the cheek. "Thank you, too, for not yelling about the dance last year."

"Oh, that. Well, it is old news now, isn't it? It can't be undone. Just be a good girl." Beatrice patted Elise's cheek.

"I will. Mom? Am I just a silly girl, and maybe Barton won't write to me again? Do you think he is alright?"

"You are not silly. Maybe you should just keep Barton in your prayers for now. If he is truly in the war, it is awful, and he just might need your prayers." Beatrice caressed her daughter's cheek.

"I think maybe you should also see if any of these things you have outgrown might fit our young Rose, eh?" She nodded toward the piled clothing on the bed and floor.

"Sure, Mom." Elise suffered a pat on the cheek and turned away from her task. She heard her mother briskly head downstairs, the stair treads creaking.

Elise felt her own heart creaking with worry for Barton Barre, but she was also glad that she had been keeping him in her prayers long before her mother suggested it. She would light another candle for Barton at church and ask the Virgin Mother, St. Sebastian, St. George, and St. Adrian of Nicomedia for his safety. Last month in confession, Elise had discussed with Father Luc about the saints protecting soldiers; he had been surprised by her question but gave her a little booklet about the many saints. Some had been soldiers, including the martyred former Roman Guard Adrian. Elise hoped that heavenly intervention might help her dear soldier.

◆ ◆

For the next week and a half, Elise and Elaine were very busy cleaning the house, working shifts at the family store, helping Beatrice put up jams, jellies, preserved vegetables, and fruits, baking loaves of bread and many pastries, and getting the large house ready for their company.

Amid it all, Elaine pulled rank and took off without permission to see Terry, leaving Elise behind to do her share of the work. One night, Elaine was caught coming home late, having missed supper and some of her chores, which Elise defiantly chose not to do. Beatrice and Édouard both were angry sentinels waiting up late for Elaine as she tried to sneak past the parlor and up the stairs. They banned her from seeing

Terry for the next month until school began. Their company was coming, and Elaine needed to be helpful and spend time with their family.

Elaine shuffled off to bed, and Elise heard her crying during the night. While she felt sad for her sister not being allowed to see Terry, Elise felt vindicated. Elaine had not gotten away with her misdemeanors and blatant disregard for their parents' rules.

The next day, Édouard also had a closed-door discussion with Terry and his father, Dr. Terrence Dillard, complaining that the young man was leading Elaine astray. She had never been out so late or come home so belligerent and sassy to her parents. He felt their relationship might tread on dangerous ground. Terry was older than Elaine—he should be more responsible for taking care of their daughter. Elaine was in ragged tatters after Terry called her to break up over the telephone! Elaine moped for the rest of the week and sullenly did her work.

When the Bonté family came to visit, she was only slightly pleasant to everyone—until Elaine met Wally Denis.

◆ ◆

Sunday, July 23, 1944

Elise ran out of the house to greet the family as they climbed out of the battered black *Chevrolet* truck at the curb. She was startled to see a short elderly woman dressed in a long skirt and fringed shawl get out first from the cab.

Beatrice trotted down the last steps from the house and walkway, taking the old woman's hands and speaking loudly in French, "Dearest Moon, we are so glad to have you here! What a delightful surprise!" She kissed the elderly woman on her wrinkled apple-round cheeks.

Moon looked up at Beatrice with delight, also speaking French. "You are kind to remember me. I am just an old widow. Give me a chair by the fire, and I'll be fine." She deferred the demonstrations with a wave.

Beatrice and Édouard both said, "Nonsense!" in unison and laughed.

Édouard greeted Moon, hugging and kissing her, speaking in another language, and both Elise and Elaine looked on curiously.

Elaine elbowed Elise and whispered snidely, "That's the old hill-people talk—ignore them." She turned away to greet Aunt Graciela in a reserved manner.

"Rosie! Look how big you are!" Elise cried as young Rose ran to meet her. They hugged and shrieked, excited to see each other again.

Reynard got out of the truck cab, stretching his long legs and shrugging stiff back muscles from driving for so long. He grimaced at the sound of the shrieking girls and passed by them to greet Édouard and Beatrice. "Wow! You'd think they haven't seen each other in years!" He ruffled Rose's hair as he went by.

Édouard greeted Rey Bonté with exuberant hugs and kisses. "Ah, *mon Bon-Bon! Regard toi!*" He quickly took him into the house, past the chattering women. Beatrice and Graciela were already engaged in conversation and locked arm-in-arm with Moon; they headed to the house.

Elise looked around, suddenly realizing something was wrong. "Didn't Didier come with you?" she asked Rose.

Rose ran back to the truck and lifted a corner of the tarpaulin off the back. "Yeah, he's still in there. I guess he didn't fall out or anything." She grinned up at Elise. "Pappy said he had to ride back here with Wally and all our junk. They were fighting something awful on the way down while Wally drove, and Pappy said he didn't want to hear it."

She giggled and stuck her head under the tented tarp. "Hey! *Mal chiens! Nous sommes arrivé ici!*" She threw back the tarp, and the girls found the two young men huddled on opposite sides of the truck amid the boxes and luggage, glaring at each other like surly pit bull dogs.

"Finally! God, am I glad!" A large, lanky, dark-haired young man clambered over the tailgate and stepped down. He stood up, glaring at the sea of upturned faces, and then saw it was two pretty girls, and his face softened.

"Hi! Just a moment." He turned away and shouted back into the truck. "*Petomane!* Get yer ass out here; we got girls!" He grinned wolfishly at Elise and Elaine. He offered his hand to Elise. "Hi, I am W-Wallace D-Denis. I mean Wally. D-Do you remember me?"

"No." Elise looked up at the tall young man. "Should I?" She did not take his hand.

He leaned down, smiling at her. "W-well, yeah. We've been swimming t-together a t-t-time or t-t-two."

Just then, the other boy vaulted over the tailgate and landed with a thump near Elise. She turned around and stared. "Didier? Oh my, you are taller than I remember." She said to the boy who stood a head taller than she did.

Didier critically eyed Elise up and down. "Yeah, well … so are you, string bean," he said churlishly. "*Je dois pisser, où-est le Looie?*" Didi announced and headed up the walkway.

"Nice manners, wolf boy! Just don't *pi-pi* in Mother's shrubbery," Elaine said caustically. She snorted, ignoring the rude gesture from Didier, and stepped over to

Wally. She batted her eyelashes up at him. "Now, why is it that I don't remember you, Wallace?" She smiled widely and took his arm. "You are just so cute!"

Wally blushed and took her arm. "Y-you think I am c-cute?" He grinned down at Elaine. "W-well, that m-makes up for being f-forgotten, then." He let Elaine take him into the house as she chattered away at him.

Elise, following in the wake of the entourage, shook her head, asking her younger cousin Rose, "Now I am confused. Who is Wally again? And what's the matter with Didier? He didn't greet me at all, or anybody even." Elise felt sad. She had been looking forward to his visit—he was her favorite cousin.

Rose stopped for a moment, letting the others go in the house. "It's a bit of a secret. Didier is in trouble. I am not supposed to say why. But Pappy made him come with us, especially since our cousin Wally is spending the summer with us. I think Didi has to make his decision this summer to either stay on here to finish school or stay at home and help with the farm and our Granny Moon." Her dark eyes were troubled as she confided in Elise. "I am to stay on for school after our vacation here. It just depends on whether Didier wants to stay, too. If he does, we have to go to boarding school. If not, I might live with you again."

Elise felt hurt by Didier's snub and nasty attitude. "I see. I don't really understand why he was so creepy to us."

Rose shrugged and tossed her ebony, beribboned braids. "Mommy said he is in that bad time for boys. You know, Pooh-ber-ville."

Elise giggled at Rose's made-up term. "Don't you mean puberty? He's a little old for that."

Rose tilted her head in thought and smiled. "Maybe, although Didi is just plain in the poohs—pooh this, pooh that, poop on you, you know. He has a dirty mouth, Mommy said." She giggled. "Papa packed extra *Lifebuoy* soap just in case!"

Laughing at the girl's joke, Elise put her arm around her young cousin. "I think I got it. Let's go in. I am sure somebody will be missing us."

It would be another day before Didi warmed up to the family. However, Elise and Beatrice saw the competition and animosity between Wally and Didi and knew there was something brewing. A storm was ahead. Granny Moon seconded the idea and waggled a furry foot on a beaded string, and said a few strange words. She then silently faded back into the woodwork with the potted ferns, subsiding in her overstuffed armchair with her bag of crochet work and sewing.

◆ ◆

Monday, July 24, 1944

Elise was to witness the storm first, as Wally and she played chess together in the parlor. They had been playing for nearly an hour, and Didi had come around a few times. He watched for a while and then grew bored and went away. Quietly humming, Granny Moon sat in her corner crocheting and silently observed the teens.

Coming back again, Didi asked Wally, "Hey, chucklehead! Ain't you done yet? God!" He slumped down on the couch with a thud next to Elise. "This is the most boring game in the world."

"It's not su-supposed to be a sp-spectator sport, idiot." Wally just glared at him and took extra time to make his move, which, unfortunately, might put him in checkmate in three, maybe four moves—if Elise noticed it. He had no other options and hoped that Didier might distract Elise enough so that he might move his king out of jeopardy using other minor pieces to protect it.

◆ ◆

Elise saw the move and watched Wally do it. She felt impolite to clobber him again, as he was a guest. She observed that even though Wally at first did not seem outwardly provoked by Didier's presence, he was soon upset. Wally chewed a thumbnail and jiggled a nervous leg. His stutter became more pronounced as he became agitated.

"D-Don't b-bug us. C-Clear off, n-knucklehead," Wally growled as he saw Didi put his arm around Elise's shoulder and whisper in her ear.

"No, I am playing. Later!" Elise shrugged out of Didi's possessive embrace.

Didi moaned and leaned against Elise, ducking his head and putting on a big, sad-eyed puppy face. "Please ... pretty please with sugar on top and a cherry too?" He smiled up at her and petted her arm. "I am lonely. Elaine and Rose are putting on makeup. Dad and Uncle Ed are busy in the garage. Come play with me." He whined, making Elise giggle.

"In a minute. Then you and I can play a game of chess after this." Elise made her move. "Check." She said to Wally with a charming smile.

Didi sat up and pouted like a truculent child. "I hate chess. It's a stupid game." He thumped the sofa with a loose fist.

Wally smiled. "Yeah, D-Didi thinks it is st-stupid because he isn't sm-smart enough to st-strategize with the brainy likes of us," Wally said boastfully and smiled.

Didi pointed at the black king. "So you say! Ha! Your king is in trouble after only one move. You lose."

Wally's smile faded fast. "Shoot! How'd I miss that? Go away!" He glared at Didier with a clenched fist.

Didier made a crude gesture at Wally, and Elise ignored it. She smiled at Wally. "If you want, I can tell you a good move. It will get your king out of jeopardy now, but you'll lose your rook." Her voice was sweet as honey.

Wally sat up tall, interested in the suggestion. "What the hell?" he blanched, glancing at Elise. "Sorry. I mean ..." He nervously wiped his sweating brow.

Elise watched as Wally looked at Didier, who was watching him cattily as if Wally was a canary in a cage. A smile played about Didier's lips. Elise knew Didi couldn't wait for Wally to lose the game to her.

"So what are you talking about, Elise?" Wally asked, studying the board and trying not to look at Didi.

"Castling. Do you know how?" Elise asked, her eyes inscrutably studying Wally and purposefully ignoring Didi.

Wally's face took on a glowing smile. "Ah ... yes ... just like this." He confidently made the move, exchanging places for the king and rook. He sat back with a broad smile. "Thanks, Elise."

Elise smiled sweetly. "No, thank you, Wally. Checkmate." She made the move with her white knight, taking his bishop and ending the game.

Wally stared at the chessboard in near horror. "You little rat! I thought you were helping me!" he griped and put his king back but checked the board for other moves. "Oh crap, I was doomed anyway, wasn't I? I was sure I had at least four more moves." Studying the moves back and forth, he asked, "How did you do that?"

"Practice, dear Wally," Elise said in honeyed tones and began to replace the pieces on the board while whistling cheerily.

Didi stood up and patted Wally hard on the back. "Too bad, old Gray Turtle. Too slow even for this little gal." He tugged on Elise's shirtsleeve. "Come on, let's get out of here. I hate hanging around losers." He stepped away from the sofa and didn't see it coming until it hit him. The embroidered silk pillow hit him in the shoulder, and he turned around, angry now. "You threw that at me?" He accused Wally, his face growing pink, ready to throw the pillow back harder.

Wally stood up to tower over Didier. "S-so what if I d-did? W-what are you g-going to do about it? R-remember, there are l-ladies p-present. And stop calling me Turtle!" He held up a tightly closed, meaty fist under Didi's face.

Elise stood up now and took the pillow from Didi. "It's a good thing I am here then. I won't have you two punching it out. What is the matter with you?" She defiantly stared at the pair. "I won't tell Maman how you abused her sofa pillow if you two will apologize."

After a moment, Wally backed down. He leaned over and took the pillow away from Elise before gently setting it back on the sofa. "I am sorry I abused her lovely pillow," Wally said smugly, "but I sure am not sorry I d-didn't hit you harder with it, you little p-pi-pissant!" Wally pushed Didi aside and stalked off with a dark countenance.

Didi, now in a fit of anger, hollered back. "Get stuffed, you big stupid ape! *Mange Merde!*" He looked back at Elise, realizing he had let go so crudely, and shrugged sheepishly. "At least I can fight without stepping all over my words like old mush-face there!"

Disgusted with the pair of them, Elise brushed past Didi and headed for the kitchen.

Didi followed on her heels. "Come on, what did I say?" He tried to grab Elise, but she evaded him.

Elise turned quickly and spat out, "You will apologize to Wally and to me for your ridiculous behavior, and then maybe you and I will talk again. Until then, I have nothing to say to you, Didier Adrian Bonté!" She let the swinging door of the kitchen do her talking as she swept past him, leaving Didier in the hallway fuming.

Granny Moon almost missed the next treble crochet as she stifled a giggle.

◆ ◆

July and August 1944

By the end of the first week of the backwoods Bontés' visit in Baton Rouge, due to the intense and attention-grabbing feud brewing between Didier and Wally, the young men were parceled out to other members of the family. Everyone hoped to keep them from acting like vicious, growling pit bulls whenever they came near each other.

Elaine took on Wally, as he was six months older than her and more suited to her interests and tastes. She enjoyed having an instant boyfriend for the summer since she couldn't go out with Terry Dillard. She still was not sure that Terry had really and truly broken up with her, and she thought he might have acted as if he had just to appease her father. Perhaps by the fall semester, they would be together again, especially after the Bonté hick family went home! Wally was at least from a civilized place, Fort Worth, Texas, and had some manners, which was more than Elaine could say for her younger, impulsive, and combative cousin, Didier.

Didier allied himself with Elise, which was usually the way it had always been in the past. They took off daily on an adventure. Sometimes, they took Rose just to keep her quiet because she would whine about being left at home. But then, sometimes, Beatrice and Graciela had other plans for Rose, like shopping and baking, or Granny Moon had Rose crochet and sew with her.

On those carefree and 'Rose-less' days, Elise and Didi skipped happily away to be alone together, running, swimming, stealing apples along the way from a house down the street, and picnicking on the city park's lakeside beach or at the river. Sometimes, they took the streetcar and went to the city gardens or to the movies—anything to be away from home. At least, Elise thought that was Didier's plan; he wanted to be far from his family and from Wally, even though he was quickly bored with Elise's idea of playing a tourist through the historic mansions, state capitol, museums, or window shopping.

After about a week of this camaraderie, it became plain to Elise that there was something more to Didi's purposeful time with her. He liked her, and she liked him back. When he was alone with her, Elise thought him handsome, romantic, dashing, and fun. His shaggy hair was glossy black, like a raven's wing, his eyes dark with mirth when he looked at her, and a small dimple lurked about his cheek, charming Elise. Didier kissed her for the first time when he rowed them out one day on the river; Elise knew there was something special.

◆ ◆

Lake Pontchartrain, Louisiana
Sunday, August 6, 1944

Didier leaned back against the seat in the rowboat and gazed at Elise. She had her eyes closed and a dreamy, tiny smile on her lips after he kissed her. He wanted to kiss her again; her lips were soft against his and tasted of cherries. They were dark red, too, like those cherries that they had feasted upon a while ago. He leaned to her and whispered, "I want to kiss you again." This time, he didn't wait for her assent and did it, surprising Elise a little. She leaned against him in the kiss, sighing gently.

He put his arm around her and pulled her in, resting her head against his shoulder to kiss her ears and neck. They were salty from sweat and the lake water, but she smelled clean from her swim. He liked how her black hair went from tangled-looking wet ropes to wild, curling waves as her hair dried in the sun. He ran a hand through her still-damp hair, enjoying the feeling of the heavy curls in his hand. Elise sighed again and sat with her head tilted back so Didi would stroke her hair some more.

"That feels good, more, please," Elise said, sounding happy and content.

"Does it? I can make you feel even better if you want," he asked, raking back another wave of hair behind her ears. He leaned to her and whispered, "I want to make you feel really, really good. Will you let me?"

Elise opened her eyes and turned to look up at him, squinting in the sun. "I feel just fine. I like the way you kiss." She reached to catch his hand to kiss his knuckles. "You have nice hands when you don't bite your nails and aren't fighting," she said boldly, with a wink at Didi.

Didi scooted closer to her side, making the boat rock precariously, thinking he would grab her and tickle Elise into submission.

"Don't dump us!" Elise yelped as she grabbed for the sides.

Didi smiled, now wolfishly piqued by her squeals. "I'll dump you if I want." He grabbed the gunwales and rocked the boat viciously, laughing as Elise shrieked. "Tell me you love me, and I'll stop!" he yelled.

"No! Don't! Didi, stop it!" She shrieked as he rocked the rowboat hard. Lake water washed over the gunwale, drenching their feet and the beach blanket. "You are getting everything wet!" She yelped, grabbing up the blanket.

"Tell me!" he barked again.

"Okay! Enough!"

"What?"

"Stop it! I love you!" Elise said hastily as she tried to regain her seat in the sloshing, rocking boat.

Didi gave the boat another hard shove port-side, letting the water splash over, and then stopped abruptly. "Do you mean it?" he asked, grabbing Elise by the arm.

Elise shrank away as his hand hovered to tickle her. "Yes!"

Didi pulled her into his arms. "Well, that settles it then—you are my girl, right?" His eyes were warm and smiling now.

"I suppose if you want me to be."

"If I say I love you, then will you be my girl?" Didi asked, looking hungrily at Elise. He could see the pulse in her throat beat nervously, and he put his hand there, stroking her throat and chin. "You say it first."

Caught in Didi's hands and in the prison of his dark eyes, Elise said timidly, "Yes, I am yours."

She barely caught her breath before Didi swooped down to kiss her again, and she thought she might faint from lack of oxygen before he released her. She had tears in her eyes. His kiss was painful yet poignant, and his roaming hands were doing strange things to Elise's body that made her tremble.

"Why are we trembling? Am I crazy? I want to kiss you again." She caught him with a hand behind his head and drew him down to her to kiss him of her own volition. After a few moments, she sighed. "Yes, I do think I may love you, but then, I think I always have."

Didi lay down in the boat, pulling Elise with him, not worried about the standing water. He laid his head on the blanket and tackle box. He held her above him and caressed her face. "I think I have always loved you, too. Maybe we are star-destined lovers like Romeo and Juliet," he mused wistfully. "I read about them last year in Mom's book of Shakespeare."

Elise shook her head. "No, I don't want to be like them. They died." She pushed back a lock of windblown curls and smiled down at Didier. "Let's just be us."

Didi traced the round curve of Elise's breast with a finger, sliding it casually under the aqua sateen bathing suit cup to stroke her silky skin. "I think it is romantic to die for another person you love," he murmured, although he was fixated on Elise's sun-warmed, round breast.

Elise wiped his hand away. "Yes, it is romantic, but I want to live and love. Isn't that better? Just think of all the things we could do and places we could go and be in love." She sighed as she sat away from him.

Didi snorted to say snidely, "Where would we go?" He resettled himself to hold Elise hard to his chest and looked upward at the pale, water-colored blue sky above them. "I only have ever been to two places in my life—here and the hills back home. That is where my life is. There, I feel like a man. Here, I am a boy, or at least that is what your father calls me." He sighed and let his hand wander absently along Elise's bare back, his fingers tracing the length of her spine. He looked askance at Elise. "No, we would have to go somewhere else or back home. Where do you want to live?"

Elise raised her head. "Here … this is my home, Didi—I mean, in Baton Rouge. Besides, we are too young to think about such things." She tried to sit up, but Didier's firm arms kept her tight against him.

"I am not. Back home, people get married younger than us. My cousin was barely fourteen when she got married to her husband, who was the same age as me." Didier countered, hoping Elise would catch on and agree.

Elise looked surprised. "But you are seventeen, and I am only fifteen. I would never get married that young. I have plans for my life. Don't be silly."

"No?" Didi let the comment go and closed his eyes to let the sun warm them. He had ideas of sliding into the cold water with sun-hot Elise and making her scream. He traced her sun-bronzed shoulder blades and let his hand wander along her spine again to the end of her bathing suit. His fingers stealthily inched under the small cavernous space between the bathing suit and the cleavage of her buttocks, resting his fingers there to let Elise get used to his hands touching her. He wanted to go further. He wanted her more than anything he could think of right now.

He wanted to force her under the water until she was gasping for air, and he would save her, kiss her, and make fierce love to her, letting Elise know she was his forever. For that matter, Didi wanted Elise to love him. But he was unsure just how far he could go before she stopped him.

His fingers slid farther down, and he stroked the top of one round, firm buttock, enjoying the feeling of her cool skin under the damp bathing suit in contrast to the sun-heated skin of her back. He wanted to taste and kiss all of it, feel the satin skin against his lips and his face. Didi wanted Elise's taste and smell in his brain.

He shifted slightly, taking the drowsy Elise with him, and made the mistake of getting her wet in the sloshing water at the bottom of the boat. Elise sat up with a jerk and swatted his hand away from her behind.

"What are you doing?" Elise looked cross with him. "I am going for a swim." She stood up abruptly and dove over the side of the boat before he could stop her.

◆ ◆

Elise felt the chilly water engulf her heated limbs and felt a cramp inside her belly as she dove under a wave. She came up for air, and with powerful breaststrokes, she swam toward the bobbing diving dock. The incoming waves pulled as she fought to get there. Elise had a strange, urgent feeling that she must reach the dock, or she might drown. Breathing heavily from the sudden dive into the water and impassioned swim, she grabbed the wooden rail of the mooring and shot out of the water to lie like a landed fish on the deck. She lay for some moments, breathing hard; her ribs ached, her stomach hurt, and her leg muscles burned. Elise suddenly felt eyes upon her. She looked up and saw Didi silhouetted against the sun, tall and rangy, looking dangerous and dripping on her. She let out a squeak of surprise.

"This is a better idea, Elise. You are a smart cookie, after all." Panting slightly from his swim, he stretched out beside Elise. Didi reached a hand to touch her, but Elise swatted it away.

"What's wrong? A minute ago, you were kissing my face off, and now you don't want me to touch you?"

Elise sat up warily. "That's right. We were kissing, and that was fine, but I got scared."

"Of me?" he asked, now biting his lip, uncertain again.

"Yes. I think I have had enough. Let's go home. I am hot, and I am probably sunburned."

"But I haven't had enough yet. Don't you want to make me happy?" Didi asked in a cajoling tone and stroked a finger along Elise's slim shinbone. He leaned to her and whispered something in her ear, then smiled.

Elise looked away and wrapped her arms around her knees protectively. "I don't know. It sounds yucky. You are so weird. Besides, I think this is going too fast. I am going home. Mother probably needs us. We have to prepare stuff for Elaine's birthday party this week." She stood up and looked back at Didi, who was still reclined on the dock. "Are you coming?"

Didi let out a resigned sigh. "I wish I was." He shook his head, mentally clearing his original naughty thoughts. "Yeah, let's go. I ain't in the mood anymore anyway." He dove off the dock and did not look back until he climbed over the edge of the boat. He scanned the water and realized that Elise had already swum across to the bank and was getting out on the beach. "Why are you over there?" He hollered across the water. "What in heaven's name is wrong with you? Elise!" He shouted, feeling spurned and getting angry.

Elise waved him away and picked up her towel to dry off. She put on her culottes and midi and sat to put on her sandals. She picked up her beach bag and the sack of picnic food and then set off for home, absolutely ignoring Didi.

Didi was on his way in, rowing the boat frantically, ignoring a few bathers as he splashed them, hollering at Elise the whole time, "Wait! *Stop!* Why are you leaving me in the middle of the stupid lake? Damn you!"

He beached the boat and scrambled up the embankment, falling into the gritty, coarse sand. He quickly got up and ran, panting after Elise. She was already on the dirt road and a reasonable distance away, and from the taut angle of her posture as she walked, Didi thought she was angry.

He caught up with her after a couple minutes of running and grabbed Elise by the arm to stop her. Instead, they tumbled off into the desiccated grass by the side of the dirt road. Elise began shrieking and kicking at him. Didi had all of a fraction of a second to think he might win before he took a whack on the head with their sack lunch. Didi sat down hard again on the ground and looked dazed. He saw a shadowed movement over him and put up an arm to deflect another incoming blow. Instead, he was bowled over by Elise again; this time, she was kissing him all over his face.

"I am sorry. Sorry. Are you all right?" She kissed his sore forehead. "Did I hurt you?"

He began to laugh and fell back into the grass. He weakly pulled Elise to him. "Boy, oh boy, did I deserve that!" He hugged Elise. "It is me who is sorry."

Elise sat up on her knees, now looking curious at Didi. "Why do you say that?"

"I am a sneaky Pete. I lost myself, and you almost got in trouble. Actually, I almost got *us* into trouble again."

"Again?"

Didi sat up. He swept the long, damp shock of hair from his forehead. "Yeah. *Je suis un puce.* I am a creep!" He reached a hand to Elise and caressed her cheek. "You can kick me in the balls the next time I try something like that."

Elise looked confused. "I have no idea what you are talking about, but you did make me very uncomfortable. I do not understand why, but I had to leave."

Didi stood up, dusting off his backside and knees, and then lent a hand to Elise and pulled her up beside him. He hugged her once and put an arm around her shoulders. "I am sorry, my girl. I won't do it again. We'll go slowly."

Elise picked up her scattered pile, handing clothes to Didi. "I am sorry. I lost my head, too."

Didier scrunched his feet into his untied sneakers. "Well, it is a good thing we found them—our heads, that is—or we would have been in lots of trouble. I want to go home, too." He shrugged into his shirt, leaving it open and unbuttoned over his wet jean cutoffs. He looped an arm around Elise's waist and kissed her temple quickly, afraid to linger, for his own passion might ignite again.

"What about the dingy?"

"Don't you worry about it—let the boatman do his job." Didi shrugged and pulled Elise along, even though she looked back in worry at the drifting boat.

They walked companionably home that afternoon from the inlet on the great lake—neither mentioning again what had happened or almost happened. Elise still felt some confusion about what had actually occurred, yet she had relaxed by the time they arrived at the lake house, enough to go to the movie show in Ponchatoula with Didier and Rose later that evening.

◆ ◆

Ponchatoula, Louisiana
Wednesday, August 9, 1944

As constant companions, Elise and Didi were making Wally and Rose upset. The cousins were always disappearing or found snuggling in dark corners, thinking they were alone or casting calf-eyed glances at each other. While young Rose, at only nine, did not fully understand it all, Wally certainly did. Elaine was oblivious to the pair, not thinking much of their relationship above ordinary friendship and mutual familial adoration. Didier and Elise had always been a duo.

Wally felt the relationship between Elise and Didier even more disturbing, especially since he now had to share a bedroom with Didier again. Didi was obsessed with Elise. Elaine had spent the past couple of weeks dragging Wally to movies, parties, picnics, and the tennis courts as an object of her affection within her circle of friends and old admirers in Baton Rouge. Now that they were vacationing at the beach house on Lake Pontchartrain, Elaine continued to treat Wally like a boyfriend and toy.

Wally was a sturdily built fellow, tall, with dark eyes, a charming smile, and thick, glossy black hair. He was easy on the eyes. Once easily swayed into Elaine's charm and her games, he had soon grown tired of the circle of giddy, giggling girls, even though they made much of him. It was the other members of Elaine's circle of friends and admirers who bothered Wally—the guys who looked with dark envy at him. Some were steely-eyed when Elaine introduced Wally to them at the tennis club or on the streetcar in town. Elaine seemed to have admiring guys everywhere!

One fellow, in particular, gave him a rough time, sneering at Wally after Elaine had passed by. Terrence Dillard had gripped Wally's hand hard; he had grimaced, feeling his bones crunch. Wally had given the same back, making Dillard wince, too. Wally did not like Dillard; in just a few minutes, they were all together, and he didn't like how Elaine flirted openly with Terry, even kissing his cheek and stroking his arm. Wally knew Elaine was a distant family member, but still, it bothered him she would go out with him and then sit and smooch with Terry Dillard in front of him.

Now that they were in Ponchatoula for a morning of shopping, Wally was shocked to see Dillard again in the drugstore. Elaine returned to the soda fountain after picking up a few purchases and dragging Terry along. She sat on a stool between the young men. Both men were exchanging spiteful glances over her oblivious head. Disgusted by the flirting couple, Wally excused himself, saying he had something to do. He took the horse-drawn streetcar as far as he could and then walked home the last miles. Feeling that he needed some quiet time, he walked along the lakeshore to the beach house. He was sorry, for in his impulsiveness, Wally had nearly been bitten by a snapping turtle, fell in the swamp and ruined his last pair of jeans, scared up a flock of squawking angry shorebirds, and, startled by it all, had run back home, only to be laughed at by the older folks sitting on the front porch.

By nearly lunchtime, Elaine showed up at the lake house, saying that everyone was going down to the beach. Wally begged not to go. He was still hurt that she had not mentioned him leaving her at the soda counter with Dillard. She didn't seem to care.

Wally eyed Elaine as she bustled about in the kitchen, already attired in her swimsuit and a short, yellow polka-dot overcoat, sandals, and a broad-brimmed hat. He watched her take out a bunch of soda pop bottles and put them in the cooler bucket.

"Here, honey, you can carry these if you don't mind." Elaine nodded at the heavy, ice-laden bucket.

"No. I said I am not going." Wally slumped in the kitchen chair.

"Don't be silly. Everyone is going. Daddy is letting us have the car, too." She glanced at Wally with an engaging smile. "Daddy said he didn't mind if you drive. He hates how I drive." She shook her head, turned to the icebox, retrieved a small jar of pickles, and handed them to Wally. "Open, please."

Wally looked soberly up at her and put down the pickle jar. "I gotta ask you something first, Elaine."

"What, honey?"

"Don't call me honey unless you mean it, okay?" he grumbled.

Elaine looked surprised. "Is that it?"

"No. Did you take me with you today, knowing you'd meet up with Dillard? So now I am your chaperone?"

She shot him a puzzled look and frowned. "Of course not, silly." She passed by Wally and trailed a teasing hand over his shoulder. "He was just there. You two seemed to get along. Isn't he nice?"

Wally made a face. "Oh, yeah, he's a real swell fella. He'd like to rearrange my body parts."

"Tsk! Now stop. Terry is sweet. He never would do such a thing."

"Oh yeah?" Wally shoved the pickle jar back across the table. "I heard about you two, and Dillard is trouble."

"And you aren't trouble?" She shot back cattily, evading the question.

Wally smiled at that. "Of course. I am always *in* trouble. I guess you like troubled guys, then."

"No, Daddy just thought Terry and I were moving too fast and getting serious. I am going to be twenty tomorrow. I should be able to choose whom I want to date, right?"

Wally shook his head. "Uh, d-d-don't get me going on that one. W-we will both lose that argument with your dad." He grabbed back the jar of pickles and unscrewed the top. "Do I have to eat those damn things?"

"You don't like *cornichons*?" Elaine asked as she speared out the pickles, making a packet of them.

"No, they remind me of little slugs or something—too salty and nasty."

Elaine reached over and swatted Wally on the head. "Sh! Mother made them."

Wally peeked around the corner of the kitchen to observe the empty hall. "It's okay. Everyone's in the living room. Your mother is playing the piano. Nobody heard us. I'll be honest. I am not into the *froufrou* gourmet junk you people call food. And I really hate that gooey, stinky cheese you people keep shoving at me, telling me it is so good. It smells rotten to me. Give me a big, fat burger any day with cheddar on it."

Elaine made a face and shook her head. "Boy, oh boy, you really are in a nasty snit. It's a good thing Mother didn't hear you. So are you going with us or not? We're going to have a little early birthday party for me." Elaine finished packaging the waxed paper-wrapped fried chicken, put it in a paper grocery sack, and stacked a bunch of grapes and apples on top in the sack.

"Will Dillard be there?"

"He might."

"You invited him then …"

"I did. Terry is my friend, after all … and he was kind enough to bring our friends to Ponchatoula," Elaine said loftily.

"Does your dad know he's in town?"

Elaine put a finger to her lips and winked. "Sh!"

Wally sighed. "Yeah, I'll go, even if it is to be your chaperone."

Elaine threw a wad of calico cloth napkins into the sack. "I hardly need a chaperone, Wallace," she snipped. "Look, if you are going to be a pain, then just stay here. I thought you might like to have some fun at the beach with me."

"You mean with you and your gang? I like fun. Fine, I'll go." Wally scooted back the chair. "I'll go get my trunks and towel, and we can go. But why are we driving again? We can just walk to the beach."

"We aren't going to *our* beach, silly. We are going out on the gulf. It should be an enjoyable time. I want to smell the salty sea air, not a stinky old lake. Besides, I hate leeches and all those icky things in the lake."

"Oh, you prefer the bigger creatures that can swallow you whole!" Wally snorted a laugh and shrugged. "Okay, I'm in then. I never swam in the ocean before!" He headed off down the hall.

Still working in the kitchen, Elaine called back. "Oh, and tell the love bugs they can come too. If anyone needs a chaperone, it's them!"

◆ ◆

Elise worriedly watched as Terrence and Wally competed in arm wrestling. Even though they were nearly the same height, Wally was more muscular. With grim effort and a grunt, he won the match hands down!

Terrence sat up sweating and rubbed his glistening biceps and elbow as if it hurt. He offered his other hand. "Care to try that again?" he asked tersely, his blue eyes sparking dangerously.

Wally shook his shaggy head. "Nah, I already b-beat you twice. What f-fun is there in embarrassing you again? Besides, ain't this supposed to be a party?" Wally got up off the bench at the picnic table and sauntered away to pick in the grocery sack, grabbing out an apple.

"Damn chicken, that's what you are!" Terrence grumbled. "Oh, you want to go next?" He then grinned at Didi, who agreed with a nod.

Didier pulled his shirt off and swung a leg over the bench. "Yeah, I do, city boy. Try to break my arm now!" He sat down hard; bent a tanned, lean, muscled arm ready for the fight; and looked boldly about the assembled group with a cocky wink at Elise.

Elise stepped up. "Don't be a fool, Didi. Terry is twice your size. He's a tennis champ! He'll rip your arms off," she stated with worry.

Terrence placed his arm on the wooden table. "You ready, runt? We'll see who's a man here."

"Yeah, I am fop. Yer nuthin' but baked wind!"

They gripped hands hard, and both counted from three to one and began. Wearing a confident smirk and with little effort, Terrence began to move the youth's hand toward the tabletop, inching slowly down. Both young men were covered in sweat, grunting and staring hard into each other's eyes. Elise held her breath, afraid for the upcoming humiliation that Didi would experience.

Elaine began to chant, "Terry! Terry!" Her friends took up the chant. Terrence glanced quickly at Elaine and smiled but then felt his opponent's hand clench his harder, and he looked back at Didier.

"Ha! Thought you'd get me, huh?" Terry grunted and squeezed his opponent's hand hard.

Didier stared, ebony eyes locked with periwinkle blue ones; sweat shone on his face and dripped from his bulging muscles as he began to press his advantage, pushing the taller man's arm in the other direction. He could tell the other man was fighting intensely; Terrence had more to lose than he did, and that made Didier fight even more. With a slight easing, he allowed Terry to push back, taking a different angle, and then, all of a sudden, Didier pressed forward with surprising brute strength and quickly mashed his opponent's hand to the table with a smashing blow.

"I win! Singing Dog is the Champion!" Didier crowed and released their hands. He bounded up laughing and kissed Elise and Elaine on the cheek. Looking down at Elaine, Didi said, "That was for Wally. Don't make him play the fool again!" He grimly stalked away toward the lone figure down on the windy beach.

Elise looked at Elaine and Terry and said, "Why do you boys always have to compete? You are ridiculous!" She saw Didi catching up to Wally, ran after the pair, and then linked hands with them. "You were both great! I never knew how strong you are!" she said with pride.

Wally tossed away the apple core and squeezed her hand affectionately. "Thanks. It's too bad your sister isn't like you. She seems to like the bright, shiny, armored kind. I saw the fancy rig that Dillard drives. And the thousand-watt, movie-star smile he shines on Elaine. He looks like Errol Flynn and is rich. He's in love with her." He winced and slunk along, now dejected. "Face it. Elaine's friends are all country club snobs. That Charlie Carpenter drives a big, shiny Buick and has a snotty, ritzy girlfriend—while I got nothin'. I'm no competition with the likes of those guys."

Elise shrugged. "Oh, Wally, you are good-looking too. Elaine was quite smitten with you. Couldn't you tell?"

"Nah. I am a p-pl-play thing." Wally walked in silence for a long moment, then commented gruffly, "Elaine is like a cat. She plays around, teases, and then gets tired of her toys too easily. Whoever wins her is gonna have a p-problem, and it ain't g-gonna be me!"

"I say screw 'em," Didi growled, picking up a tiny dead crab. He pulled Elise closer to his side. "Well, no worries with this girl. She gives her heart once and for all. Right?" He kissed her cheek, smiled affectionately at Elise, and teased her with the crab.

Wally noticed the spark between the pair. "Hey, you two better cut it out; you'll have Édouard after you. He'll rip your balls off, Didier, if you mess with Elise. Remember what Uncle Rey said, 'You ruin another girl, and you'll be hanging from—'"

"*Ta gueulé!*" Didi roared at Wally. He released Elise and stepped toward the giant youth. "Forget I ever tried to be nice to you." He said something in another language and threw the crab at Wally.

Wally's face turned crimson as he balled a fist and batted aside the crab.

Elise realized Didier had just insulted Wally again. She gaped. "Will you two stop it? Why must you fight each other? Can't you be friends?"

Wally shrugged and kicked sand over the crab carcass. "No, Elise, we cannot. You don't know what—" Wally swallowed down his insult and continued. "What the little creep has done. You b-better pray that he d-doesn't try it on with you!"

Didier shoved Wally hard, nearly toppling him. "*Gros enaelé! Tais toi!*" he snapped and then stomped away angrily.

Wally stood up, shrugging off the brief attack and the insult. He stared darkly for a moment at the retreating figure as Didier bounded into the surf. He looked at Elise and then took her hand. "Elise, I have to be honest with you. I don't want to see you get hurt. Didier is in the habit of being a big tease himself. He breaks girls and dumps them."

"He does not!" Elise looked scandalized but then gulped. "Are you telling me the truth, Wally?"

"Yes. I know Didi well, and he has no heart for love; he just wants to get what he—"

Elise interrupted Wally with a cry. "No, I think you are lying. Didi cares about me—about us. He wouldn't do that to me." She sniffled.

Wally pulled Elise to him and hugged her slight figure. "Don't take it to heart, honey-pie, please. You can trust me. I-I have only good intentions. M-Maybe Didi and Elaine are alike, just big flirts. We are more alike with good hearts, wanting others to be kind and play fairly like we do." His voice grew soft, and he kissed the top of Elise's head as he hugged her.

Elise nodded and pulled away. "Thanks for the warning, Wally, but I think I am smart enough to see things as they are." She cast a glance toward the water to see Didi swimming away through the breakers. "I think you might have hurt Didi's feelings. Maybe you should apologize to him."

Wally cast a wry brow. "Me apologize? No, let the kid swim it off. He was spoiling for a fight with anyone, me included. Don't let him pull you in and feel sorry for him; you'll make it worse. He's a fathead."

"I don't, but as a friend and because I care for him, I think Didi needs me." Elise pulled out of Wally's hand. "How about we go for a swim? Maybe it will cool us all off."

Wally ran after Elise into the waves.

◆ ◆

Sitting on the picnic table holding court among her friends, Elaine witnessed her sister and cousins swimming and having fun and decided that everyone should go too. She pulled off her swimming suit cover amid wolf whistles and led her friends down the beach to join the rest of the kids.

After a time, everyone was carousing in the water, having chicken fights—boys with girls on their shoulders, trying to knock each other over in the water. They played volleyball in the water, dove, and swam like young otters in the warm waves. But then all too soon, the competitions began again, with the young men vying each other with feats of strength and daring of who could stay underwater the longest or swim the farthest and fastest.

Just moments before, Terrence and Didi came in, swimming evenly toward the shore. But Wally burst out of a shallow wave, swimming with powerful strokes past them, and then ran up onto the beach to the pile of towels. Dragging seaweed and gasping, Didi crawled out of the water, panting and red-faced. He fell onto the sand, clutching his belly with spasms from the effort. Elaine and her friends Luella, Darla, and Kimberly were cheering and ran to meet the other swimmers as they came in.

Elise fell to her knees beside Didi and put a gentle arm and towel about him. "You are brave for nearly winning over those older boys." She kissed his cheek.

◆ ◆

Wally turned about, grinning, expecting praise for winning the race, but stopped laughing when he saw the other girls crowded about Terrence and the last two boys to arrive on shore, Charlie Carpenter and Beau Harper. Wally saw Elaine kiss Terrence and drape a piece of seaweed about his neck like a victory ribbon. Wally's good mood soured, and he strode away. He passed by their beach table and snatched his towel and sneakers. He walked to the car and left the keys on the front seat, not caring if anyone stole the damn machine! He would hitch his way home.

Later that evening, Wally met Didi on the stairs at the lake house, and he almost shoved the younger man away but restrained himself. Then, after supper, he witnessed Elise and Didier on the back porch kissing and holding hands. He grew incensed, but he wondered if it was from jealousy or from a hurt ego. He still felt the public snub from earlier. Elaine had not spoken to him since she came home from the beach. Although none of the adults seemed to pay any attention to the feuding teens, they were engaged in their own conversations, card games, and interests.

Wally was miserable. He sat in the kitchen and thirstily drank down several glasses of water, feeling so dry and parched, burned from the day in the sun and heated from the fire burning from within. Wally overheard the conversation, though it was spoken in low tones, not meant for anyone but the people on the back porch. He avidly leaned closer to the screened back door to hear it all.

"I know that I am in love with you, Elise. I am older than you, and that is why you have to do what I say."

"I am a free girl, Didi. I want to stay home and finish school. Marriage is not in my immediate plans. I cannot think about it now."

"Are you saying you don't want to marry me?"

"I didn't say that. I just mean it is too soon to think about such things. I want—"

Didi impatiently jumped on the point. "It is always what *you* want. How about what *I* want, Elise? I want you. I don't want to wait. If we go home, I have land. We can live there, build us a house, and be happy. A woman follows her man!"

"But, Didi, I'll miss my family—"

"You have a family—my mother, my father, Rose … and what about Granny Moon? She loves you, Elise! She thinks you are perfect! She says you are very special."

"Ha! Perfect? I am far from it. No, I think it's too sudden. Besides, what are you going to do for a job? How will you support us? And what job would I do without an education?"

"You don't need a job, Elise. You will be my wife, and you will take care of your family. That is plenty of work for you. You cook good and sewed my ripped shirt real well."

Wally heard Elise cry out and stomp her foot.

"I am not your maid. Besides, I don't want to marry an ignorant person. You should want better for yourself, Didier!"

"Are *you* calling *me* stupid?!" Didi bellowed.

Elise withdrew from Didier and headed for the door. "It's not the same, and you know it! You need to finish school, and so do I."

Didier grabbed Elise's arm, impeding her exit. "I hate school; it is just a waste of time. I don't need it where I live! We live by the work of our hands and the smarts of the wild—that is what is important! You can ask anyone! Even Dad will tell you how important it is to provide for your family and bring them up in our tradition." Didier growled viciously.

"That might be so, but that is for your family, not me. I have important things I want to do! I want to go to the Italian Music Conservatory in San Renaldo, Italy."

"Why go there?" Didi snarled.

"I want to study flute there. Madame Flaubert says I am that good, and she has been working to get me a scholarship to the school." Elise sniffed, sounding haughty now.

Didi sighed expressively. "That is all a silver-plated hope, Elise. What do I do in the meantime while you are gallivanting around Italy?" He slumped against the banister rail. "Besides, there's a war on over there. You gonna get shot by Mussolini?"

"I know, but there won't always be a war. You could come with me." Elise offered softly.

"I hate Italian food." Didi paced the floorboards noisily. "I don't like Italians either."

"I'll bet you never met one."

"No, and neither have you, and you don't even speak the language, you little nitwit." Didi spat hotly.

"I do, too! I have been studying for nearly two years. Plus, I know Latin and speak French, so I am sure I can get by just fine!"

Didi growled. "Well, it is all stupid ... nothing but pipe dreams. Playing the flute doesn't make money."

Wally stood, barely able to breathe, as he listened to the painful silence. He was surprised to hear Elise speak.

"*È tardi. Io sono stanco.*"

"What did you say?" Didi asked harshly.

"I said it is late, and I am tired, Didier."

He gaped. "So you really want to go to Italy instead of having a cozy life with me? I thought you loved me."

"Didi, I-I am only fifteen, and I have no idea what I want besides finishing school. Let us do that, okay? Please stay here in town and finish high school with me. Once we have done that, then maybe things will be different. We will have grown closer, and maybe Daddy can give you a job or—"

Didier backed away, sounding terse. "I get it, Elise. Yeah, and maybe you won't love me anymore. You'll probably fall for some country club jock or end up going off to your music thing in Italy and forget about me." He spun away to yell, "Yeah, and you'll find some fascist spaghetti slinger to marry instead! No, get away from me. I don't think I want to talk to you anymore tonight. I hate you!"

"But, Didi, I was only trying to be practical. Can you not see it for yourself?"

"No. All I know is that I love you, I want you, and if you can't see that for *yourself*, then why should I stay here?"

Wally jumped back from the screen door as he heard hard footsteps coming across the back porch. He dashed to the hallway and into the bathroom, breathing hard and shallowly from his quick efforts. Wally nonchalantly opened the bathroom door as Didi came by. "Hey, kid, do you want to go to the movie show with me?" he asked, trying to act as if he had not heard the revealing discussion on the back porch.

"Get stuffed, Wally." Didier shoved him aside and went out the front door, slamming the screen door behind him.

Wally heard Elise come in from the porch. "Hi. Wanna go to the pictures in town or get an ice cream?" He received a sullen look from Elise.

"No thanks." Elise scurried past Wally and ran up the stairs.

Wally heard a bedroom door slam above and winced. "Fine, nobody wants to play with Wally. What else is new?" He slunk off and joined the adults in the living room, assuming it might be more interesting than sitting alone in his hot, stuffy room in the attic. The adults were playing bridge, and Rose was sewing with Granny Moon. He sat down at the out-of-tune upright piano and tinkled a few keys, picking out a ragtime dance melody until Beatrice complained.

"Please, if you don't know how to play the piano properly, then leave it alone. You are disturbing us with that racket, Wallace!" Beatrice cast imperious, narrowed eyes at the youth.

Wally left the living room and went out on the front porch. Out of spite of Beatrice's remark, he loudly played his harmonica for a few minutes. Bored, Wally sat on the veranda for a long time, hearing the echoed laughter from the living room, a distant radio program, the shu-shu-shing of someone mowing a lawn in the twilight, and the distant rush of the wind and waves from Lake Pontchartrain. The bugs came out and buzzed and hummed in his ears and around his face as he sat on the porch glider. He gloomily ignored them all, even Elaine, who ran up the steps by him after an evening out with her 'friends.'

He supposed it was a cover-up for a date with Terrence Dillard, for Wally observed Terry popping up in Charlie's *Buick* with Elaine's friends as it raced away. Elaine looked too dressy in a flowery summer frock and high-heeled sandals for a time out with only her girlfriends. She left a seductive cloud of *White Shoulders* perfume in her wake and ignored him.

Wally felt his stiff muscles after the long walk home today after a kind trucker had left him off at the outskirts of Akers before he turned off the road. Now his sunburn hurt; it seemed a double punishment for his impulsive escape from the beach. Sighing, he lay down on the patch of dewy, short grass in the front yard. He gazed up at the southwestern sky to see the last streaks of gold and crimson fade into red and purple over the vast lake, which reflected the glory of the sunset. He watched as the stars rose in the sky, each a twinkling light suddenly popping on in the growing gloom.

He liked this part of the night. The breeze was soft upon his skin, the dewy grass cooling him, the stars smiling and twinkling above—and he felt at home finally. The stars were as bright as the city lights of Fort Worth. Along the horizon of the lake, there were other distant towns and city lights. One of them was New Orleans, glowing and filling the night sky. The sky above was different from home, the stars slightly in another place, but as Wally searched the indigo heavens, he found the constellation he wanted—his star, Sirius, rising in the night.

He ignored the few passersby on the walkway who murmured in surprise why a young man was lying on the front lawn like a dead dog. Wally also blatantly ignored Didier, who finally slunk home like a chastised kicked dog. Didier ignored Wally, too, and slammed the screen door hard as he went inside the house.

Right about now, Wally wished they were closer to Ponchatoula. He had a yen for a strawberry soda, especially since Didier and Rose had selfishly eaten the last basket of berries for dessert earlier.

He felt the night creep up about him, the ending of the day as an electrical current being unplugged; the silence of the night escalated in nearly deafening tones in his ears. He shifted on the short grass, putting an arm beneath his head. He had always enjoyed looking at the night sky. In Scouts, he had earned badges for navigation and astronomy. But Fort Worth was a bright city, and he had to go far out into the countryside to see the natural starlight. Here, though, there were not any nearby street lamps, just big, dark, ancient, mossy trees in the old lakeside neighborhood comprising a handful of simple homes, so the stars shone clearly over the southern skies.

He caught the glimmer of a shooting star—a meteorite—and then smiled. Soon, another sizzled across the southern sky from northeast to southwest.

"Ah, the Perseid Showers," Wally mused and sighed. The real fireworks of the summer were beginning, and for a week or so, Earth would be showered with bits of cosmic debris. He settled so that he could better see the show.

He lay in quiet thought, wondering what to do with his idle life. Maybe he should enlist in the military as most of his friends had done already. Some had been drafted, yet he had somehow missed it. Was there a plan for him? Wally had never been a coward, and he would have enlisted with his high school pals, but when the day came, he felt ill with dread. A dark dream had plagued him all the night before. Like his mother Benita and half-sister Bonita, he sometimes had prescient dreams. Wallace Denis was not meant to be a soldier. His mother had agreed as well, so he stayed at home and found whatever odd jobs he could to help his family. It was a good thing Bonita was engaged to a citrus grower; there would soon be fewer mouths to feed. His mother expected him to be the responsible one—it wasn't always fair.

Wally sighed onerously from the weight of the world upon him, wishing life could be less complicated. The carefree, fun days of his youth were quickly spinning by. He would be expected to get a proper job and have a family. This summer vacation was probably the last one he would experience for years to come.

His eyes rose heavenward again and tracked an incoming sparkle of light, but then he was surprised to see a pair of bare feet near him. He looked up and saw slim legs and the hem of a robe.

"What are you doing out here? It's really late."

Wally sat up and leaned back on his arm. "Come join me." He patted the lawn next to him.

"Shouldn't you be in bed?"

"Shouldn't you, Elise?"

"I couldn't sleep. It's too hot upstairs. I got up to open the window some more and saw something out on the lawn. I wasn't sure what it was."

"And you didn't want to wake anyone, right?" Wally nodded. "You are a brave little soul, Elise. I could have been a nasty old alley-gator." He patted the grass again, chuckling. "Then be bold and watch the fireworks with me."

"What fireworks?" Elise smiled and sat next to Wally. She primly tucked her robe about her legs. "I hope no one sees me like this. They will think I am a nut or something."

"Who cares?" Wally breathed deeply. "Mmm ... the night flowers smell nice—gardenias and your mother's primroses are a sweet perfume, better than smelling the lake."

Elise sighed, too, after sniffing the cooling night air. "I am glad I came down. It is so hot tonight. Elaine is snoring, and I think she came home a bit tipsy. Rose is talking in her sleep." She slicked back a handful of sweaty curls and then braided her hair. "I hope my parents don't see me, but then again, everyone is asleep but us. I feel deliciously wicked to be outside at night and alone with a handsome young man!" She was startled when Wally let out a loud cry. "Sh!"

"Hey! There's one!" Wally pointed heavenward. "Did you see it?"

Elise squinted upward. "Sort of, I think."

"Look from above the lake to the southwest, and you will see streaks as the meteorites come into our atmosphere." He sighed with pleasure. "Sometimes you can even hear them sizzle and pop. I love looking at the sky."

"Me too. Oh! There is another! Wow, that was a big one," Elise exclaimed softly.

"Yup." Wally let out a deep sigh again. "Do you want to know about the meteorites—why they come here?"

"I think they are from the Perseid constellation. I remember that from my science class. I just never got up in the night to watch them. Thank you." Elise spoke with quiet affirmation.

"Smart girl. I never met a pretty one who liked science."

"I like a lot of things."

They watched for long minutes and didn't see many streaking sparks in the sky. "Do you think there will be some more?" Elise asked softly.

"Oh, yeah ... sure. The meteors usually show up around one or two in the morning. That's when the show really starts, so you wanna stay up with me to watch them?" Wally lay back in the grass again and folded his hands under his head.

"I had better not." Elise shook her head. "I am sorry about today, Wally. I just cannot understand why Elaine is so rude and mean."

"Me either. It doesn't matter. I'll be going home soon anyway."

"But I know she hurt your feelings."

Wally shrugged. "It's not the first time. I-I ... d-don't care."

"Yes, you do."

"Maybe. Besides, nobody knows me here, so I can be and say whatever I want. I just plain don't care anymore." He looked at Elise. "So what's the deal with this dumpy old house? I like yours in Baton Rouge better."

She looked over her shoulder at the venerable clapboard two-story house she loved despite its weathered look and a sandy little yard. She offered, "I think it's a cozy place. It belongs to my Grandma Nanette. The family used to take summer vacations here when my mom was a girl. We use it sometimes because Grandma cannot come. She says the place has too many old memories, and she just gets depressed when she is here."

Elise brushed away a mosquito. "I like it, though, and the lake is pretty. I like all the loons, herons, and pelicans. They are fun to watch while they fish. Have you seen the family of Nutrias just over by the bog? The babies are so cute."

Wally shook his head with a shudder of revulsion. "Glad I missed them. Didi said they are just giant rats—yuck! And no, I don't like the lake much. It stinks. Well, the water down there closer to the swamp does anyway."

"We rarely go there, especially Elaine. She hates squishy, squirming things, always yelling about leeches. I used to like to explore when I was smaller; it was fun catching fish and tiny frogs, except I hate snakes. The last few summers have had too many water moccasins, so I don't go down there anymore. I just stay closer to the beach." She brushed back another whining mosquito and tossed her braided hair over a shoulder before looking back up at the stars.

"So that town, Ponch-Y-Houla ..."

Elise giggled. "Ponchatoula," she corrected lightly.

Wally shrugged. "Yeah, however you pronounce it. It's such a weird name. Do you like it better than Baton Rouge? I wouldn't if I were you. It's kinda dumpy, and the people are sorta like hillbillies."

"It is not a weird name. You should think it is pretty."

"Why would I?"

"It is Choctaw; it means flowing hair. Didi said you have the Choctaw and Creek families like him. That's why he calls you Gray Turtle. He said it's your Indian name." Elise said with a smile.

Wally wrinkled his nose in thought and retorted nastily, "Yeah? Well, it's stupid, and his name is just as bad—Singing Dog. I call him the Howler, sometimes, just to piss him off. I don't know any Indians. My relatives are mostly dead now. So, I am as white bread as anyone else. So what does hair have to do with the town?"

Elise looked up and pointed at a cluster of old trees lining the crushed-shell walkway of the next yard. "See all that Spanish moss hanging from the trees? The moss resembles hair blowing in the wind. When I was little, I used to climb up the trees, pull some moss off, and make little birds' nests with it. I left them on the porch for the blackbirds and starlings and the little sparrows we used to feed. I haven't seen too many birds this trip," she commented softly as she gazed about the dark, quiet yard and the indigo expanse of the lake before them.

Wally only grunted in response.

Elise, still searching the sky, asked softly, "Have you ever been in love, Wally?"

"Yes. But I don't like it."

"You are so negative tonight." Elise turned to look at him. "Why not?"

Wally rolled over and laid his head in his arms. He sighed. "I don't like how it feels when things go wrong. I don't like leaving people I love behind."

"Who did you love that you left behind?"

"My folks … and I had a girl that I liked a lot in Texas. And I can think of another one right now."

"Elaine?"

"No, someone else. The girl is beautiful and kindhearted," Wally mumbled.

"Is it someone I know?" Elise queried coyly.

Wally nodded. "Yes, but I think she might be misguided. She thinks she is in love with someone else."

"And do you think it is a mistake for her … with this other fellow?"

"A big … big mistake."

"So, do you want her for yourself?"

Wally didn't answer and rolled away.

Silence reigned for several minutes as each searched the sky and their private thoughts. Then Elise rose to her knees. "I had better go in. Mother will yell if I catch a chill out here."

"Wait, Elise. I want to tell you something." Wally sat up and pulled at her robe hem.

"What?"

He scrambled to his feet to stand above her. "Please don't let Didi bug you, okay? I-I also w-wanted to thank you for talking with me today … and just now, too. I know sometimes I lose my temper, b-but I-I w-wanted you to know h-how much I—"

"You are welcome, Wally." Elise finished with a demure smile. "After all, you are Didi's cousin; you are family. We have to stick together, right?" She stood on tiptoe and kissed his cheek. "I notice when you talk to me, your stutter mostly goes away. Maybe if we talk more, it will go away completely. I'll see you in the morning."

"I think with you around all the time, I might be cured." He smiled boldly.

"When you are, then I'll give you a proper kiss for your efforts." Elise giggled and waved goodbye. She scampered up the stairs and into the house, letting the screen door shut gently behind her. *"Bonne nuit!"* she called and left Wally alone.

Wallace stretched and glanced once more up at the expanse of inky sky studded with pale, twinkling lights. He suddenly understood why the stories of his native family had said the stars were campfires of other worlds with their ancestors looking down at them. He waved to the stars and bid them good night as a lake bird cackled eerily. With an icy shudder, Wally went inside the house, this time locking the front door after him, and went upstairs to bed.

◆ ◆

Baton Rouge, Louisiana
Friday, August 25, 1944

All hell broke loose, or as Édouard was fond of saying, "The devil is pissing on us again!" Édouard angrily paced about the front room among the sea of stricken faces and grew more irritated by the snorkeled honks and wheezes of weeping females. He saw his wife wiping her drippy nose, eyes teary and lip trembling as she watched him, afraid for what he might do. He almost relented to see her so scared but then decided he must keep his pace or lose the war.

He rubbed his forehead, now feverish and sweaty. "Let me just get this all straight here. According to Granny Moon, there have been unsavory things happening under my nose—right here in my own house!"

He stopped pacing and leveled a finger at Didier. "You have been trying to seduce my daughters? Now you come to me asking to marry my youngest daughter, Elise! Are you daft? Do you have rotten cheese for brains?" He nearly spat in Didier's face as he shouted.

"How could you?!" Graciela moaned, weeping. "I thought we had raised you better than this, Didier. How can you be so … so—" She broke off and sobbed loudly.

Reynard stood and crossed the room to Édouard. "Look, old man, I think we should just leave before anything more is said. I know my son has been a problem before." He glared darkly at Didier, who looked not in the least bit guilty, only angry and pink in the face.

"And you bring that wolf among the sheep? *My* sweet lambs?! *Non!*" Édouard moaned. "*Aucun! Je suis fatigué de tout ceci. J'ai fait beaucoup pour lui et il me verse revenir comme cela?*" (No! I am tired of this. I did a lot for him, and he pays me back like that?) He mumbled as Reynard led him from the room, nearly in tears.

Beatrice looked about the room to see Elise and Elaine silent as stones. Elise had teary eyes. "Elise, what have you to say about this? Your father does not understand and has no patience for such folly. Do you love Didier as he says?"

Elise nodded but then stood up abruptly. "I do, but I don't want to get married, at least not now!" she countered.

"If you really loved me, you would come home with us," Didi snarled and brutally squashed a sofa pillow with his fist.

"This is just a sickening situation, absolutely horrible." Beatrice began but then cast a look at Wally. "And you, young man, are behind all of this! You sit there looking so innocent, yet you are the one who has watched much of the goings on behind our backs. If you were so concerned, then you should have come directly to Édouard or me, even Rey. Why use poor Granny Moon as the bearer of bad news?"

"Me? I-I d-d-didn't—" Wally stuttered.

"Oh, stop with the innocent act and the stammering. We all know you can speak normally; we've heard you, Wallace. I have a mind to send you home with a letter to your parents about what a sneaky and irresponsible boy you are."

"Ma'am, what did I do?" Wally stood up now, aghast.

Beatrice shifted her stance to say imperiously, "For one, you deceived us by taking Elaine to places where Terry Dillard was. Now we find out that they are secretly dating again! Terry was seeing her at the lake. Elaine stole away on her birthday night to be with him in town!"

She turned to Elaine. "I am most disappointed in your behavior! I thought you were broken off from Dillard. Well, now you will be for good. You are now banished from all further outside activities. No more parties, no picnics, no movie shows, no dances, no friends, and certainly no more dates with anyone! You were deceitful and used Wally to hurt us. And you made little Rosie your accomplice in these disturbing doings—she even lied for you! Sit down, Elaine!"

Elaine had risen to complain about the punishment but subsided fearfully in her chair again.

"In fact, everyone, please sit down! I cannot think with you all standing about looking like lightning-struck cattle!" Beatrice nearly screeched. She gulped hard and blew her nose on her hankie.

She turned to Graciela. "I think it would be best if you all would pack your things and go. *Je suis hors de moi.* (I am beside myself.) I just might say something more that would break us all for good." She stepped to the bay window to stare out. "I am truly embarrassed by this terrible situation and not at all sure of how to make it all right again. This is so … so disheartening."

Graciela nodded and stood up, her dark gray eyes filled with tears. "Yes, Bea, I understand, but I must tell you how sorry I am for all of this. I just don't understand how it all got so out of hand."

Beatrice held up a hand. "Please, I cannot bear any more of this discussion."

"What about me, Mama?" Rose asked. "Can I stay on and go to school?"

Beatrice's face softened to hear Rose plead tearfully. She turned about from the window and smiled down at Rose, answering for Graciela. "Of course, my girl, you may stay if you wish. You and Elise can share her room. I think Elaine will be moving into the bedroom across from ours so that we can keep a better eye on her, as Elise can no longer be a good influence on her. Oh dear, what am I saying? Elise is not any better than Elaine is. Rose, you will have your own bedroom! I cannot have these older girls leading you astray! *Ma pauvre petite Biquet!*" She petted Rose's head as if she were Chérie. "Now go help your mother get ready to leave. I am sure there is much you will need to talk about."

Rose impulsively hugged her aunt. *"Merci Tante Beatrice!"* She ran upstairs to help pack.

Graciela looked worried now. "Please, Bea, I hope this has not ruined our relationship. I truly do love you like a sister."

Beatrice was stoic and sniffed briefly. "Of course, I still love you, but I think it is time for Didier to go. I do not want him around my girls. He is a dangerous boy." She sighed. "This is most distressing, and Édouard is absolutely disappointed in Didier. He had thought of offering him a position this year in the store. But after all that happened while we were on vacation …" Beatrice turned away with a choking sob.

"Again, I am so sorry about this. Granny Moon always seems to see through things. How did we not see what was happening? I thought the children were just out having fun, not doing adult things. Oh dear." Graciela gulped and nearly began to cry anew.

"I really do not know. But, Grace, you must take that young cad away. To think that Moon found the two of them in the throes of passion … *Oh, mon Dieu!*" She shook her head to clear the distressing image. "A beating might not even be enough for him, you know. Not that I believe beating a child is a proper way, but something must be done about him."

"Yes. I am sure Rey will see to it." Graciela sighed. "I had hopes that Didi would stay on to finish high school and learn to work in the store, but I can see he is too wild and impulsive for such things. I fear for him, you know."

"As do I. I will be sure to pray for your child's soul. He is in grave danger if he continues on this way," Beatrice proclaimed with dread.

Graciela looked contrite. "Yes, Bea. I had better go before we argue again. Thanks for everything this summer, and in spite of all that has happened, Rey and I had a wonderful time with you and Édouard."

"Yes, us too. Now go before I change my mind and call the police on your miscreant, girl-mauling son."

◆ ◆

Saturday, August 26, 1944

Elise sat at her desk, wondering if she should try to write to Barton Barre again. He had never written to her after the letter that included the photographs; she was disappointed in him. She felt hollow inside, gloomily reflecting upon the wasted summer of teenaged idleness and the brief love affair with Didier Bonté. Now that he was gone, Elise had moments to think and wonder how everything got so out of hand.

It really had to be Didier's fault; he was so impulsive, thinking that if he asked Édouard, she would be forced to marry him. Elise did not want to marry anyone. Yet, she did feel strangely attached to Didier. With him gone now, she felt loose, like a lost ribbon in a breeze, her heart slightly pained, and she wondered if that was what love did to people. It made them feel worse when apart, just like Wally had said.

Elise smiled now and doodled on her pad of writing paper, thinking that, in many ways, she almost liked Wally better. At least he never tried to touch her in places that made her uncomfortable. Didi had. It had been scary, and yet, afterward, she yearned for such physical contact. Elise did not understand such dark desire, feeling it was most likely sinful. It must be how Elaine felt about Terry Dillard because she could not stay away from him.

Elise now wanted to feel Didi's beating heart again. She liked his kisses and the way he held her close. Yet, when looking into his eyes, something was frightening in his regard. She felt it deep down inside—Didier was as dangerous as Elise's mother had said. She thought again when he kissed her goodbye, still begging Elise to come home with him.

When she said no, she sensed a hot, fierce anger in Didi—as if he would immolate her on the spot. She chastely kissed him and said she would wait for him until they were older … perhaps next summer. He had hugged her hard and then said he would never come back; he was going home for good. Baton Rouge was not his home; the hills were his home—open air, forests, lakes, and the sky were his home. He hated the city.

He kissed her again as if it was the last time, and then, with tears in his eyes, Didier broke from Elise and ran down to the truck to climb in the back with Rose and Graciela. Wally was driving with his Uncle Reynard and Granny Moon in the truck cab. It was the best way to keep the young men from attacking each other. After what had happened and the revelations and conspiracies, they were sworn enemies again.

Elise looked down at her paper and saw two large, wet drops wrinkling the delicate pink paper. Her mindless doodles were at first flowery vines that soon grew into ragged and harsh, strident, angry marks. She wadded the paper and tossed it into the trash basket below her desk. She was cross again for having wasted paper and her summer.

She would have this bedroom to herself, as Elaine had moved out the day before and into the room vacated by Wally. The room looked barren without Elaine's usual mess and her furniture. She chuckled aloud, thinking of her father's punishment, insisting that Wally and Didier help to remove the furniture up to the attic and move in Elaine's stuff before they left yesterday. As he said, "Why should I break my back for your selfishness, Elaine? You caused this—all of it!"

Elise felt lonely again. She looked about the room, wondering how to make it hers, and soon found that acting industrious cleared her mind. Rearranging the furniture to her liking, Elise hung a few pictures on the nearly vacant walls that had once held tacked-up photos of movie stars and photographs of Elaine's many former beaus. She took out some of her dolls and stuffed animals that had been in the closet lately and grouped them on her trunk, a shelf, a chair, and her bed. She arranged her chair and music stand so that she had a practice place for her flute, and thinking on it, Elise took out her mother's silver flute and played as she wandered the now-spacious bedroom.

She felt the music draw the sadness away, each note rising and falling like sighs and tears. She breathed with the music until sated and strangely serene. She stopped at the photograph of Lake Como with the beautiful ranging mountains and tranquil, deep-turquoise lake. It was somewhere she had always wanted to go, and with her dream of the Italian Music Conservatory somewhere near the famous lake, Elise played her flute, thinking about the scene aloud with her personal music. She swore—no, promised—that she would go there someday. Elise would make her dream real! She would leave this place far behind and ride the waves of her music to her dreamland. She would forsake all men to live her dream.

Elise was brought back to earth abruptly as little Chérie was barking downstairs at the front door. She put her flute away in the case and stood at her window, wondering who visited. Soon, there was a knock on the bedroom door. She opened the door to her father. He stood for a moment, looking uncomfortable, but then asked to come in.

"*Puis-je m'assesoir pour un visite?*"

"Of course, Daddy, you may come in."

He gazed about the bedroom and then smiled briefly at his daughter. Still speaking in French, he commented, "You are always the neat one of the family. Look what you have done—your room is tidy and decorated nicely! Elaine's room still looks like an upturned hornet's nest." He sat on the armchair's arm and picked up Elise's stuffed lamb. "I am sorry about yesterday, Elise." He said as he stroked the curly ivory wool.

She rushed to Édouard. "Oh, no! It was my fault! Please forgive me. I never meant for Didier to get so worked up. It was his idea, not mine, to get so serious." She hugged her father.

Édouard was surprised. "I have already. Now that the young heathen is gone, I can breathe again."

"He isn't a heathen, Daddy."

"No? Well, he acts like a right wild one—all that fighting and posting about like a young warrior. Singing Dog, indeed! Rey has his hands full with that boy."

"You were young once. I am sure you felt the same with Mother when you first fell in love, yes?" Elise asked sagely and sat in the chair next to Édouard. "Tell me, Daddy, what it was like?"

"What is love like or the other thing?" He asked, looking ill at ease.

Elise blushed. "No, Daddy, what did you do? How did you know you really loved Mom?"

Édouard smiled. "Oh, that was easy. I fell for her the very first time I saw her come into the store. She wanted some French lace for a dress she was sewing. I saw she was wealthy, and I showed her the best bolts of imported silk fabric and Chantilly lace. She glowed, and I knew I wanted her. She had exquisite and elegant taste even as a young lady. She knew what she wanted."

"That is nice. Did Mama like you too?"

"No, I was just a shopkeeper."

"So, how did you get her to like you?"

Édouard pursed his lips and thought for a moment. "Oh, I asked my father to deliver the goods to her address instead of me. He wondered why, but I told him I had other things to do. He saw the beautiful house she lived in. Her father was a banker, you know. He was very wealthy. He had an interest in the logging industry over in Ponchatoula, which is why they had the lake house there. But then, when the industry died abruptly in the twenties, he took a financial hit. Well, he never quite got over it and divested himself of the property, although your grandmother insisted that she keep the lake house."

"Really? I guess I forgot that. Grand-mère doesn't talk of him much anymore."

"That's right. Why would she? Georges Laforrêt died just before you were born. But I am glad that Nanette knows you. She does love you so."

"I know, Dad, and I love her too. So how did you get Mom to love you?"

Édouard leaned against the chair back. "Oh, I owe it to my father, really. He told Monsieur Laforrêt that he had a son and suggested his daughter might like to meet him and go to a dance."

"Really? You met her at a dance?"

"No, Monsieur Laforrêt asked to meet me first. Father was a bit impertinent to ask for such a thing without actually knowing the girl. Therefore, I went to Laforrêt's home and told the monsieur that I wanted to date his daughter. He almost laughed in my face but then believed I was serious because I had brought a basket of expensive gifts from our store."

Édouard shook his head. "I hardly knew the girl's name, but Laforrêt agreed, and instead of the dance, he invited me and Father to dinner. We went, and it was there that the Boulanger family was introduced to the Laforrêts. From then on, Beatrice and I dated once a week, only two hours for a walk in the park or a buggy ride or tea—and chaperoned, as well, by her nanny, Sylvie." He sighed wistfully and continued. "The one ball we attended was the best, and I knew then that we were truly in love."

"Then, after many months, when I asked to marry Beatrice, her father said no. I had not proven myself to be a capable businessman yet. So I waited until Father gave me more of the business, and I turned it around until it was much like it is today, a prosperous store with a large clientele. I worked hard for six months and appeared on Laforrêt's doorstep with flowers and a diamond ring I had paid for myself and again asked to marry Beatrice. He said no again and sent me away."

"But, Daddy, it must have broken your heart. How did you do it then?" Elise patted his hand.

Édouard held her hand, stroking it with a thumb. "True, I was despondent, but I knew I had to keep vigilant. I wanted Beatrice. She was the loveliest and most dear woman I had ever known, and I believed she loved me too. I was scared to death that she would grow impatient and another fellow would catch her eye, as we were both past the normal age to marry. There was always a pack of young hounds dogging her. She was funny, too; she often sent her giggly friends to our store or Sylvie just to check up on me. But I did not know at the time how much she loved me until your grandmother Nanette showed up in our store."

Elise sat up, engrossed in the story. "So what happened then?"

Édouard smiled. "Oh, that was the easiest part. Madame Laforrêt asked if I truly loved her daughter. I said I did and that I did not want to offend them by continuing to go against the monsieur's rules by taking a more avid pursuit. She indicated that Beatrice had other suitors who were more adept at such amorous games and were wealthier young men with much time on their hands to pursue her. But Beatrice was crying night and day for me, or so Madame Laforrêt said. So emboldened, I returned and gave the monsieur an ultimatum: let us marry, or we would elope and to hell with him!"

"Oh, Daddy, how romantic! And did you elope?"

"No. Laforrêt saw the wisdom of it all, for many of the other young men might have come from wealthy families, but they were not as stable as I was or as serious. The other reason is that I had never tried to take advantage of her, while others were cads and playboy types. I also think Beatrice and Nanette worked him over, and Georges finally relented. We were engaged and married within a few months despite the conventions of society and gossip. We have been happy ever since." He smiled warmly at his recollection.

"Just like a perfect fairy tale." Elise sighed with happiness.

"Yes, it was." Édouard straightened up and shrugged his shoulders. "I know I must seem hard on you and Elaine, but you are beautiful young girls. With so many wolves sniffing about, I do not wish to see you hurt." He caressed his daughter's cheek.

"I understand, Daddy. I don't want to hurt you either. I am sorry that everything was so crazy."

"No, you are not to blame. It was those boys and Elaine, and she puts these crazy ideas of romance in your head."

Elise shook her head and squeezed his hand. "No, Dad, Didier did that. Nevertheless, I think I might be over him; we do not want the same things. I believe it is crucial to choose the same things."

Édouard leaned to kiss Elise on the forehead and dropped the lamb in her lap. "You are wise for such a young lambkin. But yes, Didi is not meant for you, and you were smart to be cautious, even if it felt fun."

"It was fun for a while, but I don't like jealousy or pettiness." Elise then sighed. "I have bigger dreams than Didi does. He wants nothing more than what the moment gives him. I don't think like that. I want practical things that I can build upon and dream about together."

"I knew you to be the innocent one in all of this rottenness. I have just one thing I must ask—it is as embarrassing for me as for you."

Édouard coughed. "Um, I promised myself and will promise you that I won't be angry … but did anything happen to you, Elise? Did … did Didier hurt you or touch you?" He groaned and asked abruptly, "Oh hell, did he have carnal relations with you?"

Elise turned pink and hid her face behind her hands for a moment. "Oh, Daddy, no! But I think we might have gotten close to it. When Didier told me what he wanted to do, I said yuck!" She moaned. "I am an idiot!"

Édouard burst out laughing and held his sides. "*O ma pauvre petite lapin!*" He pulled Elise to his side. "I am sorry to laugh—it really isn't funny—but I am so relieved! Then you are still a whole … girl?"

"I think so. But I am not sure I will ever want to do the disgusting things Didi talked about if that is what sex is."

"Forget about it, my dear!" He wiped his eyes and blew his nose on a handkerchief, pocketing it. "I am so happy and cannot wait to tell *Maman* that you are still safe."

"Oh, sure … embarrass me some more, will you? Just like Mom did when she told you I got my first period."

Édouard blushed hotly. "Oh, that. Well, you are my daughter, and I should know, even if I do not need the details. I have to keep you safer now from the men who will want you. You are a very trusting girl, prettier and more vulnerable than Elaine."

Elise sniffled and wiped her eyes after the mortifying discussion. "You really think I am pretty?"

"Of course I do, and so does everyone who looks at you. I saw you in your shorts and swimsuit while on vacation. You have a figure that will not be easy to hide anymore. My girl, you will be in public high school this year. I am not sure what I should do to keep you safe. You want to be a nun?" He smiled at her startled look and patted Elise's hand. "Sorry. However, the boys will be panting after you like love-struck puppies."

"Oh, Daddy, don't be silly. They won't; nobody really does that to me now except for myopic Byron Bisbee."

"Isn't Byron our newspaper boy?"

"Yes, and a big pest." Elise shot back. She let out a sharp exhalation. "Sooo … how long am I to be punished for? And is it until school starts? And you still haven't said what my punishment will be."

Édouard smiled down fondly at his child. "You are always the little soldier, ready to take on your duty. No, Elise, after our conversation here, and now that I see none of the nonsense was of your making, I think a few days in your room will suffice. Then you can work with me in the store. I need to do inventory for the fall quarter. Since we were entertaining the Bontés, I am certain our sales suffered. I have missed you at the store, too."

Elise wrinkled her nose and giggled. "But I like inventory; that isn't much of a punishment."

Édouard smiled indulgently. "I know you don't think so because you have always liked to work at the store with me. You are quicker with the math than I am or your mother, so you are really an asset and not a hindrance." He patted her dark, curly head. "Oh, I have something for you too. Victoria Harrow next door brought this over. It seems the mailman mixed up our mail with theirs."

"Really? I have a letter?" Elise took the letter, and her eyes went wide. "Oh, Dad! I have been waiting for this for ever so long!"

"Who is it from? It looks like it's been in a war from the look of it—it's all dirty and raggedy."

"It has been in a war, the one in Europe! It is from Barton!" She squealed with excitement.

Édouard frowned and snatched back the letter. "Barton! Now, who the devil is that?"

Elise excitedly rushed through her explanation. "Mom didn't tell you? I have a pen pal, his name is Barton Barre, and I was afraid he might not like me anymore or maybe have died because I haven't had a letter from him in months."

"Go ahead, open it then. Let's see what the young man has to say to you." Édouard passed the tattered envelope back to Elise.

Elise rolled her eyes. "But it might be private things, you know."

"Oh, don't tell me you are in love with this boy now."

"Dad! Let me read my letter in peace, will you?"

Édouard sighed. "Oh, fine, keep me in the dark again. I am beginning to feel like a mushroom or a large fruit bat with this constant dark secrecy and …" He dropped to his knee to face Elise. "Please, my little darling, promise me something, will you?"

"What, Dad?"

"No more secrets between us. You can tell me anything, all right?"

Elise was caught on the visible worry in her father's teary, ebony eyes. "Yes, I will. I promise." She stroked his cheek.

Édouard kissed Elise on the forehead. "And another thing, don't grow up too fast. I miss my little girl already."

Elise kissed and hugged him back. "*Merci Papa. Je t'aime aussi.*"

Édouard rose and stopped at the door to blow his daughter a kiss. He shut the door on his precious daughter, and with a tear in his eye, he fearfully said to the hovering Beatrice, "Our time together is but a brief stay before she leaps from the nest like a fledgling sparrow." With a lump in his throat, he led the now-sniffling Beatrice to their room. "I think we both could use some quiet time for consolation, *ma coeur.*" He shut their door and kissed Beatrice heartily.

◆ ◆

Elise resettled in the armchair and tore open the flap of the envelope. She withdrew the single sheet of paper and gasped. It was blacked out in many places, and she fought to comprehend the messy scrawled message in French.

21, Juin, 1944

Ma Chère Elise,

La guerre c'est ici maintenant! Je vais à France ————— Je voudrais ————— Ne vous en déplaise, —————

242

Elise translated quickly in her head. The war was imminent. He was saying goodbye to her as he was on his way to France. He was glad that he had a brief time with her at the dance so long ago. He gave her permission to see others, even though he felt strongly about her. He was sure that Elise had strings of other beaus and should be only concerned for them. Elise gulped back tears, feeling her heart fill with love as she read the remaining words in a whisper.

> *If I were to fall for anyone, actually to say I love you to someone, then it would be you, Elise. I am foolish, I know, but I think of you often and feel deeply for you. I do not know how it is possible because our time together was so short.*

> *Thank you for your letters over the year, but I think I must say goodbye. We are too far away from each other for anything lasting between us.*

> *If one day you get a letter or telephone call from my folks in Beaumont, Texas, then you will hear the sad news of my demise. I hate to say it, but the————many people are————every day, and I might be next to go. I miss you and home, but I know that my time here is supposed to mean something. Wish me luck, Elise.*

SS Barton C. Barre

◆ ◆ ◆

CHAPTER 10

Le Lapin D'Or

Soissons, France
Wednesday, August 30, 1944

The town looked war-torn; large craters pockmarked the cobblestone streets, and tree debris and building rubble lined the avenue as Barton's company rolled through Soissons. People peeked out from behind curtains to watch the convoy of trucks pass by. Some people came out to gape at them; a few waved white handkerchiefs, pleading for peace.

Barton sat in the Jeep, taking it in while trying not to smile. He was feeling happy that they had finally gained entry to the town of Soissons. He knew and could almost feel akin to this place, as if the ghost of his father was still here. The AEF had camped here once long ago, in much the same way as Barton's division would. He kindly waved to a few folks as they stood on the streets or ran alongside the trucks, welcoming them. He glanced quickly about, wondering where his father had been. Some of the buildings were centuries old, but many were of newer designs. However, many were shattered after the conflict between the Germans and the French citizens, and then the US Army had run the Krauts out just days before, probably making the town look even worse.

There were still red-and-black swastika signs and propaganda posters emblazoned on windows, sides of buildings, and street lamps. The Germans had been here so recently that nothing had yet been cleared away, including shelled vehicles and left-behind transports; the local people still looked shell-shocked. The convoy wound through the short city streets, finally pulling up near what had once been an old hotel. The doors were blasted off, and many windows were broken out, but on the good side, the building was still intact.

Barton searched the streets as they drove through, hoping to see the sign of Lapin D'Or, but he did not see one resembling his father's description. He wondered now if the place still existed. Most likely, a place like that had been shut down. Prostitutes and brothels, while being the world's oldest trade, were not usually a secure business.

He only wanted to see if what Richard had told him about his experience here was true. His father was good at fabricating stories, especially to make a point or life parable. But then again, why would he lie about the personal things he had written in his letter? Barton wanted desperately to find that small connection to home, and perhaps he could solve his father's old mystery—what happened to Lisette, Richard's first wife and probably a prostitute herself?

In a small way, Barton did not want to find it all. To reveal such a personal thing was like seeing Santa Claus without a beard, exposing only a relative, or spotting a masked hero suddenly naked! Yet, conversely, he wanted to know that secret, intimate factor that would make his father more human and perhaps less of a righteous man than Bart thought. He wanted, in some way, to lay his father's sins at his door with the revelation of what he might find here.

He shivered in anticipation of such discoveries, wanting boldly to leap from the Jeep to roam the streets to find Richard's past here in this town. Alas, he had duties to perform and men to lead, and he stuffed all his excitement back down and continued to perform the duties of a staff sergeant. He needed to unload his trucks, settle his men, receive orders from the lieutenant colonel, and create a duty roster for their time in Soissons.

◆ ◆

The next day, Barton noticed that many of the businesses were boarded over, windows broken, and doors nailed shut as he ambled along the almost empty streets. He pitied the poor condition of the town, wondering how much damage the Fifth had inflicted on these broken people just to oust the enemy. He glanced at his buddy, M. SGT. Harlan Schmidt, who had agreed to take a walk with Barton and four other men as a police contingency out on patrol. The men in their drab olive green combat uniforms, bristling with weapons, still put the locals in a respectful and fearful mind. Some people darted from their path to walk in the street or scurried into a building; others nodded and smiled feebly at the men. Mothers pulled their children close and coldly stared at the men in passing.

Barton felt their palpable fear—he almost could not blame them. What difference was it to have one foreign army occupying their town only to be replaced by another? These people wanted to be free again and safe.

He bent to pet a scrawny cat that sauntered out from an alley, feeling good that at least an animal respected and trusted him, which said more than how these people felt about them. While the Americans were their liberators, some French citizens still harbored resentment and distrust. He continued along with the entourage of men and now felt he could speak of his personal quest to Schmidt.

"I am looking for a place, Schmidt. I don't know if it still exists."

After lighting a cigarette, Schmidt snapped his lighter shut and pocketed it, "Yeah, why?" He eyed Barton narrowly through the curl of smoke. "Have you been here before?"

Barton smiled mildly. "No, but it almost feels like déjà vu. I have a little secret confession to make."

Schmidt rounded on Barton with a sly grin. "Oh yeah? I like secrets. Do tell!" He glanced behind him to see the other men following. "Let's stop here and let the others go ahead."

Barton waited while Schmidt waved the men ahead, and then they followed at a slower pace. "My father fought in World War I here in this area. He camped here in Soissons, much as we have done. I just kinda wanted to see the town for myself."

"Hmm, well, that's kinda keen, what a fluke. Alrighty then. So what are you lookin' for, people?"

"I am not sure, maybe. Dad told me he married a girl here but then had to leave her behind when the AEF moved out."

Schmidt whistled through his teeth as if amazed. "Well, well, that is an interesting little tale. So he was with the AEF, huh? They were a rough bunch. Your old man must be a tough old nut; it's no wonder you are so tightly wound."

"Can it, Schmidt," Barton replied sourly. "I wanted to see if he was telling the truth. I want to find out if there ever was a place called *Le Lapin D'Or.*"

"Oh, is it a restaurant?"

Barton blushed. "No, man, it's a brothel."

Schmidt stopped dead. "Shee-it! Are you kiddin' me? A cathouse?" He laughed loudly like a braying donkey, which made the men ahead look back at them in puzzlement.

"Sh! You moron!" Bart elbowed the MP. "God! Why did I ever say anything to you?" he growled, now annoyed.

Choking with laughter, Schmidt spat out the stub of cigarette and wiped his face. "Jesus-Marie! You had me goin' there! Now a cathouse would be a welcome place for us! I think the gals might get rich. We got a bunch of horny dogs just lookin' for fun!" He grabbed his crotch and chortled. "Me included!"

Barton frowned. "Don't be disgusting! Forget I said anything!"

As they walked along, Schmidt wheezed with merriment. "Man, your old man in a cathouse! Now that puts a different color on you! Like father, like son, eh? You wanna go get your dickie tickled?" He pushed Barton roughly.

Barton grimly clammed up and increased his pace, ignoring Schmidt's taunts and raucous laughter. He was sorry now. Barton supposed Schmidt always would be a dirty-minded cad. Barton did not have sex on his mind; he only wanted to know if his father's story was true.

Then, as Barton thought about it, he did wonder if maybe the girl Richard Barre had married might still be there. Perhaps she was the madam now. He grimaced at the thought—he could even have a sibling living here. His father marrying a prostitute certainly did not put him in a good light, and the silvered image of his father was again tarnished before his eyes.

He caught up with the other men, no longer interested in searching for the brothel. He could still hear Schmidt behind him, chortling loudly like an overgrown turkey.

"God! Just shut up!" Bart growled.

He wanted to turn around and clobber the man. He was definitely sorry he had said anything. He hoped that if he confided in Schmidt, he might be able to help him locate the place. As Schmidt and his men were on police patrol through the area, he might run across it.

Bart took up the pace with the cadre of soldiers and shoved his previous thoughts from his mind, again on the alert for land mines, discarded weapons, and any other munitions or supplies that the Krauts might have left behind, including a more dangerous threat—missing men.

◆ ◆

August 31, 1944

That night, Barton fidgeted about trying to reach the itch on his back, but then soon another was along his ribs and his neck. He scratched but found no relief as more itchy spots seemed to erupt from strange places. He tossed back the heavy wool blanket and lit the bedside oil lamp, turning it up.

He ran a hand over the dank linens and saw minute things leaping about. He caught one between his fingers and squinted at it. *Un Pou!* Fleas … bedbugs! Barton squashed the tiny insect, leaving a bloody smear on his thumb. He got up off the sagging bed and shook out his blanket. Barton noted more things hopping and scurrying about, along with a few cockroaches scuttling under the iron bed frame. He angrily swept the filthy linens and thin mattress off the bed. He stood for some moments in agitated silence as he scratched and searched through his underwear and repeatedly ran his hands through his hair, hoping to dislodge any bugs.

"I hate fleas!" He still wore scars from fleabites from hot, itchy Texas summers as a kid.

Barton took up his bedroll, unfastened it, and rolled it out on the bed springs. He sprinkled some camphorated foot powder on it, eager to discourage any more visitors. He lay down on the bare bed, no longer feeling so good about having a room of his own. He probably would have done better to camp outside with some of the other men or even sleep in a truck. Nevertheless, the lure of a private room the size of a postage stamp and a bed had sounded good to him, including the cold shower.

He cast a wary look about the room, noticing its poor condition; cracked walls, peeling paint, shredded layers of wallpaper, and clumps of plaster were coming off from the ceiling. He could see the broken wooden laths behind the empty spaces of plaster. Staring up at the dark place, he could swear there were glittering eyes watching him.

"Oh, great. Rats? Even if the place was in good repair, I would be surprised if anyone would want to pay to stay here. *Un Sou* is too *chèr* for this dump—*c'est une poubelle!*" ("A penny is too dear for this dump—it's a toilet!") he grumbled and rolled over in his bedroll, seeking a comfortable spot. Perhaps the vermin would be less likely to attack him if he left the lamp burning.

He lay for a time, wondering who had this room before him, not that it mattered. *Was it a German soldier? A flea and lice-ridden German soldier,* Barton amended with grinning malice. He could only hope the filthy guy bought it, and smiling at the macabre thought, he turned down the sputtering oil lamp.

◆ ◆

He awoke, now chilled in the dark room; there was no glass in the tiny window, just the blackout shade. Amid the odor of mildew, he hated mildew, and there was something else sour and bitter smelling, like sweat or urine. He hoped it wasn't him. As he sat up in bed, his eye caught something gray and sinister rummaging in his pack. Stealthily, he picked up his boot, aimed, and threw it. A high-pitched squeak and the sounds of scurrying feet followed as Barton witnessed a trio of rats leaving the scene of their crime.

He grabbed up the other boot and lobbed it, hitting one rat squarely and knocking it off the pile of discarded bedding. He grabbed up his pistol and shot the damn thing!

He instantly regretted his action, for there were loud shouts and thudding feet, and then his bedroom door slammed open. He stood half-naked under the light of an electric torch amid the aim of a couple of rifles and Schmidt's pistol.

"What in the hell of Sundays is going on in here?" Major Donald Clay shouted as he parted the sea of half-dressed men in the hallway and around Bart's door. "Excuse me, let me through." The portly man gained entry, turned up the oil lamp, and stood glaring at the bloody scene in Bart's room.

Barton winced at the sudden bright light and turned hot pink as the major's shadow loomed over him. "Um, sorry, sir. I caught a rat … two of them, actually, in my kit." He looked up aghast to see the lieutenant colonel there at the door, too.

The colonel stepped alongside the major. "I see. You had to shoot it. You couldn't have thrown something at it?" Samuelson rubbed his stubbled jaw wearily and eyed the mess. He looked over at the other men. "Oh, for heaven's sake, get back to bed; there's nothing here to see." He waved them away.

The men grumbled at having been awoken in the wee hours of the morning. They were loud in their complaints, and spontaneous jokes popped up as the surly major shepherded them to their rooms.

Samuelson shouted down the hallway. "Nobody is allowed to shoot the vermin, do you understand? Save your ammunition for the human rats!" He glared at Schmidt, who was still hovering near the door.

Bart caught another joke about saving the rats for breakfast.

"Sergeant, that is all. Please return to your room." Samuelson gave lurking Schmidt a shove and slammed the door.

"So!" Samuelson turned about in the room. "I'd like to hear your take on this fine mess you have created." He stepped around the pile of bloodied bedding, and now smirking, he sat on the bare, squeaking bed springs.

Barton was still horribly embarrassed by the debacle and just shrugged. "God, sir, I feel pretty stupid. I woke up and thought the Jerries were in the room or something. I could smell them." He ran a hand around his neck and then found an itchy spot and scratched it. "I wasn't using my head, I guess."

"Clearly not. Would you also mind telling me why your bedding is on the floor?" The man nodded at the mess.

"Everything's got fleas—I was getting eaten alive." Bart pulled at his undershirt to show numerous red bites. "Look." He scratched idly and then straightened up, realizing the officer was staring at him as if he were a lunatic. "Sorry, sir. I did throw my boots at them, but it wasn't enough of a hazard. Look what those rats did to my pack." He bent to retrieve the pack and his duffle bag.

The canvas strap on the duffle bag hung limply, nearly chewed through, and there were numerous holes in his pack. One hand-knitted sock was half pulled out through a chewed hole, and its toe bore a ragged end. Barton fumed. "Oh geez, the rats ate my hand-knitted socks. My grandmother made them." He stuffed the socks back in the pack and sat down abruptly on the bed next to the colonel.

The older man smiled kindly at Barton. "You can always darn them. I have some yarn; it won't be the same color, but who cares."

Looking abashed now, Barton stated, "My sisters always darned our socks. I don't know how."

Samuelson grinned and patted Barton on the shoulder. "Lucky for you, you aren't with the regiment of Scots—they knit their own socks." He saw the incredulous look on Bart's face. "It is true. Men do actually sew and knit, Son. I do. But we can keep that a small secret from the rest of the men for now."

The colonel stood up, stretching his back and making pops and creaky noises. "So, I suppose I should be thankful that you are so quick to draw and an admirable shot, but use your head next time." He rubbed his chin as if in thought. "If it makes you feel any better, I have a story for you." He paced about the room and peered at the faded, out-of-date calendar on the wall.

"When I was in basic training, I was very young and rather proud of my expertise with a rifle. We were on bivouac out in the desert, and let me tell you, there were many things you did not want sharing your bedroll at night." He smiled wanly and then continued. "One night, we were camped in the tents, and I felt something cold crawling on my face and then shoulder and arm. I awoke with a start, and thinking maybe it was a prank from one of my pals, I rolled over in my cot. But then I felt it again. I threw back the covers and turned on my electric torch, and there in my bed was the hugest and scariest thing I had ever seen."

"Oh shit! What was it? A snake? A rat?"

"No, a tarantula the size of a dinner plate!" Samuelson said with wide eyes. "Well, without a further thought, I took up my sidearm and blew the thing to smithereens."

Barton looked agape. "Wow. The guys must have thought you were a hero. Tarantulas can give you a nasty bite."

"No, I was an idiot. I not only killed the spider, but I blew a hole in my cot, ruining it for good, put a hole in the side of the tent, and nearly shot my foot off and the company mascot dog, Digger." The officer smiled crookedly and ran a hand around his neck. "There was only one good thing to come out of all that—Digger never relieved himself on the side of our tent again." He chuckled and then sobered. "I had a good many jibes and jabs after that night, including a black eye. General Bradley still calls me Tarantula Killer."

Barton grimaced to think of his new nicknames … *Cochon* and now *Vermin Vindicator!*

The colonel stood near the door. "No, I think you can retake police duty for your punishment for the next day or two. Schmidt seems to think, and so do Wells and Sawyer, that there is still a contingency of enemy soldiers nearby. We probably didn't get them all out. You are to search every building, outhouse, cellar, attic, and barn. See if you can rout those kinds of rats, Sergeant."

"But why me? I am not an infantry soldier … I mean …" Barton complained but blanched at the look from Samuelson.

Samuelson turned with crispness and glared at him with icy blue eyes. "You are a soldier in this man's army, and if I say you do something, you do it. Understand? Besides, I need you out there among the people. You speak French. Find out what you can, listen, and act as our French spy … eh? Maybe you might find the little group of French spies for the *Resistance*. I have some information they might need."

"Yes, sir," Barton said glumly and then scratched furiously in his hair. "Oh crap, I've probably got lice now!"

Samuelson laughed. "See to it that every man gets checked out. If they have lice, they must shave their heads. We will not fight this war as a ragtag, flea-bitten, lice-ridden rabble. Understand?"

"Yes, sir." Barton shot to attention. "I'll see to it, sir."

The officer cast another look around Bart's room. "And do clean this mess up. Good night, Sergeant." He went out of the room, shutting the door firmly behind him.

◆ ◆

Soissons, France
September 1, 1944

The day dawned with heavy clouds, looking gray and sullen, much like Barton felt. His quest for the brothel had come up empty in the past few days. He might have made himself look a fool when he asked a few of the older men in the town if such a place existed. Some men had stared coldly at him and then shooed him away or asked if Barton was seeking female entertainment. Each time, he blushed profusely and said no, that he had heard of such a place and wanted to find a person who had worked there once. Barton realized asking for the place had gotten him nowhere but trouble, but to ask for a person seemed to pique interest, and the men were less likely to laugh or act repulsed by his inquiry. Also, he didn't need a date with some guy's cross-eyed sister.

He finally told a decrepit old man that *Le Lapin D'Or* was a bar. He was searching for a waitress who worked there; she had relatives in America, and he had hoped to meet her. The nearly toothless old man smiled and nodded his grizzled head. He then elbowed his equally aged friend while they sat at an outdoor café sipping watered-down wine.

"Oui. Je reconnais la maison," the man asserted.

"Monsieur, il n'es pas un maison, mais un bar … un tavern." Barton corrected the man, saying it was a bar and not a house.

"Je sais, parce que je travailler au noir à cette place dans le temps." The man waved a hand and scratched his bulbous nose. *"Les filles sont très jolie!"* He smiled up at Barton again to ask, *"Tu aimes les filles?"*

Barton ignored the man's comment that he used to work nights at the place and the question about liking girls. He was heartened to hear him comment about the girls in the present tense, so he asked in French, "Where is this place? Please tell me the street here in town."

"Non. Non. Il n'es pas ici." The man shook his head and looked at his friend, who agreed.

"Do you mean it is closed?" His heart sank.

"Oui mais il n'es pas dans cette ville, le Lapin est en la place Vieux."

"Vieux? Où?"

The old man pointed. *"Deux kilomettres la bas, Sud-Ouest … dans le pays."*

"Oui?"

"Oui!" The man nodded sharply with affirmation, nearly losing his tattered hat.

"Je te revaudrai ça." Barton smiled, thinking that now that he had what he wanted, he would offer a small reward.

"Tu as une cigarette?"

"Oui." Barton grabbed out a half packet of cigarettes from his jacket pocket. *"Pardon, ils sont Américains."* He offered a Lucky Strike cigarette to the man.

"Merci." Instead of taking one, the man grabbed the packet and took several for himself and another for his friend. *"Et ton briquete?"* His rheumy dark eyes were avariciously searching Barton's jacket.

Barton shook his head. *"Non seul allumettes."* He decided it was a good trade—a pack of matches and stale cigarettes for information, but he wouldn't give up his cigarette lighter. *"À un de ces quatre."* Bart made a one-fingered salute and, with the tip of his head, walked away with a smug smile.

"Il a de petits yeux et une tête à claques!" the old man said with a sneer to his compatriot and shared the packet of cigarettes with him as they made jokes at Bart's expense.

Barton laughed at the off-hand remark but kept walking. So the old man thought Bart had beady eyes, a face made for slapping, and that he looked like a shaved dog! Bart had what he wanted; at least somebody in the town knew about the place! It was only two kilometers away in the village of Vieux. He ran a hand around his freshly shaved neck and felt hot from the comments and the autumn sun. Now Bart just needed a Jeep and an excuse to drive out into the country.

◆ ◆

Monday, September 4, 1944

Barton had to wait two days for a storm cell to pass by; it poured rain on the countryside as if the heavens were pissing. In the drippy, old Hôtel Luxe, he passed time pacing, playing solitaire, and sketching or writing in his diary while waiting impatiently for the skies to clear and the roads to dry. He also scratched fleabites and loathed his shorn head, feeling itchy and twitchy even though his room had been cleaned and the flea-ridden bedding and mattress removed.

After his police forays came up empty in the search for German soldiers, Barton had done his other job—buying extra supplies for their company. Barton had been in the town for a short time, and he had considered its assets. After asking other pertinent questions about buying or trading supplies with many locals, Bart had a long list of what was needed and an idea of where to go. He cleared the use of a small truck and a few men to take out into the country to barter for fresh eggs, meat, cheese, and milk from the local farmers. Major Clay and Lieutenant Colonel Samuelson were eager for wine or ham and greens for salad making. So Barton added produce to the list and knew he could finagle wine from somewhere, especially if he found *Le Lapin D'Or.*

So the colonel wanted greens? Bart recalled seeing a large patch of dandelions in an empty lot—*Pis-en-lit salade* would be easy, and the fools would probably be none the wiser! *Grand-père* François always said dandelions were good for his digestion and killed any worms.

The men were eager for anything fresh; tinned or prepackaged meals were less than savory and certainly couldn't be as healthy as eating something fresh. Major Clay had agreed with Bart's suggestion and arranged for such a foray. Barton felt sneaky but happy that he had come up with the plan; after all, he was the local liaison and translator and Samuelson's *Le Cochon*. But to wait for the rain to subside was a chore for him. He despised sitting by idly when something was interesting to do.

He picked his reliable aide, PFC Dion. And chose another grunt, Pvt. Alf Lofgren, a blond-haired, gap-toothed, eager youth from a farm in Minnesota. Barton thought that Lofgren might have experience picking produce and animal products. Lofgren seemed keen on being on a farm again and out of the dismal Hôtel Luxe. Barton was looking forward to that too, yet hid his enthusiasm. The other men were cocky Lt. Rico Castellan, who would act as point man and guard, along with Pvt. Tad Dickens, a sarcastic, young, sharp-eyed nail-biter. Barton decided against asking for Schmidt as he was not sure the man would act appropriately. He felt the less these men knew, the better the results of the day might be.

Thus, after breakfast, the group set out with Dion driving, Barton riding shotgun, and the other men in the back of the truck. He felt a little thrill run through him, prideful for his creative ploy that had worked so far but also in anticipation of the day ahead, hoping to solve mysteries.

He enjoyed the bumpy ride along the primitive dirt road and still wondered if this wasn't all a wild goose chase on his part. But as they passed from the outskirts of Soissons and into the countryside, he caught glimpses of fertile farms again, autumn trees laden with apples and pears, vineyards lining the road, some still with the last of a withering grape crop. He breathed in the fragrant country air and sighed. Blond and white cattle lowed as their vehicle passed by; a giant red bull stood near the fence and bellowed in their wake; horses bolted and sprinted along the fence lines. Yes, this was a rich country. Despite the war and strife, France still had much to offer, and Barton planned to enrich their company's stores with such fresh goods as he might find.

Soon, the country gave way to a few houses, and the dirt road became a graveled one, which then became cobbled as they came into a tiny village. Barton was excited now; perhaps this was the place—Vieux. He asked Dion to slow down because there were some businesses where he wanted to buy supplies. Nodding and without a word, Dion slowed and pulled up before a brick building where Barton pointed.

Barton sat staring up at the sign, hardly believing his eyes. An aged, weatherworn sign swung from an ornate ironwork arm from the brick building, painted in cerulean blue with the silhouette of a gold rabbit emblazoned on it like a shield device. He'd found *Le Lapin D'Or*!

◆ ◆

The leaded-glass window of the tavern bore lacy curtains with a display of women's purses, gloves, and a wire mannequin head bearing a feathered red hat. Barton thought that odd for a tavern and opened the door. A bell tinkled cheerfully overhead when Barton stepped inside with Dion on his heels. He stood for a moment, surprised; there was the dark mahogany and white marble bar with the mirror behind it, but now the bar held a brass cash register and a display of women's hats. A buxom wire mannequin torso wore an embroidered blouse, a jaunty blue floral scarf, and a blue beret.

Barton almost went back outside, thinking this was the wrong place after all, but then the flowered curtain behind the bar moved, and a woman came out. She looked shocked to see the GIs in her shop and, raised her hands and stepped back as if she would flee.

"*Madame!*" Barton stalled her. "*Attends!*"

"*Vous êtes Américain?*" she asked with a fearful glance at Private Dion's carbine slung on his shoulder.

"*Oui, Madame. Nous sommes ici en paix,*" Barton said simply, glancing at Dion. "Get out, Private. I think you are scaring this poor woman."

"You sure?" He glanced around the shop and then up at Barton. "Sir, what are you gonna get here? This looks like a lot of lady stuff." He picked up a glass bottle atomizer, sniffed the spray, and then hastily put it back. "Pee-yew! That's stink-water for grannies!"

Barton shoved Dion toward the door. "Go wait with the truck. I'll be out in a few minutes." He impatiently pushed Dion out the door and turned back to smile at the woman behind the counter.

"*Madame,*" Barton began and almost choked on the title but continued in French, "I was under the impression this was a bar."

"*Non!*" She shook her head and looked worried as Barton approached the counter.

Bart took off his helmet and put it under an arm. He suddenly felt conscious of his naked, polled head as the woman stared at him. Still speaking in French, he perused the shop and stopped by a glass case displaying lace handkerchiefs and gloves.

"*Très jolie,*" he murmured. "May I ask the price?" He smiled charmingly at the woman, hoping to break her icy stance. One thing he had learned was to look interested in a product—a shopkeeper would then be faster to talk, greedily hoping to make a sale. If it cost him a few francs for information, so be it.

She came over to the case and unlocked it, asking him which pieces he wanted.

He didn't want to buy anything; he'd now wish they sold beer. He pointed and said in French, "I like the hankies with the roses and tiger lilies embroidered on them. How much?"

The woman picked up the pieces and showed them to Barton but drew them back when he wanted to touch them. "*Sale mains.*"

"*O! Pardon.*" Barton put his hand down, realizing his hands were grubby looking. He also recalled an earlier lesson about French merchants—if you touch it, you buy it!

"*Vous l'aimez?*" she queried warily, holding one handkerchief.

"*Oui, cela me plaît.*" They were pretty. He pointed to another stack of hankies and a pair of embroidered white satin gloves. "*Ces mouchoirs là aussi … trois, et les gants.*" He suddenly felt the sale might open the avenue of conversation, noting that the woman now had an interested gleam in her dark eyes. "How much for all of this, please?"

"*Pour vous, treize francs et trente centimes.*" The woman rattled off with hardly a thought.

"Cheap," Barton said to himself in English.

The woman pulled back the stack of products with a snort, complaining that her fine work was not cheap but of excellent quality. Barton understood he had offended the woman and apologized, saying that he meant her price was too low for such beautiful things. The woman then mollified, nodded, and began to wrap the articles in blue-striped tissue paper.

Barton glanced around the shop, trying to imagine his father here, and wondered when it had changed from a tavern. He avidly watched the woman packaging his merchandise. She seemed middle-aged, with dark hair tightly bound into a bun at the nape. She wore a floral print apron over a brown woolen sweater and dark dress. Her features were sharp but not unattractive. She, too, cast quick darting glances at Barton as she worked. She asked him if these were gifts for his mother or a girlfriend.

"*Oui, ma belle-mère, grand-mère, et mes soeurs. J'ai trois soeurs.*" He comically held up three fingers.

The woman laughed gently and commended Barton for his choice. She assured him that his women would like their gifts.

Barton took out his pocket change and dropped it all on the counter to count it out. The woman drew back to stare at the coins. She pointed and said distastefully, "*Non pas que. Non!*"

Barton picked up the brass medallion bearing the rabbit logo. "Do you know what this is, madame?" he asked cautiously, and she backed away.

"*Non! Non! Allez!*" she squeaked shrilly, shoving the package at Barton.

Barton grabbed her hand. "*Madame, est-ce que vous avez connaissance Lisette Lapin?*" He picked up the medallion and showed it to her. "*Vous recconnez cette medaille!*"

"*Non!*" She shook her head vehemently. "*Allez!*" Her dark eyes looked frightened, like a cornered animal.

Barton turned the medallion over and pointed to the number three. "*Lisette Lapin ... où ... elle es là?*" He knew she was lying; she recognized the medallion. If only she'd tell him where Lisette was, and then he'd be gone.

The woman, now visibly trembling, licked her lips and looked around the shop as if seeking an escape route. "*Non. Je ne sais pas!*"

Barton turned quickly as the bell on the door jangled, and Dion poked his head around. "You okay, Sarge?"

"Yes, I'll be there in a minute," he growled and motioned for him to leave.

The woman touched Barton's hand, holding the medallion. Barton turned back to her, surprised by her touch. "*Quoi?*"

"I will tell you a story, but you must come another time. Not now, *Monsieur Soldat,*" she blurted in French.

Barton looked stunned and asked, "Why not now? I want to know about Lisette Lapin. Does she still live here?"

The woman shook her head but came around the end of the counter. "*Non Monsieur, retourne plus tarde.*" She ushered Barton to the door of the shop. "*Allez maintenant s'il vous plait.*"

"*D'accord, mais quelle heure?*" he asked what time, searching her face, thinking she seemed devious.

"*Cinq heures.*"

"*Bon. Bonjour Madame ... et merci.*" Barton left the store, still unsure of what had transpired but perhaps now more intrigued than he had been before. He heard the door slam and lock behind him, and a sign popped up in the window that read: *FERME*.

"Yeah, right. You're closed to all tourists and GIs! Snotty damn Francs." Bart growled.

He put the rabbit medallion in his pants pocket and then realized he had left all his coins on the counter and felt that he had overpaid, but he would ask again when he came back later that night. Five o'clock was a long way off, and he felt disgusted now. She obviously recognized the medallion. Would the bitch honor her promise and really tell him about Lisette Lapin? Bart suspiciously thought the ladies' shop was just a front for the brothel. Maybe it was still secretly working.

Barton cast a look back at the building and up to see a curtain flick in the window above; yep, something was definitely fishy. He walked down to the truck where his men were standing about smoking and watching as the townspeople wandered past, staring at them.

Climbing in, Barton yelped, "Let's go, boys!" He slammed the door and waited for everyone to get in the truck and for Dion to start it up.

"You okay?" Dion cast a worried look at Barton and noted his harsh face. "Where to?"

"Let's head out to those orchards we saw just outside of town. We need fruit."

"Yes, Sergeant." Dion backed the truck out and sped away, once again heading out of town. He was puzzled, though, and as he drove, glancing a few times at Barton. Once, seeing Barton put a blue parcel in his jacket and then sitting back, looking sullen. The happy Sergeant Barre of earlier that morning was now a grouchy one, and Dion knew better than to jabber or bother him, so he drove, lost in his own thoughts.

◆ ◆

The men were at first treated with suspicion, but as Barton talked to the farmers, the locals relaxed and worked with him, especially when they realized the Americans were there to buy or barter and not steal or destroy as the Nazis had done previously.

At the third farm, Bart's men were there for an hour, and the wife asked them to wait while her son and farmhand loaded their produce. She also offered them freshly baked bread. Then, while they dined on cups of steaming potage of ham, peas, and potatoes with hot, freshly buttered bread, a small entourage of nearby farmers came to the farm, now bearing goods they wanted to trade or sell. The word was out that the Americans were there to help—not to conquer the French people.

However, the long delay at the Chaubert farmhouse helped to uncover a secret.

◆ ◆

The man acted wary, hesitant to answer when questioned about the farm. His hat was drawn low over his brow, and he hardly looked up or at anyone. He didn't help load the produce either and only followed the men into the house. The farmer's wife and elder daughter both acted oddly, too, casting surreptitious glances at the American soldiers crowded in their home and at the man. Although the fellow wore a woolen jacket, filthy pants, and an equally grubby shirt, the man seemed out of place.

Thanks to Lofgren for making a dirty joke about Germans and Hitler and speaking in both German and English, the odd man had lifted his head to display fierce blue eyes and a buttermilk complexion. The family members were dark-haired, swarthy-skinned, and brown-eyed; they seemed genuine, while this man was incongruous—*L'etranger!*

Barton, sitting sipping freshly pressed cider, had watched it all. He then spoke in French to the man, simply asking for more bread. The man only stared at him. Barton made sly comments to the daughter, Giselle. "Is this man deaf and dumb, or is he just afraid of us? Who is he … a lazy idiot cousin?"

The young woman looked at the man and then grabbed Barton's wrist to hiss, *"Il es Allemande!"* Barton and Lofgren looked startled. Then, with a quick nod from Bart, Lofgren stepped over to the man with the basket of bread.

He said in perfect German, "You are hungry? Have some bread. *Bitte.*"

The man's pale eyes blinked and began to water, and then he looked around at the crowded room and bolted for the door.

"Get him!" Bart yelled and was pleased to see that Dion and Lofgren were fast. They grabbed the man roughly, halting his escape. Barton stepped over. *"Tu es Allemande?"* he asked harshly. He noted that the old woman had acted too, and for now, she had pointed a hunting rifle at them all.

"Madame Chaubert," Barton cautioned in French. "Thank you, but we have him now, so you can put away your weapon."

"Non!" she shouted. Then she began spewing a horrid story about the Germans who had occupied their farm until just a few days ago when the Americans came through. She heaped fresh insults upon the man, claiming he had tortured her son and husband. The soldiers beat them all and took their good things, including killing their best milk cow for sport and taking all the meat for themselves.

Bart let out a sigh of agitation. He held up a hand; he had heard enough. "Lofgren, ask this asshole if there are any more of his friends hiding here."

With a smirk, Lofgren shook the man, demanding harshly in German. The man only stared at his feet and then barely shook his head.

"I think he is alone. Maybe he is a deserter."

Lofgren then asked the man in German if he was a deserter and got the response he wanted, for the man sagged and had tears leaking. He frisked the man and withdrew a pearl-handled derringer from his pants pocket. "Look what I found!" He held up the antique as if it were a prize and slid it into his own jacket.

Giselle now boldly spoke up. *"Il es seul, un pauvre con!"* She continued to tell of his assault upon her and that he had pleaded sanctuary in exchange for his affections and her silence. He would work the farm if they would only hide him and say he was family, her fiancé, or a refugee.

Barton could tell the man was guilty. He wore shame and fear upon his face. Although Bart should have taken the man into custody, but chose not to have the enemy stinking up his truck and taking up precious room for needed supplies. He also didn't want to cut his trip short today, keeping to a schedule so he could return by five to Vieux.

"Madame Chaubert … mademoiselle," asking the women in French, "what would you have me do with him? I can take this man for questioning or as a prisoner of war."

"Non, il es un salaud chien!" the wife retorted, and she boldly stepped toward the man to spit in his face. "He should die."

Barton looked at his comrades. "What do you say? Should we let these folks do as they will with the filthy dog? They say he is a rapist and tortured them. The guy's cohorts killed their cow and abused them all. I say we give this fellow back to the Chauberts and let him take the consequences."

Dion shivered but kept a tight grip on the escapee's arm. "But, Sarge, aren't we supposed to take him prisoner? Maybe he is a spy."

"He'll just be added useless weight and space. Some spy, look at him—he's already pissed his pants!" Barton grumbled. "I'd say he knows nothing useful."

Lofgren said something in German. The man shook his head miserably and actually wilted between the pair of men holding him. "Let these people kill him. I told him they would kill him—there would be no other end for him other than a prison camp or torture."

Barton nodded. "Good. That was smart. Take him outside." He rudely grabbed the hunting rifle from the wife and ushered everyone out of the house. He shouted in French now to the busy men and women gathered about the army truck, loading it under the watchful eyes of Castellan and Dickens. "Attention! We have found a German deserter. It is our right and the right of Madame Chaubert to see him punished for his war crimes." His voice rang out loudly as Barton pronounced the sentence upon the German soldier. "Lofgren, take him over to the hay wagon. Tie him there."

He noted some people bent to pick up stones; maybe they would stone the man to death, and Bart wouldn't have to lift a finger.

Lofgren led the man away and tied him to the wagon using the man's belt; he ignored that the man's pants drooped to his knees.

Bart called out, "Now tell him to say his last prayers and apologize to these people."

Lofgren, with a gleam in his blue eyes, swung back to the man, harshly telling him what to do. The man shouted back something, and Lofgren hit him in the face for the comment and then crossed over the dirt yard to Barton.

"What did he say?"

"I'd rather not repeat it." Lofgren looked away.

Barton studied the young man's angry, pink-cheeked face and figured it must have been a vulgar insult. Nodding, he stepped now to the young woman. "*Mademoiselle*," he continued in French, "it is your right to see him punished. Shall I have him beaten or shoot him for you? I am sorry for your abuse at his hands."

Giselle's bruised lip quivered, and tears filled her eyes. Bart studied the plain girl for a moment to see healing cuts and bruises on her cheek, slim neck, and shoulders, and he felt better that she had at least fought with the rapist. He lifted the hunting rifle to take aim as several inward breaths from the bystanders were drawn, and then he felt a hand on him.

"*Non monsieur. S'il vous plâit.*" Giselle took the rifle from Barton, checked the cartridge, and aimed it at the soldier. "*Je te déteste!*"

The loud report of the hunting gun cracked in their ears and sent the chickens in the yard up in a flurry of feathers. The recoil sent the girl flying backward, and she landed in the dirt. She scrambled to her feet and looked at the target for a fraction of a second before running into the house crying.

Barton gulped loudly, surprised by the action, and turned away. "Let's pack it in, men; we are done here!" He headed for the truck.

The men finished up their packing duty and bade the farmers and the Chaubert family goodbye. Barton commended them for being brave patriots for the cause and gave them an extra box of powdered milk in compensation for the slaughtered cow. Bart glanced as they left to see the German man naked, and people were viciously kicking him. His stomach flopped uncomfortably, hoping their revenge was sufficient.

He rode along silently as they searched for the next farm, but he could hear the jokes and several rough comments about the Chauberts that the daughter was a lucky shot or marksman.

"Right through the heart; couldn't have done better myself. I guess the unfortunate jerk got what was deserved. Maybe we should have given the family more than powdered milk. That little gal coulda earned a medal!" Castellan brayed as the men laughed.

◆ ◆

For the rest of the day, the entourage warily went from farm to farm, asking pertinent questions about the Germans in addition to doing their food searches. Barton felt a little foolish, not expecting the Germans to hide on the farms. But there had only been one deserter so far, and for him, his demise was just as brutal as he had led his life in the last days.

No one said anything more about Bart's judgment or swiftly served justice; after all, it had been the Chauberts' answer to their problem. With the aid of the US Army, they ended their illicit harboring of a fugitive enemy soldier. Barton had renewed confidence in his team. He was surprised that Lofgren spoke German and had understood French; the young man did his duty today.

The men continued on, bartering for fresh milk, cheese, eggs, bushels of pears and apples, braided queues of onions and garlic, and bags of squashes. The men gleaned the over-ripe fruit, cabbage, and cauliflower at one farm, coming away with several duffle bags full and sharing some with the elderly farmer's crippled wife.

Barton exchanged cases of American cigarettes, packages of chocolate bars, bandages, powdered milk, soap, tinned vegetables, canned fish and beef, a case of catsup bottles (which seemed a novelty to a family), toilet paper, cans of motor oil, and gasoline for tractors. He tossed in a few woolen blankets and whatever else he could use to wheedle and make a deal. Barton even traded fresh items they had just gotten for something better.

He felt much like a pioneer Indian trader, offering small tokens and goods in exchange for the better and needed fresh items. In return, the men came away with hearty goods—some potent but savory rounds of cheese, a couple of smoked and salted hams, strings of sausages, a few bottles of wine, bottles of cooking sherry, and a treasured clay jug of Calvados, a Norman-style liquor made of fermented apples. Calvados had a kick like a mule, and one looked cross-eyed after just one sip! Barton figured the medics could use harsh liquor if they ran out of rubbing alcohol!

By the late afternoon, the truck was full of fresh foods, including a cage of rabbits, crates of live poultry, a goose that honked noisily, and ducks that hissed at them. During the day, the men were offered goats and cows, a bony old carthorse for meat, and many litters of kittens and puppies, all of which Barton and his men had to kindly refuse.

Feeling they had done well by procuring fresh food, Bart ordered Dion to head into Vieux again. The late afternoon sun was going down behind the dark forest of trees nearby. Barton knew he needed to get back on the road to Soissons soon or find them a place to sleep for the night if his visit at *Lapin D'Or* took longer than he expected. He asked Dion to return to the tavern, and the young man was curious and silently did Bart's bidding.

Barton trotted to the shop, knocked, and waited for someone to open up. He put his collar up, feeling the icy chill of the afternoon breeze sliding around his bare neck and ears, and shivered. Blowing on his hands, Barton danced about before knocking again. He saw a shadow behind the curtain on the door and impatiently waved.

The door opened, and the same woman as before poked her face around it. She then stood aside for Barton to enter the shop, allowing him only a crack in the door. She shut and locked it quickly after Bart. "*Vous êtes plus tarde,*" she admonished.

Shivering and removing his helmet, Barton politely nodded to the woman yet was irked that he was only ten minutes past the hour, and she had to comment on it.

"*Je sais. Merci. Il est froid la bas. Je m'appelle Sergeant Barton Barre.*" He offered his hand to her, but she looked down at it and then up at him.

"*Je m'appelle Mademoiselle Ondine. Entrez-vous,*" she said politely but stiffly before worriedly peeking out the curtain behind him and rechecking the door lock. Ondine led Bart to the staircase in the rear of the shop and then up.

He wondered about her stilted and almost rude manner but followed Ondine upstairs and hoped she was not leading him into sin or, conversely, into danger with a brother or husband hiding, ready to beat in his brains.

Barton smiled with relief as he looked about the sitting room, noting the décor was old-styled, like last century—with overstuffed furniture and red-and-pink striped wallpaper with fancy wainscoting; red and amber glass and brass oil lamps cast a rosy glow in the room, as did the weak but cheery fire in the grate. He recalled his father's letter and suspected this room must be the madame's *Salon Rouge* Richard had described.

Barton commented, saying the room was pleasant and warm. He carefully sat in an armchair as Ondine pointed, and she offered him a cup of hot tea. Barton accepted it, grateful for its warmth, but found it weak. He drank it anyway, wishing it was coffee. Ondine primly sat across from his chair on a settee and looked about as if she were uncomfortable.

He commented gently in French, "Thank you for seeing me, Mademoiselle. Do you have a story to tell me? Maybe I should tell you one first." He sipped the last of the tea. "I was too aggressive this morning, but I am anxious to find out about a person. Lisette Lapin. She used to work here a very long time ago." He set the teacup and saucer down on the table next to the chair and opened his jacket. He took out a photograph of his father when he was a young man and then the brass medallion.

"This is my father. He was a soldier here in the summer of 1918, and a young woman named Lisette Lapin gave him this medallion." He handed the items to Ondine.

She looked at the objects, setting aside the medallion with distaste. "Your father is very handsome, but I do not recognize him," she stated politely in French, then added. "You do not resemble him at all."

"No? He was an American like me. He met Lisette, and they fell in love. He supposedly married her." Barton looked across at Ondine to see what impact his words had on her, but she was palely unmoved and sitting ramrod straight.

He continued. "It was an unfortunate time during the war, and my father had to return to his battalion when they marched out of the area. He never heard from Lisette again."

"Richard never wrote again to her either, *Monsieur*," Ondine snapped.

Barton smiled now. "So you do know her then," he commented cagily.

The dark eyes were still cold and basilisk-like upon Barton. "Yes. She was our mother," Ondine stated bluntly.

Barton felt his stomach tumble. "Our? Who else is here? Might I meet them?"

"There is only my sister Marie, and we had a brother once, Thierry."

Barton was curious now. "And where are they?"

"Thierry is dead; he died as a youth from typhoid fever. I am the oldest, and my sister is next after me. Marie is in bed with La Grippe. But my son should be here … soon!" She hastily handed Barton back the photo of Richard but then passed over a triptych frame with small sepia pictures of children. "That is us when we were children, and the woman with the boy is Maman—Lisette Lourdes Lapin."

Barton smiled, glad that Ondine was breaking. He also thought she was not above lying either—her son? What could a small child do? He now wondered about her title, Mademoiselle, noting she didn't wear a ring. She seemed nervous about being alone with him, yet she had to be brave.

"Lisette is pretty. I can see your resemblance to her." He cajoled, hoping to keep Ondine talking and answering his questions. "How old are you? If I may ask?"

Ondine blushed but shook her head. "If you are wondering, perhaps I am your sister, then no. Maman was already pregnant when she met Richard Barre. I am the bastard of a drunk," she said tersely and candidly.

Barton was shocked now. "I am sorry, madame. I did not know, and I don't think my father knew either."

Ondine hastily snatched back the picture frame and set it reverently on the table next to the settee. "No, it is a sad story." She handed back the medallion. "That was my mother's allocation. She did not want to be a prostitute, and my grandmother did not want her to be one, either. The times were difficult, and that is how they survived. Without men to protect you, it is what you do."

"I am sorry to hear that. And your mother … did she marry again?"

"*Non*," Ondine lifted her head and looked hard at Barton as if challenged. "We are all bastards—every one of us with a different man. Men promise things only so they can use you." Ondine sniffed and stared coldly at Barton. "You can imagine my shock to see that medal after so long a time. Some girls had favorite customers. They would offer them the medallions. A man could then easily ask for the girl without public embarrassment or trying to remember her name. The girls had a different name with each man; it kept them free, you know."

"Hmm, well, now I think I am beginning to understand this." He pocketed the medallion. "I did not come here seeking female companionship, but I wanted to meet Lisette … if that is truly her name, or at least see if my father told me the truth."

"My mother said your father was a liar."

Barton, taken aback by the nearly vicious-sounding statement, countered evenly, "I think that argument is old. As Richard is not here to defend himself, I will just say I don't care if he lied." Barton figured he would give his father a little help.

Ondine gazed at Barton haughtily. "You do not care that he lied? He should have taken my mother away from here. She had the life of an animal! Like a bitch dog! We nearly starved to death. No, my Grandmother was correct. The American did my mother a disservice by promising her another life."

Barton stood up and paced about the miniscule parlor, peeking into corners and peering at classical sculptures, paintings, and porcelain figurines as he talked. "Well, it seems you all did better than most. At least you had a family and a mother who cared about you. As for my father, I don't think he could help what happened. Besides, he was severely wounded in the war a short time after he left here."

Ondine looked slightly aghast, saying stiltedly, *"Mon Dieu,* we did not know. *Je regrette—"*

Barton perused a collection of gold gilt frames with miniature paintings of scenery as he paced, thinking them ritzy and *froufrou.* For the woman's complaints, the women seemed to have lived above their station in life.

He turned to Ondine. "Yes, Richard was most despondent to leave his young bride behind, but your grandmother sent him away. He could never get Lisette to speak to him again before he left. He wrote her letters to explain, but she ignored them."

He shrugged his shoulders. Seeing that he had an avid audience, Barton added theatrically, "It was a tragedy. His heart was broken, and he was nearly killed for it."

"C'est vraie?" Ondine put a hand to her mouth. *"Lettres? J'ai les lettres! Excuse moi, un moment!"* She leapt up and dashed out of the parlor, leaving Barton stunned. He plucked up a tiny gold-and-enamel inlay box, wondering at it, but then Ondine soon returned with a wooden case. Caught red-handed and unable to put it back without notice, Bart pocketed the small treasure. He eyed the woman. "So why now do you believe me?"

"I thought maybe you are like the rest—always wanting something for nothing."

Barton snorted at the statement.

She sat on the sofa to open the case and pulled from below a clutter of oddments a packet of letters bound with a red ribbon. She handed them to Barton. "These are the letters Richard wrote to her before he left, and also Mother's letters. Mother always said she loved him, but then when he left, she hated him. We found their letters among Grandmother's things after she died."

"That's too bad." Barton accepted the letters. "Why did Lisette not give Richard the letters if she loved him? He would have wanted to see her or hear from her."

"Grand-mère, I think, hated him worse for trying to steal her daughter. She locked mother away."

Barton nodded. "I see. You still want me to take these?"

"Yes. Mother kept them hidden. They are no good to anyone now. I almost burned them."

"Doesn't she want them as a keepsake?"

"Non. Elle ... est ... mort."

Barton sat down abruptly. "Oh, now I am sad. I would have liked to meet Lisette. How did she die?"

"Three years ago, in a train accident in Paris. The filthy Huns bombed it."

"That was a tragic loss then; you must miss her." Barton saw Ondine was near tears, but now she seemed moved by his statement.

"Yes, she was a strong woman; she kept us together. Mother changed this place. She always wanted to be a seamstress. She was an artist with a needle and *filet*."

Barton nodded with feigned empathy as he put the packet of letters with Richard's photograph in his jacket. "My stepmother crochets too. She will appreciate the beautiful gloves and hankies I bought from you today."

Ondine smiled feebly and sniffled. "Mother taught my sister and me to do those things, and when Grand-mère died, we closed the bar and turned the prostitutes into ladies. They were partners in our shop for some time."

"So why keep the sign, *Lapin D'Or*? Surely people would always know that this was a brothel at one time?" Barton asked with curiosity.

"Yes, that is true, but it is our family crest. The Lapin family has been here for centuries. We are known, but not always, as a house of wanton women!" She stifled a short laugh and sobered. "*Non* … times have been difficult and cruel for us, but Maman refused to spend her life on her back, and she did not want us to live like that either. We were brought up as ladies of distinction and grace, as we should have been. Our ancestors would have been horrified to know how far the Lapin family fell from grace."

Barton smiled now, and nodding, he bent before Ondine and took her hand. "And so you are a lady of grace and discernment. I thank you for your story and for listening to mine." He gallantly kissed her hand, thinking it a charming reward. "But now I must take your leave. This will be an interesting story to tell my father when I go home to America."

"Yes, please go." Ondine rose and ushered Barton to the door. "I wish you God's protection. I can see that Richard raised a good son, and you may thank him for asking after us or even remembering my mother after so long a time."

Barton smiled charmingly at Ondine. "Oh, Dad has never forgotten his first wife—he did love her. I have one more question for you before I go. Do you remember a gold crucifix that your mother might have had? My father gave it to her on their wedding day."

"*Oui*. Maman wore it always and went to her grave with it."

Barton frowned now. "*C'est bien. Tant s'en fait que j'en dise du mal.*" He shrugged away the effort. "*Bon. Merci. Au revoir Mademoiselle Ondine.*" He tromped quickly down the stairs. He stopped at the door and turned to look at Ondine. "I am sorry, but I never let you say much. Was there anything that you wished to say to my father, a message perhaps?"

Ondine came across the tiled floor to the door. "*Oui*, tell him that mother forgave him, and if he reads those letters, one of them was written shortly before she died, asking Richard to forgive her. Somehow, Maman must have sensed her days were close. She always regretted losing Richard. He was her one great but tragic love."

"I see. Well, I will pass these letters to my father when I see him. Not that anything will change or reverse such misfortune, but he has always been sad about what happened here. *Bon chance et adieu.*" Barton squeezed Ondine's shoulder and left the store. He heard the door lock after him, and the lights went out.

He felt the chilled, raw wind sweep along the walkway and stepped off the curb to cross the street to the waiting truck. He got in and simply said, "Let's go, Dion. I am starved!"

"Where?" The private dutifully started the truck.

"Soissons!" Barton now cheerfully waved Dion toward the road.

◆ ◆

That night, after the truck had been unloaded, Barton reported to Samuelson and Clay, carefully omitting the visit to the former tavern and the German soldier fiasco. He hoped none of his men said anything either. Barton quickly ate a supper of soup and fresh cheese sandwiches. He tiredly lumbered upstairs to his hotel room. He flopped on the squeaky bed and sighed. The newer mattress was thin and lumpy, but it felt like a cloud at this moment. He pulled out the thick packet of letters from his pocket and tossed the jacket on the spare chair. Then, as he fished in his pants pocket for the brass medallion, Bart remembered the gold box.

He studied the case, which was about the size of his thumb, liking the sparkling garnets among the black-and-white enamel inlay and seed pearls. On the underside, it had a deep, round dent. Curious, he thumbed the catch and opened it, hoping maybe there was a secret treasure, but found only a tiny rolled scrap of paper written in French.

He translated aloud as he read it: "Uncle Etienne Lapin's snuffbox. Born 1793, Died 1846, shot in a lover's duel with Cmte. Freneau." Bart smiled now in earnest. The snuffbox was a Lapin family historic treasure. He wondered now if the box had deflected some of the ball; still, Lapin had died. Even back then, Love came at an expensive price. He fit the rabbit medallion inside the snuffbox, snapped the lid closed, and held it tightly in his hand. Maybe he would give this to his father in exchange for the crucifix he lost to Lisette. It was a small price for a lost love. He put the snuffbox in his box, which held his letters and memories of his old life back home, now adding his own family crest—the phoenix medallion.

"Thanks, I've been lucky so far." He commented with a sigh, feeling a bit foolish for counting his safety and good luck on a piece of metal.

He settled on the bed, thinking a little intimate reading of the letters might help finish the mystery of the day. Among the letters was a faded photograph of Lisette. She was stately and very formal looking, posed with a fancy chair. She seemed older than a teen, yet the photo revealed it was taken in 1908 in Paris, ten years before Richard met her. Perhaps she wasn't so young after all and had lied to Richard about her age, too.

It all seemed so surreal, perhaps the mystery a bit too simply solved. He also did not understand how his father could be mistaken about the town's name. But then, Bart supposed, Ondine was correct; families here rarely moved away but stayed in an area. Still, he had wondered earlier why his father's letter had said he met Lisette in Soissons.

Earlier during supper, he broached the subject of Vieux and Soissons with Dion. The younger man said they found out that Soissons was a large, sprawling town built centuries ago, but during the last war, much of it was destroyed. People moved away and rebuilt what was once another part of Soissons into what the town is today, and the older other part was now called Vieux.

Barton queried, "Then why is there so much farmland between the two cities?"

Young Lofgren chimed in with glee, explaining that people needed the land and took it back for farming.

Barton had smiled at the industrious and curious fellows. He had very little information and was actually a dead-end for his father's mystery. But now, as he lay in silent repose from the day, he understood it better. Lisette and her family had indeed lived a cruel and perilous life. However, he had to admire the women for staying and venturing into a new business and succeeding. He thought more kindly of them now and of his own La Barre family motto, "We fly against the winds." The Lapins had boldly done the same and survived, with the world blowing up around them in two world wars!

He reflected briefly upon the brave Chaubert farm women. They, too, were warrior spirits, for with a bit of aid, they had persevered and vanquished their Nazi enemy—a deserter, conniving rapist, and abuser. Barton felt a bit of remorse, though; he had not done what was expected by regulations, and he hadn't reported the incident to the colonel.

Yet Barton felt the outcome was as it should have been. The Chauberts would not have hastened to oust or kill any other home intruder or thief. Because the attack had been in the guise of an army of men overtaking them, they were stymied and had to daily accept the abuse and then hide one of the fiends. There was something not fair about that.

He was glad that his men had been there to witness it all, for they seemed to find justice in what occurred, and none of them were harmed in the altercation—it all worked out. Barton was relieved that he had not killed the soldier. The young abused woman had done that for him—it would be a black mark upon Giselle's soul, not his. He knew he had killed many people by now, but it was all faceless, impersonal, and in the act of war and not out of hate, anger, or revenge. In his mind, he was exonerated for any sin in a person's death.

He yawned, feeling the excitement and fading anticipation of the day pulling at him like water swirling down a drain. Barton set the letters aside to read at another time, turned off his oil lamp, and curled up under the woolen blanket. His mind slowed, content now that he had solved a mystery, done his duty, and saved some people. And he fell instantly asleep.

◆ ◆

SIC TRANSIT GLORIA MUNDI

(Thus the Glory of the World Passes-Nothing Lasts Forever)

After the First and Third Armies' temporary halt, while waiting for the supply convoys to meet them on September 6, they regrouped and pressed forward once again into the Moselle region. The Fifth Army's tank battalions had cleared some of the way with the taking of Reims on September 1, pushing the Germans farther east toward the Siegfried Line into the Moselle Region.

Barton's division, now a part of Patton's Third Army, which was composed of parts of the Fifth, the Eleventh, Twelfth, and Twentieth Infantry Divisions, now saw daily action. They had moved their supply depots south of the camps, hoping to stay out of the way, but there were resistant enemy pockets all about them, continuing to keep a fierce stronghold along the eastern banks of the Moselle River.

Their company, under the command of Lt. Col. Lee Samuelson, along with Barton and one of the Third Army's quartermasters, met frequently to inventory and prescribe the rationed supplies for Lieutenant General Patton's army, now on a new plan of attack into Germany and Luxembourg.

Briefly meeting and witnessing the lieutenant general in action, Barton was in awe of the audacious but arrogant, brilliant strategist. The general had finally relented to listen to the logistical supply commanders, albeit with frustration, wanting to move quickly forward. Yet he was often reined in by the infrequent supply trains and the generals above him, demanding Patton to sit and stay, much like his bull terrier, William, while "his supplies" were redirected to other divisions. Barton could always sense when the lieutenant general was around, for the ground nearly shook, and the air took on an almost tangible electrical tingle. Everyone was on his best behavior just in case Patton strolled through the depot, his riding crop at the ready as if he wanted to whip his troops into shape!

◆ ◆

Moselle River
September 8, 1944

The world exploded, molten crimson and gold rained down, igniting everything within reach of the violent blast. Barton felt the fiery eye at the center of the explosion piercing him with internal fire as he dove for cover under a truck loaded with jerricans, but then he realized he was still in mortal danger and crawled on all fours toward an artillery sandbag redoubt. He ducked as shots pinged and zinged about him. He cast a quick look at his body to see he was singed at the edges and in need of a new jacket.

The three soldiers who had previously manned the gun were all dead, and the smoking machine gun was empty. Then, taking up his rifle and appropriating the dead men's ammo, Bart made ready to fire back. The Germans' offensive attack had come upon them suddenly, barely after breakfast, and Barton grimly was now in the thick of the battle. He also lost his breakfast.

◆ ◆

The 11th RCT attempted to cross first on the eastern side of the Moselle River at Dornot on Sept. 7 but were severely beaten—I hear they lost nearly fifty percent of the second battalion in the 11th Regiment in a matter of days. In the days after, the 10th Regiment crossed over the Moselle a few miles south of our first attempted crossing, near Arnaville. The First and Third Battalion of the 11th joined them, spending the next five days overcoming the Hun's defenses. The fight for the bridges over the Moselle River finally ended on September 15, when the Third and Fifth Armies (us) could cross safely. The "Red Devils" of the Fifth Division paid for it in casualties. We lost many good men over the weeks. I am lucky still to be alive, getting only a concussion for hitting my head when diving for cover! Now, I kind of think my previous wish for action and excitement was capricious and stupid. I was equally stupid for not wearing my helmet!

Barton slipped the journal into his pocket, re-sharpened his pencil, and tucked it away. He wrote in his journal infrequently, documenting the bits he could figure out. Although some days, Barton honestly had no idea of where they were and or even the date, writing his thoughts seemed to take some of the edge off of his battle-weary body at day's end.

The days for Barton were filled with tension and misery as the Red Devils kept pushing on into battle; their supply trucks were always a target or in the line of fire. Barton, at odd times suddenly wished he were back at the dirty little Caumont POL depot; at least there, they weren't being bombed or used for Nazi target practice!

He often wished he had a book to read other than the Bible. Occasionally, he read a few chapters in Richard's Bible, yet he found the stories unsatisfactory and often felt as if God were watching him in disapproval. Sometimes at night, when the war had dulled down to a silent roar, he peeked at his father's and Lisette's letters, finding them so very personal and emotional that Barton had to put them away before finishing them. He felt sickened by their unrequited love and saddened by the substantial loss that both Lisette and Richard must have suffered.

One night, he dreamed of the amorous pair among the fragrant *Muguet des Bois* and the beauty of the Belleau Woods, and his heart cried for them. He wondered what his life might have been like to have Lisette as his mother. But then Barton shook his head at the folly of such an idea—he never would have been born! And neither would the Lapin kids—well, maybe Ondine.

Barton had to let it all go after reading several of the sad letters; he bound them in the red ribbon and buried them deeply in his duffle bag, wishing instead that he might burn them, not wanting to share them with Richard. At moments, he felt perverse in wanting to add to Richard's pain; offering those letters would probably hurt the man. Then again, the letters were buried there among his dirty clothes, a silent weight, crying for the light of day for two lovers to read.

◆ ◆

Moselle Region

September 27, 1944

We are stuck—again! Patton's "war machine" has been stalled outside of the towns of Nancy and Metz. The Germans are fiercely protecting their front along the Siegfried Line, for our next march will surely drive them back into Luxembourg or Germany, thus losing precious ground for the Reich.

Metz is a pivotal city for us to win. Surrounding the old city and the area all the way to Verdun, we have seen numerous fortifications built during the past wars between Germany and France. Many fought there during the last World War. I wonder if Dad ever made it here.

Nearly every day, as Patton presses ahead, we are met with the solid wall of Nazi resistance, losing much and gaining little for all our efforts. We are beating against a wall that does not break, yet you know it should! I hate this fucking war!

◆ ◆

Metz, France
November 9–December 8, 1944

The battle began in full again after numerous and almost futile attempts had been made to drive the Germans out of the area. Patton regrouped his many troops and now would attempt to drive a wedge through the Germans' defense at any angle possible. After many days of multidirectional attacks, the city's forts were overrun. Then, on November 21, the Fifth Division captured Metz. It was a prideful accomplishment for Lieutenant General Patton and his troops. On December 8, the Second Infantry Regiments conquered the last fortification—Fort Driant. The armies could sweep through the Saar River region like floodwater and continue to push easterly into Germany. The promise of victory shone like a golden beacon brightly ahead!

◆

CHAPTER 11

Hushed Voices in the Wood

Saar River Region
Monday, December 11, 1944

The woods were ever so dark. They stepped cautiously past black, mysterious humped shapes, navigating on primal knowledge. Silently afraid to step awry, ice to crack, a twig to break, a leaf to fall, a startled bird to rush fleeing from unknown dark danger amid the soft patter of tiny-footed creatures awakened. With hearts beating loudly, afraid for others to hear, two dark creatures of the earth crept toward a grassy glade for a midnight rendezvous. Then, flinging aside caution to clasp, press lips together, breathe each other's life, search for secret places, and feel the heat of desire, lust, and life amid death. After a day of sweating and perpetual fear, the pair wanted to join for a span of breaths and thrusts. Perhaps just for the joy of living another day or to quell the inward ache of humankind, they sought compassion and companionship, and they assuaged their physical needs and love.

◆ ◆

Shivering, Barton awoke suddenly. Sitting up, he looked about the dark tent, searching yet restless after the weird dream. Unable to sleep again, tossing back the covers of his bedroll, Barton lurched up out of his cot. He had a headache behind his eyes; it had been persistent for most of the day.

The chaotic events of the day spent inventorying the confiscated German petrol, medical supplies, and ammunition were still roiling in his head, which didn't help the pain. He had been repulsed by the spattered blood on the crates. Feeling a wave of nausea again, Barton swallowed thickly and grabbed for the canteen, unscrewed the top, tilted it, and greedily drank down two drops.

Growling at the empty canteen, he knew it was his own fault; he should have filled it earlier when it was still daylight. Now, he would have to find the stream in the dark woods or go thirsty. The troops were on short water rations; they had been on the move for several weeks, usually in battle mode, and food and water were running out. He could boil some snow, but thinking about the busy encampment, he would

274

not find much pristine snow. The recent snow had quickly turned into stamped-down ice and frozen mud.

Barton fished out the slim silver flask Second Lt. Clarence MacInnes had given him as a small parting gift before Barton came over to France. He shook the flask and heard the liquid slosh. Pulling the cork stopper out, he sniffed the aromatic Scottish whiskey, also a gift from the officer. It was something MacInnes's family made and a special gift from MacInnes's father. They had shared a common appreciation for the smooth, well-aged liquor. Taking a sip, Barton felt fortified by the drink as it coursed down his throat to lay hot and alive in his belly. He sipped once more, then put the flask away, cherishing what remained.

Now, looking around the dark tent, he heard the rough, rasping sounds of slumbering men coming from the other lumpy forms in the darkness. Still goaded by thirst and an unusual lingering sense of sexual arousal, Barton grabbed up his canteen, gun belt with revolver, helmet, and jacket and then crept between the bedrolls and cots of his clerks and slipped under the awning of the tent.

He stood for a moment to suck in great draughts of the frigid night air, jammed his helmet on his head, belted on his pistol, and shrugged into his jacket as he scanned the silent camp and set out.

Tonight had been declared a silent night. Everyone needed a rest, including the convoy trucks. The men had been working nearly twenty-four-hour shifts for several weeks in an around-the-clock deployment as they steadily moved east, supplying Patton's giant war machine with the general's cache of supplies. But with precious supplies low, their company was resting at present as they waited for more to catch up.

Barton should rest, too, but after the constant physical activity, his mind would not shut down to accommodate his weary bones. He had awoken unsure why, and he now felt compelled to walk.

He wound cautiously past the tents and the heaped mountains of supplies along silent behemoth trucks. Even the men, who usually worked at night loading, repairing, and maintaining the numerous trucks as they pony-expressed their way across France and Germany, were taking a brief break tonight, having shut everything down from midnight to 0500. There would be sentries, though, and Barton stepped warily; he would alert his friend Schmidt that he was up for a while.

He glanced at his watch, noting it was after three in the morning, and headed for the sentry post in search of a bummed cigarette and maybe some water. If he could avoid going into the woods after water or taking the risk of waking others while he tried to wrangle with the spigot on the water barrel, he would do so.

He found the sentries post, but Cpl. Albert Rossini was facing Bart as he emerged from the shadows, startling him. Rossini caught sight of Bart's insignia on his jacket and relaxed with a wan smile as he lowered his rifle.

"Sergeant Barre!" he exclaimed with relief.

Bart waved aside the greeting and stepped up to Rossini. "Where's Schmidt? I thought he was on duty tonight," he said gruffly, still feeling parched and now cranky that he should have to explain his need to an underling.

"He was. He said he had to take a dump—been gone for a while, though, now that I think of it."

"Got a cig?" Barton asked and took one that Rossini shook out from a crumpled packet.

Squinting through the smoke as Rossini lit the cigarette, Barton eyed the young corporal. "So, how long has he been gone?"

"Uh, close to ten … twenty minutes, maybe."

"Hmm, well, maybe he's got a problem and needs some 'army strawberries' or something." He eyed the giggling young corporal. "I'll stand watch with you until he returns. Got some water? I'm out." He shook his empty canteen. Barton restlessly paced a bit, his silver eyes glittering in the moonlight.

The young soldier fumbled his canteen off of the canvas belt and held it out to Barton. "Yeah, here. It's fresh. I filled it earlier at the stream." He smiled wanly up at Barton. "It tastes better than the stuff in the water tanks."

Barton grabbed the canteen and took two long draughts before handing it back. "That'll do it."

He stepped over to a lorry and sat on the running board to finish his cigarette.

Rossini paced and came to stand near Barton. "I hope nothin' happened to him. I heard there are Krauts nearby. Klatch said they spotted them across the river about a quarter mile from here. Do you think they know we are here?"

Barton smoked the harsh, bitter cigarette down to his fingers, pinched the bits of paper together, and tossed the dead fag, expelling the smoke in a last breath. "Probably. They are just waiting for one of us to make a move. That's why we called a halt for the night and tomorrow. We also gotta wait for the Twelfth to catch up with us."

"Oh … well, I heard it a bit different, but you probably know more 'n me." Rossini shifted his weight, shuffling his feet and looking tired. "Man, it is cold tonight; my beezer's all runny." He wiped his reddened nose on his sleeve. "I think it's gonna dump snow or rain on us again. I ain't used to this muck and shit, and I'm used to harsh Chicago winters! How about you? Where you from anyway?" Rossini shivered with the cold.

Barton ignored the query for more information. "How long you on for, Rossini?" He stood up, stretching, feeling a bit more relaxed. Maybe he would go back for some more shut-eye. He yawned, his eyes watering, and wiped the tears away.

"Uh, Sarge said until 0300. What time you got?"

Barton glanced quickly at Rossini. "Where's your watch?"

Rossini's mouth twisted into a wry grin. "Uh, I'll blame it on the Krauts. I lost it somewhere in all the running we've been doing."

Annoyed, Barton glanced again at his watch; it was 0326. Sighing with the implied duty, he said, "I'll go see what's up with Schmidt. You stay put until he gets back. Got it?"

Rossini nodded. "Yes, Sergeant!" He stood to look dangerous again, rifle ready, his dark eyes glittering in the wan moonlight as he scanned for enemy intruders.

With a wry smile, Bart headed for the trees. The corporal was young and eager. He had just started to shave a few months before. Now, he was the company's little guard dog, 'personally trained' by Schmidt. Bart liked that kind of enthusiasm.

He padded through the dense bracken and shrubbery, placing feet carefully so as not to make a sound, thinking back on his grandfather's hunting lessons—François would be proud of Bart now. Deeper into the woods, the snow was thinner and lay in dirty gray patches on the ground. It was much easier to walk upon than trudging through knee-deep drifts and slush turned to ice.

Rossini was right in that the Germans were close, but they were on *this* side of the Saar River!

Barton heard a slight crackle and rustling and then a low growl. He crouched down to peer through the brush, searching for whatever was out there.

Someone saw and heard wolves yesterday. Now everyone was wary; wolves, snakes, and local animal life could be just as dangerous as the Krauts. A guy in their unit had been charged by an angry bull when they were traversing across a farmer's field months ago, which had sparked a bit of fun for the men in harrying the bull.

What in the hell am I doing out here trying to save Schmidt's ass?

Bart drew his pistol, scuttled through the brush, and then heard the unmistakable slap of flesh upon flesh. He crept toward the sound, thinking someone was taking a beating—not an unusual occurrence. But in the middle of the night and out in the woods—he would put a stop to this!

The sounds happened again, and then it was a low, repeated thudding of flesh against flesh. "What the hell?" Barton muttered, crept toward the noise, and stood.

There in the small glade were two dark silhouettes; one very tall and angular, the other small and bent over, leaning against a tree trunk. Hearing rustling and heavy, guttural breathing and grunting while the rhythmic noise continued—Barton's face flushed crimson and hot.

"What the hell? How did a woman get in here?" Barton muttered angrily as he continued to watch. He was ready to go yell at the pair.

The taller one was still dressed in uniform, but his pants were undone; he was having too much fun. Large hands caressed and slapped the bared buttocks of the shorter person, whose pants were pooled around boots.

The taller one moaned and thrust hard, his head thrown back. Feeling sickened, Bart knew the figure—the skinny neck, broad shoulders, and long spidery fingers caressing and slapping the white moon of small buttocks. The head lolled, and the eyes opened to focus on Barton, who was staring gap-mouthed at the edge of the glade. There was a faint quirk of the harsh mouth, and Master Sergeant Schmidt winked a glacial blue eye at Barton.

Barton felt his throat close and his gut fall to his feet as he realized Schmidt saw him. Schmidt stiffened, moaned, and fell forward, hugging the figure. With that needed break, Bart slipped back into the shadowed forest, and cautiously, taking three steps back, he turned and bolted, glad that he innately missed a thorny holly bush by inches.

His heart thudding in his chest, he ran past Rossini, who once again startled and raised his M1. Bart came to a stop, his sides heaving. "Schmidt will be here soon. Good night, Rossini!" He gasped and turned away, headed toward the far side of the camp.

Barton knew he should not be out here wandering, but he could not go back to his tent to sleep. He decided he would head to the stream anyway to fill his canteen and wear off the adrenaline shock and the revulsion he felt roiling in his gut. After a bit, he calmed himself, walking on steady, quiet cat feet toward the creek. He wound his way through the underbrush and trees, listening to the ice cracking on encrusted branches, sighing and creaking trees in the chilly wind, muffled birds, and the small things that surreptitiously crept into the nocturnal woodland.

Barton wanted to yell against the quiet of the frosty night, rage against the rawness he felt, trying to get the image out of his mind.

He knew things like this happened at times; men had needs, and for some, it did not matter how they assuaged them. But for Barton to witness it and watch them, he felt ill with the knowledge. What made it worse was that it was his friend Harlan Schmidt!

How many times had they wrestled about as friends, went to the pubs, talked about women, or made rude jokes, ogled, and lustily kissed and pinched the busty pub waitresses? They even shared Daisy Duncan's attention! Schmidt had wanted to go with Barton for a romp at the *Lapin D'Or!* Now he was scrapping together a disgusting picture of his friend, recalling that it was he, Barton, who mainly had kissed and lusted after the pub wenches!

Barton reached the stream and gladly fell to his knees. He splashed his face with the icy water, wishing it would wash out the image in his brain. Repeatedly, he sloshed the chilling water over his head, scrubbing roughly. With his hands and lips nearly frozen, he stopped to stare blearily at the chuckling stream as it coursed over the small rocks and past the frozen ferns, bracken, and fir trees. He sat back on the rocky ground, rubbing his head. Now the pain of his headache was splintering to match the soul of him, his friendship betrayed and torn asunder!

How could Schmidt do this to him? How could he not tell Barton that he was a … a … what? A fairy? A homosexual? Barton pounded his thigh angrily with the filthy thoughts. Now, he was afraid of how to go about the daily duties of meeting the man with this foul secret between them. Things would never be the same.

He felt tears of disappointment choke him—his friend was gone. They had jokingly talked about what they would do if one or the other of them died here but had never talked about how they might grow apart. He felt Schmidt was now lost to him, and he almost could wish the man dead for his betrayal!

After realizing the other person wasn't a woman, Barton had wondered for brief moments about the small person, and the truth had come to him as he walked to the creek. It was Pvt. Peter Dion. He recognized the Pegasus winged horse tattooed on the pale buttocks. He never would have thought him capable of such an atrocity.

Sure, he was small, almost petite, barely five foot four, slim-bodied, with black ringlet-like curly hair, dark, soulful eyes, and a cheerful rosy mouth. Schmidt, making a joke, had called him Pretty Dolly the first time he saw the young man. There had been rumors, yeah, that the pretty ones always got the nickname and were harassed, saying nothing of Peter Dion being of Greek heritage. Barton himself had experienced that kind of sexual harassment in training camp for his boyish good looks but fought his way up and out. No one dared lay a finger or an incriminating name on him again. Except for Samuelson, he ruefully thought.

He felt his stomach churning as if ill. He had never wanted to see such a thing, and now that he had, it was as if he was a virgin and had been raped—his inner self would never be the same. Feeling ugly inside for witnessing that kind of carnal lust.

Barton knelt again to fill his canteen, capped it, and then scooped up mouthfuls of water, again drinking and then spitting to rinse his mouth of the cotton-dry feeling he had. He slowly plodded his way back through the woods, not caring if Schmidt had relieved Rossini. That was their business; he'd hear about it anyway in the morning when they reported. Shit! He'd have to face Schmidt in the morning for his report. Barton flopped down on his cot and fell into a troubled sleep for the last ninety minutes before the new day.

◆ ◆

Later that morning, Lt. Col. Lee Samuelson ducked under the awning of the supply tent and, grabbing up the duty roster, plopped wearily onto the campstool next to the folding table. As Barton flipped through pages of supply orders, he was lost in the figures, still adding them up in his head. He jerked when Samuelson spoke.

"Sorry … come again?" Barton queried, his ears open but his mind totaling the last figures on the page.

"I said … we have a problem."

"Mmm … hmm." Bart let out a breath, wrote a figure on a scrap of paper, and slapped the packet of orders down on the table, annoyed by the interruption. He looked up at the colonel. "Did you say problem? What kind?"

"Personnel problem. Do you know about it?"

Barton felt a small trickle of sweat creeping down his brow. "Know about what?" He gulped back the reply.

Samuelson reached over, grabbed up the coffee pot simmering on the camp stove, and poured out a mug full. He noisily slurped the boiling brew, made a face, and set the mug on the ground at his feet. His eyes leveled on Barton. They were as cold and blue as the winter sky.

"It would seem our night watchmen are not where they are supposed to be when they are supposed to be there. Would you happen to know anything about that?" Samuelson crossed his arms to lean back against the stacked crates.

Barton fidgeted under the icy stare, and he returned one of his own. "Yes, sir. I was made aware that the previous night, Sergeant Schmidt reported to sentry duty late to relieve Corporal Rossini."

Samuelson picked at a split nail. "Was that all? Did he have a reason? Was any punishment meted out for his obvious derelict of duty?"

"I am not sure, sir," Barton grumbled and slammed down his pencil on the clipboard.

"I see." Again, the cold eyes assessed Barton. "Would there be perhaps any other reason as to why nothing has been done? I understand you and Schmidt are close. Yes?"

Barton stood up, disliking the direction of the conversation. "We were friends once, sir. I have had the opportunity to rethink that relationship, sir."

"Indeed!" The heavy blond eyebrows rose nearly to the man's scalp. "Then it comes as no surprise to you the rumors that are floating about the camp regarding Sergeant Schmidt?"

"I don't know, sir." Barton gulped, choosing not to give away Schmidt without his own defense, even though he knew him to be guilty of sin. "What rumors, sir? You know how men talk; one little joke gets out of control, and the lie is there whether we like it or not." Bart gave a snorted half laugh. He drank down his own cold coffee and stood to refill his cup. "Just like your nickname for me," he added in a nasty tone.

Samuelson stood now and stepped near to Barton. "The rumors are not what I witnessed." He leaned close to Barton and murmured, "I saw Schmidt engaged in personal relations with one of your staff, a Private Dion, I believe."

Barton's face blanched. "Oh shit … I mean … what …" He gulped and asked, "What were they doing?"

Leaning toward Bart, Samuelson whispered, "Kissing. And it was not all that brotherly, let me tell you."

"Oh." Bart was relieved that the colonel had not seen the men engaged in sex. "Um … You did not say what Schmidt was rumored to have done."

"Oh … gambling, the loser gets to lick his boots." Samuelson fastidiously flicked a piece of lint off his woolen jacket. "I have heard there are a few men who have experienced such … humiliation, all for the sergeant's amusement." He coughed on the last word.

"Shit!" Barton now laughed genuinely but sobered. "Excuse me, sir. But I thought it would be worse!"

"Like what I told you?" The blue eyes bored into Barton now at close range.

"Yes, sir, I suppose." Bart wiped his brow and gave a nervous, small laugh.

The officer paced about the small space, perusing the crate labels with a sideways glance as he spoke. "So what do you propose to do about it? And I'd appreciate it if you kept me informed of behaviors like this. I don't want our men gambling; it makes men hate each other. We need everybody on our side in this war. I don't want someone shooting somebody because they were cheated or lost a game and humiliated."

"Yes, right you are, sir. I will also do something about the other thing you mentioned. I'll request to transfer them both out."

The colonel's shaggy blond eyebrows shot up. "Both? No … I think just one. We need Schmidt in spite of the indiscretion. He is a hard man to beat in a fight, and so far, I believe his record is clean. This kind of thing would blemish it considerably. I do believe he is coming up soon for review and grade promotion, yes?"

"He hasn't mentioned it, sir. Like I said, sir, if it's someone on my staff, I'll see it won't happen again."

"Yes, well, see that it doesn't."

Samuelson's cool gaze unsettled Barton. He scrubbed his own short-cropped platinum-blond hair as if weary. "I know this has been a long and bloody war, and sometimes men just need to feel human again. Perhaps I was mistaken; they were consoling each other … a sad piece of mail or something, you know, brothers-in-arms commiserating."

"Yes, sir. I'll take care of it." Barton began to move toward the door of the tent, hoping the officer would get the hint, and he did.

Samuelson, being shepherded out, stopped at the doorway. "I hope we will not talk about these people again. I think we need to tighten up security around here, too. No one is to go alone into the woods. Approved patrols only, got it?" He fussed and saw Bart nod emphatically and then cast an eye about Barton's tent. "I am glad to see a man who keeps a neat tent, but you make lousy, weak coffee, Sergeant." He gave a brief one-fingered salute and edged under the tent flap to disappear into the hazy, crowded depot.

Barton let out a great exhalation, relieved that nothing more was seen by the colonel. Both men could be court-martialed for their behavior, and Schmidt being late to duty was unlike him, although Barton now knew why. If Samuelson had his say, the MP would be sharply reprimanded.

Sitting again at his camp table to sort through the file boxes, Bart looked for a transfer form for Private Dion. He was sorry to send him away; the young man was like a mascot, always chipper and ready to please. Maybe too easy to please, Barton ruefully felt. Dion was also an excellent little aide—a quick and accurate typist.

But Schmidt had his own uses, and being of a higher rank than Dion, he was more valuable. The tempting young Private Dion would have to go. However, Barton was going to make sure that Schmidt felt the sting of such action from the powers above him—the man would pull double guard duty on the day shift when he could not get away with such crap. Barton personally would think more about the man's punishment. Angry as he was, Schmidt would pay dearly for his indiscretion, even if Barton had to beat him up for it!

◆ ◆

Tuesday, December 12, 1944

Barton felt a breezy jostling at his elbow as someone sidled into line next to him amid the complaints from the men already there. He glanced sideways and saw Schmidt. Bart looked away, tugging out a meal tray; he pushed his way along, letting the servers plop various pale-colored splattered messes onto his tray—it looked like greasy instant eggs, oatmeal, and applesauce.

Schmidt elbowed him and leaned close. "I need to talk with you. Meet me at the empty table in the corner there." He motioned with a fork and grabbed around Barton for toast.

Bart ignored Schmidt, piled on three pieces of toast, and grabbed up a mug of coffee. However, he headed for a table on the opposite side of the mess tent, one which was clearly full. He stood for a moment in thought and pulled a dirty trick, seeing a fast opportunity to escape Schmidt.

"Jansen, Major Clay is looking for you. Beat it." Bart tapped the man on the shoulder and glared for a moment at the surprised face but moved aside when Jansen scrambled up with his tray. Bart sat down in the man's place. He could feel others staring but didn't care.

With his nose buried in his mug of coffee, he heard Schmidt behind him. The man leaned down, his breath hot and smelling strongly of cigarettes and onions; he spoke sharply to Bart's ear.

"I must speak with you. Buddy. It's important. Meet me outside in ten minutes. It ain't a request."

Bart waved his hand as if annoyed by a pesky insect and settled to his meal, taking a large bite of toast and shoving a spoonful of greasy yellow stuff into his cheeks. He felt, then, observed Schmidt move off. The tall, lanky man looked back once with a vengeful expression. He sat at the far table as he had suggested but now faced Barton and sent him glacial looks as he ate.

Bart had so far avoided Schmidt since that revealing night in the woods. He had made sure that he missed Schmidt when he reported yesterday to Bart's clerk, Corporal Billy Meadows, the aide saying to leave the report on Bart's desk. Schmidt had lied in his report.

Bart looked up once or twice to encounter the icy blue gaze and a quick motion that seemed to show Schmidt was ready to leave the mess tent for their talk. Barton glanced around, slightly embarrassed, as if everyone could see the friends were on the skids and there was something between them. Yet, he noted no one truly was paying attention, each man interested in his own meal or the surrounding conversation and men yawning into their coffee cups. Barton sat for a time, now finishing his meal at a slower pace. He struck up a conversation with Meadows, hoping that Schmidt would get the message Bart would not meet him.

During his conversation with Meadows over a trivial high school football story, Bart noted Schmidt saunter out of the mess tent with a stony glance at Bart, and he could not help the sigh of relief that escaped. Excusing himself in the middle of Meadow's tale, he dumped his tray and scurried over to speak with the cooks, mainly to look busy but then to check on their supply requisitions for fuel for the stoves and anything else.

Stuffing a small wad of requisitions in his jacket, Barton now headed out of the tent and into the frigid morning. He squinted against the bright sunlight filtered through the trees and remaining fog that had encircled the camp and creek this morning. There were a few rounds to make, and Barton was relieved. His head began to clear, and he felt the tension ease from his neck, glad that he had once again avoided Schmidt.

He was nearly back to the supply tent when a shadow merged with him on the ground. Barton glanced up. It was Schmidt. The man grabbed him by an elbow, then hustled him the last few paces into the tent and roughly shoved Barton into his chair. The man rounded on him with searing-intense blue eyes.

"Why Bart? Why him? What'd he do to you?"

Barton feigned ignorance and disinterest by picking up a file folder. "Get out, Sergeant," he snapped.

Schmidt leaned over him, his face inches from Bart's; spittle flecked his lips and sprayed Barton's cheek. "Tell me why you did it. He is just a kid, goddammit!"

Barton wiped his cheek with his sleeve. "You know why. You have been caught out, not just by me but also by Samuelson. Who knows who else?"

Schmidt rose shakily from the desk, his eyes wide, his angular face paled. "Did he say anything to you? Or maybe you told him about us. Is this transfer coming from you or Samuelson, then?"

Barton shrugged, feeling ill now from the greasy egg breakfast; the oatmeal lay heavily in his gut, like the guilt he now suffered. "Samuelson demanded Dion should be transferred out."

Schmidt paced about, glanced at his watch, and muttered, "I have only a few minutes before I have to report for my double shift on the road. I suppose you know about that, too?"

Barton deferred the question. His voice was harsh and full of malice as he whispered, "This is your trouble, Schmidt! You are lucky the word hasn't gotten further up the ranks, or you would have a worse punishment. Do you know what they do to people like you two?"

Schmidt shook his head, not interested in hearing the judgment, and faced Barton again. "Did you hear where Pete's going? Right to the front of the line—Ardennes! The baby-faced son of a bitch will be lucky to live out a fucking week!" Schmidt's head rose to gaze afar with watery eyes and then turned back to Barton.

"I-I didn't know." Barton shuffled his feet, wanting to get up. He felt uncomfortable with the proximity of the towering man and felt at a disadvantage should there be a physical altercation with him.

Schmidt rubbed the back of his neck angrily. "Well, maybe it is for the best. It's better than sending the kid home on a Blue Ticket. Dion would probably end up in a mental hospital." He glanced up at Barton, his voice barely above a whisper. "That's where the military sends the homos ... if they are still alive after it all."

Barton shot to his feet. "Look, get yourself together, Schmidt. I can't have this crap going on around here. We are due to move out tomorrow, so that's your cue to settle this." He lowered his voice and spoke in an ominous tone. "Because we were friends, I tried to cover some of this up, but I won't do it again. It goes against my very being, as well as military law. I refuse to go down with you—not on my watch! So it's your choice; live right or die, man."

Bart saw the fight coil up in Schmidt, and he drew back a fist and punched Schmidt in the face before he could react. Bart spun away, fists clenched, expecting a fight.

"Get out," Bart ordered, "you are late for sentry duty. I will give you a pass."

Schmidt looked down coldly at Barton, his lip bleeding. "Don't bother. I am a big boy." He put on his helmet, and at the tent flap, looked back at Barton. "I am sorry. Are we still friends?"

"I don't know. Right now, I am dismissing you and everything else that has to do with this fiasco." Barton turned around now, not caring to look at the broken man or acknowledge that Schmidt was actually a higher rank than he was. He heard running feet, and his own heart trembled for his actions.

◆ ◆

Wednesday, December 13, 1944

The depot camp was chaotic as the new supply shipments came in. Barton was engaged in keeping everything circulating and deployed, trying to juggle the newest with the old and get supplies out to the troops on the move. The once-swift Red Ball Express in this corner of France was on the move again, heading northeast deeper into the former German-occupied territory. The men quickly sank back into their long, tiring shifts almost happily, as if relieved for the idle, peaceful days to be over. The camp thrummed again with the cadence of industrious enterprise—trucks roared, and gears clashed. Soon, the roads had once again been churned into mud, and a smoggy haze of dust, diesel exhaust, and oil fumes ringed the camp.

Barton had become used to this sort of army perfume, relishing it like a heady fragrance. The diesel fumes bit his sinuses, making him sneeze and cough, but he loved it. It meant the US Army and Allied Forces were on the move again. So caught up in the chaos of his work, he mentally set aside the previous arguments and events.

He passed Schmidt and Dion each a few times during the day but ignored them both, no longer concerned by their problems. Dion would be sent on ahead as Lieutenant General Patton's battalion swept by them to refuel and restock their supplies. The snaking arm of the eastward movement continued gathering resources as it went.

◆ ◆

Wednesday, December 13, 1944

So it was that on the last night, as the rest of their company was packing up to break camp in the predawn hours of the morning, all things good went badly, and the bad things went to hell.

Barton was busy speaking with Lieutenant Colonel Samuelson outside the supply tent and became annoyed when Corporal Meadows came rushing up, saying that men were fighting in the woods and that they had to come. He was breathless and pink-faced with the effort of running. The corporal murmured it had to do with Private Dion and Sergeant Schmidt; someone was going to kill them! Both officers, with a knowing look at each other, briskly trotted after the corporal, who swung a flashlight toward the glade that Barton now recognized. They arrived in a break of the trees to find Corporal Rossini armed with his carbine, shouting at Schmidt.

"So this is what you do, Sergeant Schmidt? You said you were taking a shit! Well, look, you got the shit on you now!" he gave a nasty laugh.

"Corporal, stand down!" Samuelson shouted. He stepped into the snowy glade, now looking warily at the trio of men. "What is this?" He started toward Rossini, but the man leveled the rifle on him. He blanched white.

Rossini's voice turned high-pitched and quaking as he rasped, "No. No. Nobody's gonna take this from me. Sir, I am reporting that these men have been—" He ran out of gas and turned pink.

"Have been what?" The colonel brusquely turned to Dion and Schmidt. "What are you doing out here? Don't you have duties?"

Schmidt lowered his hands. "Yes, sir. Well, no … we are both off duty. We were just saying goodbye, sir. You know Private Dion transfers out tomorrow, joining the Fourth."

Rossini's excited, squeaky voice mocked Schmidt. "Saying goodbye to your girlfriend is more like it! You damned liar! I saw you!" He turned slightly to face Dion, tears streaming down his face. "Why him? I thought you were my friend!" He began to sob and relaxed some, taking a faltering step backward. He blubbered. "You did this just to get a promotion! You ass kisser! You liar!"

Dion stepped forward with an outstretched hand. "Stop! I am your friend. Please … put down the rifle, Al. We can talk it over—"

"No!" The young corporal swung back, leveling the weapon again on his target. "Don't you ever speak to me again … you lying, perverted piece of … you both make me sick!" Spittle flecked his lips as the corporal yelled with tears streaming down his cheeks.

Schmidt yelled, "Don't be an ass, Rossini, nothin's goin' on!"

Dion, nearly in tears, yelled back, too. "You are the one who lied! Rossini, you are a two-faced, selfish creep!"

Samuelson, clearly upset, stepped cautiously toward the armed young man, his voice calm as if settling a distraught child with a cookie. "Stand down. At ease, Rossini. You are not going to make anything better here by this action. Come on,

Son. Why don't you come with me and tell me what you saw, hmm? Let's have some coffee and talk … I promise I will help you …" He crept closer, now putting out his hand slowly to take the barrel of the M1 from the corporal. "That's it …" His hand was inches away, and suddenly, Rossini swung the rifle to face Schmidt and Dion, with Samuelson in between.

"No! I am takin' them out! We don't need shit like this in our army. No, sir!" Rossini fired, the barrel smacking hard against the colonel's outstretched hand. The explosion of the rifle sounded like a cannon in the forest, followed by two simultaneous echoes.

Everyone ducked except for Schmidt. Bart pushed the colonel aside to protect him as Bart's shot hit Rossini high in the chest. Schmidt's hand, surreptitiously on his sidearm during the argument, snaked out and fired before Rossini could shoot again. Both gunshots hit the young man nearly at once.

Rossini's hands went limp, and the rifle tipped forward and slipped to the ground. Barton scrabbled across the frozen ground and grabbed the piece up as the man tottered, eyes wide, a dark crimson stain spreading across his jacket. Rossini crumpled to his knees and fell backward into the short, dry grass amid the clumps of snow; his helmet rolled away with a hole shot clean through it.

Intending to lead the young, wounded corporal away, Samuelson got up from the ground, shaking out his numbed hand. He stepped past the awestruck Corporal Meadows, who could only make incoherent noises.

"No! Oh! Al!" Private Dion rushed to the fallen young man's side and cradled the head of his friend in his lap, finding a bloodied graze above Rossini's right ear. He stared down into the pink-cheeked face. "Why did you do it?" he asked with a tear-choked voice.

Rossini opened an eye and frowned. "Pete. Why … aren't you … dead?" Blood bubbled on his lips between words.

Dion gave a small laugh and shook his head. "You cross-eyed fool! You have always been a lousy shot, Al. You tried to kill a tree!" He stroked the stringy black hair away from the corporal's brow and sat, gently rocking him.

"*Per favore. Fatemi un favore …*" Rossini mumbled as his hand feebly struck at his chest.

Schmidt came over and stood stiffly nearby, looking down at the young man lying in the ragged, frozen grass. The blood seeping into the dirt and snow looked like black oil in the dim light of Corporal Meadows' electric torchlight, making the scene surreal.

"Damn shame. Let's get Al outta here. Maybe we can save him, although I don't know why we should," Schmidt snarled. "I feel like kicking the little asshole." He holstered his sidearm and refastened his belt. Schmidt stepped around the scene to pick up his jacket and helmet from the ground. "I'll get the medics."

Samuelson looked up at the tall, lanky MP to find his face impassive. "Why did you shoot him, Sergeant? I almost had him there." He spun to Barton. "And you too. Why did both of you shoot this poor boy?"

Barton holstered his revolver. "Sir, he almost shot you! You were in the line of fire!" he spat hotly. "It was self-defense."

"I had to shoot Rossini. He shot at me, sir. He's crackers!" Harlan chimed in.

"He shot at me, Harlan." A soft voice from the ground arose. "It doesn't matter anymore; he's gone," Dion said simply, then patted down the jacket of his friend, taking out a blood-streaked and dirty folded letter from a pocket. "I'll write to his sister and mother, Violetta, in Chicago and tell them he died bravely." Dion wiped his eyes and then stuffed the papers in his own jacket pocket.

Schmidt snorted derisively and spat. "Brave! The little runt wanted to go off half-cocked and report us to Samuelson here for nuthin'. Show him what I gave you, Dion. Do it!"

Dion sat back on his heels and hesitantly reached into his jacket. The colonel shrank back, not expecting a long knife. "Sarge gave me this as a going away present, sir." He held it up to the light.

Samuelson flinched from the dark stain on the tarnished metal of a wicked-looking serrated blade and hesitated to touch it. "I see. Well, it was all a big mistake then, wasn't it?" His face contorted into an uncomfortable grimace, the shaggy brows frowning. "Well, let's get him up then." He turned away. "I cannot bear to see my young men fighting for nothing. Rossini deserved better."

"No, he didn't." Schmidt snorted again in laughter and lit a cigarette. "I took that knife off a Kraut I found dead in the woods a few days ago; been wearing it myself. But I thought our little man here might need it at the front."

Suddenly, there was a loud popping noise, and the cloudy night sky lit with a red and amber glow.

"*Oh shit! Incoming!*" Schmidt yelled and ran away toward the camp, long arms and legs windmilling. The colonel and Corporal Meadows followed suit, fast on Schmidt's heels with the corporal's flashlight winking through the trees.

Barton scrambled into the trees and then heard the wild screech of a mortar as it hit and exploded in the woods twenty yards away. Showered with dirt and debris, he shook the dirt from his head as he looked back at Private Dion, who was still holding

Rossini. "Get your ass out of there before you are a corpse … like your friend! Move it!" he ordered. Bart was relieved to see the young private give a quick kiss on Rossini's face and scurry away into the trees to join him.

He gripped the young man's arm as they ran low to the ground, weaving through the trees to head back toward camp as the sky lit with the white and red incendiary flares and the forest ignited into flames under another barrage. Bart fell heavily on top of Dion as another mortar showered debris and shredded foliage on them. He murmured aloud, *"Mon dieu help me!"*

Dion looked askance at Barton, "You want me to help you?"

"No, idiot!" Barton griped. Moments later, they stood and ran the last yards into the camp.

The next thunderous mortar shell neatly buried Cpl. Albert Rossini, making him once again a part of the earth.

◆ ◆

4 miles west of Saarlaurten, Germany
Friday, December 15, 1944

Days were spent making zigzagging movements across a blasted country—sometimes retreating, other times in a diagonal direction to get away from their persistent enemy. At one point, some of the Twentieth's armored tank cavalry rescued them. Finally, the journey brought the supply train to a halt in low hills. The supply company made camp protected on two sides by a rocky escarpment; a nearby creek bubbled in friendly tones. Across the shallow Saar River valley were the remnants of burned-out farm buildings and a few cottages. The frozen land had gone fallow, but upon exploration, several men found squashes, icy grapes, and an apple orchard and returned to the encampment with duffle bags full of their gleanings to share among their comrades.

The apples were a welcome treat, and Barton, while perusing his requisitions and inventory sheets, chomped noisily on a small, mealy apple. He was relishing the break in his tent after a busy morning of his staff reassessing the trucks and taking inventory. After the last attack days earlier, they had lost three trucks, blown to smithereens along with their crews and jerrican cargoes. There were numerous missing pallets, some of which had been new supplies. Everyone was searching through the hastily scrabbled-together provisions to see what remained. Medical supplies were short again. They lost one of the medics in the first nighttime raid. It was as if the Krauts knew precisely where to hit their camp, taking out a battalion medical tent along with four sick men and two injured ones. After the fast escape into the dark countryside that night and for the following days, Barton had put aside all thoughts of what had transpired in the woods.

He heard that Dion had gone back to retrieve Rossini's body but could not find him; there was a pile of dirt and a crater six feet across where they had all once stood that horrible night. According to Billy Meadows, who was now Dion's new friend and confidant, Dion had not even found Rossini's dog tags; there was nothing left of the man! Somehow, they had miraculously all escaped death, except for Rossini; he was already dead.

Barton had not spoken to Schmidt or Samuelson about anything of that night. It was as if a dark shade had been pulled down, hiding the ugly deeds from which they had barely escaped. But he knew there would be something soon; once things settled, a report would have to be made, and letters would need to be written to Rossini's family. It saddened Barton still; the entire filthy scene would not be something he would forget for a long time.

He knew Dion was to be sent on now that the supply convoy had stopped running from the Jerries. The Fifth Division's tanks and troops were just over the hill in a strategic placement meant to keep the Germans out and allow the slow eastward movement of the US troops toward the damn wall. The tanks and troop convoys would funnel through the valley to refuel and take on supplies as they headed toward the German front lines.

Currently off duty, Barton wondered if he had time for a nap. He felt weary, but his stomach rebelled and won, so he headed to the mess tent for lunch. Standing in line to pick up a bowl of tepid vegetable soup, biscuits, some sort of pudding that had been hastily cobbled together with some of the better apples and stale bread, and a pile of brown glop, which turned out to be overcooked canned baked beans. He no longer cared; food was food. He was that hungry!

Barton considered the idea of writing a letter to his family. He could no longer remember if he had written since he'd arrived in France. He recalled the early days and how quickly the chaos of the Red Ball Express supply train had sucked him in. Barton had lost track of the days.

Sometimes, he felt as if he were in a whirlpool, going around and around but not getting anywhere, as he fought to keep his head up. There were times he would like to give in and get sucked down into the swirling abyss. But his innately stubborn pride would not let him succumb to such weakness.

Barton bussed his empty meal tray and plodded wearily back to his tent. He was off for the next few hours and should probably sleep, but as he lay down on his cot, the noise of the surrounding universe was too full of strife. Clanging and jangling metal, strident shouts, and dust crept into his tent, making him sneeze and giving him a headache. He sat up, rough and miserable. He rubbed his jaw and felt the stubble of three days' growth of a beard and thought, *What the hell. I'm going to let it grow, even if Samuelson hates it.*

He grabbed up his jacket and helmet, pulled on his gun belt, and headed into the woods. He walked for a short time, still within line of sight of the camp, and found a somewhat dry, sunny spot where he sat down with his back against a fir tree.

The weak winter sunlight was dappled, the distant voices were muted, and the air here was clean. The sound of the bubbling creek and twittering birds soon lulled Barton to sleep. He fell asleep deeply for the first time in however long he could remember, with the scent of *Muguet des Bois* in his nose.

◆ ◆

She was there; the gentle breeze lifted a black strand of hair and blew it across her cheek, and Barton smoothed it back. He held her face in his hands to look at her angelic smile—her dark eyes sparkled, her finely arched brows were light wings, her cheeks flushed with desire, and her lips felt warm upon his. Barton could taste her; she was like wine, intoxicating and sweet. Feeling lightheaded and giddy, he reached to put his arms around her and press her seductive body to his, but the sunlight was in his eyes, blinding him. Her face became a blur. She no longer tasted of sweet wine but of peppermints and cigarettes. Barton pushed away the vision, and his hand hit something hard—his instinctual reflexes fought back.

"Easy … I wasn't hurting you!"

A hand grabbed his, squeezing hard, which brought Barton awake. He opened his eyes, shielding them against the ray of sunlight, to find Private Dion kneeling before him with a wry smile on his full lips.

Barton looked around, suddenly afraid. "W-what are you doing?"

Dion gave a little laugh. "I came to say goodbye to you. I also want to thank you, Sergeant."

Barton sat up now, embarrassed, and rubbed his hands vigorously along his scratchy cheeks. He wiped his mouth—he could still feel her kiss. He clambered up and stood, now wobbly and muzzy-headed.

"Oh, are you leaving now?" he asked shakily.

"Soon. I wanted to … well, say thank you for saving my life the other day." Dion dropped his head bashfully. "Twice. If you know what I mean," he said, casting coy, dark eyes with absurdly long, dark lashes at Barton.

Barton looked down on the diminutive young man. He put a hand on the private's shoulder. "That's all right; you would have done the same for me, I am sure. We were all lucky to get out. It's too bad about Rossini."

Dion stood up tall, made a little sniffle, and wiped a grubby finger under his nose. "Yeah, that too. It was my fault, too, I guess."

Bart noted the pink shade rise on Dion's face and felt his own chagrin. "I know. Just keep yourself safe, Dion. Don't repeat it if you understand my meaning. You might have to use the Kraut's knife to save Pegasus," Barton said huskily, trying to be amusing and not maudlin. He found it was always hard to say farewell to his staff or men for whatever reasons parted them. And he now found it more so with the dark secret between them.

Dion's face rose, now with a big smile. "Thanks, Sarge. You've been really good to me. You were the best boss. I'll make you proud, you'll see." He put out his small, dirty hand for Barton to shake.

Barton perused the hand, and feeling the emotions of the past days, he took it and the man's forearm; he gave Dion a hard pound on the back and drew away. "May good luck go with you, kiddo." He commended the private.

Dion looked up and smiled widely. "Thanks. I need it. Oh, and you kiss real nice." Giggling, the small private happily bounded away like a jackrabbit through the underbrush and snowdrifts.

Barton stood stunned and put a hand to his lips. His dream of Elise Boulanger had felt so real!

"Damn! You little pervert!" he shouted after the kid. He felt disgusted, nearly hysterical, wanting to spit and wipe the young man's kisses from his lips, but instead, he swiped a hand over his mouth, embarrassed, and headed back to his tent. He needed to write a letter, feeling the need even more now. He would write to Elise to let her know he was very much alive.

◆ ◆

Some minutes later, in his tent, Bart sat at the folding table and retrieved a couple of sheets of writing paper. He caught sight of the calendar and closed his eyes for a second, counting the days of their advancement into the Moselle and Saar Regions, and realized that they had missed Thanksgiving Day in America, and Christmas was looming near now. Yet nobody had said anything, and he wondered if others realized it, too.

His mouth began to water as he thought of savory turkey or roast goose and stuffing, creamy mashed potatoes, or wild rice swimming in sage gravy. A myriad of flavors invaded his mouth and mind—Mémé's bacon and green bean cassoulet, sweet potato pie, pumpkin pie, decadently sweet pecan pie, spicy mincemeat, baked yams …

Barton felt his stomach growl, complaining about the poor diet of late. C-rations were a miserable excuse for food, and the newer K-rations were scarcer and not much better. Barton left his tent and headed to the mess tent, hoping to have a word with the company cook, Klimowski—they had a private understanding.

Corporal Billy Meadows was there instead, peeling onions and sniffing audibly with eyes streaming.

"You crying?" Barton asked huskily.

Meadows looked up, surprised. "Uh, no, Sarge." He swiped a damp hand under his nose and eyes.

"Idiot, you just wiped onion juice on your face!" Barton snatched up a damp rag and handed it off to the corporal.

"Uh, sorry, sir." He swabbed his running eyes and face with the rag.

Barton sniffed about and paced around the kitchen tent, hoping to find evidence of a decent meal. He glanced at the pile of shredded onions. "So anything good on the menu?"

"What else but cigarette soup. I hate it."

Bart frowned. "Me too. So, what did you do to get KP today? I wondered where you were earlier."

Meadows smiled weakly, sniffled, and then climbed off the stool to join Barton at the table with the steel pan full of the onions. "I kinda screwed up and told Samuelson I was going to miss the private around here. Dion was a nice guy."

"So what?" Barton snatched a piece of raw onion and munched it with relish while leaning against the worktable.

Meadows rolled his eyes emphatically. "Well … the Colonel thought I might be having similar thoughts about Dion that Rossini had, you know, them bein' Blue and all. Samuelson busted me here to the kitchen to think about it. It was either that or digging latrine holes." He held out reddened hands. "Look, I got blisters already from scrubbing pots and cutting these damned onions!" he complained. "I think fat Kookie Klimowski is a Nazi bastard!"

Barton almost laughed. "So, have you changed your mind about the private?"

The corporal's eyes went wide. "Hell yeah. I mean, yes. I ain't a Nancy boy!"

Bart sobered and gruffly whispered, "Look, that was a bad night for all of us and stuff nobody should know about. Rossini and Dion were um … friends … Hell, I don't want the rest of the camp to know."

"Know what? That they were doing the nasty or that you killed Rossini?" Meadows retorted, then regretted it.

Barton snatched him up by the throat. "Don't you dare say a damned thing! I didn't kill him. It was self-defense. Rossini was a nutcase! Got it? All of us would be dead if I had not intervened," his eyes glittering icily upon the short corporal.

"Yeah, I got it. I'm sorry." He grinned weakly up at Barton, gulped, and then asked, "Do you think we are gonna be camped here very long … because I want to work for you again!"

Barton was relieved, almost felt compelled to ruffle the shorter man's yellow hair, but resisted the urge, recalling he had never liked it as a kid. "I'll see what I can do. I guess we gotta stick together and keep this crap to ourselves." He stood again after releasing Meadows. "Maybe you can tell me if Kookie is planning a holiday feast soon or not."

"What holiday?" Meadows shot Barton a stern look and then clapped a hand to his mouth. "Well, hell, is it Thanksgiving already?" he gaped.

Bart laughed, then shook his head. "No, we missed it. Don't tell me I am the only one around here who knows it."

"You might be. I'll betcha we are gonna miss out on Christmas too!" Meadows whined and stomped his foot like a temperamental child.

Barton snagged another sliver of onion. "Well, that is depressing." He chewed the onion. "I'd say that it's bad for the morale of the men to deprive them of a holiday meal. Maybe I should check with the colonel and see if anyone else is doing something for the upcoming holiday. Maybe there's something already planned, all on the QT." He shoved away from the table, grinning.

Meadows wiped his abused hands on his stained cotton apron and followed Barton to the door. "Yeah, and tell that stuffed peacock Patton to feed his damned troops with some decent food, or we'll leave him like Napoleon's troops did!"

Barton put a finger to his lips and grinned wickedly. "Hush! Them's fightin' words and will get you court-martialed or at least a week in the can. Patton might personally smack you upside the head!" He shook his head and shoved the corporal back away from the door. "Idiot! I never heard you say that. And you remember what I said, or you are dead meat, kid." Bart strolled away now with purposeful steps and a smirk on his face.

◆ ◆

The Fourth Army was besieged in the forests of Ardennes near Luxembourg. The Germans violently attacked them at dawn on Saturday, December 16. Mother Nature was brutal, sending blinding freezing sleet and snowstorms, compounding forward movements on both sides. Many troops froze in the woods, unable to get help, retreat, or move forward. The bombers of the 101st Airborne were grounded during the days of the storm, and their aerial support was crucial to observation and barrages.

After days of repeated and concentrated attacks, the encircling Germans held all the roads leading toward Bastogne with their Panzer divisions. They were demanding the United States admit defeat because their troops were closed off, their munitions and supplies were low, and much of the Americans' medical staff and supplies had been captured in the previous days. The Führer hoped that this offensive would force the Allies to make a treaty or admit defeat. The other troops along the Saar River were sorely in trouble, too.

Not ready to end the fight, many other US divisions were on their way to help. The Third Army, too, was summoned to bring relief to the beleaguered troops of the Fourth. The Fifth Division, which had been barely holding on near the town of Saarlaurten, was ordered to move and turned northwest to Luxembourg on December 20. Patton happily headed for the fight, ready to aid 101st Airborne's General Anthony McAuliffe.

After a harrowing, freezing one-hundred-mile trip along perilous muddy and ice-covered roads, the Fifth arrived in the city of Luxembourg. They viciously struck the southern region of the Reich's front door to drive the Germans back across the Sûre River.

On December 22, McAuliffe audaciously replied to the German Kommandant, who in days previous demanded the Americans surrender.

"Nuts!"

Gen. McAuliffe humorously shared the presumptuous and overly confident German Kommandant's demands in a Christmas letter to his troops. McAuliffe's simple answer fueled their troops with the needed spiritual impetus and support to persevere.

In the days between, the Fifth relieved the Fourth, allowing some men in the battle-weary units to rest in Nancy for a few days. The Fifth Infantry continued to push, wiggle, and worm their way through the newly gained Luxembourg borders. Patton planned for a significant push for the Fifth and Tenth Infantry Divisions by December 23 to help reinforce the recently gained areas. The 945th continued to daily pound the region with fresh artillery, shelling roads, bridges, small towns, and farms along the German frontline, hoping to oust the stubborn enemy.

However, in the days that followed, the Germans were hard-pressed by the latest fierce American retaliation, and the Fifth Army recaptured much of the Fourth Army's confiscated materiel. Surprisingly, they then took hundreds of German troops as prisoners, abruptly stopping their southern attack along the borders.

General Patton, for the past months, was concerned about the continued harsh winter weather that brought freezing snow and sleet and was slowing his armies considerably. Most days, the heavy cloud cover kept the airplanes of the 101st from providing surveillance on the Germans' maneuvers and stopping air-supported advanced bombing and strafing raids. The audacious general asked the Third Division's chaplain, James O'Neill, for a prayer to stop the brutal weather. Patton wanted to win and not have Mother Nature confounding his plans at every turn.

Regardless of the bold request, the chaplain penned a prayer, asking for better weather and God's help to continue in their valiant fight. The prayer pleased Patton; he had 250,000 copies printed on index cards. As his personal Christmas greeting to his troops, everyone in the Third Army received a card on Christmas Eve.

Upon Patton's orders, on Christmas Eve Day, the 945th, Twelfth Corps, and the Third Army spent the day firing interdiction and white phosphorous salvos along a ten-mile border. There were returned hostile salvos in kind. Patton was disappointed that there was far too much German activity and resistance in the newly freed areas.

Then, on Christmas Day, Patton gave his back-line troops a proper hot Christmas turkey dinner, and he spent the day meeting with many of his men. The men on the frontline were only to get cold turkey sandwiches, a welcome change from field rations.

In the middle of holiday festivities, the Fourth reached the Bastogne region and again took heavy casualties. It would be two days before supplies and medical help could meet them. The 945th, now in Eschweiler, fired the new POZIT (proximity fuses), a uniquely designed shell timed to detonate about thirty feet above the ground, killing more in one blast than their weapons previously used. The German troops were terrified, as they had witnessed examples of this secret weapon during the battle in the Ardennes Forest weeks before. Patton was pleased with the new deterrent, citing that they took seven hundred German casualties near Echternach when the Jerries were caught out in the open. He now had a dynamic weapon to help him win.

Lieutenant General Patton's Christmas prayer miraculously worked, and like a blessed gift, each day continued to dawn clear but bitterly cold. The air support could continue, raining terror from above. With morale high, Patton moved forward along the frontline once again with confidence and full cooperation in their advance bombardments.

The Battle of the Bulge was to continue for weeks, ultimately driving the Fifth Division (Twelfth Corps) to cross the Sûre River on January 18, 1945. Then, they prepared to cross Our River past the Luxembourg-German border with multiple assaults and forays along the bordering rivers and bridges of the Kyell, Sûre, and Moselle at strategic points. Thus, this created a new front from which the Third Army and its many divisions could move into Germany.

Patton was ready to drive his army right down Hitler's throat!

Happy New Year, Herr Führer!

Putting away his journal, Staff Sergeant Barton Barre hoped and now prayed that it was the beginning of the end.

CHAPTER 12

Retribution

Sûre River Valley
January 20, 1945

The morning was sullen gray, "cold as a dead Kraut," as newly promoted Corporal Lofgren quoted, or "cold as a witch's tit," as Sergeant Schmidt often said. However cold, it was of no relevance to Barton as he read Lieutenant Colonel Samuelson's report of last month regarding the "disgusting display of indecency and immorality, poor soldiering, and perverse callousness in the recent death of Corporal Rossini."

Feeling feverish, Barton continued to read and felt his gorge rise. His throat burned with acid, and he swallowed it down. He angrily lay the report aside, wondering how in the hell he would get out of this.

Samuelson implied Barton should be demoted in rank, as he had allowed such behavior among his men and was most likely a part of it, too. Samuelson also felt his staff sergeant should be put up against a tribunal court for shooting a fellow soldier, which Barton surmised might eventually lead to military prison or hanging. Barton ran a trembling hand along his jaw, feeling that Samuelson was too harsh. After all, he had shot Rossini to protect his own ass and Samuelson. Bart believed he should stick to his story that he had fired in self-defense against a crazed man obviously suffering from battle trauma. Where the hell was a good lawyer when needed?

Hell, last year, Lieutenant General Patton had done less when he slapped a soldier silly, accusing the hysterical, traumatized man of cowardice for admitting he was scared in battle. However, the general later had to recant his vicious attack and publicly apologize to the soldier and the battalion and subsequently lost his command for a time. Still, Barton did not believe he had done anything wrong by shooting Rossini.

He let out a long-held breath, wanting to rip up the report. Someone should listen to him first before going off half-cocked on a vengeful tear to accuse Barton of such indelicacies or inaccuracy! There had to be a way out of this.

During the weeks after the incident, Samuelson was silently dispassionate and reserved with everyone involved. Barton had thought perhaps the event would be pushed under the rug or that Corporal Rossini would be listed as a casualty in the war, not reported as murdered! *Damn, it wasn't murder! It was Rossini's fault that he was dead. If he was that miserable, he should have shot himself and saved everyone the trouble!*

Barton stood and paced around his nearly empty tent, clutching the old rabbit's foot in his pocket as if it could alter this terrible fate. If they had not been on the move and in battle for so many weeks since the incident, he was confident that the lieutenant colonel would have arrested him before now.

He could almost hate the man, feeling the colonel acted so smugly superior and prim about the delicate affair and then turned about-face to write a report that would clearly destroy Barton and Schmidt! Schmidt deserved the rotten treatment, but not Bart.

Barton hated this war, and he could not believe that he had been spared in so many battles, skirmishes, and challenging days only to end his military career this way—sitting in prison for murder! It wasn't honorable! He wondered how Schmidt felt about it all. Banished and under guard in his tent, Barton supposed it could be worse—he might be sitting in the frozen latrine that the MPs sometimes used for a prisoner or outside in the cold digging foxholes under the laughing guards as punishment.

There was a guard outside his tent. Barton peered through the crack of the flap to see he was smoking and coldly pacing about. The cigarette smoke blended with his frosty exhalations. Barton wished for a cigarette now.

Their division would move soon, and Barton wondered what would happen. Would the colonel send him to the front as he had Private Dion? Would he be sent to the rear to a military police detainment area or prison? Would his trial be sooner or later—maybe after the war? Barton hoped that the Lieutenant Colonel and others felt he was valuable enough to keep. Although, much as he would like, he would dearly love to get out of the war, he certainly could not go home with a dishonorable discharge or a prison sentence! His father would absolutely puke and die of shame. Barton would rather be dead than suffer that humiliation! But a self-inflicted million-dollar wound was not his style either. He laughed at the irony—so much for being a hero!

Consumed by his upcoming woes, Bart again sat on his cot to rummage in his duffel bag, looking for the Bible his Father had given him so long ago. Although he had grown up in the Catholic Church, he'd never had much use for reading the Bible or saying prayers when he grew up, thinking them like childish bedtime stories and rituals. But now he thought prayers might be a place to start.

He found the venerable Douay-Rheims 1898 French-American edition of the Catholic Bible and shoved his bag off the cot. He then lay down to page through the ragged book. Recalling his father's letter when Richard felt the world coming at him with sharpened teeth, he turned to his Bible and found solace and peace. Bart was unsure he might experience all that but hoped it might make the time pass quicker as he waited for Samuelson's decision.

His eye caught the passages describing Moses' journey into the wilderness. Barton felt like the dethroned prince, a man now without country or home and lost in a war-torn wasteland. He skimmed speedily through the story and snickered as he read the Ten Commandments, thinking that he had abused all of them at some time in his life. And indeed, now the part that read, "thou shalt not kill," struck him ironically funny.

Millenniums had passed since the commandments were supposedly written, yet for every generation through those times, armies rose to conquer and fight, killing millions and destroying notable civilizations. How could God let them do it? If man wasn't supposed to kill another, then why were there wars? Why all the sinful greed, and why was the Golden Rule so blatantly disobeyed? Did God take sides amid the horrors of war?

Barton felt his world get a little smaller, tightening around his neck like a noose. Why would God let him get this far if He meant for Barton to die? Why put him in a place and time that would make him fight for his life and then punish him for it if killing was so damned wrong? It wasn't fair!

He slapped the book shut and laid his head on the pillow with the Bible on his chest. He noticed the various colored ribbons and pieces of paper stuffed between the pages of his father's Bible. They were markers for what Richard felt was needed at the time he read his Bible. After several minutes had passed, now curious what those passages might reveal about his father's spiritual life, Bart thumbed through the book again to find a page marked with a faded red ribbon.

It was the story of the twin brothers Esau and Jacob. Each greedily sought praise, material comforts, and rewards from their aging father, Issac. Barton snorted derisively, wondering how this story had helped Richard. Had he used it to learn patience with his own envious and combative children or in how to best punish them?

Bart skimmed through the pages and found some of the psalms marked with ribbons and one with a bookmark. In that psalm, King David was beseeching the Lord to save him and smite his enemies, counting their evils like sins to God. Yet in the subsequent verses, the king felt anguish in doing so, asking for forgiveness and for the Lord to deliver him from himself!

Bart could almost relate to that, for earlier, he had been wishing for a way out of his current troubles. He could only come up with a few bad scenarios that might befall Samuelson before he could file the incriminating reports to their superiors. Bart took an interest in finishing the psalm and then read more. He did feel akin to King David, trying to reason that his own sins of failure were more critical than the sins of others. He ruefully gulped back tears now, not wanting to admit his own role in Rossini's murder.

He had not cried for Corporal Rossini when he shot him or when the young man was conveniently blown to smithereens minutes later, covering the evil deeds of the night. Barton had been more afraid of the jealousy and sexual aspects between Schmidt, Dion, and Rossini than the shooting. And now, he had to admit, his case did indeed look grave!

He wondered if there was a way to keep quiet any rumors that might arise from the report about Schmidt and his boys. How could they put a kibosh on the entire rotten, damned mess and not have any of the mud hit him in the process?!

He lay for a time reading and then, upon turning a page in the Bible, found the Christmas prayer Patton had issued his troops. Barton reread the prayer, thinking it was an impudent and arrogant thing for the general to do, yet somebody upstairs seemed to have listened. For nearly all the days since Christmas Eve, the weather had improved, and Patton's army had been victorious in their forward movements!

Now Barton wondered if he should ask for divine help. If King David and an audacious American general could demand victories and deliverance, then so could he. Barton found his phoenix medallion and put it on. Then, holding it in his hand, he closed his eyes and lay silent for a few moments before whispering his prayer. "Please deliver me from my enemies. I do not know what saint to pray to for this problem, but God, listen to my prayer. I did nothing wrong. You gotta help me."

Then Bart recalled the proper way to make a confession and said aloud, "I am heartily sorry for killing Corporal Rossini. I liked him. He was a good kid—" He choked on his tears. "I didn't mean to kill him, just stop him. I tried to save the Colonel when I did it. God, I don't want to die for that. Tell me what to do … I don't know anymore what I should do."

Thinking he might throw in a few Hail Mary prayers for good measure and wishing he had his old rosary, Bart broke down to weep and could not say the rest of his penitent prayers audibly. Clutching the Bible to his chest, he rolled over on his cot and cried into his pillow, now weak, very alone in his misery, and sorry for himself.

Suddenly, a new hope sprang up, and he cried anew in his plea, "Mama, you gotta help me. Please tell God I need help."

◆ ◆

The sounds of screaming artillery overhead, running feet, and shouting brought Barton back from his prayerful reverie. In the next moment, he heard the thunderous explosion nearby; it threw him from his cot as dust from the canvas tent rained down on his head. He crawled back up and hastily put on his jacket, helmet, and sidearm; the MPs had confiscated his carbine. He could hear explosions now coming at regular intervals, pounding the camp. Swallowing his fear, he stepped out of his tent, ready to defend himself. He found the MP guard lying on the ground outside the tent.

"Hey, Flynn! Are you alive?" Barton queried as he quickly searched the man's limbs, looking for injuries.

"Oh, hell! What a noise!" The man shook his head and looked blearily up at Barton. "I passed out, I think."

Still filled with adrenaline, Barton nodded. "I think so. Look, I can't sit here and wait to get shelled, can I? I've got the right to fight or at least protect myself."

"But you are under arrest, Sergeant," the MP stated. He tried to sit up, rubbing his head.

"Too bad. I won't sit around like a wounded duck, and if you are smart, you'll get the hell out of here, too!" Bart yelled over the next volley of explosions. Ducking, he grabbed up the man's Thompson M1. "Let's go liberate Schmidt, too, if he's still alive!"

Another round hit close by, showering them with dirt clods, and the MP surged to his feet and followed Barton on a zigzagged track between the tents. "Hey! Gimme my Chopper!" Flynn yelped.

Bart tossed the submachine gun over and withdrew his own Colt 45.

Some tents were on fire, and a Jeep nearby had exploded. The men were racing about like ants, putting out fires, scooping up fallen comrades, and some falling behind sandbags to fire at the Germans.

Barton looked around and did not see advancing enemy troops. The barrage was coming from above—the Germans were shelling them from far away. He passed a frenzied man firing away with a Browning .50 caliber into the woods.

"Soldier, stand down!" he shouted.

He fell in beside him, behind the redoubt. "Cease fire!" Barton yelled over the chatter.

The man looked about at Barton with shock. "But, Sarge, they're here!"

"No, they are not! Have you seen anyone? Did you shoot anyone?"

"No … but they have to be out there! They got Private Arnold!"

Barton glanced for a second at the soldier, now understanding his furious fight. "Their infantry is probably advancing, yes, but not so close as to be hit by their own artillery. Stay here and keep watch. Don't waste any more ammunition until you actually see a Kraut come out of those woods! That's an order, Nicks!" he warned the private and then fled the redoubt headed toward Schmidt's tent. "Friggin' peeshwank! The Germans shoulda got him instead of Arnold." He shook his head and continued through the camp.

Schmidt hid behind a truck some yards away from his flaming tent and a burning troop transport. He smiled as if relieved when Barton slid to the ground beside him. Barton pushed Schmidt's M1 carbine down. "Don't bother. Nobody's coming through those woods until they stop shelling us. It's all coming from above." He grimaced and shook his head, his ears still ringing from the nearby explosions.

"I am glad to see you too, Buddy. I almost didn't get out alive." Schmidt smiled wanly at Barton as he held up a singed jacket.

"Where's the MP?"

"Dead," Schmidt said hollowly.

"You?"

Schmidt grinned lopsidedly. "Nah, I wished I had, though. The damned bastard wasn't going to let me out. I trained that son of a bitch. Then when the transport next to my tent blew, I ran out along with the other poor fools from their truck. The shithead almost shot me, but the Krauts got him instead." He leaned against the tire. "Couldn't have done it better myself—shrapnel right across his neck." He made a finger-slicing-across-his-neck motion and grinned at Barton.

"You are a sick puppy, Schmidt." Barton made a face. "Where'd you get the rifle? That isn't yours, is it?'

"Where d'ya think?" Schmidt nodded at the corpse of the guard amid others. He shrugged into his jacket and settled against the tire, pulling out his lighter and a pack of cigarettes. "So where is your Boy Scout? You shoot him to get out?" He lit a cigarette.

"No, I saved Flynn's scrawny ass and told him to run for it. I guess I lost him over there somewhere," Barton said glumly and then accepted the lit cigarette from Schmidt, taking a drag before passing it back. He cringed when another round pounded the earth, taking out another tent full of supplies. "Hell, if this continues much longer, we'll all be dead, and it won't matter about the colonel's damned report," he shouted through the din and falling debris.

Schmidt nodded and swiped dirty sweat off his face. "Yeah, I've been thinkin' on that some. We might have a way around it." Schmidt sounded confident as he held out the cigarette to Bart.

"How so?" Bart took the cigarette, smoked it down the last half inch, and then tossed it away toward Schmidt's burning tent.

"I see it like this. Samuelson has to say what he saw."

Barton ducked as more dirt rained down on them from another barrage. "Yeah, so what?" He squinted through the grime.

"We-e-e-l-l," Schmidt drawled, "the Colonel would show derelict of duty to keep such stuff quiet for so long. Don't you think he'll be in hot water, too, if he blabs this shit? I mean, he has been sitting on this thing for a long time … and I figure he's biding his time to get us both. You know, I never did like the prick, especially for what he did to Pete." Schmidt's voice was gruff, and he cracked his fisted knuckles as if readying for a fight.

Barton considered the man's words and stoically said, "That could be. However, as Samuelson is our superior, for him to report us at all, gets the CO's attention. Colonel Rice will probably believe him over us. No, I say we have to nip it now or just tell it like it is and suffer the consequences."

Schmidt gripped Bart's arm fiercely. "I ain't sufferin' nuthin'. You know, he said I'm gonna be demoted two ranks below my current rank and get a trial too, but not for manslaughter like you, only for firing upon an unarmed man and behavior unbecoming a soldier!" Schmidt gazed blearily at Barton. "Don't that beat it all to shit? Do you think Rice knows about Dion?" Schmidt sounded wounded and scared.

"I don't know. Probably not, or Rice would have done something by now. He's that tightly wound. They all are." Barton shook his head and pulled away. "You know, I really don't appreciate getting dragged into your shit, Schmidt. I told you to leave it be." Barton glared at the scrawny man and watched him squirm.

Schmidt made a face, frowning, and stated with petulance, "Well, I liked Private Dion. He was a good soldier and a sweet little friend. He … listened to me." Schmidt's voice cracked.

"I think you may have liked him too much. You caused this crap. Now we gotta clean it up, and right about now, I am in no mood or inclination to save your sorry ass."

Schmidt ducked his head and picked at his long, dirty nails. He coughed and spat. "I know, and I am sorry, Bart. A man can never have too many friends, you know. I need you to be mine. Please?" He looked over at Barton; his blue eyes glittered with tears. "God! I hate this damned place! Fucking kill me now!" He moaned and put a filthy hand over his eyes. He shuddered as another mortar exploded in their camp.

Bart shook his head. "You take the cake, man. You couldn't get away with this crap back home, either. They'd stomp your guts and string you up faster than a naked nigger with a hard-on. Sorry, that's mean and racist—you know I don't mean it."

Schmidt laughed now at Bart's crudity. "Oh, don't I wish!" He sobered. "Hey, do you think Dion is still alive?"

"I have no idea. Dion was supposedly sent to Ardennes—but maybe Samuelson took pity on him. He might be safer there than where we are now!" Barton jested grimly. "We both know it was a terrible place to be."

Schmidt nodded. "I hope he is in good hands and has found a friend." He looked over at Barton and then offered his hand to him. "Are we still friends? I kinda thought you might still like me since you came to find me."

Barton reluctantly nodded. "Yeah, I guess we are still friends. I don't have anyone else who listens when I complain!" He banged a fist against Schmidt's shoulder and then, groaning with the effort, rose from the crouched position by the truck and began swiping dirt from his uniform. "Let's get a move on—"

"Are you loco? Where are you going?" Schmidt looked up with alarm at Bart.

"Haven't you noticed the shelling has stopped? I am going to find Samuelson and see what I can do about our problem." He glanced back at the man he had called friend moments before. "You wanna come try to save your sorry hide?"

Schmidt sprang up from the ground. Shouldering the rifle, he said, "Hell, yes, I am tired of sitting here like a duck waiting to get shot or hung out to dry."

Barton nodded and punched Schmidt in the arm. "That was my thought exactly."

Together, the men traipsed through the wrecked camp. Feeling full of purpose and vitality again, they helped carry men to the medics' tent. Barton let Schmidt swipe some of the grime off in his tent, and then they went in search of Samuelson, once again on a joint mission for mercy.

"Hey, has anyone seen Samuelson?" Bart asked in the mess tent, knowing the colonel's schedule of having coffee with his clerks and aides about this time. However, the men were busy putting the spilled supplies together and righting tables and benches.

Corporal Chas Carlton was a soggy mess. Carrying a rag and bucket, he made his way over to the men. "No, not recently, but Jensen said he saw Major Clay leave just shortly before we got shelled. Did you hear Stan Arnold and Zane Gustafson bought it? Corporal Lofgren's gonna be really sad about his buddy Gus. Kookie got hit too—took a chunk outta his arm."

"Where was Clay headed?" Barton asked, fearing the worst and not bothering to stay with the corporal's wounded report.

Carlton scratched his chin thoughtfully and then turned about to yell. "Jensen! Where was Major Clay going?"

Jensen trotted over, his hands covered with brown, dripping goo. "Uh, I think up to Regimental. He and Samuelson had some business with the Colonel. You can ask Browne; he'll know."

Barton and Schmidt exchanged quick, worried glances. "Jensen, if you happen to see Samuelson, you tell him I am looking for him," Barton ordered and turned about to leave.

Jensen attempted to wave with the dripping hand but stopped and simply nodded. "Yes, Sarge." He then turned to wander away.

Schmidt yelled after the man, "Hey, what is that stuff on your hands?"

Jensen stopped and looked back at Schmidt. "Oh, this? Pancake syrup. I am afraid there won't be pancakes for a while until we get some more syrup in. The dang Krauts got it all!" He grinned and headed back to the kitchen.

"That's okay. Klimowski makes lousy pancakes," Barton retorted.

"Hey, I like pancakes," Schmidt shot back as he trotted to catch up with Barton. "So what do we do now? Sit around here?"

"I think we should find the major's aide, Browne—see if he knows anything more before we go running after everyone," Barton said, trying not to let the disappointment show on his face.

Schmidt stalled Bart with a firm hand. "Let me go. You'll just piss off Browne."

"Be careful. I don't know how many people know that we are supposed to be under house arrest. Ha! Tent arrest, I mean!" Bart joked. "If we were smart, we would just sit tight and wait." He clapped Schmidt on the back to send him running.

"What a wild goose chase. I feel like a complete moron," Bart grumbled as he continued on to his tent, afraid he might find it under guard again. The post by his tent flap was empty, the ground littered with cigarette butts. He wondered where the MP guard was; maybe Flynn had been hurt in the minutes after Bart lost him. He checked inside to find it empty, then put on his wool jacket, leather gloves and pulled on his knitted wool cap, topping it with his helmet. Bart's ears were still ringing from the noise and the cold. He made sure everything was tidied away, neatening his blanket on the cot and shaking the dust off his pillow. He wondered now if he would receive extra punishment for leaving his tent. But then he figured the powers above him should allow for such a reprieve. Bart was nearly run down by Schmidt as he stepped from the tent. He pushed Bart back inside.

"I got news—it could be good, could be bad," he announced in a breathy voice, rough from running in the cold. He coughed. "Yeah, Major Clay did leave about ten minutes before the shelling began. They are out on the road about nine miles away. Samuelson's driver radioed back that they got a flat, and his command vehicle's sitting off the road."

"So what? They have probably fixed it by now and are already at Regimental," Barton stated with acidity. "We are shit out of luck now."

"Nope, we got lucky. The spare was flat and had a round in it. Those guys are sitting out there like lame ducks on the pond. Wanna go duck hunting, Buddy?" Schmidt grinned at Barton.

"Do you think we should?"

Schmidt's pale blue eyes glittered with mischief. "I don't see why not."

"We could point out that everything was a mess here, and we were the only ones off duty who they could afford to go help them." Barton continued as Schmidt nodded.

"I am the noncom superior at the moment, and so are you. Lieutenant Sweeny is in surgery. Captain Grimm bought it." Barton paced for a second but then pounced on the idea. "Yeah, let's go. Tell Samuelson's aide that we'll go help them. That way, somebody knows why we are gone and not AWOL. Get some supplies in case we get stuck out there for the night, and be sure to grab a new spare tire! I'll get a Jeep."

The men briskly went about their implied duty, glad to have something to do and hoping to thwart the arrival of Samuelson's report.

◆ ◆

Later, as the pair drove along in the speedy little Willy, Barton announced, "It is starting to snow again, damn!" Shivering, he then wondered aloud. "I just hope we aren't making this all worse for us. Samuelson will probably bust us for leaving our tents! He's such a hard ass."

"Nah, I think this is count number two in saving our Colonel's butt. He might forget about it all."

"I doubt it. Samuelson's got an elephantine memory." Bart shook his head, glancing at Schmidt. "I do like your reasoning. However, I think Samuelson has a chink in his shiny armor—he despises crap like this. He's about as tightly wired as Patton is and feels there is no excuse for bad soldiering or mistakes. You follow orders, no matter what! No homos allowed."

Schmidt, with a foot propped on the door sill, leaned back in the seat. "Ha, who's a homo? Is he gonna accuse me of being one? 'Cause I ain't."

Barton eyed his friend harshly. "No? Come on, I saw you and the private."

Schmidt pulled out his Smith & Wesson MP45 and inspected it. "Yeah? And what did you see, and how are you gonna prove it?" He glanced at Barton through the pistol's sight. "You got the guts to describe shit like that?" He saw Barton wince. He put the gun down but then silently aimed it out toward the passing trees and road sign. "It was nothin' but brotherly love." Schmidt smiled nastily.

"That is not brotherly love. You ever had a brother?" Bart glared at Schmidt.

The man shook his head and looked back with a frown. "No. Had a sister once, though, and she was as mean to me as an addled rattlesnake. No drop of human kindness in that bitch." Schmidt sat up and polished the pistol with his jacket sleeve as he spoke. "I read once that Alexander the Great was a great lover. He had boyfriends all the time—all those famous Greeks and Romans had 'em. It's called brotherly love." He shot a glance at Barton. "So don't go tellin' me I am a faggy-fairy. I ain't."

Barton shook his head. "I think you are speaking of filial love, moron. That is love for your brother, your fellow man. It's not about screwing him. I have brothers, and we never did that crap."

"Well, whatever you call it, you can just leave me alone about it." Schmidt yanked on an ear and dug in it.

Barton grimaced at the filthy gesture. "Haven't you ever been with a woman?"

"Yeah, lots of times—not much fun, though. They tickle you a little and make you think they like you, take your money, and shove you out the door with your dick in your hand. That tart, Daisy liked you better'n me." He winced at the memory. "No, a guy you can talk to—"

"Then you have been with the wrong ladies. It's a great feeling." Barton shifted uneasily in his seat, wanting to laugh because he never had to pay Daisy for fun. "Stop talking about this. You are getting me upset. I think you have dragged me about as far into this mess as I care to be or need to know. I'm gonna be lucky to get out alive!"

"Fine. You brought it up," Schmidt grumbled.

Barton sighed. "I won't be your shit screen, Schmidt. I have no idea what to say to you anymore," he stated harshly.

"Nope … I think you are gonna keep quiet about it all, just like I will about you shooting Rossini."

"Extortionist, that's what you are. You're a perverted sodomite and a bloody blackmailer," Bart retorted with spite.

"Yeah, maybe I am, and you are a bloody Peeping Tom! If you didn't like what you saw, then why'd you stand there gawkin' like you enjoyed it? It weren't no peep show."

"I did not!" Barton yelled at Schmidt. He quickly clutched the steering wheel, jerking it hard to avoid a shell crater in the road.

"You don't gotta kill us over it!" Schmidt yelped and grabbed the seat.

"Look, just shut up about everything. Let me do the talking. Got it?"

Schmidt sighed noisily as he recovered from the swerving Jeep. "Yeah, I suppose." He waggled the pistol at Barton. "But you say anything else about me other than the truth about that night and us shooting Rossini, and I'll shoot you dead myself. Nobody's got to know nuthin'. We'll see how far you'll go with a few holes in you. You'll be dead meat," he snickered wickedly.

Barton looked askance at Schmidt. "You know, for a sergeant, you sure need to brush up on logic—you make absolutely no sense. You're an idiot," he griped.

"Yeah, well, I'd rather be a walking, talking idiot than a stuffed-up priss-pot, kissing everyone with a stripe above him. I know about your kind, too … ass licker. Dang it! Dion thought he'd get around me for that too, conniving little—" Schmidt put his feet down and holstered his sidearm. "Before you go spoutin' off again, you be lookin' sharp 'cause they're gonna be around here somewhere. We're at the nine-mile mark."

Barton shook with restrained anger, hating Schmidt once again for his remarks. It just proved that he could trust no one but himself. Now, he was unsure about himself, too. He had worked up what he wanted to say to the colonel over the past hour, but now his earlier brave resolve waned. He just hoped that maybe Schmidt had a point.

◆ ◆

Amid the flurries of snow, they could see black smoke curling above the trees, and Barton felt his heart leap. The Germans had recently shelled the road. There were still smoking craters in the road and burning trees all around. Barton had to navigate slowly around them. He pointed at the smoke as they came around the bend. The Willys Jeep with the truck bed and short trailer lay tipped upside down and precariously nose down in a ditch, although it was well off the road with black smoke roiling from the undercarriage.

"We-e-e-l-l … look at that. Maybe we won't have to worry after all. The crafty Krauts got the Colonel." Schmidt whistled and grinned wolfishly as he bopped Bart on the shoulder.

Barton stopped their Jeep and stepped out; he stood for a moment in thought. "It might be our lucky day, but we had better check for survivors, Schmidt. Watch my back—there might be snipers around."

"Oh yeah, I've got your back," Schmidt said mulishly and stood ready with his rifle.

Barton felt the hairs on his neck spring up with the words but then took out his sidearm and crept along down the hill. Looking warily about, he ran across the muddy, slushy field to the vehicle.

"Hello! Anyone here?" he called out, testing the wreck. With a quick glance back up at Schmidt, who remained with their Jeep, he shook his head. The trailer lay on its side, but the canvas was heavily soaked with something. A few crates had spilled from the Jeep and were now lying broken open on the ground. He could smell the wine and gasoline before he even saw the damage. He picked up one unbroken wine bottle and inspected it, finding it was a German Riesling. He almost laughed at the irony of it all and bent to retrieve another, greedily stuffing it in his coat.

"It's his loss, my win," Bart chuckled. "Guys run off leaving good stuff …"

He looked about the wreck and then noticed a tan coat lying under the vehicle. He bent down and began to pull on the coat, thinking it belonged to Samuelson. "Well, the idiot is going to be one cold son of a bitch, leaving his coat behind. Why didn't he just stay here with the truck?" Barton mumbled. As he yanked on it, he heard a rip and tugged harder.

"You bet I am flipping cold. Stop stealing my coat, will you!" An angry, pained voice came from under the Jeep.

"Colonel Samuelson?" Shocked, Barton let go of the coat and sat down abruptly on the muddy ground. "Where are you?"

"Get this damned thing off me. My driver ran off to get a tire and has yet to come back. I tried radioing the camp, but nothing happened. The Jerries hit us after he left," the man groaned.

"Are you hurt?"

"Of course, I am hurt …" There was silence for a moment, and then the colonel's voice sounded weaker. He coughed. "I have been freezing out here. I don't know if I still have legs or not; I can't feel them anymore."

"Is Major Clay with you, sir?"

"Not anymore." Coughing, the colonel added, "I am sure Dan is dead … He hasn't said anything for a while."

Barton reached past the rocks under the vehicle and felt about. He then felt cold flesh and griped it, feeling it was a hand. "Is that you, sir?" He felt a slight squeeze, and feeling relief, it wasn't Clay, he added, "I have Schmidt with me. He'll help me. I'll be back in a jiffy."

"Oh great. It would have to be you two. That's why it took so long …" Samuelson groaned but then added weakly, "Get on with it, Sergeant."

Barton sprinted up to the road, handed off the wine to Schmidt, and then ran to get the tools and the jack out from the vehicle. "Major Clay is dead, Samuelson is hurt … the driver took off to get a spare."

Schmidt goggled. "Quincy left them like that? What a gold-bricking idiot. I always hated that squirrel-brain."

"No, they were shelled. Never mind … grab the first-aid kit and help me get Samuelson out." Barton was stalled by a hard hand on his arm.

Schmidt looked down at Barton with brittle blue eyes. "Is he badly hurt? We could leave him, and nobody would know. Did you find his report? If not, we could blow them to kingdom come," he said huskily with dark meaning.

Barton looked pained with the thought and then shook his head. "Don't be a fool. Somebody would know. I don't know how hurt he is, but if we left Samuelson, he might survive and tell somebody that we didn't help. We've got to do this." He glared up at Schmidt.

"I say we shoot the bastard, leave them and go. Who's to know the Germans didn't get him."

Barton surveyed the wreck and then shook his head. "Look, let's call it leverage. We save his ass, and Samuelson saves ours—right?"

"Yeah, I already said that. But what if he doesn't?"

Barton shrugged out of Schmidt's grasp. "Well, I am not going to pay a higher price just to find out. Now move it." He grabbed out the collapsible shovel and headed down the incline and across the field to the overturned Jeep in the ditch.

"Sir, I am back. Can you hear me?"

"Yes. I don't think I can move much. I've got one hand free. Can you see it?"

"No. Don't worry. We'll get you out. Stay still." Barton waved to Schmidt, who reluctantly came down the slope and crossed to the Jeep.

"Thank you, Sergeant Schmidt."

Schmidt looked hard at Barton. "Uh, yes, sir." He whispered to Bart, "How'd he know I was here?"

Barton shrugged and handed Schmidt the jack. "Here, put this on a piece of the crate so it doesn't sink into the mud. Jack this end of the jeep up some, so I can get in under there and find Samuelson."

Schmidt nodded and silently set to work. The vehicle groaned and creaked as the side shifted, lifting.

"Argh! It's crushing me!" Samuelson screamed from under the Jeep.

Barton ran around the other side and saw a booted foot sticking out, pressed upon by the angle of the vehicle. "Stop! Put it down some. We need to get the other jack and some rocks to lift it and wedge it on this side!" he yelled to Schmidt.

The pair worked, lifting the vehicle by inches on each side, with Schmidt grumbling about Bart's ideas and Bart yelling for him to shut up because he was a college engineering major and knew what he was doing.

"Oh! Good Lord, I have Laurel and Hardy rescuing me!" Samuelson groaned. "I smell smoke. Something is burning!"

Barton now realized that the Jeep had been smoking when they arrived and that there was obviously spilled gasoline. He shoved Schmidt. "Go check and put it out. The ground's soaked with fuel."

Schmidt fell backward from the shove. He rolled to his feet and looked about. "Yeah, I see it—it's a burning tire. So what am I supposed to put it out with?"

"Get some water, throw dirt on it, or piss on it for all I care—just do as I ask! Unless you want to get us all blown sky high in the next few minutes—" Bart let the threat hang as he pushed several rocks under the frame of the vehicle.

Schmidt was like an automaton, moving in slow motion as he took up handfuls of the ditch water, ran up the embankment, and threw it on the flames, but it was like spitting on the fire. Finally, he grabbed up handfuls of mud and turf and threw them on the flaming wheel; it sputtered and went out.

"*Got it!*" Schmidt shouted back, sounding proud of his work. He then slithered down the ditch to join Barton again.

The young men struggled to keep the heavy vehicle from sliding farther into the ditch and the icy water that ran there. Together, they slid part of a crate under one side of the Jeep and then jacked up the other side some inches and wedged a large rock and broken log under the frame to use as a fulcrum.

Schmidt walked around the vehicle. "We're gonna lift this? This is a heavy sucker. I say we put the winch on it and pull it over with our Jeep."

"*No!*" Barton and Samuelson yelled in unison.

Barton made a slicing motion with his hand to Schmidt. "Sh! Don't be a fool; you'll kill him."

Schmidt rolled his eyes at Barton.

Barton crawled in the swift-running ditch water under the narrow space beneath the vehicle and felt about. "Sir, give me your hand." He felt movement and the hand. "Good, now I will pull you out." He grabbed hold of his wrist and coat sleeve, then pulled. As he did so, he felt resistance and heard a loud snap.

"Ow! My arm! I am stuck," the man said despondently from the dark shadows. "I think my foot is hung up in the steering wheel." His voice wavered. "I don't want to die. You must get me out quick before I freeze to death here! I hate snow!" The colonel went on mumbling imprecations upon the men.

Bart scrambled out and stood up. He paced around the vehicle, afraid to put more pressure at any angle by raising the vehicle any higher. Determined, he grabbed up his shovel. "We'll have to dig him out. If we jack this thing up anymore, it's going to come crashing down."

There was a low moan from under the Jeep.

Schmidt got down on his belly to peer under the Jeep and hooted, "I can see you, sir. We'll get you."

"Fine. Just do it quickly, please."

Together, Barton and Schmidt dug with a shovel and a piece of broken wood from a wine crate. Soon, they had a shallow trench under the Jeep to the wounded colonel. Bart shimmied his way under the vehicle and slid the man into the trench. Then Schmidt and Barton both pulled Samuelson out by his coat.

Samuelson blinked at the pair like a newly dug-up mole. His face was covered in blood, smoke, and mud. He began to cry but with joy. "Thank you! Thank you, God!" He put a hand over his face and lay silently weeping.

They pulled him up from the water, and Barton knelt by the man. He felt along his legs and arms. "Probably broken." He confirmed. He took his handkerchief from his pocket and wiped the man's face, cleaning away the filth and the tears. He put some Mercurochrome and a loose patch on Samuelson's forehead, where he had a bloody gash. Samuelson thrashed about in pain and yelled vile expletives.

Bart smiled down at the gasping man, surprised by the filthy words. "Sorry, sir. Let's get you back to camp." He ran back to his Jeep and took out a spare sleeping roll. He and Schmidt carefully wrapped the colonel in the bag and carried him back up to the Jeep on the road, which in itself at first seemed a simple thing to do, except for the deep muddy ditch that they slipped and fell in a few times. The hillside was now slick with the powder of snow.

Samuelson was oddly silent as he lay curled on the backseat during the trip back.

Bart turned about once to find Samuelson staring up at him. "You all right?" he hollered and glanced back again.

Samuelson nodded but said nothing.

Schmidt gave Barton a dirty look and ran his finger across his throat in a silent warning to Barton.

Barton ignored him and continued to drive. "Someone needs to get the major later. We couldn't do it. I've been wondering where Quincy is, sir. We should have passed him coming out here, and certainly, by now, we should have seen him. Where did you say he went?" Barton glanced back at the Colonel.

Samuelson shrugged, and then, moaning at the effort, he closed his eyes.

Barton drove along the slick road. He murmured to Schmidt, "Keep an eye out for Quincy. Maybe the Krauts got him."

He slowed as they passed the blackened craters in the road, and Schmidt pointed toward the ditch, where there was a flash of green amid the winter skeletal shrubbery. "Hey, what's that?"

Barton came to a complete stop and looked in the direction of Schmidt's finger. "I don't know. Go find out, will you? I'll watch your back."

Schmidt glared at Bart. "Fuck You. You say that to me?" He climbed out and scrambled down the ditch. He disappeared into the underbrush and then came back up with a man over his shoulder. He plopped the limp man on the floor in the back with Samuelson.

"Sorry, sir. He's a goner," Schmidt commented drily and got back into the Jeep. He waved to Barton to get going.

"You sure got a fine bedside manner, Schmidt," Barton said sourly.

"I hate picking up stiffs. It gives me the creeps."

"Oh, and you think I like it?" Barton griped back but then asked, "What happened to him?"

Schmidt paled. "Gutshot … bled out in a mortar hole all by his lonesome," he stated flatly.

Samuelson spoke now from the backseat. "I am so sorry, Quincy." He began to weep silently.

Barton was angry for all that had transpired and felt as if the accident and Clay's and Quincy's deaths were now heaped upon his plate as extra sins. Bart could smell something rotten and looked at Quincy and then at Schmidt. "What is that smell? Is it Quincy?"

Schmidt wrinkled his nose and turned about to sniff the air above the dead man. "Maybe he shit himself, but it could also be me. I fell in the ditch." He settled with a small smile again in the seat.

Barton's nose rebelled. "God, man, you stink! Don't you ever bathe?"

Schmidt made a nonchalant shrug and swiped some mud from his knees. "Sometimes. It ain't like we got much time."

Samuelson weakly lifted his head and asked, "Sergeant Schmidt, when was the last time you had a shower?"

Schmidt ran a grubby finger under his nose and then answered. "Soissons, when we stayed in that fancy hotel." He nodded and turned to smile down at the colonel. "I liked them showers, all the pretty tiles in the bathroom—not like takin' a shower with cold water in a tent or spit washin' outside in a frozen crick."

"Oh, good heavens, man! You can at least wash every day. How do you shave?"

Schmidt turned about and grinned. "I got a very sharp knife."

"Then, Sergeant, I order you to take a shower, and for God's sake, use some soap! Get a fresh uniform, too." He subsided to grumble. "Ugh, disgusting creature."

"Yes, sir," Schmidt moaned and glared at Bart.

Barton rolled his eyes at the ridiculous conversation and hurried along the road.

Soon, they came into their camp. It looked only mildly better than when they'd left it a few hours before. The dusting of snow was already melting. A few new tents stood, and men were looking purposeful in their duties and not as frenzied as before. He slowed as they passed along the rows of tents and stopped in front of the medical tent. Bart and Schmidt carried Samuelson in, dropped him off with the attendant medics, and then had orderlies carry Quincy in and leave him. They had no idea what to do at present, but filthy and covered with mud, blood, and sweat from their efforts, the pair headed to supply for fresh uniforms and then to the shower tent.

Leaving together, feeling clean and wearing fresh uniforms, the men joined others in line at the mess tent. The pair ate supper together in silence and then retired to Barton's tent. Schmidt left for a half hour to report in with the MPs but came back, saying he was back on duty in the morning. He settled on the new cot set up by Barton and laid back upon it with a sigh.

"What a shitty day, huh?" Schmidt stated and stared up into the dark.

After brushing his teeth, Barton spat outside his tent and came back. He wiped his face on a towel and settled on his own cot, shut off the lantern, and snuggled down under the covers. "Yeah, it's been a hell of a day and one I hope to forget."

"Do you think Samuelson will forget it, too?"

"I have no idea, Schmidt. Quit beatin' yer gums about it. I have had enough." Barton lay for long moments in silence and then yawned. He stretched his legs and rolled over.

"Hey, Bart, if we are friends, how come you always call me Schmidt? Why not Harlan?"

"I don't know. Schmidt fits you." Bart yawned noisily. "God, I am tired. Just go to sleep, will you?"

"Yeah, sure." Schmidt yawned, and his cot creaked as he turned over. "Hey," his voice was soft in the darkened tent, "I was really proud of you out there today. You got moxie, Bart, and yer smart."

"Oh. Well, it was nothing."

The cot creaked as Schmidt rolled over again to face Bart in the dark. "Nothing, huh? You probably saved our butts and the colonel's too. Nope, it's got me thinking about what you said earlier about brotherly love."

"Drop it, will you? I don't want to talk about that again. G'night," Barton rasped.

Silence wafted through the tent on a chilly air current for a moment.

"Thanks, Brother. G'night." Schmidt yawned and rolled about noisily in his cot.

Barton felt his guts grip, and he lay for a long time in the dark, thinking about the onus of Schmidt's simple words.

◆ ◆

Sunday, January 21, 1945

Barton rose early, dressed in the dark, and was eating his breakfast in the mess tent all before sunup. Schmidt came along looking disheveled and as if he had slept in his uniform. Bart knew he did, for all of Schmidt's uniforms and possessions had been lost the previous day in the tent fire. The MP was homeless. Barton was not sure if he wanted Schmidt as a temporary tent roommate, for the man relentlessly snored like a chainsaw. He also farted and talked in his sleep. Bart was definitely rethinking this friendship, feeling on the verge of abandoning Schmidt once again, but only after the mess with the colonel was resolved. He hoped to God that Samuelson would remand his report since Schmidt and he had saved his ass—Then Sayonara Sergeant Schmidt!

Schmidt sauntered by Bart's table with a food-laden tray and stopped at Bart's place. "Hey, can I sit here with you?" He plopped down on the bench before Barton could say anything. Schmidt sipped his coffee and then dug in, forking fried SPAM into his mouth. He slurped his coffee again and looked at Barton. "Sleep good?"

Barton chuckled, rolling his eyes. "Oh yeah, like the dead." He shifted away from his friend, who already smelled of cigarette smoke and dried sweat. He wondered why it had never bothered him before. He thought distastefully that it was no wonder Schmidt had no luck with women; he was a slimy slob and had no manners at all. He watched for a moment as the man gulped down his food, chewing like a cow on cud. Barton's stomach rebelled at seeing the mouthful of food still in Schmidt's mouth when he spoke.

"Yeah, Browne came by with a message from Samuelson this morning. We have to meet with him right after breakfast," Schmidt announced hurriedly and then shoveled in another forkful of food.

"Oh." Barton swallowed thickly. He glanced at his watch—it was 0650. There was no escaping it. He drank the last of his coffee and forked the remaining cloud of powdered eggs. "Is he still in the med tent?"

"Yeah. I guess we'll get interrogated from the Colonel's hospital bed." He leaned to Bart, whispering, "I still sorta wish he hadn't made it. We shoulda done somethin' permanent about that problem."

"That is old news, so, fuck it. Just stand up for yourself. Maybe Samuelson won't bust you to private." Barton frowned and drew back from Schmidt. "Get cleaned up before you go. You know how fussy Samuelson is … after yesterday, he might not take any pity on you if you go looking like a ragbag. Have some pride in yourself, Soldier!" Barton snapped and rose from the table.

Schmidt watched his friend walk away—Bart's back and shoulders straight, his uniform neat, his tie tucked in his shirt, cap on straight, and boots polished. He shook his head and then looked at himself. Yeah, he was a mess. Barton was right. He hastily shoveled the last of his food in his face, dumped his tray, and dashed away with purpose—to get spiffed up for his meeting.

◆ ◆

Lee Samuelson tried to eat his breakfast with his left hand but found it shook as he lifted a spoonful of tepid oatmeal from the bowl. His right arm was in a sling at an acute angle to his shoulder to relieve pressure on his broken clavicle and once-dislocated shoulder. He was not accustomed to using his left hand for much of anything except to punch somebody, which he would love to do right now. He got the spoonful close to his mouth, and it dribbled down his chin. Frustrated, he slammed down the spoon and grabbed the napkin to wipe his chin. He felt like a ninny!

Staff Sergeant Barre dared to show up just then when Samuelson felt his most feeble state. He almost yelled at the young man, but to see him step up and snappily salute, looking bright-eyed, pink-cheeked, efficient, and eager to report, stopped Samuelson from saying anything snide or derogatory. He returned the salute clumsily with his left hand and offered Barre a nearby campstool.

The young sergeant sat primly and put out a hand, lightly touching Samuelson's hand. "How are you feeling this morning, sir?" he asked, sounding unusually solicitous.

"Oh, just dandy. Here I sit with a broken leg, fractured clavicle, and a broken wrist, and my sciatica is playing the devil with me," Samuelson snarled. "Not to mention, I have a hundred-piece drum corps marching through my skull. Yeah, I feel—"

Barton nodded with a wry grin. "That good, huh? At least you still have a sense of humor."

Samuelson almost barked back a retort but then saw the amused glint in Barre's clear gray eyes. "I suppose you find it amusing. My wrecked shoulder is your fault, you know."

"Sorry, sir. Pain is never amusing. At least you are alive. But I must say that you don't look quite yourself this morning, not all spit-polished. Is there anything I can do for you, sir?"

Samuelson frowned and looked down at himself, finding a glob of oatmeal on his pajama front. With a frustrated hand, he brushed it away with the napkin. "No, and I am in no mood to eat this muck. There is nothing wrong with my stomach. Tell the orderly to take this tray away. I wanted my usual ... bacon and eggs!"

Barton stood and took the tray. "I'll be back, sir." He went across the tent and dropped the tray on a cart. He came back bearing a cup of juice. He handed it to Samuelson. "Here, sir. Some juice might sweeten your mood for the moment. Shall I ask the orderly for something else for you?"

Lee drank the juice in a gulp and handed Barton the empty metal cup. "No, I am fine. But thank you for your concern." He settled against the pillows, shifting his sore hip and the awkwardly raised bound leg.

He eyed Barton. "So … you are here to meet me. I can say that I find your unflinching service somewhat annoying to me now in light of all that has happened lately." He sighed audibly and grabbed back the cup, putting it on the bedside table to stop the young sergeant from fiddling with it. Lee could see that Barre was trying hard to keep his anger and emotions in check, and he could honestly give him kudos for it. Samuelson was not sure how calm he would be if he were in Sergeant Barre's boots. He let out a sigh again and decided to finish this.

"Sergeant, please pull the curtain there," Samuelson directed. "I want to speak in private with you."

"Yes, sir." Barton rose and pulled the folding curtain divider around the officer's bed. It was silly; anyone beyond the divider could hear them. He sat again.

Samuelson leaned on his left elbow, propped up by pillows. He noticed the young sergeant trembled and looked peevish; just one wrong word, just one dismal look, and Barre might lose his breakfast.

Samuelson whispered harshly, "I am at a disadvantage here, Sergeant, but I will tell you my feelings on what has happened recently." He cleared his throat. "Might I ask you a personal question first?"

"Yes, sir."

"Are you in any way involved with Sergeant Schmidt or these other men, Private Dion or Corporal Rossini?"

Barton froze. He looked straight on. "Sir, I am not sure what you are asking me."

Samuelson leaned in toward the sergeant, and he whispered, "Is there something you need to tell me? You may be honest with me, Son."

Barton gulped hearing the word '*son*.' "Sir, if what you are asking is what I think it is … then … no. I am not personally involved with anyone. Private Dion was my aide, and Rossini was under Sergeant Schmidt's orders. I have been only a friend to Schmidt since we met in England last year. I disagree with the rumors, and I do not feel for any of the men in … 'that way.' Sir." Barton gulped.

"I see. Then what do you think we should do about this messy affair?"

Barton sat up straighter. He passed a hand over his sweaty brow. "I think, sir, that we should drop it all. As a service to our fallen comrade, Corporal Rossini, his family should receive a letter saying he died in action."

Lee pursed his lips in thought and glanced harshly at the sergeant. "But he didn't. Must I remind you of the night?"

"No, sir. But who is to say that the corporal wasn't killed when the shelling began? As we couldn't find enough of him to put in a box and ship home, I think we should be kind and leave it there. His family will be hurt enough to find out he is dead." Bart eyed the officer's stern face and continued hurriedly.

"To add a report that Rossini behaved poorly or was unstable would diminish the corporal's service. Could you actually write to his family and say that Rossini was killed because he was involved in an unwholesome and indecent relationship with his comrades? Then, in a jealous rage, he shot at his fellow soldiers … who had to return fire?" Barton left off, waiting for the colonel to catch up with the idea.

Samuelson rolled away a bit to think. "You are correct, and I think perhaps more astute than I have given you credit for, Sergeant." He looked back at Barre. "How do you feel about shooting a fellow soldier?"

Barton trembled and looked away for a second. "I wish I hadn't, but then we might not be here to talk about it, would we?" His voice evenly calmed, Barton finished. "Corporal Rossini wrote his own death sentence by firing on us. I was only protecting us, sir. I think I must remind you that I did it to save you!"

"Have you ever shot anyone before?" Lee glowered at Barton and added with a smirk, "Other than rats."

Barton caught himself from smiling at the old joke. "No, sir, and I did so only at the enemy in battle. I used to hunt birds with my dad and grandfather." He hastily swallowed the thought that he had almost shot the German deserter, too.

"You have a sharp eye and fast reflexes. Maybe I should be thanking you," Samuelson countered, yet did not look at Barton.

Bart noted that he almost seemed … what? Embarrassed?

Barton nodded firmly. "Sir, I was only acting out of duty. If I could take that night back, I would. I regret it all. Except that I think, other people besides Rossini would be dead now, possibly all of us. I have made my own peace with God, and I have to live with Rossini's death on my conscience. This has all been a difficult time. Perhaps the army has trained us too well. Here we are killing the enemy, and yet we are to be punished for an accident and doing our duty. That is hardly fair, sir." Barton looked dismal. "It wasn't exactly friendly fire that killed Rossini. He did it himself."

"My father gave me this, sir." Barton reached into his jacket and pulled out the worn Bible. "He thought I might find solace in here." He put the Bible on the officer's cot.

"And have you?"

"Not really. But I did ask for forgiveness, and I have asked for Rossini's."

"I see. I am surprised to find you humbled and a religious man, Barre."

Barton deflected the comment with a shrug. "I grew up in the church, but it never made much sense to me. I have been reading this of late, and while this war makes no sense either, I at least feel I am in the company of others who have felt the same—hating the killing but knowing I have to do it for the sake of others. It is my honorable duty for my country that I do what I have to." Barton looked up at the officer, hoping he'd said enough.

"And you did that? You didn't shoot Rossini for any other reason? Not in anger or perhaps jealousy?"

"No, sir. I meant only to wound him in the arm."

Samuelson was quiet and thoughtful for a moment. He picked up the Bible and clumsily thumbed through the dog-eared pages. "You could have left me out there to die with my blown-up vehicle, Sergeant. Knowing what I could do to you with my report, why did you save me?" His azure eyes glittered dangerously as he stared at Bart.

Barton swallowed hard and barked, "Sir, you are above me. You deserve my respect and my duty. It would have been criminal for me not to come or at least send someone to help you. I suppose I cannot hide my true feelings on this matter, but I figured I had already saved your life once; I could do it again."

"And I would forget about your tribulations, right?"

Barton hung his head. "Yes, sir." He looked up with misty gray eyes. "When I found you, I knew I had to try and help. It would be an unchristian thing to let you die alone out there—maybe worse than shooting Rossini."

Lee nodded. "Yes, it would."

"Perhaps it was fate that you were blown up, and Schmidt and I rescued you. If you made it to the regiment headquarters, everything would be different now, right?"

After a prolonged moment, Lee put out his left hand. "I would like to shake the hand of my savior, twice over. Consider my report amended."

Barton clasped Samuelson's hand and pumped it eagerly and happily now. "I kept thinking about my father and what he would say about me coming home and ending up in prison for a mistake."

"Yes, and what would he have done?"

"Hate me for the rest of my life. We don't get along very well as it is."

Samuelson smiled kindly, the hard edge in his voice gone. "Son, I think he would be proud of you. Before this nastiness, I never had a complaint of you, except that you were sometimes too tough with your men. You do know what they call you, don't you? BTO Barre and a prick."

Bart smiled wanly. "Yes, sir. I don't mind, though. I am not in the army to make friends. We are here to fight an enemy, and if I gotta be tough, then I will," Barton stated tartly.

Samuelson nodded. "All right then. Good job. But just don't let them hate you too much—far too many men are killed by friendly fire, if you grasp my meaning … just as our young corporal."

"Yes, sir. Are we finished, sir? I have two questions." Barton's eyes now glittered with hard light.

"Yes, I think so. What is it, Son?"

Barton leaned to Samuelson. "What about Schmidt? He did fire on Rossini for the same reason I did."

"I understand. I'd like to think that you have some influence over Schmidt. I know he doesn't care much for me. But as you said, we are not here to make friends. What do you think of his situation?"

"I think you should drop the charges against him too. He does a good job as long as he is kept busy. His men look up to him; he is tough too and an asset in other ways. But I think he has a personal problem. I think maybe transfer him out of here. A new commander and unit might get him back in shape. But then again, I don't think he has many friends, and he certainly has nowhere to go. He lost everything in the shelling yesterday."

"So you want him to stay—because he is your friend?" Samuelson queried softly.

"No, put Schmidt in a different capacity … give him a different duty."

"I'll see. So are we good now?"

"Another question, sir. Why did you wait so long to arrest us or write the report?"

Samuelson looked stunned for a second and rubbed his chin thoughtfully. "Let me say that I have given these recent events much thought, and I felt something had to be done. Our battles of late have not made my job any easier in deciding what must be done according to military law. You have proven yourself, Barre, to be, at most times, a valiant soldier and a capable staff sergeant for this regiment and company. You have done your duty to keep the supplies moving and the men well-organized. It has been very distressing for me to decide to remove a valuable man during an important time of great need. However, the behavior of my men falls upon me, as well as you, Sergeant Barre. I had intended to earn my full colonel rank in the next month as promised."

"So you were willing to be reprimanded for us?" Barton asked quietly as he searched the officer's face.

Samuelson's blue eyes were narrowed and hard, like ice chips, as he answered, "No, but it was the right thing to do. Do you understand?" He stared at Barton then added, "I think you and I are a bit like-minded. We understand what must be done at all times, yet there are times when an intervention of sorts must happen. Fate, as you said, puts us in compromising situations that are not of our making. I don't think we shall talk about what happened in Soissons regarding a certain deserter."

Barton's eyes went wide, but he nodded. Then, looking a little relieved, he commented, "You know … I am sorry about that too. Well, I hope that you will continue to have confidence in me, sir. I promise to keep things going while you are out. So how long are you laid up?"

"Indefinitely. As for you working for me, I must tell you now that you won't." Samuelson shifted uncomfortably on the cot.

"What? Sir!" Barton gasped. "I thought we were—"

"We are even. I have asked for a transfer. You will be under another commander."

"Is it because of your injuries or what happened?" Barton asked warily.

Lee Samuelson let out a heavy sigh. "All of it. I think we have a top-trained company, and it is to my credit and yours that you will maintain it under the command of Col. Ed Rice. He will be arriving in two days, God willing."

"So … this is it?" Barton nervously looked for his escape route as he stood.

"Yes." Samuelson's hand shot out to still Barton. "Oh, I do have another question for you … I have been meaning to ask—"

"Sir?"

"Well, it might be indelicate, and in view of the recent problems, I want to ask you something. Call it my own curiosity. When we were in Soissons, there was a rumor that you were looking for a brothel. Is this true?"

Barton turned crimson with anger and embarrassment. "Uh, no, sir."

Samuelson's eyebrows rose in silent query.

"Well, yes, but it wasn't for me ..."

"I see. So you were looking for entertainment for your men?"

"No."

"Would you mind clarifying what you were doing then?"

"It was personal, sir," Barton shot back quickly.

The officer's blue eyes narrowed again to icy slits. "Sergeant, I must remind you that nothing in the army is ever personal. And from what your men say, it seemed rather important to you to find a brothel. Is that where you went when you requested the truck?"

"It wasn't a brothel. At least, not anymore, it isn't."

"I see." Samuelson eyed the young man before him. He sighed. "Well, I do understand that young men have their desires. However, Privates Dion and Lofgren said they weren't invited in, and the lieutenant was left to watch the truck. They all said you were gone about twenty minutes." He gave Barton an odd look. "Quick lover, aren't you?"

Barton looked down at his fidgeting hands and stilled them. "Sir, I was looking for someone my father knew a long time ago. Perhaps you recall that I told you he fought in France in the last war?"

Samuelson's eyebrows shot up, and he looked intrigued by Barton's words. "Oh? Your father? And did you find this mystery person?"

Barton regarded him with clear gray eyes, now telling the truth. "No, sir. She was dead." He looked away now with chagrin.

"Then I am sorry." Samuelson studied the sergeant for a few moments and then commented, "I did not mean to pry, but your actions also affect your men. You must remember to be a good example to them at all times and not lead them astray."

"Yes, sir." Barton stood and snapped to attention and saluted. "Sir, thank you, sir. I shall remember that."

"Were you also aware that the shop was suspect?"

"How do you mean?" Barton slumped from saluting.

"It is a sanctuary and meeting place for the Resistance. We intercepted several radio *communiqués*, and your name was mentioned."

"No! *Merde!*" Barton gulped, feeling ill. "No wonder Ondine Lapin was so skittish."

"Yes. Thank you, Sergeant Barre, for finding them. You are not involved with them?"

"No, sir!"

"I suppose I am relieved now to find your quest was innocent, or so you say."

Samuelson continued harshly. "Well, then, I think I would be remiss in my duty to let this all slide without any punishment. I have decided that you and Schmidt must each write a letter to Rossini's family. I'll let you tell them what happened in your own way. I have also noticed that you don't get mail, Barre. So while you are at it, write your father. I don't expect you to tell him of recent events, but at least let him know that you are still alive. You are restricted to quarters until then. Oh, and perhaps a visit to the chaplain might help that conscience. Dismissed."

Barton saluted smartly and turned about on his heel but then remembered his Bible and came back, snatching it up. "I think I may need this. Goodbye, sir."

He left the medical tent, wanting to leap and dance about with joy. His prayers had worked, and so had his snappy military demeanor and the respectful "sirs," always keeping the colonel ahead and in wonderment so that he would not feel undermined. Barton's plan worked, although he still felt awful about Rossini. He was shocked by the news that the former brothel was a hotbed of intrigue. He was once again a free man! Barton jauntily stepped along to his tent, ready for a morning of writing letters.

◆ ◆

January 21, 1945

Dear Family,

So much has happened, and I cannot remember when I last wrote. I won't bother to catch you up with every detail. Let me just say that I am still here in Europe. We are again camped close to Germany's border. We have had so many attacks and battles in the last two months as we came through France and Luxembourg that I cannot count them.

It has been freezing cold this winter, and I have worn the hats, socks, and gloves that you sent me last Christmas. I could use a new pair of knitted socks. I had to kill the rats that chewed on them. I did get a new pair of gloves from a Red Cross package, along with a bag of M&Ms and other fun and needful things. But I missed your special Christmas package—I guess times are tough for you, too.

By the way, we had a turkey dinner on Christmas Day courtesy of Lt. Gen. Patton. Although I have to say it was not as delicious or as memorable a meal as the food back home. I do miss Thérèse and Mémé's good cooking. I think

I have lost some weight, but I cannot tell—there are no mirrors. But I had to get a smaller-sized blouse and pants this last time. My stomach always bothers me because the food is lousy. But by mealtimes, everyone is so hungry and thankful there is food that we eat it all, even cabbage water soup. (You know how I hate soup!) I was dreaming the other day of Mémé's garlic and bacon green beans, lamb stew, and fresh buttered bread. I woke up feeling so hungry for it, but then I was disappointed to find we were having SOS (chipped beef on stale biscuits). C'est la vie et c'est la guerre!

Times have been tough of late. Life is hard for me. There are many days in a row when I have been so pressed into duty and busy running and fighting for our lives that I cannot take even a moment to think about the natural beauty of the season or countryside. Right now, everything is frozen. The snow is no longer pristine but filthy gray with the marching of our troops and vehicles. Some days, we are almost up to our knees in muck. However, I think I am luckier than most because I am not in the infantry marching every day and fighting in the trenches. Life in the quartermasters and POL transport divisions offers us a tiny fraction of comfort and some security.

Yesterday, our camp was shelled. We had thirteen casualties (including two POWs) and ten wounded. We lost a great deal of forwarded supplies in the shelling and a few vehicles. But I made it in more ways than one. My friend and I helped save some men from near death, and that felt good. But this war is clearly not at an end, and I am afraid I will be here for a long time. We are due to cross into Germany soon. It's too bad I know little German. But I am glad that I speak French, as it has given me an advantage many times.

Well, that is all for now. Here is my division address—please use it. I would enjoy hearing from you all.

Yours,

Staff Sergeant B. Barre

Barton reread his letter and decided he'd said enough. The colonel had said not to tell all, but at least his family would know and understand the dire dangers Barton had been in of late and that he had not been lazy in writing them nor frighten his family. He was now glad of Samuelson's decision, and he let out a sigh of relief, feeling the shadow of Albert's death finally fading, primarily after he had written the letter to Rossini's family.

He took the letter out of the envelope and reread the short missive.

January 21, 1945

To the Rossini Family:

I write with grim duty to inform you of the death of Corporal Albert Rossini on the night of December 13, 1944. We regret that his death could not be reported to you sooner, but we have been engaged in heavy fighting for the last month. He died when our camp was fired upon by the enemy. We are equally sorry to inform you we could recover nothing of Albert, and we tried. From dust to dust and ashes to ashes, so he has been commended to the earth again.

On a good note, please know that Albert was a good soldier, obedient and dutiful. He was witty, had several friends, and kept many in his unit laughing even though the times were grim. Albert was not directly under my command, but I knew him and thought kindly of him. You should be proud that he served his country well. I am sorry for your loss, and his unit will miss him.

May you find solace in your grief!

Sincerely,

S. Sgt. B. Barre, 5th Quartermasters Div.

He glanced at the two balls of wadded paper on the floor—earlier attempts to write a letter to Rossini's family. He knew this one was a keeper. He stuffed the letter in the envelope, thinking he had been courteous, kind, and brief to Rossini's family. Nearly everything he said was true. Bart felt Rossini's family did not need to know the embarrassing truth of the corporal's demise. He sure wouldn't want his family to get such a letter.

Bart sat back against his duffle bag, took a sip of water, and then shivered a little in the cold tent. Since returning to his tent, he had yet to see Schmidt and hoped Schmidt passed the colonel's interrogation and would see some kind of freedom, too. In some ways, Bart thought Schmidt should not be in charge of other men. Although Schmidt trained them well, he was not always a decent example of soldiering, as he was sloppy and often irreverent at inopportune times. He also sometimes shirked his work if it didn't please him.

During the troubles, he was surprised, though, to find that Schmidt shared Bart's silent innermost wish for Samuelson to die. But after careful thought, Bart realized it was the coward's way to wish evil upon the colonel. Samuelson had only been performing his duty, no matter how unfair it seemed. Barton also thought he had behaved dutifully and adequately with the officer, and that had helped to diminish his punishment. However, his punishment actually went further than the letters; it was the ultimate humiliation of being under house arrest yesterday and today, and the former written reprimand with the colonel's harsh judgment still rankled. For Samuelson to feel he was such a wicked person had truly hurt Barton. But now he thought God was looking out for him after all—Barton had been in the right place at the right time to save Samuelson. He had won his freedom and his pride. Perhaps the lucky legacy of the Barre third son had finally saved him from a terrible fate. He felt the weight of the gold family crest upon his chest and sighed with relief.

Feeling better now, he took out another sheet of paper. Balancing his writing kit on his knees, he sat for a few minutes, lost in thought, wondering how to write to Elise Boulanger after so many months had passed. Then Bart fell upon an idea and wrote quickly.

January 21, 1945

Dear Elise,

> *I think you may have forgotten me since I have not received more letters, but I have never forgotten you. I have so many tales to tell, yet they are not the kind I wish to speak of with you. The months have passed quickly since my last letter, and I honestly have forgotten when that was. So much has happened, and being in the middle of a war does not allow one much time to think of happy thoughts and times, let alone write them. After all these months, please accept my words and know that I have thought often of you.*

> *We passed a field of fragrant white flowers last summer outside Chartres; I recognized them as Muguet des Bois, and I thought of you. Their perfume suits you, and it has stayed with me ever since our meeting. We once saw a field that was all purple—it was lavender growing amid the blasted farmland, along with bright fields of orange and red poppies. The fields were in stark contrast to the war-torn lands with the ominous shadows of the bomber planes flying above them.*

> *When I passed along a beautiful river bordered by a field where dark horses grazed, they ran alongside our convoy as if they wanted to race with us.*

Their majestic dark manes and beautiful liquid eyes recalled you to me. At that moment, I sent you a greeting and a kiss. The horses were lithe and sleek like you. I loved them.

As each month passes, I keep asking myself, why have I not written to you? I want to, yet I think, 'What do I have to say to a beautiful girl?' All I know here is hard work, enemies, sorrow, and death. My words fail me. The life of a soldier is bleak, but I shall say this—my memories of you and the few letters you sent to me have kept me afloat when I have felt alone. I always keep your photo with me as a reminder of a merry time once upon a long time ago—it feels like a fairy tale. I have never liked fairy tales, thinking of them as sappy and silly, but the one about you seems a keeper and one I shall think about often. You are my princess, Elise.

I shall close as the light is fading. It is late afternoon, and I must go eat supper. But I shall leave you with these thoughts—I think of you often, wish I had known you better, and hope that I might meet you again one day. For now, please think of me as your friend, and I hope you will take pity on me and write to this lonely man who feels very far from home and lost in the woods. Please note my division address in case you misplaced it.

God bless you!

Fondly yours,

S. Sgt. B. Barre

Barton impulsively kissed the paper and thought it was a proper letter without sounding too mushy. He knew he was feeling homesick for her and any attention, but then, after the horrible events in the past two days, he felt overly emotional. He hastily shoved the letter in the envelope, addressed it, and, taking up the other letters, went out to post them before he changed his mind about being a romantic, soggy fool.

He trotted along, feeling as if a weight had been lifted from him. The air in the camp was crisply cold, with a slight taste of wood smoke, and for some reason, Barton smelled vanilla ice cream. He could smell the mess tent even at this distance. His mouth watered for the savory scent of onions and whatever the wounded cook Klimowski had prepared for their company's supper.

Barton got in line at the mess tent and looked about at the dimming sky. The setting sun had left streaks of crimson blood among pale pink and lavender clouds pasted thickly in the sky. It was beautiful. It was going to snow again. Barton sighed with an inward joy, thinking that his life of late had no happiness, but today he had a reprieve.

The inclement winter weather was perhaps God's natural reminder of all that was good in the world. Tomorrow would be a new day, cleansed with fresh snow. Barton stood for a long moment to enjoy the last rays of the sunset. The dark shadows of night fell upon the camp as the lights came up in tents and on the overhead lights and trucks. Yet, in that moment, he knew they were friendly shadows and no longer sinister. He gladly left it all behind as he entered the mess tent, warm with crowded bodies of his comrades, and the aroma of food wafted deliciously. Barton was free.

◆ ◆

January 23, 1945

Col. Edmund Rice rapped on the tent pole as he entered the supply tent. "Good morning, Staff Sergeant Barre." His voice boomed in the quiet of the early morning. He stamped off snow-covered boots.

Lost in thought while taking inventory, Barton stood up too quickly and staggered a bit.

"Had a little nip, did you?" The colonel's ruddy mustache twitched with amusement.

"Uh … no, sir." Barton stood to attention and saluted the colonel. "Good morning, sir."

"I see you are engaged in something here." The colonel brushed snow off his coat, then paced about the tent, perusing the cases and crated supplies neatly stacked.

"Yes, sir. I wanted to get a quick inventory so you will have the latest counts for the first staff meeting," Barton stated stiffly, still at attention.

The colonel sat on Bart's campstool. "At ease, Barre."

"Yes, sir." Barton relaxed and put his hands behind his back, waiting for the rest of the colonel's speech.

"So, are you finished with your report?"

"In a few minutes."

"That is just fine. Samuelson said you were a rather efficient and neat fellow. I can see he wasn't joking," Colonel Rice stated with a smirk as he looked about the tent and removed his gloves. "So, I was wondering … do we have any German contraband? I understand Lee had you confiscating such things as we move along."

"What kind of contraband, sir?" Barton's ruddy eyebrows rose with interest.

"Oh, maybe a little wine, cheese, or Russian caviar perhaps?" the Colonel smiled at Barton now. His jade green eyes were amused twinkling in the dim sunlight. "Surprise me."

"I happen to have some Riesling left behind by him. I also have some vodka we found among the Germans when they left the last town we took. It's Russian, so they must have engaged with the Ruskies somewhere. Do you want to see it?"

The colonel tilted his head to the side as he listened to Barton. "You speak French, do you?"

"Yes, sir. *Oui.*"

"Good. *Spreichen sie Deutch?*"

"*Nein.* Not much, other than sauerkraut and frankfurters and *Mox Nix!*" Bart added wryly.

The colonel's mustache twitched. He rubbed his hands. "Too bad. Well, then, get me the wine; I am not much into vodka. Please."

"Yes, sir." Barton retrieved a bottle, one he had gotten from Samuelson's overturned vehicle a few days ago. "It might be a good year—before the war, 1938."

The colonel's eyebrows rose as he took the bottle. "Well, yes … this is a very nice vintage! In fact, I have drunk this very one before the war back home."

"You are kidding, right?"

The colonel shook his head. Smiling, he explained. "No, my father-in-law owns a wine import business, and we had this very wine before I shipped out over here in 1941. Interesting coincidence, yes?"

Barton nodded and leaned stiffly against the crates. "So you have been involved in this mess since '41?" Barton whistled through his teeth. "Wow. And they haven't sent you home yet?"

"Nope. I did have two weeks leave in London. My wife flew over, and we had a good time until a blitz. I sent her home faster than I could kiss her." Colonel Rice set the bottle aside on the table. "She went home with a little souvenir—another daughter!" He chuckled, now full of mirth.

"You must miss her."

The colonel exhaled loudly as he stretched his lanky legs out, folded his hands over his stomach, and looked up at Barton hovering nearby. "I do. I write to her every week, and she writes to me too—she keeps me up on the country club and our friends, as well as the older girls' activities in school. The kids send me pictures they've drawn. I find having a piece of home is a minor diversion from this ungodly conflict."

"That is nice, sir," Barton commented, leaning at ease against the stack of crates.

He was surprised that the colonel was so chatty for their first meeting. Rice seemed a fair and likable fellow. He was well groomed, his wavy hair a chestnut-red color with flecks of gray at the temples and a stubborn swath of curl swept rakishly low over his brow. The colonel had pushed it back up twice already. Barton thought he resembled an older version of the movie actor Van Johnson and figured he must be in his early fifties. He was tall, almost six-foot, with an athletic physique. Colonel Rice talked with his hands, often gesturing when searching for a word or idea. He seemed intelligent, and Barton hoped they would get along.

He listened as the man spoke about his home in Baltimore, Maryland.

Barton popped up again from his private thoughts. "I have family in Baltimore. My uncle is an investment banker."

The colonel eyed the younger man with interest. "Really. Do you know the bank?"

Bart shook his head. "No, sir. It has been a while since I saw him. He has a bunch of kids, and his wife is a music teacher. Nice folks."

"But you aren't from there, are you?"

"No, sir. Texas—born and bred."

"Really? Which part?" The colonel looked with renewed interest at Barton.

"Beaumont. It's a little town … about eighty miles northeast of Houston."

"Nice town."

Agog Barton asked, "You've been there?"

"Yes. I have been just about everywhere. That's what a life in the military does for you. I was at Fort Sam Houston once, a long while ago. I knew Lee Samuelson back then, too."

"I see," Barton stated flatly, thinking the men must have been friends.

"Are you planning on a career in the military, Sergeant?" The colonel studied his trimmed nails for a moment and then looked up at Barton.

Barton shifted his weight and looked away for a moment, surprised by the changed direction of their conversation. "Not really, sir. I am hoping to go home after this war. I had other plans."

"So what were they? Are you planning on going to college then?"

Barton smiled with pride now. "No, I already graduated."

"You look like a kid still. How old are you? From where did you graduate, and what was your major?" Colonel Rice leaned forward again, smiling now.

"I will be twenty-two this April. I graduated from the Agriculture and Mining University of Texas in May of '43 in mechanical engineering with a minor in petrology."

"You are still a kid. So you were an Aggie—that's impressive." He looked up at Barton with a smile. "When you were a boy, did you ever play with firecrackers?"

Bart's eyebrows curled as he thought about the odd question and replied with a wary smile. "Um, yeah. Black Cats and cherry bombs were my favorites. We put them under cans so they would launch like little rockets. My brothers and I had—"

Rice cut him off. "So, how did you end up in this man's army?" The colonel leaned back in the chair and steepled his long fingers, still watching Barton as carefully as a cat watches a bird.

Barton smiled ruefully. "Let's just say I did something stupid and signed up with my friends."

"Are you boys still together?"

"No, sir. One friend is dead, got shot in Italy saving a comrade."

The colonel's smile faded. "A hero then. You keep good company. How about the other friend?"

"I don't know. We were separated in England last spring. He was sent to Slapton Sands, and I went to East Whitcliff's Army Air base."

Rice sat up now, regarding Barton, his eyebrows raised. "Slapton, did you say? That was a bloody mess. Your friend didn't survive, did he?"

"Why? What happened?" Paling, Barton stood up straight and approached the colonel.

"You don't know? There was a mistake in communications. They were practicing crossing the Channel, getting ready for Operation Overlord, and the entire entourage was sunk by German U-boats. Only a couple of rescue boats made it back to the beach. We lost a lot of valuable men and equipment that day."

Barton went white and looked unsteady. "I never knew. That means that both Garrett and Louis are dead. We were friends back home in Texas. God, I feel a bit sick now."

The colonel stood up and went to Barton, "Here, you can have your chair back before you faint."

Barton sat reluctantly on his camp stool. "Sir, thank you for the news. I just never knew about it."

"When did you come over?"

"July ninth ... at Utah Beach."

"Then you have been here since almost the beginning. Have you ever had a leave?"

"Not really, sir. We have been on the go since I got here. Being the staff sergeant, I have to keep things rolling." Bart smiled wanly.

"Maybe it is time for a break, Son. I read Samuelson's report, and he has good things to say about you. But he warned me about you."

"He did?!" Barton looked up, shocked. "Why? What have I done?" he asked, feeling anger rise in his blood and hoping that Samuelson had not left behind any of the reports about their recent tragedy.

"He said that you take everything far too seriously. You often seem to overlook what is in front of you. Now working hard is a good effort, Staff Sergeant, but if it makes you indifferent to your men or unapproachable, that is a problem. Your men should look up to you and view you with confidence, knowing that they are in good hands and you have wise judgment."

"But, sir! I have done all that. You name just one man who thinks I have been unfair or—" Bristling with indignation, Barton sprang to his feet.

The colonel waved a hand. "Don't get defensive, Barre. I am not complaining, only pointing out that you must keep your men happy as well as safe. If you are deaf to their concerns, then you are not serving them well. I have also noted that you have not signed paperwork for anyone's promotion. If you do not think them worthy, then that is one thing. However, I think Samuelson was rather proud of this company. Do you understand?"

"Yes, sir." Barton looked up at the colonel. "Am I being demoted?"

The colonel laughed. "Is there a reason I should? Oh, now you have little faith in me."

"I hardly know you, sir." Barton gulped nervously.

"I think a little R&R would be just the ticket. We'll be moving out tomorrow. Once we get to Trier, you are to take a rest while we camp there."

Barton wanted to complain. He felt a shadow again upon him like a spectral ax over his neck. "What about Sergeant Schmidt?"

"I understand he is your friend."

Barton relaxed his guard a little. "Yes, sir. He's been through a heck of a lot more than I have. He was in the Twelfth in Italy before we met."

"I saw that. Well, upon Samuelson's recommendations, the sergeant has been transferred to the Ninth."

"Is he still an MP?" Bart asked, thinking that perhaps Schmidt had been demoted.

"He is no longer of my concern or yours, Sergeant." Colonel Rice adeptly feinted the question aside.

"And me?" Barton groaned. "I feel you are not being honest with me, sir. Am I being transferred too?"

"That depends on you, Sergeant. If you continue to complain, I might get sick of you and ship you off to the front. I don't like complainers on my staff." The colonel's eyes were hard on Barton.

"Yes, sir. Thank you, sir."

Colonel Rice picked up the bottle of Riesling and smiled at Barton. "Well, now that we have met properly, I have rounds to make and visits with my other men. This has been enlightening. Have a good day, Staff Sergeant Barre." He smiled at Barton, tipped his cap, and then ducked under the tent flap, striding away quickly.

Barton felt his stomach flop over, feeling disappointment. Rice had asked him everything he could have read in Bart's records. Why all the chattiness, odd questions, and false interest? The worst of it all, Schmidt was leaving. Bart would be alone again, and he felt friendless suddenly. He had not seen Schmidt since breakfast two days earlier. Feeling a sense of urgency rise along with stomach acid, tasting the undercooked, greasy sausage from his breakfast. He had to find Schmidt and make sure they were on the same page; they had a secret between them. He hoped Schmidt did well with Samuelson the other day!

However, the blizzard for the next three days and the war impeded Barton's personal plans, for he soon was caught up in duties for packing up and moving out. He had new duty rosters to prepare for Colonel Rice, with amendments due to recent changes in personnel and divisions being moved along the front. Barton began to feel the pinch as the days of lax freedom between camp commanders were finished. Their company snapped back into shape, once again ready to roll under the command of the new colonel.

Bart never saw or said goodbye to Schmidt.

◆

CHAPTER 13

Operation Wood Duck

Winter 1945

From the North Sea to the outskirts of Cologne, Field Marshal Sir Bernard L. Montgomery commanded the British Twenty-First Army Group, holding the Germans at bay. Also under Montgomery, the First Canadian Army fortified the left flank of the Allied line, with the Second British Army in the center and the Ninth US Army to the south. The Twelfth Army under Lt. Gen. Omar Bradley, who also had command of the First Army to the north and the Third Army to the south, was pocketed in the middle of the Allied lines. In the southern perimeter, Lt. Gen. Jacob Devers commanded the Sixth Army, which was composed of the US Seventh Army and the First French Army; they held the borders to the Allied divisions south, to the borders of Switzerland and Austria.

Nearly a 450-mile front along the western Rhine River valley was entirely composed of US and Allied troops. With daily bombardments and pincer-like precision, the armies launched their attacks. Constantly trying to out-gun and outfight the beleaguered German Army, they hacked away at the remaining resistant troops. Crossing the Rhine was the goal, and once done, Germany was a prize plum waiting for the Allies to devour once they conquered Berlin.

From the Eastern front, the newly Allied Soviet troops had cleared through Poland and invaded Hungary and Czechoslovakia, brutally advancing with decisive victories as well, circling and bringing in the armies of the Reich much like the shepherd herds a flock to slaughter.

During the bitter winter, the fight for the *Wehrmacht* cost the German Army dearly, and by midwinter, some of the enemy troops were voluntarily standing down—low on munitions, weapons, and food supplies, they allowed the Allied Forces to capture them and the area. All along the Rhine River border, the German resistance waned as their supplies and reinforcements were weakly diminished by the persistent Allies.

◆ ◆

Moselle River
February 14, 1945

The overcast sky with gray, moody clouds hovered over the landscape. A chilly wind arose from the Moselle River behind them as the convoy of company supply trucks trundled along what was supposed to be a road. To Barton, the road looked hardly more than a donkey trail through the wooded landscape. Everyone before the supply train and after was on the lookout for enemy sniper fire. Parts of the Fifth Division had come through in the days earlier, cleaning out the vermin in a sweeping, two-mile-wide battle, pushing back the enemy forces into Germany as they pressed ahead. Barton noticed that the landscape had hardly changed when they crossed the borders from Luxembourg into Germany. However, the dangers were still there.

The imposed month of peaceful times, once the Allies and the US Army had vanquished their enemy from Luxembourg's border, was over now that they were in Germany. Advanced forays were clearing the villages, forests, and roads ahead, working toward the goal of overtaking the Rhine River and the lands east of it.

Meanwhile, another danger and death from the sky hit when the British RAF bombed Dresden, an important industrial and railway hub city for the Germans. Following as a cleanup measure, the USAAC rained death from above. Nearly 250,000 citizens were killed, and almost eleven square miles of Dresden were destroyed. The towns of Misburg, Bohlen, Chemnitz, and Magdeburg were also hit by the series of bombardments. Hitler's Fatherland was seriously wounded and compromised.

◆ ◆

The Eifel Region
February 17, 1945

Barton's days were consumed with work from dawn until late at night. In the beginning, Colonel Rice seemed to be a casual and blithe fellow, but now he was a demanding man who was not easy to please with strict military directives. One too many times, Barton had found himself under the crosshairs of the impatient colonel's displeasure and angst and battling wits with his aide, SGT. Stacy Philips.

The constant push forward into Germany also proved to be a life of duress and daily danger for them all. Thrice, they had been under severe fire and had to pull back toward the river border behind them. Each day was an incremental step forward and sometimes two steps back in the macabre dance with the Germans.

All of a sudden, Barton found himself summoned to the colonel's headquarters, and with trepidation, he went to meet Col. Ed Rice.

There were other men in Rice's command tent, and as Barton saluted the colonel, he was motioned to sit alongside the group of men. He was nervous by the summons but now felt as if there was some relief, thinking that perhaps he was not in trouble for something. He glanced to his side to see a slim, medium-height man wearing a British officer's uniform helping himself to a decanter of liquor on the colonel's desk. Another man was a tough-looking Australian with a broad jaw, much like a bulldog. The third was a silver-haired French officer, and the fourth was the colonel's personal aide and unit commander, SGT Phillips—a man Barton truly disliked.

Barton looked around the tent to see a map displayed on a board. It looked like Germany. Squinting, he noticed several names encircled—Coblenz, Boppard, Oppenheim, Bitburg, and other German towns. And wondered why he was here.

Colonel Rice was on a field phone, not talking much, nodding a lot, and responding with single-syllabic responses. Finally, he ended with a, "Yes, sir, and thank Hilton Railey for the loan of his Ghosts." He hung up the phone, and his office assistant promptly took away the field phone and then sat at another cluttered table across from the colonel.

Considering the cold, snowy day outside, the crowded tent was warm. Bart felt a trickle of sweat running down his ribs, tickling as it went. He shifted uneasily on the campstool. His eyes kept bouncing off the open decanter, and the wafting aroma made his mouth water for the Scotch whiskey. He licked his lips, wishing that he might have a snort; it had been a very long time since he'd had liquor. However, as only one man was drinking it, Bart felt he was excluded.

The Brit looked almost out of place here in the grubby field tent with his freshly pressed uniform and pleated pants. His shoes were polished, and he had a clean-shaven look about him with the pleasing scent of bay rum. The other two Allied men, although neat, looked fresh from the field, their boots dusty and a fusty smell about them. Bart surreptitiously sniffed himself as he shifted his weight on the campstool. He had bathed that morning and shaved, but his uniform was not fresh, and his boots were muddy.

The deep winter snows were melting, and all about them were grassless fields of churned-up mud. The tanks that came through a couple of days earlier had incised three-to-four-foot-deep ruts in the field and roads. Many of the lower-profile vehicles had to move off the road, or else they were easily high-centered or mired down in the viscous mud. Barton had spent part of the morning on the muddy road, redirecting the traffic of supply trucks and vehicles along other routes and going to the previously cleared and inspected roads.

The armored battalions and their trundling trailers with massive guns were their saviors, yet they took a toll on the roads, destroying everything as they moved along somewhat like a stampede of elephants and swarms of locusts. Days before, Bart had been witness to beautiful, spring-green fields that were now marred by lines and circles deeply etched into the landscape by the processions of tanks and the Fifth Division's armored regiments. For a second, he recalled the verdant fields of his ancestral plantation and felt the wounds to his core. These scars would be incised in the earth for perhaps a generation or longer. Barton felt a poke in the ribs and crossly came back to the conversation about him.

"… will cross at these strategic points here, here … and here. Colonel Claude Lefoy's special Sixth Division will cross first at Sauer River, moving into position. The Twelfth has been holding the Siegfried Line there. The enemy's attention will also be diverted to this two-mile-wide corridor along the Kylle, for there will already be a buildup of artillery positioned there from the Twelfth Corps. They are hoping to take the area soon." The colonel turned about to face the assembled group.

"Captain Lawrence, Sergeant Major Dunston, and Staff Sergeant Barre will team up with half a company from each of their divisions to move through with supplies as fast as possible behind Lefoy and get as far inland or upriver as possible at each crossing. Operation Wood Duck will then be put into action. While there, temporary supply depots will be set up to fuel and feed the invasion forces as they come across each of the river crossings or bridges. So far, there has been serious opposition along the western side of the Rhine. A little air raid from the Ninety-Fourth should clean out the rats if the weather clears." He smiled wanly at his remark but then waved at the map with his pointer.

"The Fifth will be ready to strike as they cross over the Rhine near Oppenheim. By March or sooner, General Irwin intends for the Fifth to take Oppenheim and Frankfurt and enter into the Ruhr Valley here." The colonel stabbed the map with his pointer.

Barton avidly watched as the colonel then outlined the plan to cross the mighty Rhine River. There were strategic points that must be cleared in precisely timed order to surprise and push back the German forces as the Allies took over bridges and towns. It was basically a feint—pushing a little this way and letting the Germans fight back hard, pooling their forces in pocketed areas, depleting their weapons and strength at each turn. All the while, the massive combined strengths of the Third and Sixth Armies, Fifth and Twelfth Divisions would amass behind and around for a giant push into the German stronghold east of the Rhine.

Barton quickly assessed the troop diagram; it looked like a massive ploy in chess. He noted there were a few holes along the defensive line where the Germans might gain advantage again, but Barton would not blurt that out and look a fool. In their race to cross the Rhine first, Generals Bradley, Patton, and Irwin seemed to have left a portion undefended. Barton blanched to hear Colonel Rice's further comments. Oh hell, Bart and his comrades were heading for the damned hole in the wall!

After about an hour of strategic planning for the troops, the Colonel turned the meeting over to Brig. Gen. Marshal Greene. The man had crept in to stand at the back of the tent while Colonel Rice had been outlining the plan; he now strode forward to the map.

Greene, one of many commanders in this endeavor, was overseeing their move into Germany for the collaborated Allied armies that were taking part in the invasion spearhead and Operation Wood Duck.

Barton listened, thinking the officer a braggart as the swaggering general outlined the supply train movements and requirements, slapping the maps with his quirt. After his initial speech, he handed each of the men a packet of orders, requisitions, and other pertinent details.

Marshal Greene was a heavyset man; Barton thought he resembled a dark-haired Santa Claus. His round belly jiggled when he gesticulated with the quirt on the map. Greene's dark khaki shirt was heavily stained under the arms, as he sweated profusely while he talked. Every so often, he dabbed his cheek or brow with a worn handkerchief, taking care not to muss his oiled hair, which was styled in a little wave over a balding pate. A thick, curled mustache twitched as he talked.

Bart found his eyes wandering to the quivering mustache and the large, dark mole on the man's cheek, and he tried not to find amusement in it. The man seemed to be another copy of Lieutenant General Patton in his terse speech and condescending attitude as he paced about, smashing things with his quirt for emphasis, making everyone startle or grow nervous. Barton, though, felt as if his brain was turning to mush. There was too much information all at once, and he found it difficult to focus. He sat up straight again, discovering that he was slouched in the chair.

However, Greene's voice was unlike dynamic Patton's tone, which commanded attention. Instead, his voice slid into monotone rumblings, and the pedantic way he delivered his plans was putting Bart to sleep. Bart's eyes flickered once, and he tweaked his leg to stay awake.

Bart suddenly stifled a yawn and looked about, feeling guilty and afraid that the Colonel and others could see he was fighting the wave of sleepy boredom. Yet, Colonel Rice and Sergeant Phillips were standing by the door of the tent, engaged in a heated, hushed conversation. Bart tried not to focus on them. He turned about to listen to the general.

For now, Greene's plans had somehow rolled into a sermon with a lot of bold sentiments. "God has ordained us to be victorious."

"It is our eminent right to be here." Greene outlined the historical relevance of the march into Germany and that the Americans and Allies would be victorious. "Our vast resources and distinguished and committed military force will make us indomitable—we shall win this war!"

"Crossing the great Rhine River alone will be a monumental and historical feat not achieved since Napoleon!" Greene continued. The short, round man slapped his quirt on the table, again demanding the attention of his men. "We have more troops and superior weapons than little Bonaparte, so we are due a glorious victory!"

Blinking sleepy eyes after the sermon, Bart sat up straight, stifled another yawn with the packet, and was relieved when the general soon dismissed them. Bart stood up, feeling as if he had been sitting cramped on the campstool for half a day; he glanced at his watch and found it had been nearly two hours—it was no wonder he felt overwhelmed. His hunger pangs signaled his missed lunch. He'd get only coffee now unless he begged like a dog for scraps.

Stretching and putting on his jacket, Bart prepared to exit out of the colonel's tent. He was handed another packet and told to put the insignias on his uniform per the attached diagram. Feeling overwhelmed, Bart headed toward the mess tent. He heard his name and spun about. The Brit and the Aussie were hailing him. They trotted up to him.

"' Ello, Sergeant … Barre, is it?" the Aussie offered a hand to him. "I'm Sergeant Major Montague Dunston. This is my mate, Captain Lawrence, and we would like to have a luncheon with you." He peeked at his watch, adding, "Although it is almost tea time. Blast! But no worries."

Barton glanced at the men. "Uh, sure. I have nowhere to be until 1400, but I think we missed lunch."

"No worries. Take a brief trip wi' us, and we'll set you up right proper, even if it is only tea cakes. You look fair starved." The Aussie laughed as he redirected Bart across the field toward the Allied camp. The captain was silent as he walked beside Bart and Dunston.

Bart decided to make a few inquiries about the latest plans. "So … this is a big deal, huh?"

"You can say that again, mate. However, mum's the word until we move. General Greene has given us almost carte blanche for whatever we require. We thought"—Montague gestured between the captain and himself—"we'd sit down and read through this rubbish together. Then, everybody will be on the same page. Am I right? Right?" Dunston chortled low as he stepped around a backing lorry loaded to the rails.

He yelled suddenly, "Hoy! Hoy! You, stop there. That load is not tied on properly; you'll lose it in the middle of the road the first bump you take!" Dunston jumped out almost in front of the lorry and banged on the driver's door. It came to a squeaking, lurching halt. "Get down and do it right, or you'll have boxed ears from the general for it!" He watched as the driver got out looking mutinous, but the man did as Dunston bid.

Pointing a finger at the man, Dunston added, "You be glad you followed my order there, mate. The Huns don't need to get those supplies because you were too lazy to pack them properly. RSFSL—Remember Safety First, Stupidity Last!" He lectured the younger soldier. Dunston stepped around the truck and back on his original course across the Allied camp. Soon, they ducked under a canopy and entered a spacious field mess tent.

Bart sniffed the aroma, and his stomach complained noisily. He noticed a few officers and men sitting at tables eating and drinking tea and coffee. Now, in the Allied camp, Bart felt almost as if he was in England again. He sat at a table in a corner with the Captain and the Sergeant Major. A man came by and asked what they wanted to eat.

Barton laughed and said, "How about a rare steak, yea high." He put up two fingers, showing the imaginary thick steak. "No, I am kidding. I'll eat whatever you have." He smiled up at the mess orderly.

The Captain shed his jacket, laid his cap aside on a vacant chair, and then smiled at Barton. "I could go for that too; however, I think we might only have corned beef or kippers today."

"Corned beef will do. I am a Texan—I miss my rare beef. Canned, ground-up meat just doesn't always cut it." Barton grinned at his little joke while the men put in their orders. "You know what they call beef in our mess? Tiger meat. What we have lately tastes about as bad as a fricasseed cat!"

Dunston laughed. "Ha! We got ourselves a genuine cowboy, then! We'll have to find you some raw meat! We passed by a lovely meadow with a fat bull just this morning. Wanna go have a wrestle? I'll hold 'im down while you cut a slab!"

Barton blushed hotly, feeling as if the man teased him too much.

"But first things first, me boys. We need a drink!"

Bart was disappointed to see Dunston grabbing up mugs and a metal teapot. He poured dark tea into the cups and set them out. He offered the milk pitcher. "I know you, Yanks like your tea straight and plain, but ..."

"Yeah, I'll take some." Bart poured in a drop of milk. He then passed it to the captain. "I was stationed in England before I came over here. I am used to milky tea." He dropped in some sugar and stirred the tea. When it was ready, he slurped it, feeling suddenly good. He smiled at the men over his cup.

"Yep. Nothing does a man better than a cuppa." Dunston smiled as he drank his tea. "Makes you feel civilized again."

Barton turned to the Captain. "I didn't quite catch your name there, sir. So, how do you feel about all of us working together on this operation?"

Captain Lawrence set his cup down. "I am used to running things myself; however, I am game for this. After all is said and done, it is for the greater good that we collaborate."

Barton was surprised that the man did not have a heavy British accent; in fact, he sounded more like a stuffy Southerner from the States. However, his stiff demeanor and the way he politely sipped from his tea mug were upper-crust British.

The man had light, golden-brown hair and a pencil-thin mustache; his navy-blue eyes were large and seemed to punch through Barton with a singular glance. His manicured hands were elegant, and the movements were graceful, like conducting a symphony and not stirring tea. The man resembled a society playboy, not a rough-and-tough soldier.

Barton ended his silent appraisal of the man and was pleased when a soup plate appeared under his nose, steaming and piled high with slabs of corned beef, wedges of cabbage, and chunks of carrots, potatoes, and onions all swimming in the pale herb broth. The orderly brought a basket of thick, warm bread and a dish of butter.

"Real butter?" Barton eagerly slathered his bread with it. Biting into the dense bread, he closed his eyes as he savored the sweetness melting on the warm bread. "Oh, this is nice." He tucked into the meal with hungry dedication and talked little; instead, he listened as Lawrence and Dunston spoke in low tones meant only for their table.

Occasionally, they asked Bart pertinent questions or commented on the Fifth's previous battle prowess—the Red Devils were famous. He only nodded and made a few comments as he ate. Then suddenly, he finished his meal, but the orderly traded his bowl for a small dish of egg custard. Barton ate that, too, with unabashed delight. Feeling better, he sat back, his stomach full and his senses sated by the hearty, flavorful food. Their repast was better than what was served in his camp.

"That was perhaps the best Brit meal I've had in a long time. I am glad it wasn't kippers or dried salt cod. I had my fill of those last year!" He smiled at the men.

"Where in England did you serve, Sergeant Barre?" Captain Lawrence asked as he neatly laid aside his cutlery, having finished his meal.

"I was at Amstead-on-Devon first, then East Whitcliff Army Air Base. I came over here last July."

"I see." The captain nodded. "I assume you have seen a lot of action."

Bart nodded. "I have seen more than I would like to have experienced, but I suppose you both have seen enough, too."

Dunston grinned lopsided and jerked a thumb at the Captain. "Oh, me more than 'im. The Cap's a pencil pusher, that one; keeps 'imself all clean like a show pony, the tin-arsed Pom. But I tell you wot, tho; 'e's a dunny rat all right-o in a pinch." Dunston patted his chest and tossed his head, exclaiming, "Me, I don't mind a little excitement now and then. And me? I'll happily shoot those Nazi blighters any day." He tucked into his custard with a leering smile.

Bart observed the Captain's face grow taut, his lips pressed together as if he stopped himself from commenting. There was a slur somewhere in Dunston's comments.

"Sir, I noticed that you are, um, very neat. I mean, you don't look like us guys in the field."

Lawrence chuckled as he passed a slim hand over his brow. "Well, no. As our good mate was saying," Lawrence passed a critical blue eye over Dunston, "this is my first time along the front. I just came down from Montgomery's headquarters."

"Pissed someone off, did you?" Dunston quipped between slurps of custard. "I knew it when I saw you. Seems you lost a stripe, too."

The captain let out an exasperated breath. "That is none of your concern, Montie-Duntie."

Montie winced. "Oh, me mum used to call me that. Cripes, don't do it." He slapped his napkin down on the table.

The captain actually smiled, looking pleased with his remark. "I know," he responded. He took a spoon to eat his custard but leaned a little to Barton. "Montie and I go back a long way; a little good-natured joshing puts him in his place. He's my old Humpty-Dumpty friend." He eyed Montie and ate his custard in silence.

Montie leaned to Barton. "I say, in private, we all use our informal titles be there are too many sirs and layers of commands here. You can just call me Montague and him Lawrence. What about you?"

"Oh, Bart is fine." Barton leaned his arms on the table now that he was finished eating. "I have a question. I am wondering why I was picked to do this operation. Certainly, there are others more qualified."

Montague answered quickly. "Perchance. But if you read your packet, you'll find the three of us speak fluent French, and since we are to work with Lefoy, who conveniently speaks lousy English, then—snappo—we are it! Then Handsome Harry there, and I speak German and Dutch, so it is a straightforward deal to see where we are going. Operation Wood Duck will be a pivotal maneuver in bringing across our troops and keeping them fed and pampered. It won't be anything like you did before, mate."

"Oh, I thought maybe it was some kind of suicide mission—throw us in front of the wolves or something." Bart grinned now. He poured out more tea, this time without milk.

"Ha! More like those Nazi Panzers! Yeah, we'll be right behind enemy lines with our bums bare in the air!" Montie snorted.

Captain Lawrence looked away from Montie with disdain and pursed his lips. "I think you have hit the nail on the head, Barre. While we all have something of value that is useful to the Allied's needs, we are either *persona non grata* or superfluous within our individual companies."

Bart choked on his tea, sputtering. "What? I don't understand what you mean!"

"Your Colonel Rice is transferring you to be under the command of the Allies and Lefoy. This is not a bad thing, but your days of being a cozy little staff sergeant and dogs body to Col. Rice will be at an end." Lawrence coolly eyed Barton with the information and looked amused. "I see you are sweating. Now you are upset?"

"I am being demoted then." Sounding petulant, Barton thumped a fist angrily on the table. "Damn! I knew it—he doesn't like me." He grumbled, nearly silently, "Fucking Samuelson—"

The Captain laid a gentle hand on Bart's fist. "No, think of it more as a promotion with more men under your command, along with our concerted efforts to supply the armies converging along the *Wehrmacht.* However, the days ahead will be more dangerous than before. You will no longer be sitting safely on your pretty little behind at the tail end of the army. We will be in the forefront, taking over newly conquered areas as Lefoy pushes ahead, which should prove to be exciting. We'll have some fun. Montie is an expert in demolitions!"

Lawrence's voice took on an imperious tone as he continued. "Greene has it right when he said the crossing of the Rhine would be monumental. Do you realize the scope of such an operation? Now the map we studied was only a portion of this area, and you saw how much was going to be required just to take the Germans' border around here. Can you imagine this operation is tenfold that? Both up and down the Rhine, most of the Allies under Montgomery and your armies under Bradley and that audacious Patton are all hitting the Germans hard from every vantage point. After we cross the Sauer River, the Rhine will be even more eventful, I am sure. We'll soon be knocking heads in the Ruhr Valley. We are going to win this war."

Smiling, Lawrence took the teapot and filled his cup. He sipped it dark, found it offensive, and poured in milk and a spoon of sugar. "Yech, you Americans have lousy taste in tea."

Montague held out his cup, and Lawrence filled it. "Yup. I think this will do it. Shove a hot poker right up their bum; they'll pay us attention then."

Captain Lawrence cast him a baleful eye. "Please. Do you have to be so distasteful and crude?"

Montague shrugged. "Hey, mate, you make this operation sound like we are on holiday. You haven't been in action yet. This is no Sunday School outing with the lambs. People are going to be dead, maybe you and me and 'im!" Dunston jabbed a thumb at Barton, who cringed.

"But, yes, I would say this is as good as any plan to overtake the Huns now that we are on German soil. Did you see that last town we drove through? Maybe nobody was smiling, but they were waving hankies and white flags at us. These people have seen enough war. Me too—I got worries back home and a pretty Sheila waiting."

Barton sat quietly in thought, absorbing the men's conversation. But his mind also roiled around the words that Lawrence said earlier—they were all *persona non grata.* What the heck? He thought the colonel liked him, and Barton was sure he had done an excellent job for the man.

Barton grew angry. He felt the ghost of Rossini rise and laugh in his face. Perhaps Samuelson had not amended his report enough, and Barton was still under suspicion. Maybe this was his long-anticipated punishment. *Great! I am heading into harm's way!* He felt his stomach lurch in fear. He shoved aside his dessert plate and cup and took up the packet of papers from the meeting, hoping there was some kind of explanation.

After their lunch and the logistics meeting, Barton left the Allied camp and headed back to his own in search of Col. Rice. He had to wait, as the man was in meeting again.

Bart went about his job, actually arriving late for duty, but no one was there to complain. He kept glancing at his watch, wanting to break and confront the colonel. Suddenly, the day was over, and dinner was approaching. He had to spend time tonight to read through the orders he had received earlier at the meeting and sew on the new operation insignias for Lefoy's Sixth. He would report to Colonel Lefoy tomorrow morning with the British Captain and the Aussie Sergeant Major.

◆ ◆

Spring 1945

As March unfolded, the reports coming from the front and from the Allies were changing the strategies the Supreme Allied Forces Commander Gen. Dwight D. Eisenhower planned to conquer Berlin. It was the belief that the Soviet armies were on the eastern front just hours away from Berlin. The Americans would not be the first to conquer Berlin!

The other rumor was that Hitler's loyalists were planning to fight from the Alps near Austria as their last stronghold. However, the *Wehrmacht* was suffering such brutal defeats at every point that they could not adequately hold their mountain frontier or those in their homeland boundaries against the invading armies with such scattered forces.

Adolf Hitler put out the call for every able-bodied young man to enlist and citizens to fight for their beloved homeland. Millions rallied to his call to build a series of defensive walls around the city of Berlin, hoping to thwart the Russian tanks.

Thus, as the days progressed, and after each victory by the Allies and the US armies, Hitler's troops were devastated, and their numbers diminished by thousands. Their supplies ran low along the Rhine Valley, costing the German Army dearly. Some of the enemy troops were again voluntarily standing down, allowing the Allied Forces to capture them and the area as they invaded. The towns that flew white flags of truce, asking for peace as the Allies marched through, were humanely spared. As the troops moved forward, it gave them a sense of pride to see the German people suddenly bowing to the greater force of the Allied armies.

However, the German high command was not taking their defeat lightly. Many officers were harshly reprimanded, demoted, or shot for treason in allowing the enemy to win.

American General Courtney Hodges overran the Germans, plowing them under, and by March 7, the Ludendorff Bridge at Remagen along the Rhine River had triumphantly been overtaken. From there, a fierce weeklong battle ensued as they struggled to reinforce a wide lodgment area from which the Twelfth could safely deploy and cross. Over eight thousand men crossed the first day, including Lefoy's Boys, as they were now called. The Ninth, Seventieth, Eightieth, and Ninety-Ninth Infantry Divisions victoriously crossed in the days after with swift success.

As the Germans retreated once again toward the fatherland, realizing that their days were numbered, they began to wire the bridges along the Rhine with heavy explosives, ready to destroy them at the first sign of invasion. This was a last desperate action to keep out the invaders.

After discovering several instances of wired bridges, the Allied engineers checked each of the bridges for explosives before crossing. It was often a race for time and supplies, with the Germans barely finishing before they were pursued and overtaken by the Allies. For every Allied win, there was a painful defensive retaliation as Hitler tried to keep his troops strong and push back the invaders. Hitler's own aerial counteroffensive on the bridge at Remagen was off the mark by many miles, but due to the many battles for the bridge, the venerable wounded Ludendorff Railway Bridge collapsed on its own on March 17, taking with it the lives of many of US Army engineers and soldiers. That sad day seemed like an embarrassing defeat for the Americans.

Hitler's pride was wounded, and many of his generals and officers involved in the failed Remagen assault were arrested and condemned to death for their failure and mistakes.

By the middle of March, General Eisenhower, impressed by the swiftness and force of Patton's Third Army as they swept through the southern frontiers of Germany along the Saar-Palatinate regions, revised his plans once more for crossing the Rhine. Eisenhower felt that with Montgomery in the north pounding away like a ramrod at the Reich's door, he would send his forces along the southern routes through the Ruhr valley to clean up and push hard into the strategic sectors of Germany, which still had substantial German resistance and industrial strengths from which the Germans could draw.

With glory looming large for Patton's forces to cross the Rhine in an assault and before General Montgomery's foray into the north, General Patton pressed his plan to cross the Rhine on March 21 with Eisenhower's approval. Using supplies stockpiled in the Loire Valley from his war front the previous autumn, Patton was ready to go, sending forward supplies, troops, assault boats, pontoon bridges, and river-crossing equipment. His plan was to cross the Main River, which was about thirty miles east of the Rhine near the town of Maintz. However, he suspected the Germans would be ready for him there. They made a feint there while crossing at a few other strategic points, such as Neirstein and Oppenheim, with the Twelfth Army. Then, at the Boppard and St. Goar, twenty-five miles northwest of Mainz with the Eighth Army, Patton himself finally crossed over the Rhine on the night of March 22.

The Germans' offensive action was surprising. There was little resistance in some areas, but while crossing the only bridge left standing outside of Oppenheim, Patton's forces were engaged in heavy shelling by the Germans and fierce machine gun fire as their assault boats crossed the river. The Twelfth Division had set up artillery along the flat lands between Neirstein and Oppenheim, along with counter barrages, and after a bloody battle with significant losses on both fronts, the town of Oppenheim was conquered.

◆ ◆

Six miles southeast of Remagen
Sunday, March 24, 1945

The lodgment depot camp was eerily too quiet today; even the sibilant hiss of the radio in the communications tent quickly blew away on the breeze. Barton strolled along the eastern bank of the Rhine River, peering past the heavy trees and scrub. Something seemed amiss despite the calm morning.

Before they camped here, the days had been busy and fraught with battles and fast movement as they dodged engagements with the enemy. They had lost one truck coming across the Sûre River. As part of the bridge suddenly exploded under artillery fire, the vehicle had veered, crashed through the bridge side rails, and went over into the swirling water, taking with it the precious supply cargo and six men. The men did not survive; some were trapped in the sinking vehicle, and two were killed while swimming to shore by the enemy on the opposite side of the river.

The new depot camp was six miles away from the last bridge they had crossed. For several days, there had been a continuous march of troops and convoys of supply trucks, some dumping part of their loads and taking on fuel and some bypassing them. During the early days in camp, Bart's new company was busy directing shipment traffic, inventorying, and arranging the supplies, making them ready to go for the infantry divisions to pass them. But nothing had come by in nearly two days.

The sound trucks from Lefoy's unit had already moved on upriver, and the staged "troop movements" were no longer heard here. Barton had thought it was ingenious once he heard it all. For a day after most of the traffic had ceased, the sound truck had blared the continuous noise, and Barton thought it really did sound like a massive army on the move, complete with muted conversations, tanks' clattering treads, sloshing mud, laboring engines, and the whine and clash of gears. Barton knew all the noises to be realistic because he had been a part of such movements for months. Whether it would fool the enemy, he wasn't sure, but anything now was worth trying to keep an advantage. Brigadier General Greene and Colonel Lefoy's ploy might work. So far, Operation Wood Duck didn't seem like much of a big deal, mostly the same as Barton had experienced before—SOP as they sat about waiting for new orders or deployed materiel.

Barton and his men were getting itchy, though, wanting to work. Yet, with everything done and nothing happening, they were sitting on their thumbs, playing cards, smoking ciggies, eating rations, and a small cache of confiscated Swiss chocolates and dry sausages. Barton felt as if it was surreal in some way after the rough days of the hard push before. He did not know many of the new men well; most came handpicked for their skills from various units in the Twelfth, Twenty-Third, and Lefoy's Sixth Armies.

Barton pinched the cigarette butt tightly between his fingers, putting it out and then placing the dead fag in his pocket. They were warned not to leave much litter or evidence that they had camped here. Orders were that Barton would be relieved by another unit, and his unit would move northeast in a few days.

Supposedly, there were still pockets of the enemy and snipers about. A guy taking a leak in the woods had been picked off, and now nobody was to wander in the woods alone, patrols only. Second Lieutenant Steven Kells had agreed with Barton that they were still in danger. They must keep a tight watch over their camp, even though nothing had seemed to go on for the past few days.

Barton had been on patrol the previous night. The woods had been eerily calm, every tiny noise amplified by the echoing trees, canyon hills, and rocks. He had felt his skin prickling all night as if the camp was being silently observed, and he surmised it was. Even the continuous dialogue of the two radio men in the communications tent had sounded too loud, echoing about the woods at times. He told them to clam up, hearing them laugh and joking with someone on the radio. He received only terse nods and odd looks. The men continued their dialogues but were less noisy.

From the coded radio news he heard, it sounded like Lefoy was really moving forward fast and leaving behind depots for the troops. His armored battalion escorting the supply trucks was making good headway east into the *Reichland*. Barton hoped that was the advantage needed and thought that perhaps the war would soon end when they all invaded Berlin in the surprise attacks. Let Hitler get caught with his pants down!

He snickered to think of such a thing. One of the radio men kept a sketchbook with caricatures—he had made one with Hitler taking a beating from General Patton with his dog William chewing the Führer's boot. In another, General Eisenhower whacked Hitler with a baseball bat, and one sketch had England's Churchill spanking Hitler with a giant cricket bat. Everyone got a big laugh.

Barton veered away from the riverbank and headed back to the camp. He noticed the sky above was a dull, flat blue, like faded paint; the air was sticky with humidity, and the sun looked like a faint eye in the sky. In Texas, if this were summer, it would be ominous signs, getting ready for nasty rain, a tornado, or a hurricane—the calm before the storm. Here, though, they were probably going to be pelted by rain later in the day; it was oppressive, and he did not care for it at all.

A rough wind dragged across the river, bringing with it the stench of sewage and death. During the fight, many villagers were killed. The Nazis also killed their livestock and burned the town, thinking that if their enemy did make it across, there would be nothing to pillage and no people to take prisoner.

Barton snorted—his laugh derisive; Americans did not pillage … much. Lefoy's men had, though, taking great pleasure in confiscating the wines and various foodstuffs in a couple of destroyed cafés and stores along the way. And Bart's men, although advised not to take things other than needed supplies, had somehow taken whatever they pleased as they trekked across the devastated landscape and through the war-torn villages and towns. Sometimes they plucked grenades and war souvenirs from dead German soldiers. Barton supposed he was no better, for he had a bottle of expensive cognac he had traded with a young GI for some cigarettes and French soap in the last town.

He would like very much to go to his tent now and relax with that bottle; however, he was on duty for the next half hour, the man in charge. At this moment in peaceable times, he liked that role. In the weeks before, Barton had really hated his command and his commander, Lefoy. Barton had worried that his own decisions might be wrong in a fight compared to the impetuous Lefoy. Then, he had argued too many times with Sergeant Phillips and Second Lieutenant Kells over seemingly petty and trivial things.

With Phillips gone ahead with Lefoy, Barton now felt like he had earned the respect of his men and colleagues, Captain Lawrence and Sergeant Major Dunston, since they all seemed to think the same. He talked with them daily by field phone in coded messages or by meeting up with them; Lawrence and Dunston were encamped farther south along the river at strategic points where troops were still crossing. Colonel Lefoy's camp kept moving in crabbing increments inland every couple of days from the original location of their Rhine River crossing at Remagen, with little relief depots along the way.

However, Barton's new colleagues and their companies had suffered far greater dangers to date, as Colonel Lefoy had led them ragtag through the countryside. The British captain lost a substantial number of men. Lawrence had recruited nearly half from Barton's company and some from Dunston. So far, Barton felt Operation Wood Duck was a bust—they still had to cross the eastern plains and mountains of the Rhine River valley. There continued to be significant resistance at every place. It was only the weeks and days leading up to the invasions over the Rhine that had been interesting yet deadly.

Barton initially did not enjoy playing the role of bomb maker and deploying them along the way. Dunston and US Sergeant Ben Kent, the Mad Boomer, had taken Bart under their wing to help build and distribute explosives. Often near bridges or entrances to towns, they left booby traps for the Panzers that plagued them daily. Now Bart understood the odd questions regarding fireworks in Colonel Rice's interview. Rice had set him up.

While it was exciting to see the bombs go off and take out a flank of infantry or a tank, Bart was always nervous he'd blow up himself or Kent. But after several of these wild escapades, he had respect and liking for the surly Sergeant Kent and wise-cracking Dunston and had learned a great deal. But that was during those weeks in transit, and now his unit was sitting here once again, waiting for orders and something to do. It felt all too like the Caumont POL depot last year—he was a chained guard dog eager to be set loose.

With a final surveying glance at the quiet camp and riverbanks, Barton let out an exasperated breath and ducked under the canopy of the supply tent office. He found a pair of his men playing poker. They looked up with somber faces, dreary with the tedium of having nothing to do. Barton sat on a campstool next to Cpl. Jimmy Hyer and peeked over the man's shoulder at his cards. He shook his head at the man.

Tech Cpl. Dan Fine, taking a break from the communications tent, rubbed his beaky nose and caught the silent message between the men. He upped his ante. "Two. You in Jimmy?"

Jimmy grimly traded his cards around in his hand and looked at the pennies left in his pile. He shoved three across. "Yeah, I see you and raise you one. What do you got?" He grinned now.

Tech Cpl. Fine met the bid and then splayed out his cards: an ace, king, queen, and jack of hearts. "Suck on that!" He leered at Hyer as the younger man laid his cards out—a pair of jacks and the rest muck. "Well, thank you," Fine noted, sweeping a hand over the pile of pennies and pulling them toward his side. "Your deal, loser."

Barton spoke up then. "Hey, the winner is supposed to deal." He glanced at Hyer who was picking up the cards. "Do you know how to play this game?"

Hyer nodded. His gray eyes were twinkling as he put a finger to his lips and then began to shuffle the ragged, worn cards.

Barton reached into his pocket, figuring he had a little time to spare. "How much to play?"

"Five bucks." TC Fine spat out a piece of tobacco. "These *Gitanes* don't draw, man! Where'd you get 'em?" he asked Hyer as he sucked down another heavy toke on the thin, floppy cigarette.

"Took 'em off a dead Kraut. They taste better than those *Gauloises*," Hyer said as he dealt out the cards to each man. "I wish we'd get some *Camels* or *Strikes* in. I hate those Frenchie fags. Okay, Five-card-drop-yer-drawers—you go first, Sarge." Hyer chirped cheerfully with a smirk.

Barton laid a five out. "I thought you guys were playing for pennies. What's up with the fin?"

Fine cackled, "That's what we start with. If you are lucky, you'll get to keep it. We've been playing a long time and just got pennies left." They each put in five pennies.

Barton shook his head. Peeking under the cards, he said, "Oh, what the heck. Hit me."

"One?" Hyer looked at him dubiously.

"Yeah."

"Oo, big man here thinks he has a hand," Fine sneered nastily at Bart and then shoved cards across to Hyer. "Three."

Hyer passed the cards over and took two. He looked over at Barton expectantly. "You lead off, Sarge."

Barton looked about the table. "So what am I supposed to do here, throw in my five? Why can't I put in pennies like you guys?"

Hyer shrugged but Fine spoke. "Hey, man, it's our game. Don't like your cards, then you can fold and say *arri-ve-derci*, baby."

Barton hesitated for a second. He could see the avarice on Fine's face and the innocent look on Hyer's and wasn't sure if he was being played for a mark or if they were just idiots playing a stupid game by their own rules. It felt suspiciously like his brothers teasing him again. "Fine, here's my fin. Meet it."

The men resigned and laid down their cards. Barton had the highest hand. "Okay, that was easy-peasy, boys." He swept up his fiver and the pennies. "*Adios*, boys." Barton stood up and shoved the money in his pocket. He put his helmet on and ducked under the tent. He could hear the men laughing as he went.

"Shit, he only won ten cents. What a maroon! You'd think he won a million bucks!"

Barton's jubilation soured. That's what he got for playing nice with a bunch of dolts and bowsers. Hyer and Fine were decent soldiers; however, as of now, Barton thought they might be on woods patrol tonight. He headed to his tent to make up the work roster for the next couple of days.

While in his tent, Bart again decided to write a letter to Elise. He never heard from her the last time he wrote. Perhaps his mail had been slow in getting to the States; no one could rely on anything these days except for more chaos.

He wrote swiftly for several minutes, asking her how she was and even about the weather and then telling her about the recent snows and rainstorms … dang! Barton realized he sounded like a weatherman. And the stinking Brits—they were always consumed by talk of the weather and their health. Bart crumpled up the paper and got out his worn leather writing kit, taking out a single sheet of paper again. He then sat for some long minutes, trying to come up with something witty to write.

He heard a few birds twittering and the river rushing along the banks amid the murmur of the camp, and despite the tranquil moment, Barton felt restive. He was bored and sorry to say that he was ready for a fight again. He'd even take a scary trip with Kent just to do something meaningful. But Kent was with Lefoy, probably recruiting more guys for his Boom Squad.

He rested his head on his knees, thinking of the past weeks. He had fought more in this short time than in all the time he had been involved in the war. Captain Lawrence was correct; they were no longer on the back lines—now they were moving behind enemy lines, knocking over Germans at every turn. Barton had to wonder if the name Operation Wood Duck was genuinely relevant.

Lefoy had led them on a merry chase after crossing over the other rivers, and once in the German interior, the supply convoys had nothing but a fight nearly every day as they zigzagged across the countryside. Barton had felt as if he had primarily done a lot of ducking for cover.

Barton, however, had enjoyed his prowess in fighting with the machine guns, sitting in a sandbagged redoubt or building and popping off little German heads, luridly watching as their helmets flew away or as the men ran toward him. He was the Grim Reaper, luring them to their deaths.

But it was after such fights that the nightmares came —the black blood spurting from bodies, parts falling off, the faces of the dead, pale and bloodied, looking back up at him. When he walked on the death patrol, shooting the nearly dead who begged for it or rousting out the simply wounded men for prisoners of war, Barton felt powerful, like God in some ways, able to give or take away life. Yet, when he was under fire, he ran like a scared rabbit for cover and laughed when others did the same in his crosshairs. Sometimes, he wondered if the war was making him vicious—an apathetic, overly efficient killing machine.

The first man he had knowingly shot had been fellow soldier, Cpl. Albert Rossini. Barton didn't count the German deserter; he would have been his first, but the abused Chaubert girl had taken that man's life. Yet, the German soldier and Rossini's death were grim guilty shadows in Barton's mind.

Sometimes, the sound of the artillery and mortars rang in his head like echoes from that terrible night in the woods when Rossini died. Then he'd awaken to another day of the same, except that this time, it was reality. At times, Barton wanted to run away and hide. He wasn't a coward.

He hated to see the devastation of the beautiful countryside and the forests where battles were fought, thinking it was all such a terrible waste. Spring was trying to emerge in this once-frozen land, and the scent of blooms and the sight of the delicate trilliums, harebells, edelweiss, lilies of the valley, and other blossoms in the forests were invigorating. Barton viewed them as a sign of hope. It was sickening to see the stately trees blown into splinters and stunted or uprooted by the powerful screaming shells and the earth pitted and pocked, sometimes bearing gruesome things in the deep holes.

He felt much as Schmidt had; he hated to bring out the dead. Some men were so damaged that there was hardly anything left of them to show or say they had been human once. He supposed the Germans suffered the same to find their troops dead. Barton often felt squeamish as they overtook a village after a battle. Pitying the civilians and the animals, they were just as vulnerable as the soldiers were, sometimes more so. Then the sneaky snipers were everywhere, and a single shot could ring out and bring instant death for somebody, even someone innocently pissing in the woods.

Bart shivered and looked back at his clean white paper and wondered how he could write about any of this. The war was filthy and horrific, and he was a part of it all. Reluctant to admit it, but Richard had been right about war—it was the worst thing Barton had ever experienced. He tried to recall a pleasant poem, and stanzas from Wordsworth leached into his mind as he wrote to Elise.

> *'Therefore, I am still a lover of meadows and the woods and mountains, and all of that I behold from this green earth—both what I create and what I perceive. I am well pleased to recognize the nature and language of these senses. The anchor of my purest thoughts, the nurse, the muse, the guide, and the guardian of my heart and soul of my moral being is all tied to you. To think of you is my only beauty in this ravaged world and offers me any peace.'*

> *Elise, I am grateful you do not judge me. I am harebrained in my attempts to say nice things. My world is not pretty; there are few pleasures other than to know I still breathe and go on living. At this moment, I miss you. The men here are good soldiers, but not to make them my friends. A sergeant owns few friends. Some days, I wonder why I bother, for all too soon, they are gone; men die daily or are moved on to other duties. You are my best friend at this time. I hope you are well. Forgive me for not writing more often, but then I have little to say to a beautiful girl.*

> *My kind regards,*

> *Yours—BB*

He quickly sealed the letter and stuffed it in his pocket to post later. He didn't want to reread it—he would probably be embarrassed for his weak sentiments and poor memory for poetry and tear it up. He put the writing kit away in his duffle bag and settled on his cot. He batted away a droning insect, scratched idly at an itch, and noted the time on his watch. Now off duty, Bart rolled over with the pillow over his head, wanting to think of something else than the war. There was nothing left to do for a while, and he wasn't concerned that LT Kells was technically now on duty. He felt a brief nap was in order on this lazy day.

◆ ◆

A couple of hours passed in lonesome bliss, and suddenly Barton was awakened by someone shaking him roughly. He growled and rolled over. Opening his eyes, he looked up, ready to complain, but saw it was Captain Lawrence crouched beside him. Lawrence put a finger to his lips and motioned to Barton, shoving his gun belt and helmet at him and gesturing for him to follow. Barton did so and crept out of his tent, following the captain. Crouching low, they wound their way through the camp, past awnings and makeshift supply tents, and headed uphill into the woods. There, they met up with a baker's dozen of Bart's men. He scanned the assembled group, noticing that many were missing; they looked frightened.

Hunkering down behind some rocks and brush, Bart whispered harshly to the Captain, "What in the hell is going on?"

"Sh!" The Captain motioned downhill toward the camp. "Nazis."

Barton gaped. He saw a string of men dart from tent to tent, taking cover. He peered through the brush and looked upriver to see at least four more armed men slipping behind a supply truck. They were carrying a machine gun on a tripod and grenade launcher; they were prepared for a fight. He could no longer hear the radio tent, and he felt a pain in his chest.

"Oh … hell. How did they get here?" Barton turned about to look at his men; a few shrugged but one knelt by Barton.

"Sorry, Sergeant. They took us by surprise—they were like ghosts. Jackson, Sayles, and Crosier are dead —throats cut. Damned assassins!" Private Gene Slade shivered as he spoke; he then motioned between himself and PFC Tom Emery. "We got out real fast and passed the word."

"You were on woods patrol then?" Barton asked.

"Yeah."

"Where are the rest of the men?" Barton asked as he watched the increasing snaking line of green-clad soldiers moving quickly from tent to tent and standing guard by the company truck.

"Some are here, and I think the rest are dead … or got away. Oh, crap. Look! They found Hyer and Fine!" The private pointed to the camp.

Four enemy soldiers dragged the men out of hiding from behind some supply crates—they were shaking them and passing them roughly around the circle of men. Barton could hear some shouted words and rough laughter. He looked to Lawrence. "Can you make out what they are saying?"

"A little. The fat one is asking where the commander of the camp is." The captain's voice was tight with emotion, his watery blue eyes fixed on the scene below. "Oh, please don't tell them …" He quivered, his hand sliding to his sidearm. "This is very bad. I thought Lefoy cleared us. Oh, damnation!" he cursed quietly with fervor.

Barton peeked over the rock and then looked at his men about him. "Do you all have weapons?"

"Yeah … but nothing much. Look, there is another group coming in now." Corporal Neil Swanson nodded downhill. "Looks like a mucky-muck … he's in a car."

A tall man stiffly climbed down from the gray utility vehicle, casting a wary look about the camp before crossing toward the supply tent office with his little entourage. He waved to the men holding Hyer and Fine, and they shoved the captive men to kneel on the ground.

Observing it all with pocket binoculars, Lawrence commented, "Looks like an SS officer. He's got tall boots and a cap. Sounds like one, too; he's asking Fine if he is a Jew." He spoke softly and then swept a hand over his eyes. "Oh, now he is asking him where his commander is. Um, he just called you something foul."

A loud shot rang out, and the men witnessed Fine falling over. Hyer yelled out in shock, and a man clubbed him with his rifle.

"The bastard shot Fine!" Emery growled and then pulled off a grenade from his belt. "Let me get them, Sarge! God damned pigs!"

Barton put up a hand to still him. "Everyone shut it! If you throw that, you'll kill Hyer too."

Emery sniffled. "But you can't let them get away with this." He looked down. "Oh no … they got Kells now."

"I know." Barton shook his head at the rough treatment the second lieutenant was getting. He glanced at the captain. "What are we going to do about this?"

The captain drew in a deep breath. "We might be able to take them out if we can do it quickly. Otherwise, we are all dead men up here. Option two: we head north upriver toward Lefoy. I came to warn you that there had been enemy sightings along the river. We thought you might be ready to move down with us; we are heading inland tomorrow toward the Third."

"Nice of you to inform me of that now." Barton eyed the captain with derision. "And what do we do about the supplies down there and the rest of my men?" he queried with worry.

"Screw 'em," Tech Private Jim Leonard rasped. He leaned near Barton. "I say we take 'em, and to hell with the consequences."

The men flinched, as they heard an echoing shot. The company's Second Lieutenant Kells was gone.

"Man, these guys don't give anyone a chance." Barton pushed away from the group, and crouching low, he slipped through the woods, hiking farther uphill among some brush. He hissed, and the men followed him. "From here, we can see the road and the bend of the river. If you want to make a run for it back to Lefoy, then stay in the woods away from the road." He glanced at the Captain. "I think I want to stay and see what happens."

"Me, too," a few men echoed.

"Hyer is dead unless you walk down there right now." Lawrence pointed to the tall officer. "That man means business." He put a hand on Bart's arm. "I don't think you want to see him killed, or risk yourself do you? I say we go now."

"No. But I was thinking that we might be able to take out that group." Barton gritted.

Lawrence hissed back with barely held anger, "And then you will only alert the rest of their patrol to swarm like bees around us. You will not give away our position! Consider this a loss. We don't have enough men or armaments to withstand their weapons. There are too many of them. This is not your Alamo; just give it up."

Barton bristled at the comment.

"Hey, Sarge, something is happening." Private Slade shook Bart's shoulder. "It looks like they found more guys, and that officer is breaking into the crates."

"See, they just want supplies, the greedy swine," Corporal Swanson said and then grinned weakly. "Maybe they'll take what they need and leave."

"I seriously doubt it. Hyer and those men are either prisoners or dead men. That commandant is a nasty piece of work." Corporal Alf Lofgren offered sagely.

Barton nodded and sounded sad now. "If I go down there, I'll be one too."

"Then let's just shoot them!" Emery slid down the hill a little. "You cover me, and I'll throw this; let them feel a little heat. You guys can pick 'em off like they did Sayles and Crosier."

"Halt! Get back here; nobody is to do anything!" The captain reached out and gripped the man by the collar, yanking him back. He looked back up at the circle of worried faces, hissing, "I am taking command here. Everybody head uphill and keep moving northeast. Don't look back. Tell Lefoy what's happening; let the Sixth send them some heat. *We* can't do it! Keep on guard, though! Go!" He watched, as the men slowly resigned and began to drift away, silently sliding undercover from bushes and trees until the forest swallowed them.

Barton moved to higher ground and looked down on the camp from a better vantage point. "If we had machine guns or a bazooka, we could take them," he said to Lawrence, who, like a silent ghost, suddenly joined him.

"I know; however, it isn't worth it."

Barton looked sharply at the Captain. "You obviously have not had to decide who is gonna die on a mission. Everybody is worth it. This is gonna look bad on me." Barton swept a hand over his face. "I'll be lucky if I don't get demoted for this."

"You are wrong, Barre. I have lost more men than you have in the past weeks. But we must carry on."

"How in the devil did they sneak up on us?" Barton questioned.

"They came on the river, I think. Nobody has guarded that bridge front since it collapsed." The captain finished softly as he checked his ammunition.

"But how did your camp not see them? Don't you have patrols?"

"Yes, but we had bad fog conditions this morning."

"Well, so did we, but it burns off by lunchtime," Bart argued.

"Yes, but in that fog, a good many men can get by us if they are quiet enough."

"Crap." Barton watched the camp below, noting the soldiers were still breaking open crates, smashing some of the radio equipment, and throwing goods in the back of the supply truck. "Boy, what I wouldn't give for that grenade launcher now."

"Yes, it would make a pretty display of power for all of one second. Then all hell would be upon us." The captain slid his pistol back into its leather holder. "You are so insistent on a fight, like a bulldog."

Barton elbowed the captain. "Sh! Look! What in the heck is that?"

"What?" Lawrence peered down at the camp where men were dragging out long things with strings from a broken crate.

"Those. Are those weather balloons? And … antiaircraft buoys? Shit!" Bart gripped the man's forearm. "Something stinks here. Most of those crates are just filled with excelsior—they are friggin' empty or filled with junk!" He glared at the officer. "They were supposed to be food and ammo supplies. What kind of game are they playing with us?"

Captain Lawrence shook his arm away from Barton. "I think it should be obvious. Your camp is a dummy."

"A … d-dummy? We are decoys?" Bart's voice rose, and he backed down. "My men are dying for empty boxes and weather balloons?" He moaned with despair and incredulity. "No wonder they all had special codes on the inventory list. I thought they were secret weapons or something. Damn!"

"Sergeant, please calm down." Lawrence pressed Barton to the ground. "Your job here was important to create the illusion that the troops were landing and crossing near here on the treadways. But now they are miles away. You have supplies; they just aren't essential, not like mine or the other depots. Why do you think you had a communications tent with those radio men reading scripted reports?"

"What? I don't believe it!" Barton struggled with the lightweight captain. "You sons of bitches made a fool of me!" He kneed the captain in the belly, hissing, "Get the hell off me." Barton rolled away and lay upon his stomach to watch the angry German officer as he kicked at the smashed crates, sending up clouds of excelsior and yelling at the men. He heard the captain slither over to him.

"Might I remind you that you just struck a superior officer and—"

"To hell with you." Barton spat harshly. "You people make me sick."

The officer had a moment to look surprised. He sounded the word out as if it were something awful-tasting in his mouth. "People?"

"You are a friggin' wimp. My men were right—we should have done something."

Suddenly, a shot echoed through the hills, followed by another. Their attention was instantly drawn to the scene below. The German officer had just shot Hyer in the back and head; the man lay quivering and jerking for a moment as blood spurted out, then he lay still. The seven other men tried to break and run, but they were quickly gunned down.

The German commander looked up into the hills and, turning about, he yelled into the air, tossing away a sheaf of papers. Then he stomped over to his vehicle, climbed in, and waited for his assistant to drive him out. Barton and Lawrence watched as the soldiers clambered into the supply truck and drove away with it. The air smelled of truck diesel and sulfur; a dirty, slight haze hung ominously over the camp.

Lawrence let out an exhalation. "Do you want to know what the officer said?"

Barton shifted away. "I think I can figure it out myself." He swiped a hand around his neck, feeling it cramp from his prone position. "That's it. I am going down there. I have my camp to fix up and men to bury. I can only hope most of the others got out. I hope to God my field radio still works."

"I'll help you."

Barton slid down the hill a way on his butt and then stood and walked boldly back into the depot camp. He avoided the mess that had been Corporal Hyer and the others, snatched up the papers scattered like leaves on the ground, and studied them for a second before wadding them up. "Fricking liars!" He then strode through the camp, looking at the devastation.

The enemy soldiers had sliced through the tents and canvas covers; they had spilled gasoline on some of the tents and empty crates as if they had intended to burn the camp. A few tents held dead men with their throats cut, still lying on their cots or on the dirt floor. The Germans had been silent and deadly. There had been hardly a fight. Perhaps Bart was lucky that Lawrence had shown up when he did. As much as he wanted to be grateful for the officer's help, he was angry as hell about losing his camp.

He kicked through mountains of yellow and gray excelsior and packing wool, and he wondered now just what his men had actually guarded in the camp. The tires, truck parts, and petrol supplies were gone, as were the pallets of ammunition. The Nazis had found little else of worth. The food stores were gone, and the confiscated Swiss chocolate, canned milk, and cases of toilet paper were missing. Ha! Barton hoped the Germans got sick. He had reserved some of the food crates because they were outdated.

"Let the Jerries eat rotten canned tomatoes. I hope you all die of ptomaine poisoning!" Barton muttered sourly as he surveyed the mess.

He found two of the outpost men brutally slain. Tech Corporal Fine was sprawled on the ground in a pool of blood. Some asshole had pissed on him and cut a crude star on his forehead. Barton looked away; he felt his gorge rise, and he suddenly threw up. He could not look anymore at the horrific mess.

Dashing into his tent, Bart found many of his possessions strewn about. The bastards had taken the cognac! He jammed the remaining items in his duffle bag and took up any other supplies that he could think of, including some of their recent orders and files. He grabbed up the field radio even though it was broken; he might be able to repair it along the way. Bart met Captain Lawrence outside.

"Let's go," Bart said despondently. "I had hopes of finding someone still alive, but everyone is gone. There is nothing left." He shrugged his pack, the field radio, and duffle bag on his shoulders and stepped away.

The captain stood his ground. "What about your men? Aren't you going to bury them? I pulled some of their tags so we can report them." He dangled the bloodied metal dog tags.

Barton flinched at the sight and looked away. "No. Let Lefoy's Goons clean up the mess; he caused this," Barton snarled and headed for the forest.

Captain Lawrence cast a quick glance about the devastated camp, pocketed the tags, and then snatched up a pair of rifles from dead guards and followed closely on Barton's heels into the forest. They walked for some minutes in silence as they trudged uphill, their footfalls and heavy breathing the only sounds.

Lawrence spoke up as they walked. "I am sorry about your men, Sergeant Barre." He tripped over a tree root but caught up with Barton. "They died heroes."

"Like hell they did. They were slaughtered like sick animals. Nobody was a hero today, especially me and most especially not you!" Barton glowered at Lawrence. "I think you had better get away from me. I just might take another swing at you, and I don't need to end up in the stockade."

"Point taken." The Captain haughtily stepped away some yards but hiked along evenly with Barton.

They hiked for close to two hours, each buried in their thoughts, but whenever Barton looked over at the officer, he found the man's face immobile, almost innocent. Periodically, Lawrence checked a compass and adjusted their direction with a grunt. As they walked, Bart's attitude sank, now morose, and he felt ill that somehow this mess today was his fault.

There was a low rumble of thunder, and Bart looked up. The clouds were dark and ominous above them. He felt a splat of cold wetness on his face. A steaming shower dumped on them. It was all bad luck.

"I'd like somebody to explain to me how we made a difference today. If our camp was a decoy," Bart's laugh sounded brittle. "Now I understand the name—Operation Wood Duck—we were just sitting ducks, waiting for somebody to take potshots at us! I am right, aren't I?" Bart growled. "Well, somebody is going to pay for this mess, and it isn't going to be me! I didn't do anything wrong except to follow orders." He finished by asking, "How in the heck did you get in without the Jerries seeing you?"

The sodden captain huddled under his jacket and then passed a rifle to Bart. He now strolled quickly along as if he was on a Sunday outing. He stepped through some low, dry bracken and sidestepped prickly holly bushes. He looked over at the reddened face of the sergeant. "It was easy. I came by Jeep on the road from the other way. Lefoy sent me."

"You knew they were around here?"

"We suspected they were. However, I did not see them coming up from the river until I walked into your camp."

"So, where is your Jeep? Why are we walking?" Barton stopped now, angry again.

Lawrence jerked a thumb over his shoulder. "Oh, it's some miles back that way by now. I came in on foot, just in case. But I am sure the Jerries have already found it. No, we will have a few blisters for our pains." Lawrence tossed off his comment blithely. "Don't worry. We can walk the kilometers we have left. I promise not to get us lost." He shook out his cap, and the wet sluiced off.

"Oh, that's just great. I … oh, never mind. I have no idea how you got to be a captain, but your command really stinks. Kells was better than you, and he was a junior asshole!" Bart's voice rose as he faced off with the officer.

"And why is it that you sound like an American? Are you some kind of spy? No! I know, you are a bumbling idiot like the rest of these idiots who make up stupid plans like this. General Greene can kiss my pink ass. Operation Wood Duck! Operation Fucked up beyond all recognition—FUBAR is more like it!" Barton started to stomp away but then stopped; he looked at his watch and then the sky, blinking against the rain. "We have about a half hour of daylight in the forest here. We better be getting close to Lefoy's battalion," he said bitterly.

The captain nodded as he glanced at his compass. "Yes, we are close enough. Do not worry, Barre; you will get your supper. You Americans whine if you aren't fed properly."

"Yeah? Well, you piss and moan if the damned tea is cold!" Barton shot back as he tromped ahead of the captain, angrily splashing through puddles.

The captain laughed softly, like an echo. "That we do. It is a wonder that the British Army can survive such inhumane conditions while at war. But we are tougher than we look." He stepped closer to Barton. "You Yanks are a tough lot, too. However angry you are with me for what happened today, I will be truthful and tell Lefoy that you are brave and honorable. So are your men."

"Thanks for the favor; however, I mean to report just how ridiculous this was. Talk about a giant *snafu!* We could have taken those men! We might have saved Kells, Hyer, and Fine at least."

"Yes, perhaps you might have saved them for a few minutes, but then you would have put us all in jeopardy. You can thank me now for saving your arse. And we at least saved some of your men from further calamity." Lawrence tossed his head, pushing away the soggy forelock of hair over his brow. He smiled at Bart.

Barton spat on the ground as he walked. "I will not. You cost me too much. And Lefoy is going to hear about this crap. Did he know we were nothing but a decoy camp?"

"Yes, of course."

The answer took the fight out of Barton. "Oh … well, I still don't understand it all."

"Don't worry. You lost little, and what are a few men against the greater good of all?" the officer stated loftily. "I will offer you back some of your men to help round out your loss when today is over."

"Step off, Lawrence!" Bart snapped, but then turned to the man, annoyed. "Just what in the hell is your first name anyway?"

"Uh, no. Lawrence will do fine." He smiled wanly at Bart. "You Yanks have such a wonderful bluntness with speech."

"Your argument and the rain are making me crazy. Stop calling me a Yank. You make me sound like a jerk-off." Bart gritted as he kicked at some pinecones on the ground, secretly enjoying that they caromed off rocks to explode or spun dizzily away.

"Ah, yes … a wanker." The captain laughed softly. "I think we Brits are more colorful and less direct in our, shall we say … expletives."

"Stuff it, you bloody moron. Sod off, you pretentious, sniveling wanker," Bart angrily grumbled and then bent and scooped up a pinecone. "How's that for your colorful epithets and expletives?" He impulsively threw the pinecone at the captain, hitting him squarely in the chest. "Just get lost for good … before you kill me too. I have a job to do." Bart stepped up his pace almost to a trot, creating some space between the British officer and himself. Lawrence's laughter rankled Bart's raw nerves as he ran away.

After a long time again in mutual silence, the captain raised his head. Sniffing the cool, wet air, he quipped, "Oh good, there we are. I smell dinner—I do believe we are having lamb stew tonight." He ran to come even with Bart again. "You know, I think you might be in for a surprise. Lefoy isn't going to care much about what happened. In fact, he might like it … except for the part about losing your men."

The captain looked at Bart, watching for his irritation, but then he continued, "Everything with you is so pessimistic, Barre. You are a half-empty-glass man. I've seen you with your men, Barre. You don't give a fig about them. You are a boor and a sanctimonious young man only out for your own glory; it pleases you to have men to command. You are not their friend. You don't need to put on a show for me or for Colonel Lefoy with your facetious empathy and displaced anger."

Bart stopped and turned to Lawrence. "I am not any of those things. You are cold if you think that." He swept away hot tears. "I cried for them. Those men are dead because we did nothing for them! It is my fault because I listened to you!" he shouted.

The captain laid a gentle hand on Bart's shoulder. "Nothing could be done. You must learn to fight your own battles, not those of your men. It was their fate to die today."

"Great. I get stuck with a presumptuous, stick-up-the-butt prick. You are cold as stone. Just stay away from me, Captain Lawrence. You are bad luck." Bart skirted the man and raced ahead. He saw smoke rising above the distant trees and tents ahead in the dim light of the forest. It was a welcome sight.

"As you wish, Sergeant Barre."

◆ ◆

Lawrence had been correct. Colonel Lefoy took pleasure in the report that Barton had carefully prepared and that the captain had reiterated and supported. Lefoy had actually laughed that the ploy had worked, for while the little skirmish happened, they had been moving deeper into the valley, preparing to meet up with the Third Army and the Twelfth. What was left of Lefoy's camp here would deploy in the night after dinner.

After a briefing with the Colonel and new maps and directives, Barton met up with the remaining men from his company of once sixty men at the start of their operation a month ago. They greeted him reservedly, with only one man coming forward to shake his hand. Corporal Lofgren clasped his hand and pounded Bart on the back in greeting.

"Thank you, Sarge. We would be dead by now if not for you and Captain Lawrence."

Emery spouted off, "Yeah, but at least we'd be with our pals and glad that we had gotten revenge."

Some of the men laughed. But Barton did not. He sat on a cot and took off his boots, wincing at his blistered and swollen feet. "I need about fifteen minutes of shut-eye here and some quiet. We are moving out after dinner, so be packed and ready to go." Bart lay down, feeling his bones weary from the long trek through the woods.

"Uh, sir?" Private Leonard popped up, raising his hand like a schoolboy.

"What?" Barton grumbled.

"We don't got anything to pack."

Barton sat up. He scratched through his wet hair. "Oh, yeah. Well … then, report to supply and get what you need. Someone will have to go back with the Goons to collect all your gear tomorrow. The Nazis made a real mess." He yawned, then added, "We'll meet later in the mess for dinner and talk. Dismissed."

"Yes, Sergeant."

"Thank you, Sergeant Barre." The men echoed and filed out of the tent, leaving Bart miserably alone.

His thoughts were mutinous as he stared at the red duck emblem on the green patch with the tiny blue, white, and red French shield emblazoned on his shirt sleeve.

"Stupid sitting ducks!" he grumbled and closed his eyes.

◆◆◆

CHAPTER 14

A Wounded Fatherland

March 1945

The following days were chaotic as the various supply units pulled together to form a snaking convoy behind Lefoy's troops. He led them quickly along the miles left between them and the Third Army. Making camp a few miles away from Patton's war machine, they waited while his troops joined in, ready for the big push through Oppenheim, creating a fifty-mile-wide cleared bridgehead along the Rhine.

Barton felt somewhat relieved that they were now again a part of Patton's troops. He liked Old Iron Guts, admiring him for his audacious moxie and tenacious bulldog attitude. Barton secretly wished he had the authority and power to be like him. Maybe if he had that power, none of Bart's men would be dead, and he never would have been just a decoy camp, something for people to joke about at breakfast!

As he sat in his tent, he wrote briefly in his diary, describing the past couple of weeks and his disappointment about the last failed project. He felt some pride again that he had new recruits and a nearly complete company again of seventy men, some filling in from the Third and the Twelfth Infantries. A few new, fresh-faced recruits were put on patrols and camp guards with some experienced men. The rest comprised workhorses, as well as fetching and deploying matériel to various companies.

The Rhine River crossing continued to be dangerous, and Patton's troops were still traversing at various points along the river, using pontoon and treadway bridges and ferrying across supplies and men. Lefoy's battalion kept the supplies running. In the days since March 7, all along the Rhine River, the armies were battling and crossing, creating safer bridgeheads and more expansive lodgment areas for the invading troops to deploy as they moved inland.

March 28, 1945

General Bradley is overly proud of his Twelfth army for crossing the Rhine. He has boasted that the mighty Rhine River has been taken without air support or air battles and that thousands of troops could freely cross anywhere along the Rhine. However, Montgomery in the north is preparing to take the

Rhine River with the aid of numerous air strikes. Perhaps Bradley has forgotten what happened at Remagen with our own preliminary airstrikes. Yeah, we lost that bridge for good!

The city of Oppenheim is still dangerous, even though Patton has conquered it. My men and I have spent hours on bridge patrol, seeing that the convoys of supplies safely make it across the bridges and through the city.

The town looked terrible when we got here; buildings gaped with holes in their sides, some had collapsed, and many were still burning. People were still recovering bodies lying along the rubble-filled streets. I rode through the other day with a truck of supplies. It is difficult to see children and their pets dead and their families weeping for them. I don't particularly enjoy kids, but I feel sad for them—their future is gone.

Despite the ruin here, there are still sniper potshots and explosions nearby occasionally as we rout out the rats of resistance. We are to be wary even of the children. Some of the citizens are still allied to Hitler. Across Germany, young boys and old men are lining up to enlist. Just yesterday, a thirteen-year-old boy shot at us and yelled a bunch of propaganda garbage. He was caught, roughed up, and is a prisoner now. He won't be going home to Mama.

Oppenheim has suffered. The city reminds me of the Lord's vengeance upon the cities of Sodom and Gomorrah. Were these citizens so terrible that they had to die? Hitler must now be a hated man among his people for causing so much ruin and death. God! I hope we can find him and kill him too! End it, finally.

I must get ready for my day in the trenches here, too. I hope I will see dinner tonight. I hear we actually have some fresh beef for goulash!

◆ ◆

Oppenheim, Germany
March 30, 1945

With the conquest of the area, men were resting up and trying to put aside their months of battle fatigue. Barton, too, was able to rest. He had an actual bed and a shower with hot water, got a haircut, and received new razor blades for a clean shave. The dowdy, smelly, torn uniforms were replaced with fresh ones, and he was issued a new pair of boots. The boots, though, felt loose in the wrong places, and Barton soon had blisters, but at least they were dry and did not smell like a moldering gymnasium!

He now wore double socks to help his feet and comfortably strutted down the street with a group of his men toward a tavern. Barton had been thinking about what Captain Lawrence had said to him about doing only for himself and not acting like a friend toward his men. So today, he was a chum with his men, offering them their first drink. He enjoyed the camaraderie and light jesting with the men, feeling a part of something again rather than a lonely Sergeant Barre.

They each drank several steins of heady German beer, ate rich sausages, hard-boiled eggs, and slabs of dense black bread, and felt like kings. Barton was unsure how much food the tavern had because they emptied the jar of eggs. The German people were poor, too, after a prolonged war, with no jobs or money. The American men wanted entertainment, but the people who owned the tavern were withdrawn and suspicious and offered nothing. A few men got up and sang some rowdy songs. Barton just clapped in time, not knowing the words. He laughed at their jokes and silly antics of leaping over the benches and chairs, dancing on the bar top, and trying to kiss the old proprietor's fat, homely wife. The men were drunk and foolish with vainglory, eager to squander their recent pay on earthly pleasures and wish for more.

Barton took a drink to toast his father, Richard, on his forty-fifth birthday, sending him good wishes across the air and missing him a little.

Soon, he had to calm the group when he observed Captain Lawrence and a few officers come in. They sat on the other side of the room and ordered bread, cheese, and wine. Barton felt contempt for the man, and his wry humor soured. He rounded up the men's money and paid off the tavern owner. He offered the woman a few chocolate bars, which she vehemently refused because they were American. She did not want to be unpatriotic to her fatherland. Bart let it go.

He rousted his boisterous men out and down the street. They wobbled and sang loudly and off-key, happily drunken with new freedom and good beer until a singular gunshot echoed through the street. Everyone took cover. The men quickly sobered, and they quietly dispersed through the streets like wraiths in the night to return to their encampment. The fun was over.

The next day, Bart's company rolled out with the Twelfth Army Corps, and he was no longer under the command of Lefoy. However, there was a contingent infantry of the Brits following along and among some of the Ninth Army as they pressed forward into Germany's southern Ruhr region.

For the following weeks, each day was a battle for supremacy. Armed with powerful artillery and fresh tanks and with help from the Allies, Patton's directives kept them rolling deeper into enemy territory, striking terror at every point.

With Colonel Rice's advance recommendation and pleased by Bart's participation in Operation Wood Duck, Barton and a few handpicked men were soon part of Sergeant Kent's latest group—The BOOM Squad. With his previous experience, clever engineering skills, and now a demolition expert, Bart trained the men on making incendiaries, Molotov cocktails, trip-wire explosives, and running mine pits for enemy tanks and transports. Every town along their route was carefully observed and assessed, and traps were laid. The days that followed were harrowing but exciting for Barton. Yet, that dark shadow hovered like a pesky raven, keeping him ever more wary—afraid of the end.

With Berlin no longer the target, Leipzig was the new prize. The plan was to join up with the Soviet Army near the Elbe River and break the resistant German troops, with many of the Allied and US forces coming at them at once in a multidirectional assault.

◆ ◆

West of the Mulde River
Friday, April 13, 1945

Barton heard the pounding Allied Howitzers and defensive shrieking *Infanteriegeschütz* from miles away as they traveled, but now, up close, the screaming explosions and blinding fiery fury as the ground exploded near them was reality. The truck shuddered in the aftermath of the explosion of a nearby shell. Barton shifted the gears a little too quickly, grinding them with a complaint, and swerved away from the giant crater that suddenly gaped ahead. He gritted his teeth as another mortar hit nearby. He looked askance at his companion, a young West Point Lieutenant two weeks in fresh from the States, another ninety-day wonder. His face showed terror as his white-knuckled hands gripped the doorframe.

Bart shook his head, trying to clear his ears, which now rang from the constant barrage exploding near them. He couldn't stand any more of this; they were in direct fire. He wondered how they could continue ahead.

"Get somebody on the line and tell them we're in a shitload of trouble here!" Barton yelled to the young man.

Lieutenant Ethan Shaw bent to grab up the field radio and hit his helmet on the dash as the truck lurched. He glowered at Barton. "Hold it steady, will you?"

Barton glared back. "TS Shaw. Tell them to get us out of here!" he shouted again. He watched a bit as the fellow cranked up the radio but had to watch the road and the other trucks ahead and behind him. He was lost in grim thoughts, thinking that today might be his day to die, when he felt a tug on his jacket sleeve.

"What?"

The Lieutenant leaned nearer and hollered over the lumbering truck engine and the screaming artillery. "They know about it already."

"What are we to do then?" Barton asked. He didn't like the expression on the lieutenant's face.

"They said to stick it out. Help is coming!"

"Oh, hell." Barton looked ahead and peeked up at the sky. It was cloudy, and there were no airplanes in sight for any aerial support.

"This is like Tennyson's poem," Shaw stated loudly as he lit two cigarettes.

"What are you talking about?" Barton slowed and veered away as the trucks ahead skirted a burning transport truck. "Poor fools," Barton commented as they passed the blazing truck with burned and dead men scattered about.

The lieutenant passed Bart a lit cigarette. "Here, Sergeant. Remember the poem about the 'Charge of the Light Brigade'?" He flashed a bucktoothed smile at Bart. "And into the valley of death rode the three hundred …" He pitched his voice to sound like a theatrical baritone orator.

Bart glowered at Shaw as he took the cigarette. "That was six hundred, and they all died. And we are hardly charging along here."

He wished for a moment that he was on horseback with rifle and lance, and he would ride the other way about now! Not to be a coward, but there was no surviving the Infanteriegeschütz mortars and long-distance guns when they were aiming them at you! He stuck the cig between his lips and grimly tightened his grip on the steering wheel.

"… cannon to the right of them, cannon to the left of them, cannon in front of them, volley'd and thunder'd." The lieutenant rambled through the poem.

Bart's mind switched gears. In the months since his problem with the death of Corporal Rossini and his recent BOOM Squad antics, he had flirted with the idea that maybe he should read his Bible more often. He had read a little last night before their convoy deployed in the wee hours. Perhaps it was not relevant to the day, but a few lines from Jeremiah kept threading through his head as if an omen.

"The terror you inspire and the pride of your heart have deceived you, you who live in the clefts of the rocks, who occupy the heights of the hill. Though you build your nest as high as the eagle's, from there, I will bring you down," declares the Lord.

Barton had read little more in the book of Jeremiah last night before sleep claimed him. He awoke in the early hours and had risen with the rest of the camp to move out. Now, thinking of the verse, he hoped that the 'you' and the 'eagles' were the enemy and that they were going to have the vengeance of the Lord upon them for this!

He cursed loudly, braking suddenly as an explosion just to the right of his truck hit the back end of the transport ahead. Suddenly, there were men on the road ahead of them … actually flying out and landing on the road. The truck moving ahead was in flames, and Barton's fast maneuver in the blinding flash took his vehicle off the opposite side of the road and nearly overturned them.

He was deaf! He was blind! Barton felt as if his lungs were filled with pepper. With his eyes streaming with tears, he elbowed his way out of the cab of the truck and fell heavily to the ground. Blindly, he then quickly crawled away and rolled down into the muck of the ditch alongside the road. He lay panting for a long moment before his vision began to clear. Through the watery waves, he saw his own supply truck engulfed in flames, the canvas cover on fire like a funeral pyre. The lieutenant hung limply from the truck window. Barton climbed back up to his feet. He wobbled a bit as he approached his truck, and from a short distance away, he noted that the cab and windows were blown out. He also saw the lieutenant was clearly dead; blood streamed from a ragged hole in his helmet—shrapnel had gotten him.

Other trucks in the line were burning, and people were yelling. Men raced about, with some taking shelter along the ditches as fiery hell continued to rain down upon them. They were sitting ducks out here! Barton, without knowing why, made the sign of the cross, wishing he still wore a crucifix. He rashly hoped his phoenix medallion would help. He staggered away along the ditch.

Barton knew he could not get to the field radio in the inferno of his truck, and still blinking away watering eyes, he made his way back along the line of stopped trucks. He spied men taking cover in the ditch; there were only open fields and no places to hide. They waved him in, and Barton saw they had a radio. He dove in alongside them.

"Staff Sergeant Barre!" he yelped, saluting briefly as he sat upright in the ditch. The Brit had more stripes than he wore. "My truck and Lieutenant Shaw are gone. Have you been able to reach Command?" Barton yelled over the exploding barrages nearby.

The shelling continued, and amid the din and roar of the explosions near them, they hollered at each other. "Yes. They know about this. The First Division is trying to maneuver away, maybe take some heat off us. We just have to hunker down here for the moment," the British Major hollered back.

Barton clapped his hands to his ears and bent low into the muddy bank as another shell screeched overhead, landing some thirty feet away and showering them with dirt. "Nice way to begin a day, isn't it?" he shouted at the officer, who lay only inches away.

"Right-o. I think I'd rather have lousy cold coffee than a shell up me bum!" He grinned back. "Damn Jerries—don't they ever sleep?" He glanced at his wristwatch. "The sun's just barely up." He scooted closer in the ditch to Barton. "What company are you with?"

Barton told him and saw the odd look on the man's face.

"You were involved in that Operation Wood Duck thing with Dunston?" He ogled Bart.

"Yeah ... biggest mistake of my life."

"That's not what I heard. You got bollocks." The Brit buffed Bart's shoulder with a gentle fist. "Good one, that."

Barton felt his mood sour further. Operation Wood Duck's fiasco still bit him hard. He lost the camp and far too many men—twenty-seven deaths were, to him, a blatant failure. But somehow, others thought the operation was more than that. Barton was going to holler a retort back at the Brit when he heard a different explosion coming from their side toward the river.

"Hey, there they go—that's what I want to hear." The major yelled down to his men cowering in the ditch. He glanced back at Barton. "Your trusty cavalry is coming." He grinned but ducked again as earth and rocks showered them from another nearby hit.

They lay for nearly a half hour under fire, and then silence reigned. The field radio squawked, and the officer grabbed it up. His mud-streaked face bore a smile, and he winked at Barton. "We have a corridor cleared ahead. We can go." He smiled as he relayed the message. He waved an arm and clambered up out of the ditch. "Move it out, lads; pack it in. We are a *go!* Hup! Hup!" he shouted.

Up and down the line of the convoy, a little cheer went up. Men scrambled to pick up their wounded and the dead where they could. They searched through the rubble for any supplies still intact, and then they clambered back into the remaining trucks. Barton, after thanking the major for the support, trotted ahead toward the trucks in his company. He was grateful there were some left. The men were glad to see him, and he grabbed a front seat in the second truck in the line.

"I'm letting you drive for a while. I've been driving for four hours straight, and the last hour was under fire," Bart jabbered to the driver. He felt relief to know that some of his company remained. They had been closer to the front of the convoy today, and he'd lost probably ten trucks, not to mention the troops and supplies with them.

He shook off the adrenaline rush, feeling his nerves and muscles now ache and burn with sleep waiting to claim him. He closed his eyes for a while as they drove; he could feel the direction of the convoy changing as the eastern rising sun no longer was in his eyes. Soon, they entered a wooded area with a rough road bordering a river, and he felt them stop.

Barton sat up and rubbed his face, wondering where they were. "Are we stopped?" he asked the Private driving the truck.

"Yeah, there's a roadblock ahead." The man suddenly sneezed and fished in his pocket.

"Is it theirs or ours?" Barton asked as he peered around the leading truck ahead of them.

"I think ours. We got off the main road an hour ago." The PFC blew his nose loudly out the window and wiped it on his jacket sleeve.

"Thanks for the ride. I think I'll take a walk up and see what's happening." Barton jumped down from the cab. He still felt achy from the long night and the accident as he strode along the parked trucks. A few men leaned out and waved or greeted him, asking for information; he waved back.

He felt a chill in his bones, for the air was cool and dewy in the spring morning along the shady wooded road. He would love some hot coffee. Arriving at the front of the line, Barton found a roadblock and a gang of men about it. They were a mixed group of Brits, a couple of French officers, and a few American officers. He sauntered up, wondering about the plan.

Feeling someone near him, Barton turned to smile and greet the man, but seeing that Captain Lawrence stood at his elbow, his smile faded. Lawrence coolly nodded at him in acknowledgment. Barton turned back to hear what was going on.

The bridge on the main road was out. The Germans had blown it up that morning. The diverted supply trains were now going across the countryside to join up with a division from the First to cross over the Elbe and then come around into Leipzig from the north. Barton listened for a while as logistics and a map were explained. Then the commander—Barton did not get his name—announced that they would take the next two hours for a meal break. It was just rationed stuff, but he felt the men needed it before they crossed over the river. They might have another big fight ahead of them.

Barton nodded as the commander dismissed them all. He turned on his heel and started to return to his company, but then he heard his name. Lawrence! He stopped, even though he did not want to, and waited for the man to catch up with him.

"So we meet again, Staff Sergeant Barre." The man sounded cordial. "I am glad to see you alive after the routing we had this morning." He plucked at Bart's filthy uniform. "A bit singed around the edges there, aren't you?"

"Me too … I mean … to see you in one piece." Barton sounded sullen. "So what wild operation are you on this time, Captain?"

Lawrence laughed. He rubbed an ear and squared his shoulders. "Oh, I am just a soldier today like everyone else. If we make it into Leipzig alive, I wanted to ask you to dinner."

"Dinner?!" Barton snorted. "I don't think so. I think Colonel Darnel has better things for me to do." Bart tried to be brisk in his answer and walk away, but Lawrence put out a hand to detain him.

"Look here, Barre. I am trying to mend bridges with you," he sighed, sounding a little wounded.

"Why?" Barton looked almost eye to eye with the captain.

"I know the last time we were together, some bad things happened. I guess I wanted to prove to you that I am not a bad sort of fellow. My mates and I thought we'd meet for dinner tonight. I wanted to include you."

Barton felt suspicious all of a sudden, and his eyes narrowed. "Trying to recruit me for another one of your bloody blunders?"

"Ha! No … just dinner." The captain ducked his head, his cheeks pink. "*Touché*, I think." He coughed and smiled back at Barton. "Whether we get to Leipzig or not tonight, come round to the Sixth. We have a little celebration planned."

"For whom?" Barton asked, now curious.

Lawrence looked around and then back at Barton. "Keep it on the QT, but today is my twenty-eighth birthday, and my friends and I are celebrating … if we can. Some of the men are doubtful since it is an unlucky day."

Barton squinted up at him. "How is the day unlucky? Oh, you mean what happened this morning?"

Lawrence rubbed his chin. "Ah, not exactly that. It is Friday the thirteenth. Most folks would rather stay in bed than venture out." He chuckled lightly and patted Barton's arm. "Maybe we should have all stayed in bed."

Barton eyed the captain dolefully, not catching the joke. "I see. Well, maybe if I am not previously engaged, as in running for cover or shooting at someone—"

The captain pounded Bart on the shoulder. "Good. See you around seven."

"Right." Barton spun on his heel and directed his attention now toward his men.

◆ ◆

After a hastily put-together lunch of freshly traded K-rations, Barton felt somewhat better. His stomach was full, and they had been safe for the past few hours. He walked patrol with a few of his men and took a quick inventory of what was left of his company. He worked with his men, but all the while wondered about the invitation to dinner with the captain that night.

He could almost like and admire Captain Lawrence. He was a nice-looking fellow with a charming smile and an easy way about him. But there was something darker that hovered about the man as if a shadow. Bad luck! It was no wonder—the man had a birthday on Friday the thirteenth!

Bart had never wanted to believe in bad luck. His father had always believed in good luck and felt that people made much of their own luck by their choices. Barton had often wondered, though, how much of his time in the service thus far had been his fortune. Or perhaps Providence or God was looking out for him. Or maybe it was that Barre legacy and charm that kept him alive.

Barton pridefully owned a sense of heroism and tried to be a stalwart soldier and worker, following orders, if only to keep out of trouble. But if someone gave him a crappy order, he hated it. At times, Barton had given officers a ration of his opinions, but so far, maybe he had been lucky that the officers had either agreed with Barton or remanded the stupid order, so nobody would look the fool for giving a crappy order. He felt superior to his inexperienced team, many of whom were just out of high school. Barton, though not that much older than many of his comrades, had always felt there was more to offer them. Yet, he rarely did offer them anything other than what he told them to do, and that was based upon orders from a higher command. Barton mostly felt as if all the men were nothing more than a bunch of trained dogs.

He knew that Captain Lawrence had hit him squarely in the gut when they had argued that fateful day in the forest. Bart only wanted others to think he was better than he was; he worked hard to show that hardened façade. But at night, when alone, Barton felt the fear and loneliness like a cancer eating away at him. By day, he was tough and tried to not let things get to him or around him or through him. Bart grinned at that thought—he had survived the day so far while his company lieutenant and many of his men in their company bought it. Was it good luck? Barton did not know. He engaged himself in duty, shaking off the pervasive dark thoughts, and soon, they were on the road again, trundling along the wooded track.

He felt the passing breeze tickle the longer hairs on his neck and whistle in his ears as they traversed like rumbling oversized beetles across the landscape. They passed destroyed farms where horses and cattle lay bloated in the spring sun when they should have been enjoying the bounty of the lush grasses. Barton felt the melancholy drip over him again like dirty oil; it coiled about his heart. Despite the men about him and an army of thousands behind him, he felt alone in his misery.

◆ ◆

That night, they camped beside the Elbe River, and Barton excused himself from his men to wade through knee-high verdant fields toward the Allied camp. He could smell food and coffee. The amber illuminated tents in the British camp ahead were a welcome sight. Laughter and cheering, rowdy men's voices caught his attention as he headed for the officer's mess.

Captain Lawrence, the center of attention, saw Barton peek into the tent, and he waved to him. "Men, here is my friend, little Sergeant Barre!" he shouted.

An unruly cheer went up, and a few men rushed to the doorway, pulling Barton in. He felt like a new kid at school, unsure of what to expect: bullying, teasing, or flattery and interest. He also didn't care for the diminutive remark. He sat at a table near the captain while a couple of men passed down a glass of beer and some bread. Another familiar face appeared on the opposite side of the table—Sergeant Major Dunston! Barton greeted him with a warm smile and tapped glasses with him. "Hey! Montie!"

"Good to see you, mate' glad you could make it." Montie laughed as someone in good fun draped a cloth napkin over his head. He pulled it off and winked at Barton. "Bunch of drunken sods, eh?"

"I am surprised. It isn't even dinner yet," Barton commented and sipped his beer. He licked the thick foam from his upper lip. "This is German beer?" he queried and took another taste.

"Yup, fresh from the brewery."

"Brewery? Where?"

"Oh, found one on a raid. We've been cutting loose a bit here and there, makin' friends with the sheilas and blowin' a few doors off. Pinched a few kegs to make the blokes happy."

"Sheilas? You mean German ladies?"

"A few." Dunston chortled and winked again. "I've been there and back again and around the bend, like to feel dizzy most days."

"Are you still with Lefoy?" Barton queried, wondering if he was treading on the man's toes.

"Nah, that operation is over; however, I rambled a bit with the Sixth coming in. A bunch of us headed down to Austria for a month. Hey, I heard you had some fun too … blowing up the Jerries' Panzers."

Barton was surprised Montie knew about the new demolition squad. Before he could respond, Montie's interest changed as he watched the antics of giant men hand wrestling.

"Two bobs on Hatcher!" Dunston yelled across the tent.

A large-set man hollered back, "Yer arse! Hatcher is nae but a wee babe! Our man is Donegal! Donnie! Donnie!" He caught the group up in a chant as the two men, Donegal and Hatcher, sweated it out. Hatcher won, and the large man, Captain Athol "Buster" Breen, grumpily slapped down money in front of Dunston's nose.

"Yer lucky this time, mate!" he growled and ambled away toward the wooden keg of beer. "Beer to the loser—we must fatten ye up, yer but a wee bairnie!" He beckoned the brawny loser with arms the size of small hams to the keg.

Barton chuckled, still feeling reserved among strangers. He smiled at Dunston. "You are a lucky man if you have survived all that you have. We had a tough day today. Somehow, the Krauts knew we were coming and exactly where we were. They wiped out a bunch of us today."

"Yeah, mate, I am sorry about that. But if it makes you feel any better, my mates and I took a chunk out of their front line this afternoon." The sergeant grinned back over his beer mug.

"Well, that's good." Bart finished his beer in a long slurp and ate a chunk of heavy bread, enjoying the yeasty, salty taste with the last of the beer. "It makes me wonder if those Krauts are sitting around a beer right now, too, and saying the same of us and how many we sent off to Valhalla or they sent to hell!"

Dunston pointed a thumb at his chest. "Ha! Me—I am lucky to be here to tell you about it, young Barre. I almost bought the flower farm meself. Big Buster Breen dragged my sorry carcass out." He yelled now across the tent, "Hiyo! Breen! A toast to the man of the day!" He held up his cup in a toast.

Breen laughed and waved down the applause. He poured out another cup of beer. Smiling into it, he murmured with good humor, "Arseholes like you make doin' me job a picnic."

"So what happened?" Barton asked, now curious. The man before him looked fine, uninjured.

"Ah, I won't tell ye. Let's just keep the night for celebrations." Montie held his cup up again. "Mates, let's have a round for the birthday man. Cheers!" he yelled and got up to toast his friend Captain Lawrence.

Lawrence blushed, although amid cheers and wishes of good luck and a rowdy rendition of "For He's a Jolly Good Fellow," he came over to the table where Dunston and Barton sat.

Lawrence pulled up a stool near Barton. "I am glad that you came tonight. Thanks." He sighed as he settled down.

"Sure. If I had known you were serving beer, I'd have said yes a heck of a lot sooner!" Barton raised his glass and tapped it against the captain's metal cup.

"Oh, so you are a beer man then? A bit of ale?"

"Guinness."

"Ah, see … I knew I liked you." Lawrence confirmed with a nod and a chuckle, "Although you did seem rather dismal after losing your precious cognac to the Nazi blighters."

Barton shrugged with indifference. "Guinness, cognac, whatever gets you over the hump and helps to forget this place." He laughed with the men.

Dunston turned his head again to Bart. "So, old man, what did you do before the war, eh?"

Bart sipped his beer and set it aside. "I had just finished college and was looking to get a job,"

"Oh? A working bloke, eh? Not like our bonny friend here." Dunston winked and patted Lawrence.

Lawrence frowned slightly and then asked evenly, "So what type of work are you interested in, Barton?"

"I have a mechanical engineering degree. I was thinking of using it toward … um, maybe the oil industry or something like it. I have some designs I want to patent …"

Dunston caught on. "Oh, so you are an inventor then?"

Lawrence asked instead, "Oil, you say? That is quite interesting."

"So he says. He's never seen the broadside of an oil well outside of what he puts in his sexy little sports car." Dunston thumbed a derogatory jerk at his friend and laughed roughly.

Lawrence looked nearly haughty at his friend. "Everyone has to start somewhere. Well, now, how about another drink there, Barton?" Lawrence smiled anew, ending the conversation and motioning for Barton's empty glass.

"I shouldn't." Barton had sobered. "But thanks for inviting me. I think I needed a bit of cheering. My company lost quite a few men today."

Dunston patted Barton hard on the shoulder. "Say no more." He stood to make an announcement. "Men, there's something we should be doing tonight … Let's 'ave a moment of quiet for our lost mates and then cheer them on to a good place, shall we?"

"Hear! Hear!" The men sobered, and bowing their heads, they stood still in respectful silence. Then, a lone voice sang the first verse of "Amazing Grace," and everyone joined in.

Barton hummed and mumbled the aged familiar words, thinking it odd that it was one of Richard's favorite gospel hymns. He felt his heart beat hard. Some of the men he had not known well; they had been some of the newer replacements, but their deaths bit him, as did the lost lives of Corporal Swanson, Tech Private Leonard, Tech Corporal Fine, Private Emery, and Lieutenant Shaw. Three had been with him since before the beginning of the Operation Wood Duck fiasco. Barton, at that moment, also recalled some of the other men he knew who had died months before, including his childhood friends, Garrett and Louis Guillot, and was damned proud he was still alive.

He sucked back a sob and ran a hand under his nose to catch a drip. He felt someone put an arm around his shoulder, and he wanted to cry more. He cried not just for losing his men, but he felt, perhaps, that he cried for losing himself—the carefree Barton Barre he used to know. He was an adult now—these were not kid's games with pop pistols and dirt-clod grenades. The war was real.

These men meant something to him. He glanced to see others sniffling and wiping their eyes as they spoke the names of the dead and sang the old hymn. These soldiers were tough, hardened, and brave, but they took this moment to remember their fallen comrades fondly. The song ended on a weak, sour note, as many of the men were almost choking in tears. A few blew their noses and wiped their faces on kerchiefs or sleeves.

Then Captain Breen held up his cup and led them in a rousing song of "God Save the King," all to get them back in the mood again. Barton moved away and refilled his glass with beer. He returned to the captain's table. "So, did you invite me for dinner or a beer bust?" he asked, laughing over the glass.

"Oh, yes, dinner." Lawrence roused from his melancholy moment and called across the tent, "McFee! Serve up the dinner you made for us, will you?"

A thin, angular fellow snapped to attention and dashed away but returned soon with another orderly; they set up a serving table and asked the men to line up. Barton followed Dunston to the ragged line of boisterous, inebriated men, and although he did not know what to expect, he was pleasantly surprised by trays of fresh steamed trout. He accepted a fat little speckled trout along with some boiled potatoes and turnips and then grabbed up a dish of cake studded with raisins. Happily, he set to eating the feast at a table with a cluster of men. Lawrence and Dunston flanked him on each side, and Barton soon felt part of the entourage.

"This is a delicious surprise. Where did you get the trout?" Bart asked between bites.

Lawrence laughed. "We have been camped by a stream all this afternoon and evening; some of our boys are having a feast, too. Delicious things ..." Forking a delicate white flake of fish into his mouth, Lawrence chewed with relish. He opened his eyes and smiled at Dunston. "Reminds me of the bream we used to catch as children."

"Oh, yes. Mum used to cook them nice and tasty."

"So you grew up together?" Barton asked as he picked out a needlelike piece of bone and sucked off the tender flesh.

"Oh, we had some rough-and-tumble times as boys," Lawrence stated as he sipped his beer and patted Dunston's dusty shoulder.

Now curious, Barton witnessed the silent knowledge that was shared between the men and suddenly felt envious. He had no one to talk to about his childhood, at least no one who knew him then. He talked about fishing on the plantation.

"Oh, I hear in Louisiana you can catch crocodiles. We got 'em back home." Dunston chuckled as he sucked his fingers.

"Not crocodiles—alligators. There's a difference." Barton corrected him.

"Oh, these alley-gators, are they just as nasty-tempered as crocs?" Dunston licked his fork and looked at his nearly empty plate; he speared the last chunk of turnip and dredged it through the fishy sauce on the plate. The fish skin and bones were piled on his napkin, which he obviously had no intention of using.

Barton wiped his lips with his napkin, hoping that Dunston would take the cue. "Yes. Although I never had much run-in with them—snakes, though, I've met a few of those nasty creatures. Don't ever let a rattler or water moccasin see you. They'll actually chase you!"

Lawrence shuddered. "Oh, all this talk of reptiles makes me ill. Here, Humpty, take the rest of my fish. I am full." He shoved his plate toward the sergeant major.

Dunston dumped the remaining chunk of fish on his own metal plate. "No use in wasting good fish. Me lovely mum always said—"

Captain Lawrence rolled his eyes in mock boredom. "There he goes on about his mum—you would think she was the Queen Mother."

"Hey! Me mum is a good woman!" Dunston retorted amid a mouthful of fish.

"She is to put up with the likes of you." Lawrence patted the sergeant on the head, again with affection. "Just for that, I get your treacle pudding." He grabbed up the saucer of what Barton thought was cake.

Barton ate a bite of the dessert and decided it was a cross between bread pudding and cake, a little dry with currants, raisins, and sticky, dark, bitter caramel threaded throughout. He ate it with gusto, anyway. It was better than tinned peaches and canned chicken soup, which his men were eating tonight.

"So, do either of you know what is ahead for tomorrow? Are we all going to take Leipzig or what?" Barton asked.

"I don't think so. *We* are coming around the other side. The Twelfth and the First are going to try to cross into Leipzig ahead of us. We might not see each other for a couple of days after tonight." Captain Lawrence confirmed the plan. He sounded a little morose. Looking at his fingernails, he said, "That is why I asked you to come tonight, Barton Barre. Just in case we don't make it. I wanted to say thank you."

Barton's brows rose. "For what? I haven't done anything."

"You have been a decent fellow to have in a pinch. You are a good soldier, and I am touched that you do share our empathy with our fallen friends."

Barton felt the sling like a gut punch. He laid his fork down and wiped his face and then resolutely scooted back his stool and stood. "Of course I do. I have to write some letters tonight to their families and tell them they died. I should go."

Lawrence nodded. "I understand. Still, thank you, and I do hope that we can meet again."

"You blokes," Dunston shook his shaggy head, still looking like a stubborn bulldog, "why not trade addresses and be pen pals, Nathan? Gor! I need something wet." He staggered away like a leaning stork.

Barton wanted to laugh at the ungainly and slightly drunken man. He looked back at the captain, caught now by the name.

"I am not sure that I have been entirely kind to you, but thanks for your thoughts and for the invitation tonight. Dinner was great, and so was the company." Bart offered his hand. "I better go. Good luck to you, Nathan Lawrence." He boldly tossed the name out to see the man's reaction and shook hands with the captain. He felt a little wave of kindness as the captain smiled at him. "Keep God on your right side and the devil at your backside, and I'll meet you on the high side," Barton quipped, amused by his offbeat blessing.

The captain nodded and laughed softly. "I shall do just that. I'll be in Loch Lomond before ye …" he sang the end of the refrain.

"Huh?" Barton did not know the song but said, "Happy birthday, Captain Nathan Lawrence." Then, dismissing himself, he waved to the others as he left the tent. Some yelling, "Keep calm and carry on!"

Barton laughed at the stodgy British slogan, meant to be an inspiration, and stepped out into the night headed back to his division camp.

Bart felt a bittersweet pang when leaving the captain's party. He had met some friendly people; they were good men, and if this wasn't a war, he felt sure he could make them his friends. Dunston was an irascible but doggedly wry man and seemed stolidly a friend. Barton had a rare few loyal friends like Dunston because he usually outgrew people either by need or interests.

The captain was another matter. He seemed to have a heart and a genuine feeling for Barton. It was Lawrence who'd held him while they sang and wept. Bart was unused to such feelings of empathy, mainly directed at him. He had almost shrugged off the touch, but at that moment, he had witnessed many of the other men with arms about each other or holding hands and had decided it was all right for the moment. He had never cared for demonstrative affection; even his family used to embarrass him. But tonight, Bart felt it was different; they were men at odds with the world, and together, they were of a like mind and feelings. The image of Harlan and his boys flashed in Bart's mind, and he almost rejected the demonstrative attentions of the Brits. It wasn't the same thing. These were friends, not lovers.

Barton slept well for the first time in a few weeks, and the next morning, he rose early, ready to do the work of the day—conquer Leipzig.

◆ ◆

Monday, April 16, 1945

Damn! The lead truck was broken down! Now the trucks in the convoy were trying to go around it on the narrow lane leading through the wooded area and getting stuck. But regardless of the breakdown and the true chaos of the moment, as men scrambled about to move the truck off the road and get it going again, the enemy decided it was an opportune moment for a surprise barrage from above.

Men ducked and took cover in the trees and around the trucks, yet Barton felt as though he were again a tin duck in a shooting arcade as he watched men go down around him. Trees exploded into sawdust and matchstick kindling; men turned into unrecognizable bits of mush. Barton slithered out of the stopped vehicle, arming himself with as much as he could carry and yelling to his new corporal aide, Milt Sheldon as they joined others in the roadside trees.

Captain Lawrence skidded to a stop beside Barton, his breathing labored from running in the chilly morning, his words steamy exhalations. "The road ahead is blocked," he announced. "They've got a Panzer sitting like Cerberus at the gates of hell. We cannot go that way."

He grabbed out a ragged cloth map from his pocket. "Command said we should try for this route. We need about a dozen trucks full of munitions, supplies, and men to get over here." He stabbed the map with a dirty finger. "Once there, we'll set up a little rendezvous point. Then over here"—his finger slid a bit across the map to a squiggle showing a creek—"with part of the Third, they should draw their fire away from this road. Colonel Darnell suggested you and your demo squad should do a little reconnaissance and light up a few interesting spots. Maybe we can get that watchdog to move along with a more tempting bone."

Bart winced as they heard another explosion, this time followed by the return ragged chatter of Thompsons and the Brits' M2s. "Oh hell, this is another damn ploy, huh? Playing decoys again, are we?"

Captain Lawrence eyed him with a smirk and a twinkle in his blue eyes. "Not quite, but we are only sitting ducks here, just biding our time until the Grim Reaper takes us all one by one." He put a hand on Bart's shoulder. "Come on. Chin up, Sergeant. Let's get these lads on the move! We have some work to do today, and I, for one, plan to live out the day!" He scampered away through the underbrush like an eager bird dog in a field.

With grim duty, Barton rallied his men, shouting orders as they set up to deploy on another road, this time cross-country, with a new attack and diversion plan in mind.

◆ ◆

Tramping through the woods and then into green farm fields, the men noted several homes and outbuildings, some engulfed in flames. A detachment was made to check for the enemy and survivors. Some reported back that what appeared to be family members were shot or dead; even children, pets, and farm stock were slain.

Barton exclaimed, "How could the bastards kill their own people? Are they spies?"

One man fidgeted in a pocket and drew out a small object. "Sergeant? I found a packet of these in a man's hand." He passed it along to Barton and the captain.

Captain Lawrence observed the capsule with distaste. "Cyanide. We have been hearing reports for months now of officers and townspeople taking their own lives. Why, just a week ago, rumor has it that the Hitler Youth were passing these things out like candy at a symphonic concert. The Germans are not taking their defeat very well."

Muttered comments ranged about the circle of men until someone stated baldly, "They call it *selbstmord*—self-murder. People are doing it everywhere. It is the latest fad!"

"Mass hysteria is more like it," Barton grumbled.

Someone else laughed and made a joke. "Ha! Instead of dropping propaganda flyers on the enemy cities, maybe we should rain down instructions on how to commit suicide. Hey! We'll help them all with mass suicide by distributing cyanide instead of relief food! We would definitely win the war then!"

Laughter and groans rang about the group, but then the captain and newly arrived Sergeant Major Dunston, with new men and trucks, called the rally to a halt. Soon, they were on the road again.

◆ ◆

As Barton's company traversed across the countryside, there were many signs of advanced bombardments by the British RAF, and as they neared the outskirts of Leipzig, there was evidence of heavy damage to the city. Mounds of rubble lay along the roadways, and the streets were mostly empty, except for a few brave souls who were pillaging what was left or pulling corpses from the ruins. As the Allied soldiers approached, many people scurried away like rats; some shouted perhaps a warning, for within moments, Barton's company was fired upon. They all took cover, and some men retreated to come again from another direction.

The roar of artillery, the chatter of gunfire, and the rattle of tanks were distant echoes as Bart's men dashed through the haunted, empty streets and past bombed-out houses in the suburbs of the city. The US Third Army was giving the enemy a heavy pounding today as they made crucial advancements into Leipzig from several directions. Barton's company and the British company found their rendezvous point and set up a temporary depot in time for more troops and trucks to come limping in.

◆ ◆

April 17, 1945

Despite the coolness of the day, under the rising sun, a miasma of warm mist rose from the nearby creek to swirl eerily about their small encampment. Barton swiped his face, feeling damp and gritty from their long march and the demolition work of the past days. He peered through the glare of the watery sunlight, thinking he saw movement across the creek on the road. He retreated to report activity.

They were on the outskirts of Leipzig, and while this portion of the town mainly seemed deserted, about a half mile up, there was a stone bridge across the creek with a broken cobblestone street, which Barton assumed led to the heart of the city. There, it was reported that another watchdog sat waiting for them. Barton's men were anxious while waiting for further orders if they were to move ahead into the city, at least not until it had been cleared of the enemy. Surveillance troops had been dispatched into the burg, searching out survivors or stubborn enemy holdouts.

Yesterday morning's discovery of the suicidal family remained a grim reminder that the war was not all about the military factions. For Barton had seen so many horrors to date—people tortured for consorting with the enemy; rumors of prisoners of war being killed, abused, or denied basic human needs; the assorted reports and pictures of starved labor camp workers, including the abuse of citizens of the Reichland. He could not imagine how the cruelty of such a sort could continue. The Germans were pulling young children from school to be in the army. Teens were flying planes and fighting before they had hardly known a life. And now that the US and Allied troops were all converging on Hitler's homeland, rather than fighting, some of the local people were convinced to die by their own hands rather than taken as prisoners!

Perhaps Private Goode had it right—let the Jerries kill themselves, and there would be no one left standing to fight! Maybe then, all the evil would be gone from the world. Barton shook his head from the maudlin thoughts and headed off to organize the supply trucks.

◆ ◆

That afternoon, they were given the order to advance, and Barton and his little contingency of US and Allied troops made their way on foot into the broken suburb of Leipzig. As they neared the stone bridge, there was the clatter of heavy metal, and Barton made a sign for his men to disperse along the creek edge.

Suddenly, the screaming of a shell zoomed overhead. It took out the transport in a blossom of fire with debris raining down upon them. Everyone ran for cover, leaping into the ditches and behind piles of dirt, stone, and brick rubble.

Barton and Captain Lawrence, who had been leading their men, looked about with dismay. Hearing the roar of another mortar, they could only duck down in the mud. They lay for what seemed an eternity, yet it was probably only minutes as they listened to the barrage coming from above and around them. There were nearby shouts and moans of pain, and Barton knew they were in peril.

"I say let's get the hell out of here! Retreat!" he shouted at the captain, but the man only ducked his helmeted head into the muddy bank and let out a moan.

"Damn it! I lost Montie!" the officer wailed. "We are bloody well doomed now!"

Then, as if Nathan's voice had pinpointed them in the murk of the afternoon, a crater explosively opened up near them and sent the pair flying toward the creek bed.

◆ ◆

Formavit igitur Dominus Deus hominem de limo terræ, et inspiravit in faciem
ejus spiuraculum vitæ, et factus est homo in animam viventem.

The Lord God formed man of the slime of the earth, and breathed into
his face the breath of life, and man became a living soul.

◆ ◆

He lay for what seemed an eternity while the words of the Bible threaded through his confused mind. He tried to make sense of it. Yet it was probably only minutes he lay on the ground. He felt as if all his bones were broken. With the air sucked out of his lungs, he painfully fought for oxygen and opened his eyes. Bits of dirt and debris continued to rain down upon him. His fingers clutched the smoking dirt, and he was glad he could move and breathe again. He rolled as much as he could over onto his stomach to shelter himself from the fallout but then slid headfirst down into the creek bed.

After a few minutes of lying in the mud, Barton lifted his bare head, rubbing his ringing ears. He peered into the mist, not trusting any longer that he was safely hidden by it or by the reeds. He found his destroyed brain bucket and then slithered away to hide deep in the muck.

The Krauts were systematically shooting men as they walked along the embankment, and a sniper from a higher vantage point made sure his aim was deadly. Despite the ringing in his ears, Bart could hear Captain Lawrence calling for help, one hand up in the air waving like a flag. He was afraid that the Krauts would hear him, so he crawled to Lawrence, thinking that he might get him unstuck or whatever the man needed. Along the way, Barton traded jackets with a British Major lying nearby, for his coat was burned and shredded. Barton painfully felt the burns and lacerations on his body but knew he had to move as he snatched the man's helmet, for Barton's was ruined. Shivering with exhaustion and damp cold, he bent to the wounded captain, hoping to silence him.

Nathan's bloodied face swam before Barton's eyes. A huge gash across one cheek ran down his jaw and over his neck and shoulder, splaying the captain's flesh open to the bones. The man was spurting blood like a weak fountain alongside a large splintered blade of metal lodged in his lower neck and shoulder as if meant to behead him. Barton quickly thought to leave him behind. The terrified look in Nathan's blue eyes scared Barton to his very core. The man's words were more chilling and persuasive, and Barton found himself moved to act.

"Save me, Barton Barre," Lawrence whispered.

"I can't. I don't know what to do, Nathan!" Barton put a hand over the torn neck wounds and looked away, feeling squeamish as the blood seeped through his fingers. He knew if he pulled out the metal shard, he would most likely kill the captain immediately. Maybe that would be merciful.

"I thought you were a Boy Scout." Nathan smiled weakly amid bubbled blood flecking his lips, reddening his teeth and gums.

"No, I am n-not." Barton gagged, sickened by the gore.

"If you do not help me now and I live, I will hunt you down"—Nathan gritted amid the pain—"and kill you myself, Barre."

Barton sat back, shocked by the vicious words. He took out his handkerchief and a spare woolen sock from his singed pack and wrapped them against the man's neck, trying to stem the blood, but the impromptu bandage was soon soaked.

"I feel terrible," Nathan moaned.

"You are gonna die, Lawrence." Barton miserably shook his head. "I can't do anything. I gotta go … The Krauts are coming back this way." He glanced nervously away to look up the embankment, hoping he had time to get away and hide.

Barton gasped when bloodied hands grabbed him by the throat, and bloody spittle sprayed his face.

"No! Don't leave me! You help me now, or I will kill you. Get me to the bleeding medics now!" The man's hand slipped from Bart's neck to his sidearm. "Do it now, or I'll shoot you dead where you sit, and I don't care if I go to bloody hell with you for your death!"

"Why? You are a mess—just rest." Barton pulled away the man's hand, carelessly crushing Lawrence's fingers. He moved away, ready to leave.

"I cannot … I have important …" Lawrence groaned and gritted his teeth. "Just get me to the medics, damn you!"

With disgust, Barton grabbed an arm, swung the wounded man about in the mud, and dragged the captain as quickly as he could scoot, pulling him along the ditch. There was the stone bridge crossing the mud-filled old streambed. Despite the shelling, it was still intact, and he hoped to get there before anyone from above could see him. He stopped to breathe, hiding behind some dead brush and dry reeds. He cast a quick look at Lawrence, feeling his actions were futile.

"How're you doing?"

"Oh, just lovely. I'd like some tea and strumpets. Can you call room service?" Lawrence coughed painfully.

"You want crumpets or whores?" Barton smiled at the levity of the man who was below him, a bloodied mess. He wondered if the shock was perhaps making Nathan hallucinate and giddy.

Barton shifted, trying to ease the pain in his leg, wondering why it was hurting. His leg hadn't hurt so much before. He wiggled his foot and found it did not work so well. Willing his foot to move, he pulled his pant leg up out of his boot and gasped when he felt severe pain and the stiff, muddied fabric caught on his shin. He pulled the fabric up and then found a piece of shinbone lay like a broken shingle bulging under his skin; the skin was already reddened to a dull bruise, and a sharp piece of the bone protruded near his knee. He suddenly felt the pain, and Barton groaned with it. He never should have looked. He took out the other spare sock and clumsily tied it around his leg, thinking it might keep the bone from moving too much as he slid and crawled to safety.

He glanced at Lawrence, hoping he was out of misery by now. The man looked terrible. What was left of his face was pale and waxen. Yet he was still alive, a pulse beat steadily in his throat along with the oozing dark blood. The blood was no longer a spurting fountain; perhaps the captain was almost dead.

"I gotta see if the bridge ahead is safe. I'll be back," Barton whispered harshly in the man's ear.

"No, you won't. I know you are trying to dump me. I'd like to see thirty, please."

A hand grabbed Barton's arm, and he looked down at the man. "I will be back," he assured him. "I can't go very far; I've got a broken leg."

Captain Lawrence smiled weakly, his eyes closed as he murmured, "Oh, goodie for you. The lame are leading the half-dead." He squeezed Bart's arm and opened his eyes. They were bright blue and lucid as he gazed up at Barton. "I promise you with my very life that if you get us out of here, you will be rewarded. My family is rich."

Barton smiled now. "Rich, huh? Well, so is mine. They've got a plantation." He snorted a short laugh.

Lawrence opened his eyes wider. "No, mine are so wealthy that they pay people just to wipe their bums." His smile was tremulous, and he breathed hard, trying to endure the pain of his wounds.

"Well, I ain't gonna wipe your ass, Nathan." Barton chuckled. He almost laughed loudly but hunkered down now. "That rich, huh?" He wiped his runny nose on a sleeve. "So what will you give me if I help?" he whispered harshly.

Lawrence nodded and opened his eyes again. "Got you, didn't I? I will see that you have whatever you want. I can help you get a business started after this bloody war is over," he hissed softly.

"A business, huh? What if I just wanted money? How much is your life …" Barton began harshly but then stopped and looked about. "Someone's near the bridge. Sh!"

"Money isn't everything. You gotta earn it … B-Barre … bloody hell. I c-can't talk anymore …" The captain choked, and blood bubbled anew from his lips. "J-Just get us the hell out of here, Barre. That's an order!" he rasped.

Barton gave him a 'one-fingered' salute, and with a glance up and around to see the way was clear, he said, "Yes, sir!" Barton pulled the wounded man along beside him as he painfully crawled and slithered along the muddy ditch from bushes to bracken and through the dried cattails and reeds, wincing at their rattling noise.

They reached the stony ramparts of the diminutive bridge, and Barton heard trucks on the move from the road above, their engines laboring and gears whining in the distance. He couldn't say if the vehicles were American or German as he lay near Nathan with a hand over the man's mouth to shush him. The effort of moving him was painful for them both.

He could hear voices above, too. Barton rolled over the captain to hide under the bridge, leaving Lawrence in the open, theorizing that the sight of a bloodied man who looked dead was deterrent enough to keep the Krauts from searching along the ditch or under the bridge any further. After sweating for long moments and finally hearing no more noise from above, thinking himself safe, Barton slid down the bank and undid his pants to take a dump in the muddy creek.

After a temporary respite, Barton heard voices again, and then vehicles approached the nearby road and began to cross the bridge. He scooped up his pants, trying to fasten and belt them quickly, but then two 'stonelike objects' plopped in the muddy water near him. Shying from the wet splash, he then heard mortar fire and sheltered under the bridge, hoping it was safe cover.

Volcanic hell erupted from the water, and Barton hit the bridge buttress and then flew into the air. Feeling a body near him, he blindly grabbed it, only to roll down into the ditch. There was hardly a moment between the first explosion and the next two when he was peppered with fiery debris, and molten fire erupted about him. His skin was burning, and he painfully rolled in the soupy mud of the ditch to put it out. Then he caught sight of Lawrence a few feet away; the man's upper torso and arms were engulfed in flames, and he threw himself on the screaming Nathan.

Barton remembered nothing after that, only pain and a sense of loss as the world continued to explode about him. Abysmal darkness swallowed him whole. His last thought was, "I repent."

◆◆◆

CHAPTER 15

Unsung Heroes

Beaumont, Texas
Monday, April 30, 1945

Richard sighed impatiently as he listened to the doorbell and persistent knocking at the front door. He rose from his desk in the bedroom, wondering why no one else bothered to answer the door. Glancing in rooms along the way and finding them empty, Richard trotted down the stairs. He hurried along the hall, slipped on the rug, and bashed his way to the front door, grumpily answering, "Yeah, yeah …" as the doorbell rang again. He yanked open the door with a squeak. His mind noted now that his lower back hurt from tripping on the rug and the door hinges needed oil, but then the sight of a uniformed man on the front porch jerked his mind back to the moment. He switched on the porch light.

"Yes? What is it?" Richard demanded.

The man peered at a clipboard and asked in a dry-sounding voice, "Is this the R. Barry residence?"

Richard frowned at the mispronunciation of his name. "I am Richard Barre. What is this … another jury duty summons or some stupid community-watch survey? No, I have not seen any Japanese boats or subs on the river or anyone looking out of place!"

The man coughed lightly, removed his peaked hat, and tucked it under his arm. "Sir, I perhaps have news of your son, Barton Barre."

Richard back-stepped. "Barton … is … did-did something happen?" he choked out.

"Might I come in, sir? The news would be better in private rather than delivered on your front porch."

Richard held open the door and stepped aside for the man to enter. He noted now the dark green uniform. On the darkened porch, the man resembled a deputy. Now, he recognized the insignias and stripes of the US Army along with a black band on the man's coat sleeve.

"*Oh, merde!* I mean, what has happened?" He led the uniformed man into the living room, turning on a lamp. "Here, have a seat. Can I get you a drink?" Richard paced back to shut the front door. "Oh, I should get my wife … right?"

The man sat on the sofa with his briefcase in his lap, setting his peaked cap aside. He nodded. "It would probably be wise for her to hear this too."

Richard stood dumbly, tears crowding his eyes as his throat tightened, but then he bolted down the hallway and into the kitchen, bellowing, "Thérese! *Viens ici, maintenant!* Thérese!"

The sewing room door popped open, and Thérese looked out. "What, Richard?"

Then she spied the man in uniform on the sofa. He smirked and pointed a finger toward the hallway. She dashed out and suddenly crashed into Richard in the hallway. He grabbed her hard by the arms to steady them.

Gulping a heaving breath, Richard barely could get the words out. "I need you. S-S-Some … th-thing has happened to Bartie." He bent his head to hers. "Oh God, what if he is dead? I had that horrible dream."

Thérese now felt a chill overcome her. "Oh, Richard, is that who the man in the living room is? Is he … is he here to say …" She couldn't finish. She tugged him around. "*Allons-y,* let's be brave, *ma Coeur.*" She led him into the living room again. Richard sank into an armchair, and Thérese perched on the padded arm, still holding his arm.

"I am sorry, but I do not know your name, sir. I am Thérese Barre, and this is my husband, Richard," Thérese commented as she nervously arranged her dress skirts over her knees.

The man set his briefcase and clipboard on the sofa, stood, and reached to Thérese, hand outstretched. "Yes, um … thank you, ma'am. I am Lieutenant Ian Fletcher, and I have come with news of your son, Staff Sergeant Barton Barre." He gripped Thérese's hand gently. "You'll probably want to sit for this news, ma'am."

He eyed Richard, who remained sitting, looking grim and pale. His dark eyes were glassy. "I am sorry. You look shell-shocked already, sir. What I have to say is rather grim."

Fletcher nervously shrugged his shoulders, smoothed his woolen jacket down, and removed a packet from his attaché case. Opening an envelope, he began to speak.

"I shall read it for you first." He cleared his throat. "Dear Sir or Madame Barre." He glanced at the pair, noting they held each other tightly; Richard's hand was nearly white-knuckled as he gripped Thérese's fingers.

"This letter is to inform you of the possibility that Staff Sergeant Barton Barre, Service number …"

Richard's brain went fuzzy as he listened.

Barton was dead. The words swirled darkly in Richard's brain … Barton was missing in action but could be dead …

"How could he go missing? What did he do, just walk away?" Richard asked bleakly. Then, with a sickening laugh, he queried, "Are you saying he is AWOL?"

The lieutenant swallowed hard. "Uh, no, although he could be, but if you would let me finish this letter from his regiment commander here …"

Thérèse patted Richard. "Please don't make it worse. Just listen," she hissed in his ear in French and then smiled wanly. "Please finish, Lieutenant."

"Yes'm." Fletcher continued in a gravelly voice.

"If it is any consolation, SS Barre was last seen with the unit of a British officer and troops leading a convoy of US and Allied trucks and with men on foot on April 16, 1945, near the outskirts of Leipzig, Germany. It was rumored that they were to rendezvous with more of their regiment to take the city. No further information is available after this date.

"The resultant battles that week for the 2nd and 69th Infantry Divisions were victorious in the taking of the city of Leipzig. However, many souls were lost on all fronts in the heroic hand-to-hand battles that ensued. Finally, many of the city's citizens were overwhelmed and ultimately greeted our troops with white flags of truce, and the remaining German troops surrendered.

"This department is making every effort to find more information, but at this time, Staff Sergeant Barre has not returned or reported to his commanding regiment. Unfortunately, everyone in his unit and truck companies perished in the battle. If we find more facts regarding his whereabouts, we shall confirm or recant our findings.

"At this time, we are sorry for your loss and any confusion as a result of these war times since information with warring countries may be unreliable. The term "Missing in Action" only implies that this person has not reported to his commander. He has not been found dead or alive on the battlefield. He may also be a prisoner of war or lost. Often, such persons are recovered; however, it has been some time since this battle, and the War Department does not wish to imply that this case is closed. Thus, every effort will be made to recover your son.

"Congress has enacted legislation that enforces the service pay to continue to families and dependents during this time. Thank you for your patience in these matters and for the dutiful service of your—"

Richard held out his hand before the man was finished. "I want the letter, please."

"Of course." Fletcher passed both it and the envelope to Richard. "I am sorry, sir. I do hope your son is found."

"Alive, you mean?" Richard snapped as he studied the letter.

"Of course."

"What if he went AWOL or is lost and has amnesia?" Richard asked, sounding lost himself. "He could be lying wounded somewhere, and no one knows where he is. He doesn't speak a word of German! *Mon Dieu!*"

"Yes, sir. It often happens." The lieutenant gathered his cap and briefcase and then stood. "I am heartily sorry, sir and ma'am. If there is anything we can do …" He stood dumbly for a moment and then realizing no one seemed ready to escort him to the door, he finished. "I will take my leave now."

With that, the man left, his heart pinging to hear the Barres weeping. "Good Evening and Good Luck!" Fletcher called as he shut the front door, escaping into the chilly evening.

◆ ◆

A short while later, Thérese rose, blowing her nose and wiping her eyes. She noted they were alone now. "Richard, *chéri*, please, you need to stop all these tears. This letter does not say our son is dead, just missing. I want to be hopeful that he will be found." She took the crumpled letter from Richard's fist. "We must put this in God's hands now. We can do nothing else for Bartie except to pray."

Thérese folded the letter and put it in her smock apron pocket.

Richard dashed away the wetness from his ruddy cheeks. "*Je sais, mais …*"

"*Non, bébé,* you should only be strong now for him and us," she spoke softly in French. She hugged Richard again and then took his hand. "Come, let's get some tea and talk sensibly about this, my love."

"I knew Barton made a grave error in enlisting with those ill-fated Guillot boys— they are both dead. Now look at what has happened! How can this be possible?" With a heavy exhalation, Richard groaned as he rose from the low chair and rubbed his hip. "Where did that lieutenant go?" he asked, looking about in the hallway.

397

Shrugging away the question, Thérese linked her arm with Richard's. "Probably to another family to give them bad news. What a grave and terrible duty he performs to go to families with such news. It is positively macabre. He is like the Angel of Death."

"Ha! I feel like the angel has visited us." Richard held the swinging kitchen door for Thérese. He followed her in and then sank into his chair at the table.

"Oh dear, and we were so rude! We should have offered the poor fellow a drink or food," Thérese tsked with concern.

Richard looked wide-eyed and then slapped his hand on the table. "*Merde!* That is what I forgot! I offered him something and then just ran about like a crazed squirrel." He rubbed his face while he heard his wife giggle as she prepared their tea. "Don't laugh."

He slumped glumly in his chair. "And I would like to know just where you and the girls were that no one could answer the door? Why is it that I must run higgledy-piggledy from upstairs? I even tripped on the damn rug in the hallway. I hate that rug—get rid of it!"

Thérese shook her head and sighed. "Richard, you are just being an old grump. Isn't our news bad enough? Why must you cry foul on everyone?"

"Where are the girls, then?"

"Studying with their friends at Helen's house. Camellia and Sadie Beth have a term paper due next week, so the girls are together. I thought they might enjoy a little fun."

"Oh, but …" He accepted a plate of tea biscuits and then stated, "Well, call them home. This is important."

Thérese brought over the steaming teapot and their cups, setting them on the table. She kissed Richard's cheek and sat next to him. "Just let them alone for tonight. I think they need time with their friends right now. They will be distraught by our news."

"I don't care," Richard said mulishly and splashed the watery, weak tea in their cups.

Thérese blotted the wet spots on the tablecloth. "I do. I do not relish sitting up half the night with crying girls and answering the many unknowable questions I expect they will have. No, it is better to tell them tomorrow. Drink your tea, and then let's go to bed. The night is getting on, and nothing we would do or say will make anything better for Barton. We just must have hope and faith that God will save him." She patted her husband's hand and gripped it for a moment. "I believe things will be set right very soon."

Richard did not comment, but as he took a sip of tea, his eyes rose to the kitchen calendar. His heart leaped in his chest. "Oh crap, talk about bad timing. Bartie probably died short of his twenty-second birthday!" He gulped and felt fresh tears rise and burn like acid down his cheeks.

The photo on the calendar was a lovely garden scene; however, it was the advertisement that overloaded Richard's mind and heart—Magnolia Mortuary and Cemetery. There would be another Barre family member laid to rest there.

The La Barre family curse was again a valid omen, and Richard felt it strike deeply into his soul. "We are cursed!"

◆ ◆ ◆

AFTERWORD

As younger generations grow up to learn about war, it is perhaps disheartening for them to know that man, in general, is a warrior and often seeks conflict wherever it may be found. Humankind should remember the experiences and lessons learned in the past if it would keep us from war. World War II was a devastating time in our world history.

Sadly, the generations that survived the Great War in the early nineteen hundreds expected that there would be peace. And yet, hardly twenty years later, the same enemies were spoiling for a fight again—this time, with more significant consequences than before, costing millions of lives and ravaging the entire world, sending it into darkness and pain. Winston Churchill called those years from 1914 through 1944 'The Thirty Years' War.'

Many of the influential heroes and enemies had their start fighting in World War I. Benito Mussolini, Adolph Hitler, Joseph Stalin, and Japan's Hideki Tojo all rose to power to right the wrongs of World War I and ultimately break the Treaty of Versailles, for which they felt cheated.

After World War I, Germany was condemned to more than $200 billion in war debt for causing the war, which caused a great depression in Germany. It was during these sad and dissolute years that Adolf Hitler began his campaign to regain the honor and pride of Germany, secretly creating his private military and advanced war machines. Japan, which had allied with the United States in the previous war, was cheated out of payment for its support and lost promised territories. They soon became a new enemy. Mussolini was ready to bring about a new age of the Roman Empire. Stalin, with the help of Vladimir Lenin, fought to bring Communism to his Mother Russia and make them once again a great and powerful military. With these vengeful legendary leaders becoming an Axis of power, Hitler felt he could conquer the world using them all to his ultimate glory for his empire of the Third Reich.

This year, in particular, 2014, marked the seventieth anniversary of the greatest amphibious assault ever—D-Day. Also, at the time of this revised publication in 2024, it is the eightieth anniversary. For those millions who served on all fronts, some people still live and remember how it was during the most devastating war ever. They fought both on the home front in the country where they lived, and many were soldiers in a foreign land, but all were warriors for the cause of freedom.

For them, this book is but a glimpse of those experiences in how those we love on both fronts must endure, survive, and move forward through the pain of absences, war, hardship, and afflictions of the heart.

This book is not intended to be a treatise on war, nor in how we fight or survive, nor find glory or shameful defeat. But it is an honest telling of events with all the natural twists and turns of the plot and the characters bound up in real-time, with a bit of fiction thrown in. For some people, it may feel all too real. Sorry for any *cauchemars* (nightmares). The author apologizes for the slang and language used to malign the enemy, but these were the opinions of the times and were widely used among the populace.

Some events were fictionalized to tell the story. Yet, it should not deter us from the truths behind the devastating months that our character, Barton Barre, fought in Europe. Operation Wood Duck and the many participants, Brigadier General Greene, Colonel Rice, Colonel Lefoy, Sergeant-Major Dunston, and Captain Lawrence, was fiction, yet it is based upon truth, and it is only mentioned about Captain Railey and his Ghosts.

These creative men, many of whom were artists or craftsmen from the film industry, made up the Twenty-Third Headquarters of Special Troops under Captain Hilton Railey. They cobbled together many months of study, sound recordings, and surveillance photos and then artfully created grand deceptions, convincing the enemy that troops of immensity were advancing or encamped, often in unprotected areas. The British had made several such subterfuges in the early years of the war in Africa, hoping to gain any intelligence or advantage. Railey's Ghosts had inflatable tanks, unmanned vehicles, planes, and empty tents—anything to make a camp look real from the air or distance—yet it was all a decoy, such as General Patton organized and guarded in the days before D-Day.

Troop movements played over loudspeakers sounded as if thousands of men were on the move or engaged in battle. Unknown to the Germans and most of the American/Allied troops, there were many places set as decoy camps, often in unprotected pocket areas. The German intelligence fell prey to some of the deceptive tactics and advanced, thinking they had intercepted radio signals or heard the troops and hoped to be on the line waiting as they came over.

It was a successful defensive ploy and allowed thousands of Americans and Allies to cross over safely into Germany or move up the lines into position, with little to no conflict in the areas suddenly unprotected by the enemy. The Twenty-Third occasionally took some flak on their side as enemy shells pounded fake camps, camouflaged dummy tanks, and useless artillery. By the time the enemy arrived, the ghost camps were already gone, and the Germans' perceived victory was hollow and futile. The Ghost Army was a classified secret, and only in 1996 was part of this information brought to light.

It is interesting to note that the author initially wrote about Operation Wood Duck and decoy camps in 2009 without knowledge of the Ghost Army and prior to watching a documentary in 2014. Afterward, the author cleverly dropped in a few more hints as to the Ghost Army's types of deception to make it all seem real. Barton Barre's camp was a decoy near a bridgehead, with sound trucks playing for a few days, fake "spoof radio" conversations blasted the airwaves, and supplies that were unimportant stored to make the camp look like a real lodgment camp for advancing Allied and US troops. Poor S. SGT. Barton Barre was not up on the game but, unfortunately, lost when a German army unit actually found them. We witnessed the anger and disappointment of the Nazi officer, thinking he had found something helpful, perhaps secret weapons, and discovered it was only a decoy.

During the war, on every front, whether friend or foe, much was gained despite the tremendous losses of life. New systems and intelligence logistics were put in place, and technologies were invented; unfortunately, so were new ways to destroy and kill. But overall, the six years of the general war brought nearly every country of the world into the twentieth century through these advanced war technologies.

Today, we may look back on these modern marvels and methods and laugh at their contrived simplicity, yet for the time, they were genius and are the foundations of many of the technologies we use today in the military and our daily lives. For example, The Ghost Army's usage of decoys, recorded troop movements, and radio scripts became classic subterfuge. The metal recording reels were the forerunner of audio tape. The Enigma and Encryption machines were the concepts for supercomputers and secret military coding. The Navajo Wind Talkers, who created their own code based upon their ancient native language, which no one could break, were ingenious and soon widely respected in the Pacific theater.

The Red Ball Express, thought up by Allies using a platoon of Negro men pulled from various units and divisions, was resourceful. These brave men, along with the many quartermasters from US and Allied divisions, ran the trucks for eighty-two days, surviving the worst of the war while supplying the Allied troops and Lieutenant General Patton's war machine on all fronts. The incredible foresight and planning of the Express helped to build future logistics programs for the military and shipping.

Include then the fast and deadly fighters, mighty bombers, jet planes, and rockets; sonar, radar, and radio tech; U-boats and submarines, all of which created super advantages in both war and for later advanced technologies in transportation and safety.

As a society, generations later, we have much to be thankful for both on the technological front and the innovations in our daily lives. The world is indebted to these derived legends of war who took America and the world from outmoded ideals, decades of economic depression, and bitter, devastating war and transformed them into a new world, ready for freedom for all.

BOOM!

❖

ACKNOWLEDGMENTS

Thank you to the inspiration of the heroes we encounter, whether through daily circumstances, on the evening news, from historical reference, in books, or from other media and movies—these men and women are legends.

As in the dedication, this particular book is in part loyal to the stories of millions who endured the years of World War II on all fronts, each trying to find his or her way back to harmony and peace in their private Garden of Bliss amid the tumultuous days of the war.

We may fondly recall our personal legends of war: siblings, parents, or grandparents who fought in many ways during those terrible years. My parents, as youths, lived in America through those times. They knew economic hardship and, yet, experienced simple adolescent joys, while their friends and relatives who lived or fought in Europe suffered various woes and depredation, and some tragically died.

My dear friend Lily lived in France during the German Nazi occupation. As an impressionable teenager, she and her family lost much during the dark and dangerous days of the war. Afterward, she rarely spoke of the painful times (except for her hatred for dark-green or gray clothes—Nazi and German Army uniforms). Yet it was easy to guess from other historical evidence what she might have experienced. For her, those times of impoverishment, military tyranny, and wartime danger perhaps fueled her lifelong need for freedom, self-expression, justice, and an independent, creative existence. Lily was my silent muse for this book.

Thanks to another legend, WWII hero W.G. Johnson, a former Flying Tiger pilot in China. He offered suggestions and some anecdotes regarding military salutations, flying, and life on the Army Air bases.

Thank you to the many survivors who have told their stories about the war, sharing them in history books, movies, and on the internet.

Thank you to the publishers, advisors, and editors for their assistance. My readers can thank them for convincing me to divide Legends of War in half and make it affordable and more exciting. You will note the new book title, *The Road Home*—a mystery waits in the next book in this series.

Thank you to my friends and family, who are patient and attempt to understand my devoted and fragmented energies as I persevere to create this lasting La Barre Legacy series.

Grace á Dieu!

Books in the series by C. A. Portnellus

Sparrow Wars in the Garden of Bliss—A La Barre Family Saga

**Prelude to War: Book One*

**Legends of War: Book Two*

**The Road Home: Book Three*

**Things of the Earth: Book Four-Parts I & II*

Back to Earth: Book Five

Raw Earth's Secrets: Book Six

Garden of Bliss: Book Seven

The Days of Distant Thunder: Book Eight

Echoes of Thunder: Book Nine

Thunderstorm: Book Ten

Biting the Big Apple: Book Eleven

Sparrow Wars: Book Twelve

Alpha And Omega: Book Thirteen

*Denotes current published books available in paperbound and E-book formats.

*An Excerpt from The Road Home, Book Three in the Sparrow
Wars in the Garden of Bliss: A La Barre Family Saga*

◆◆◆

CHAPTER 1

Guardian Angels Keep Thee

The sound was deafening. Rolling thunder shook the very ground he stood upon and then collapsed, sending him flying. Clouds of smoke and debris shrouded him for a time, and then there he was as if the clouds parted and the very light of heaven shone upon him.

He was dead.

Screaming demons of war fought with the angels of peace for his soul, clawing and pulling at him.

*Formavit igitur Dominus Deus hominem de limo terræ, et inspiravit in faciem
ejus spiuraculum vitæ, et factus est homo in animam viventem.*

Suddenly, he breathed in life again.

The ebony-scaled demons cursed the light and Giver of Life and then slithered away to claim other souls.

◆◆

*"Blessed be the heroes who die in honorable duty for their country. Blessed be the heroes … St.
Adrian of Nicomedia, pray for their souls … St. George, pray for us in the hour of our need …*

Give us solace for our tears …"

"No! No! Barton!"

Elise rose, screaming. Tears streaked down her cheeks, heartrending sobs filled her throat, and she fell back upon her bed, clutching her pillow. All of a sudden, her bedroom door was thrown open. She screamed again. The light in the hallway revealed her father.

"Elise! What happened?"

"Oh, Daddy!" Elise began to rise from her bed, but Édouard swiftly came and sat on it. He hugged her close.

Édouard petted her head, smoothing back the sweat-damp bangs from her face, and then used his hankie, wiping her tears. "What is wrong? Are you ill?"

"Non. J'ai une cauchemar. Je suis stupide," she said brokenly.

"Is she all right?" Beatrice's worried voice asked from the door.

"I've got her. Just a bad dream is all, Maman. Go back to bed, *ma chérie.*"

"Where is Chérie?" Elise asked all of a sudden and then pulled away to look about the dark room, afraid again.

They heard a skittering noise, and the little poodle poked her tiny nose out from under the bed ruffle.

Beatrice chuckled. "Well, you frightened everyone, it seems." She scooped up the black teacup poodle, dropping her in Elise's arms. She tugged the coverlet and linens back in place. "What were you dreaming? Your bed is a mess. Were you fighting off dragons again?"

Elise let out a shattered sigh. "No … it is probably nothing."

Édouard kissed her brow and patted her cheek. "Dreams cannot hurt you. It is all silliness of the mind. You rest easy, little love. The angels will sing and kiss you to sleep." He glanced at her alarm clock. Smiling, he added, "The night is still young. It is not even two yet. *Dormir Bébé.*" He stood and pressed past Beatrice. "Let her sleep now. Come back to bed, love."

Beatrice hovered for a moment. "Are you sure you are fine now?"

Elise nodded and curled up with her pet. *"Oui Maman."*

Beatrice smiled and began to close the door. *"Fait un beau rêve, chacque temps."*

Elise heard the words but felt they were odd and like déjà vu. Yes, she needed to make a beautiful dream this time. Elise lay for a moment, trying to still her heart and slow her mind to sleep again. She could still see him … lying in the mud, the mist curling about his singed body.

She wondered at the Latin verse and scrambled out of bed to retrieve her Bible. Switching on the lamp, she quickly wrote the words on paper. She felt she might never forget them; they were ingrained in her heart and mind. She translated the words and then found them in Genesis 2:7, when God the Creator breathed life into Adam.

"The Lord God formed man of the slime of the earth, and breathed into his face the breath of life, and man became a living soul." She read aloud, then sniffled tearfully. "Oh God, please don't let him be dead." She turned off the light and lay again in bed. Fearing the darkness, she hugged her Bible close.

This time, she prayed to the patron saints of soldiers until the words ran out, and perhaps the angels kissed her to sleep.

About the Books and Author

C.A. Portnellus is the author of Sparrow Wars in the Garden of Bliss: A La Barre Family Saga series.

As an avid reader and lover of history and fiction, Portnellus has offered the reader an honest, gritty, and yet charming tale of family legacy with intriguing characters set in some of America's most notable recent decades.

Spanning eighty years and six generations, each book in the series brings us into the real world, much like our own experiences, yet unique for all that the La Barres and their descendants and fateful connections have become. Hoping to kindle readers' interest in historical eras, these books are rich in detail and scope. The stories are more than a meandering trip down memory lane; they are a part of each of us. For the characters, there is hope amid darkness and faith that there will always be a new day, bright with promise and love. At the heart, these books are love stories, each of an era representing the changing mores and family values of the time. The dark legacy of the Barre family curse will have intriguing consequences for generations to come, casting some into dangerous situations or destroying everything they value. Forgiveness and redemption will keep them together.

It is the author's audacious hope that these books will become new modern-American classics, following the storytelling traditions of John Steinbeck, Ernest Hemingway, and James Michener.

When not writing or researching for the next book in the La Barre Family Saga series, one can find Portnellus following creative artistic pursuits. With a love for all things old or set far into our futures, the author enjoys period costuming for theater, reading, and going to the movies.

Portnellus shares daily life with a delightful life-mate and the resident feline. The author enjoys traveling to interestingly beautiful, relaxing destinations and devoting time to natural gourmet cooking, fiber arts, painting, photography, making music, and the pursuit of peace and charitable efforts.

You may leave kind comments for the author via e-mail:

Csparrow.bliss@Yahoo.com